BORN IN THE WAYEB

Other books by Lee E. Cart

The Cracker Book: Artisanal Crackers for Every Occasion
The Paper Trail: Useful Charts to Organize Your Writing

BORN IN THE WAYEB

BOOK ONE OF THE MAYAN CHRONICLES

LEE E. CART

Ek' Balam Press
Wellington, Maine

Ek' Balam Press
15 Taylor Cemetery Road
Wellington, Maine 04942

Cover design by Brandi Doanne McCann

Printed in the United States of America
Library of Congress Control Number: 2014915996
ISBN-13: 978-0-9906765-0-8

Publisher's Note: This book is a work of fiction. Names,
characters, places, and incidents are either products of the
author's imagination or are used fictitiously. Any resemblance to actual persons, living or dead, events, or locales
is entirely coincidental.

To my boys, Yule, Johann, and Finn, with all my love,
always

Cast of Characters

The city of Mayapán

Ajelbal: Member of the Xiu tribe betrothed to Satal; a flutist.

Alaxel: Chachal's secret lover; a prince.

Alom: Mother to Yakal, wife to Q'alel; a servant.

Binel ja': Younger sister to Yakal; a river or brook.

Bitol: Commander of the Gates and uncle to Yakal; a builder of ancient pyramids.

Ilonel: Lead raider employed by Satal; a spy.

Imul: Younger sister to Yakal; a rabbit.

Kubal Joron: A member of the council; a water jug.

Kux: A member of Ilonel's group of men; a weasel.

Lintat: A young boy helped by Naʼom; a little boy of three to eight years of age.

Masat: Younger sister to Yakal, servant to Satal; a deer.

Matz': A member of the council; an ear of corn with few grains.

Memetik: A slave boy; to bleat like a goat.

Nimal: Head of the regiment; a leader.

Q'abarel: Owner of the bar, The Drunken Blackberry; a drunkard.

Q'alel: Father to Yakal and husband to Satal; a military leader.

Sachoj: Great-grandmother to Satal; a viper.

Satal: Wife of Q'alel, mother of Chachal, member of the council; a black wasp.

Tarnel: Owner of the slave market; a bodyguard.

Tikoy: Younger brother to Yakal; a frog.

Uskab: Wife to Yakal; a honey bee.

Xik': The fletcher of fine arrows; a feather.

Yakal: Father to Naʼom and son of Qʼalel and Alom; a stonemason.

The village of Pa nimá

Ajkun: The village midwife and herbal healer, grandmother to Naʼom; a witch who heals.

Banal Boʼj: A village member; a pot maker.

Chachal: Mother of Tzʼajonel and wife of Chiman; a necklace of colored stone.

Chiman: Leader of Pa nimá, father of Tzʼajonel, and husband to Chachal; a shaman.

Ekʼ Balam: Jaguar friend to Naʼom; dark or black jaguar.

Kemonel: Mother to Mokʼonel, Poy, and Tzeʼm; a weaver.

Kon: A young friend to Tzʼajonel; a stupid person.

Mokʼonel: Kemonelʼs older daughter, under the tutelage of Chachal; a robber or thief.

Naʼom: Granddaughter to Ajkun, daughter to Yakal; to have felt or sensed something.

Pempen: A village member; a butterfly.

Potzʼ: A village member; a blind or one-eyed person.

Poy: Kemonelʼs younger daughter; a doll.

Setesik: A village member; a large round basket.

Sijuan: Young female friend to Mokʼonel; a female friend.

Tajinel: Late husband to Ajkun; a farmer.

Tuʼjanel: Wife of Yakal, mother to Naʼom; a new mother.

Tzʼajonel: Son of Chiman and Chachal, friend to Naʼom; a painter.

Tzeʼm: Kemonelʼs newborn son; a laugh.

Yukanik: Leader of the convoy from Pa nimá and other villages; to scar.

The Mayan Gods

Acan: The god of wine.

Ahalgan: One of the thirteen gods of the Underworld; the god of pus.

Ahalpuh: One of the thirteen gods of the Underworld; the god of pestilence.

Camazotz: One of the thirteen gods of the Underworld; the god of bats.

Chac: The god of rain and lightning.

Cinteotl: The god of maize.

Hun Hunahpu: Father of the Hero Twins, who gave his blood to produce humans.

Itzamná: The supreme Mayan god who taught his people to grow maize and cacao.

Ixchel: The jaguar goddess of midwifery and medicine.

Kukulcan: The plumed serpent god.

Patan: One of the thirteen gods of the Underworld; the god of blood vomit and lung disorders.

Xic: One of the thirteen gods of the Underworld; the god of blood vomit and pneumonia.

Yum Cimil: One of the thirteen gods of the Underworld; the god of death.

SATAL

It was the first night of the Wayeb. The rhythmic pounding of drums vibrated through the thick stucco walls as Satal pulled her pack basket off a copper peg driven into the plaster. She set the basket on the tile floor before approaching the mummified head of her great-grandmother, Sachoj, who was tucked into a rough-carved niche on the far side of the room. The puckered brown lips of the head moved in the sputtering candlelight, and Satal nodded to the old woman.

"I know, I know, you don't have to remind me," Satal muttered as she placed a coconut husk full of jequirity beans and her four-inch long, dark green obsidian knife in the basket. She added a lump of charcoal and a small copper bowl. Then, she picked up a piece of cotton cloth, carefully wrapped the shrunken head in it, and gently laid the bundle in the basket before covering everything with a folded, blue woolen blanket. Satal put a tiny leather pouch in the pocket of her skirt, slipped a black shawl around her shoulders, and stepped into her leather sandals. She pulled the straps of the basket onto her back and shrugged to shift the load. She stopped to look around the room, to see if she'd forgotten anything. Even through the layers of fabric, she could hear her great-grandmother urging her to hurry. "Everything's packed, and I'm on my way. Satisfied?" Satal said to the cool night air.

She heard a faint "*je*" as Sachoj whispered yes.

The beating of the drums grew louder as Satal made her way by candlelight to the large front room in her palace. The twelve-foot-high ceiling remained dark as the candle flame flickered off the stucco walls. Painted against a lurid yellow background, larger-than-life Mayan men, dressed in leather battle gear, raged at each other, their brown bodies and black obsidian spearheads dripping blood as they fought to gain control of a limestone *cenote* filled with dark blue water, the only source of fresh water for miles. The candlelight shimmered when Satal crossed the room and cast odd shadows that mingled with the mural of the warriors in their perpetual conflict.

Satal moved out into the darkness of her inner courtyard. The drums echoed off the thick walls of her house and pulsed in her ears. She blew out the candle to let her eyes adjust to the dim light of a night sky peppered with stars. A thin crescent moon hung by one point, threatening to spill its contents onto the thousands of Mayans attempting to sleep in the city of Mayapán. Satal found the reed cage she had purchased at the market the day before and lifted it with her right hand. The hen inside shifted and squawked as it felt the earth move beneath its feet, but soon settled again as Satal whispered to it and adjusted the cotton cloth that hung over the cage.

She hurried along the narrow passageway that separated her house from her neighbors. When she reached the corner of the open plaza in front of the Temple of the Warriors, Satal stood in the shadows and checked for any soldier who might be patrolling the area, as all women and children were forbidden outside their houses during the Wayeb. She saw the large ceremonial bonfire blazing at the base of Kukulcan's pyramid. The multi-layered, four-sided pyramid reached toward the moon, its apex still just a rough jumble of limestone blocks. The high priests of Mayapán stood on the second tier of stone steps of the pyramid, chanting their magic into the flames that carried their words up to Itzamná, the supreme god. Hundreds of the city's men, dressed in simple loincloths, their black hair flattened against their skulls with peccary fat, circled the bonfire flames, moving in quick unison to the beat of the drums. Young apprentices stood in a group to one side, ready to serve a sweet sip of mango or pineapple juice to any man who faltered from the rapid pace of the dance. The doorway to the five-day Wayeb was opening as one year transitioned into another, and the men danced to keep the gods of evil, pestilence, and death at bay. Meanwhile, the women and children hid indoors; they were too afraid to venture forth, to cook hot meals, to comb their hair, or to bathe.

"Pray all you want, but your words are meaningless," Satal mocked. "The portal to the Underworld is about to open, and it's time to summon my friends, the gods of Xibalba." She pulled her shawl up over her head, adjusted the cage in her hand, and headed toward the wall that surrounded the entire city. Twenty feet high in places, the only access to and from Mayapán was through one of the twelve arched entranceways that penetrated the wall. The main gates, located in the northeast and northwest walls, were wide enough for four columns of people to pass through with ease. But Satal headed toward the least-used opening, tucked into the far corner in the south wall.

"Halt, no one is permitted outside the walls during the Wayeb," a young man said as Satal approached.

"Idiot, it's me," Satal said and dropped her shawl just long enough for the youth to catch a glimpse of her brown face and scarred lips. She tossed the leather pouch with its ten cacao beans to the boy. "Leave the gate unlocked, and I'll fasten it upon my return," she said.

The boy nodded and pulled back the wooden bar. The door swung open on its copper hinges, and Satal stepped through into the cornfield outside the city. She felt the air move behind her as the door was closed, but didn't turn around.

She took a deep breath of the damp night air and let it out slowly before picking her way through the corn stubble toward a small ravine on the far side of the field. Satal glanced back toward the city just once before half-stumbling over the steep edge into the gully below. With the rainy season still two months away, the ground was dry, and Satal's feet sank into the powdery gray-brown dirt. But she had no trouble finding the small opening that led underground. She carefully put her basket down, sat on the cool dirt, and turned onto her stomach. Her feet barely touched the rungs of a wooden ladder as she wiggled her gaunt frame through the gap and down two steps to the floor of a tunnel. The air was suddenly very cool, and Satal was glad she'd brought the extra blanket. She reached back up through the hole and pulled down her basket and the chicken cage, then felt around for the torch she had left the last time she'd been there. Using her knife, she knocked it against the rocks and created enough sparks to light the torch. The sudden brightness bounced off the low ceiling of the passageway and cast high shadows on the earthen walls. A small bat, disturbed by the glare, flew farther into the dark.

"Hurry, Satal," Sachoj urged, her muffled voice echoing in the tunnel.

Satal adjusted her sandals, hefted the basket onto her back, lifted the chicken cage, and holding the torch in front of her, set off in the direction of the bat. As she moved deeper underground, the hammering of drums faded until it was less a sound and more a vibration that Satal felt beneath her feet. The shaft she was in sloped gently downhill, curving left and right; other tunnels branched off from this one, but Satal knew they were all dead ends. Water dripped from the ceiling, and the walls were covered in patches of grey-green moss. Satal moved more quickly when she heard running water. A few more yards and the warren opened into a limestone cave the size of a small room. It was her own personal sanctuary, close to the gods of the Underworld and far from prying eyes.

Stalactites jutted from the ceiling like so many teeth, and bats rustled overhead as Satal illuminated the space with the torch. A pool of clear water burbled up from the ground before disappearing into one of the many passageways that connected this underground brook to a network of flowages that twisted and turned through a vast labyrinth of caves and caverns. With no rivers or lakes in the region, the cenotes or sinkholes were the only aboveground access to this hidden system of fresh water. Tiny villages and large cities were built near them, and through the millennia, many battles had been fought for the rights to drinkable water.

Satal set the end of the torch down in a crack in a large stone. She unwrapped her great-grandmother's head and carefully placed it on the rock altar she'd built several years before. She felt Sachoj's eyes watching her as she filled the copper bowl with water. She placed it on the altar in front of Sachoj, next to the lump of charcoal, the jequirity beans, and her knife. Then she knelt in front of the chicken cage and extracted the hen. Holding it by its feet, she quickly slashed the hen's neck open with her knife and let the fresh blood drain into the bowl of water. She tossed the still-thrashing carcass to one side.

Satal picked up one of the red jequirity beans. Tipped with black, they looked like bugs—small, deadly bugs—but they served a dark magic purpose. She nicked the end of the bean with the bloody knife and touched the split bean to her tongue. Instantly it went numb, and the rest of her mouth began to burn and tingle. Grabbing the bowl of blood-water, she drank deeply before settling herself on the dirt floor in front of the altar.

"Slowly breathe in and out," Sachoj said. "Let the essence of the bean flow throughout your system."

As the toxin worked its way through her body, Satal felt hot, then cold, then hot again. Her great-grandmother's face drifted in and out of focus, and Satal gripped the edge of the altar with her hands to keep from tipping over.

"Call to the gods of Xibalba," Sachoj ordered. "The doorway to the Underworld stands wide open."

"Camazotz," Satal said, calling on the god of bats, "Come to me; bring your friends, the gods of pestilence, Ahalpuh and

Ahalgan, and the gods of blood vomit, Xic and Patan. Your year-long wait is over. Unleash your vile powers." The air around Satal blurred and rippled as the spirits of Xibalba emerged from the tunnels and passageways with the giant bat, Camazotz, in the lead. His great wings thrummed the air, matching the faint vibration of the drums, and the few drops of bloody water in the bowl jiggled and bounced about.

Sachoj laughed and Satal could see the two, brown-stained, filed teeth that remained in her mouth. "Well done, my dear, well done," Sachoj said. "You truly are a child of the Wayeb."

As the toxin of the jequirity bean continued to pulse in Satal's veins, a harsh buzzing filled her ears, and she felt herself growing thinner and longer. She looked down to see her skin shifting, twisting. Her brown arms became segmented and turned black, her fingers elongated into claws covered in tiny black hairs. Her back ripped open and sprouted iridescent greenish-black wings, which Satal slowly opened and closed in the cool cave air. She lifted up off the ground and looked back with beady eyes at the body of a woman lying on the dirt and rocks. Somewhere deep within the recesses of her insect brain, Satal recognized the human form.

Camazotz beat his giant wings, and the air rippled around Satal's wasp-like shape. "You summoned me, my lady?" he said.

Satal addressed Camazotz. "Search the city and surrounding areas for any women in labor and kill the newborns. I must retain sole access to the Wayeb."

"Come with us," Camazotz whispered. The other nightmare gods nodded their sickly gray-green heads in agreement. "Tonight's your birthday, Satal. Come celebrate with us, and be free of this earthly realm," Camazotz urged.

Satal was torn between following Camazotz and the others to the surface to spread fear and pestilence over Mayapán and returning to the body on the ground. Her transparent wings beat in rhythm with those of Camazotz, and she moved closer to the huge bat despite the stench of damp earth and disease that rose from his black fur. He tilted his head toward the ceiling of the cave, and the hundreds of small bats hanging there began to flit around the cavern. They swirled around Camazotz and Satal, enveloping them in a black cloud of leathery wings.

"Stay away from her," Sachoj hissed to the giant bat. Her mouth opened wide, exposing her two fangs. "She has more work to do here on earth before she enters Xibalba."

Through her insect eyes, Satal looked at the shrunken head and back at the clouds of bats. She watched as the hundreds of creatures clustered around Camazotz and flew as a group into the tunnel leading to the night sky.

"Come with us, Satal," Camazotz insisted.

A piercing whistle penetrated Satal's brain, and her attention snapped to her great-grandmother's head on the altar. Sachoj's eyes were focused on the prone body on the ground. "Satal," the head called. "Satal! Listen to me! Eat the charcoal. Your work here is done; come back to me, come back."

With reluctance, the great black wasp sank back to the ground, grasped the charcoal, and forced it into its mouth. The bug chewed on the dry, gritty carbon and swallowed it piece by piece. Over the course of two hours, Satal felt herself return to the cold and aching body lying on the cave floor. She crawled to the pool of water and drank several handfuls, trying to wash the potent bean from her system.

Shivering with cold and exhaustion, Satal pulled the wool blanket from the basket and wrapped it around her shoulders before hunkering down against a large rock. The room tilted and swayed, and Satal knew several more hours would pass before she'd be strong enough to return to the city. She shook her head, trying to remember what had just happened. But the night was a blank. She stared into the wrinkled face of her great-grandmother. "Did it work?" she asked.

"Yeeesss," Sachoj hissed, and Satal grinned.

Yakal

It was the last night of the Wayeb. Far to the south of Mayapán, in the small village of Pa nimá, Yakal shuffled counterclockwise around the bonfire to the beat of a solitary drum. He glanced at the hooked, beak-like nose and black obsidian eyes of the carved limestone statue of Itzamná placed on a flat rock pedestal outside the temple. The shadow of the foot-tall Mayan god loomed larger against the wall of the village shrine than the silhouettes of the twenty men who circled in front of it. Itzamná's stone eyes stared outwards, but followed Yakal as he struggled to dance. Beads of sweat trickled down Yakal's back, and he ached from his teeth to his toes. He was grateful the five days of ceremonial fasting and dancing were almost over. He needed food, drink, a bath. He longed for the feel of his wife's round belly, full of his first child, cupped under his hands as they snuggled in bed. Yakal stumbled and brought his thoughts back to the blaze in front of him.

A young boy of ten held out a gourd to Yakal, and he stepped from the ever-circling group of men to drink the sweet mango juice. He looked at the dark sky overhead and knew dawn was still several hours away. He wasn't sure he had the stamina to continue praying and dancing until daylight. As Yakal took another sip of juice, he thought back to his childhood in Mayapán, of watching from the shadows as his father, Q'alel, and other warriors like him had moved in rhythm to the beat of thirty drums to keep the evils of the Wayeb at bay. His father had never faltered, never showed any sign of weariness, nothing like the fatigue that plagued Yakal.

He shook his head to clear his thoughts; he needed to be strong, as he wanted nothing to do with the Underworld. He handed the gourd back to the boy and stepped back into the circle.

The drumbeat slowed, and Yakal and his fellow tribesmen watched as their shaman and village leader, Chiman, tossed three balls of *copal* into the flames. The resinous incense sparked and burned, sending its pungent smoke into the air. Chiman reached into a bamboo cage near the idol and grabbed a squawking rooster by its feet. With one swift slash of his obsidian knife, Chiman cut the rooster's throat. As the dark blood dripped over the sculpted head and face of Itzamná as an offering to the ever-hungry god, Chiman prayed out loud. "Itzamná, our lord and protector, send Camazotz and his friends, Xic and Patan, Ahalpuh and Ahalgan, and the evils that lurk in the four corners of the world back to Xibalba, back to the Underworld for another year." Yakal watched as Chiman tossed the limp chicken into the flames, then reached into a small satchel tied to his waist, and pulled out a handful of sacred dried corn. He tossed this into the bonfire as well, and the red, black, white, and yellow kernels popped and sizzled in the heat.

With the idol glistening blood-black in the flickering firelight and the smell of roasted chicken and corn drifting in the wind, the drum picked up its pace again, and Yakal shuffle-stepped sideways with his friends as his empty stomach grumbled in protest.

A few moments later, the eighteen-year-old youth caught sight of the village midwife, Ajkun, heading toward his hut on the other side of the small village square. Ignoring the looks of the other men and Chiman, Yakal stepped away from the fire and hurried after the older woman. He arrived at his house just as Ajkun was beginning to examine his young wife, Tu'janel, who lay on the narrow bed.

"Surely it's too early for the child to arrive?" Yakal asked as he watched Ajkun rub her hands over Tu'janel's distended belly. He noticed the concern in the older woman's face.

"My daughter's not due for another two weeks, but all the signs point to this child arriving tonight," Ajkun said.

"You must stop it from coming," Yakal said. He wiped a wet cotton cloth over Tu'janel's sweaty brow. "We're not out of the Wayeb; this is no time for my son to be born."

"For the love of Ixchel, I wish I could delay this birth, but the goddess of childbirth will do as she pleases," Ajkun said as she hurried to grab an earthen pot from the corner of the small hut. "Now get out of my way; I have work to do."

"I'm not going anywhere," Yakal replied. "Surely you must have herbs that can halt this labor until tomorrow."

"Yakal, your place is at the bonfire with the other men. But if you plan to stay, at least make yourself useful," Ajkun said as she pushed the handle of the glazed pottery into Yakal's hands. "Build up the fire, fill the pot with water, and set it to boil; we'll need plenty for this birth, as I fear the baby is upside-down."

Yakal just stood, staring at his fifteen-year-old wife. She was the first and only woman he had ever been with, and he could see the panic on her face at Ajkun's words.

Ajkun swept aside the rough blanket covering the doorway and pushed the young man outside. She glanced quickly around the dark jungle before releasing the curtain. The candles in the hut flickered in the slight gust of wind, and one went out with a hiss.

Yakal paused in the small courtyard in front of his hut. He could hear the drum and the chanting of his neighbors as they continued to pray for a safe new year. He knew he should return to the bonfire, but he was too worried about Tu'janel. He drew a deep breath in and felt the cool night air against his bare, muscular chest. Tilting his head skyward, he searched for the night star and prayed to Itzamná that the baby would not be delivered until morning. As a child, he had listened to the stories told by the priests of Mayapán about the dark forces that appeared during the Wayeb that turned good soldiers against their leaders, caused mothers to beat their children, or men to vomit blood until their bodies turned hollow and their brown skin turned white. He shuddered as he heard Tu'janel groan. He hurried to stoke the embers in the fire pit and threw several small pieces of kindling onto the flames. Then he removed the large water gourds hanging on the outside wall, poured their contents into the pot, and placed it carefully on the three cooking rocks.

With nothing to do but wait, Yakal slumped against the adobe-covered wall. He concentrated on the good stories his mother had told him about the Wayeb, about how the malevolent powers of the Wayeb lessened as each of its five days passed, and the evil spirits were sucked back into the Underworld as the portal closed. And for the priests and shamans, this transition period at the end of the yearly calendar was a time for deep reflection and introspection. After training for years, many powerful shamans embraced the last day of the Wayeb as a time of spiritual growth and invited the more benevolent spirits from the Underworld to visit to gain insights into the ways of the multidimensional world.

But no innocent child should be born while the portal remains open, especially my firstborn son, Yakal thought. And he knew no child was safe while Satal sat on the council in Mayapán. He had seen some of the witchery his father's legal wife was capable of and knew she demanded immediate sacrifice of any child born at this time. No, he didn't want his son born this night.

He felt the rough stucco wall of the hut against his bare back and shifted his weight. His eyes fluttered, and he jerked them open. He concentrated on watching the flames. He would wait at the house to greet his son when he appeared at dawn. He was so tired, though; all he needed was a few minutes sleep. His eyes closed, and his head slumped toward his chest. Images of black shapes rushed at him on flying wings, and he was jolted awake.

AJKUN

Tu'janel groaned, and Ajkun placed her hand on her daughter's swollen belly. She raised Tu'janel's *huipil* and could see that the baby was struggling inside as Tu'janel's stomach moved and wobbled in the dim light. Ajkun felt movement behind her and twisted on the narrow bed to see Yakal standing in the doorway.

"Get out, Yakal," Ajkun said as she turned to face her son-in-law. "The childbirth bed is no place for a man."

Ignoring his mother-in-law, Yakal approached the bed. "I'll leave if you insist," he said to his wife, "but I want to stay and help you if I can." He looked into Tu'janel's eyes, but she shook her head no. Then she let out another moan as a small contraction bore down on her.

"Easy, my daughter, it's not time to push just yet," Ajkun said. She stroked her daughter's forehead, wiping away the sweat. "Yakal, fetch me the hot water; she needs some thistle tea."

Taking the hot pot from Yakal, Ajkun mixed herbs into the water, added a spoonful of honey, and then strained the mixture into a pottery mug.

Ajkun placed the rim of the cup against Tu'janel's lips. "Drink," Ajkun insisted when Tu'janel turned her face away. "The honey will give you strength for what lies ahead." She placed the half-empty cup on the floor and stood up. Taking Yakal by the arm, she guided him outside. "Make more hot water, lots of it, and stay outside," she added as she pulled the covering over the doorway.

Ajkun walked to the small clay statue of Ixchel in the far corner of the room. The midwife offered the goddess of childbirth a piece of tamale. "Dear Ixchel," Ajkun prayed, "help my child through this difficult time."

Tu'janel clutched at the edges of the rabbit skin blanket as another contraction hit her. Her brown face paled, and Ajkun hurried to help her daughter sit up.

The older woman pulled off Tu'janel's cotton shift, exposing her high, rounded belly. Taking a glazed pot from her leather medicine bag, Ajkun dipped her fingers into the salve inside. She rubbed the peccary fat mixed with white sapote on the taut skin, smoothing her hands around and around in a circle. For over an hour, Ajkun took turns rubbing Tu'janel's belly and wiping her sweaty brow.

Suddenly, Ajkun felt the baby move under her hands. "What's happening?" Tu'janel said.

"The baby's dropped into the birth canal; come, you must get onto the floor," Ajkun said as she began to lift Tu'janel under the arms.

Ajkun motioned that Tu'janel needed to squat. "Lean back against the bedframe and let me take a look." Ajkun knelt in front of Tu'janel.

"Push, Tu'janel, push," Ajkun said.

Ajkun felt warm fluids dripping from her daughter's thighs onto her feet, and she ground her teeth as Tu'janel screamed in her ear. One tiny foot appeared and then another, and Ajkun grabbed the child and pulled it the rest of the way out. "It's a girl, Tu'janel," Ajkun said as her daughter slumped on the floor.

She turned to see Yakal standing in the doorway. "It's a girl," she repeated.

"What, how can that be?" Yakal cried. "All the signs pointed toward a boy; by Itzamná, what cruel joke is this?"

"The gods have their own plans," Ajkun said as she wiped the infant quickly with a rag and wrapped her in a cotton cloth before laying her on the bed. "She looks like you," Ajkun added while she helped Tu'janel back onto the bed. "I'll need the rest of that hot water to clean the baby and your wife. Come and help me fetch it, while we let Tu'janel rest." She guided the boy back outside.

Ajkun breathed in the dark night air scented with the sweet smell of vanilla pods drying nearby. Just a touch of light was visible in the east, but sunrise was at least an hour away. She watched Yakal kick at the sticks piled by the fire, scattering them in several directions. She could still hear chanting and the single beat of the drum and knew the Wayeb hadn't closed. That wouldn't happen until the rays of the sun touched the statuesque face of Itzamná in the square. *The child was born while the entryway was still open,* she thought.

Suddenly Tu'janel let out a loud cry, and Ajkun hurried back inside.

Tu'janel held out her hands to Ajkun. They were covered in blood. She stepped forward and could see blood seeping through the thin blanket. "Will I be all right?" Tu'janel asked.

"Only Ixchel can say for sure," Ajkun mumbled as she gently pushed her daughter back down on the bed. *I'll do whatever I can to keep you from the Underworld.* She turned to the doorway. "Yakal! Fetch me that water. I must help Tu'janel and wash the child."

Motioning to Yakal with one hand, Ajkun pointed to the basin set on the floor, and she watched as he poured in the water. "Go now, rest, I'll wake you in a few hours," Ajkun said. Using a soft cotton cloth, Ajkun helped Tu'janel clean her hands and body. Then she took a small deer hide bag from a shelf and added pericón to the remaining warm water. The small yellow blossoms filled the hut with the spicy scent of anise. She removed the cotton cloth from her new granddaughter and inhaled the perfume of the newborn, like honey in milk. She sponged the infant with the warm water, washing away the last remnants of the birthing. She tied a clean rag between the baby's legs, bundled her in a black monkey skin, and handed the child back to Tu'janel who nursed the infant for a few minutes before falling into an exhausted sleep. Ajkun picked up the umbilical cord and afterbirth and took them outside to throw into the fire.

Over the next few hours, Ajkun moved back and forth from the hut to the fire to burn the bloody padding from between Tu'janel's legs. Each time she stepped outside, she noticed Yakal hunched on the ground, his head against the hut wall, wrapped in his gray squirrel cape. His eyes flickered in his sleep, but he didn't wake, despite the numerous trips she made. Even the stringent smell of yarrow that drifted outside failed to rouse him. It was only when she held a vial of peccary urine under his noise that Yakal woke with a start.

Yakal looked up into his mother-in-law's face and noted the tears crowning in the corners of her eyes. "What's wrong?" he said as he pushed himself upright. He hurried inside and saw Tu'janel with the baby tucked in by her side.

"She's gone . . . I'm sorry," Ajkun said as she turned to face him. She swiped at the tears coursing down her face.

Yakal scanned the room and noted the earthen pots of bloody rags. "How did this happen? You're the midwife and healer of this village; you're supposed to have saved her."

"There was so much blood," Ajkun cried. "I tried to stop it with every herb I could think of, but nothing worked." She sat down on the hard-packed dirt floor and wept into her hands.

Yakal went to Tu'janel's side and held her cooling face in his hands. "My love, we've only been wed a year," he said softly, "come back to me." He kissed her on the lips. But Tu'janel remained silent, her spirit headed for the land of the ancestors. Yakal motioned for Ajkun to approach the bed. "We must delay the news of this birth until the drum has stopped. The baby was born after the Wayeb closed, is that clear?"

"But Yakal, you know I can't lie to Chiman; how will he predict her destiny in life if I lie about the time of birth?"

Yakal grabbed Ajkun's arm and held it tightly. "There's no time to explain; even as we speak there's someone who may sense the baby's presence in this world and wish her harm. Just promise me you'll protect her."

"I don't understand, Yakal, there's nothing to fear," Ajkun said as she pulled her arm from his grasp and stepped away from the youth. She headed toward the doorway with the baby in her arms.

"Stop, Ajkun," Yakal said as he stepped in front of the woman. "Promise me we'll wait for the sunrise before anyone sees the child." He gently led the woman back to the bed and pressed her to sit down, the infant still cradled in her arms.

"I'm too tired and sad to argue with you," Ajkun said as she laid the baby on the bed and bent over Tu'janel's still body. She removed the hand-carved black jade necklace from around her daughter's neck. "This will belong to your daughter one day," she said as she kissed Tu'janel's brow.

Yakal did not look up. "No matter what I say or do out there," Yakal said as he flicked his hand toward the doorway, "remember your promise."

When the drumbeat ended, the silence pressed on Ajkun's ears. Yakal stood up and crossed to the doorway. "Go outside now, and tell Chiman of the birth while I deal with the dead."

Ajkun cradled the infant in one arm and grabbed her medicine pouch with her free hand. She turned to take a last look at her daughter. The baby whimpered, and Ajkun held the tiny face to her own, sun-wrinkled one. "Little one, do not fear, you're not alone," she said. She straightened her sore back and faced her son-in-law. "I don't know what you have in mind, but you'll need to take care of your child; it would be what Tu'janel wanted."

"I must leave the village at once," Yakal replied. "You have to raise the child. Perhaps my sacrifice will help hide this curse the gods have brought today," Yakal said.

"How dare you call this birth a curse," Ajkun said. "Leaving is no great sacrifice; you're just protecting yourself. Ixchel and the other gods have called my daughter home, and I share in your grief, but you can't abandon your own daughter."

Without saying a word, Yakal pushed the older woman aside and went outside. Ajkun followed on his heels. Several of the women from the village were up in the early morning; they were starting their cooking fires and grinding maize on grindstones to make corn gruel for breakfast. The Wayeb was over, and all the men needed to be fed. When they saw Yakal and Ajkun appear outside, three of the women hurried over.

"What happened?" Potz', the one-eyed woman, asked. "We heard angry voices."

"My wife just died while bringing a child into the world," Yakal said as he scooped up an armload of firewood. "I can't stay here in the village without Tu'janel by my side."

Potz' looked at the bundle in Ajkun's arms and then at the midwife. "When was the baby born?" she asked.

Ajkun stared into the woman's lined face. "Only a few moments ago," she said.

Potz' shook her head and silently returned to her cooking pot.

Kemonel, who had her own infant daughter wrapped in a shawl strapped to her back, lifted the edge of the blanket to peer at the newborn. "She looks like Tu'janel," she said and smiled at Ajkun. She placed her hand on the woman's arm. "May the gods help you with your loss, my friend."

The third woman, Pempen, gave Ajkun a quick hug.

Ajkun nodded. "I'm on my way to see Chiman. As shaman of the village, he'll know what to do."

Pempen said, "I'll go get him for you," and hurried off.

Ajkun watched as Yakal went back to the hut, dropped his bundle of wood, and reentered the house. He swept the floor with his bare feet, clearing the dirt room of any remaining birthing debris. He was just beginning to chop into the hard-packed soil with his digging stick when Chiman appeared at the hut.

Chiman nodded at Ajkun before approaching Yakal. "Pempen has spread news of the birth and death through the village, my friend," he said. "We must pray for the safe passage of Tu'janel through the Underworld. She fought bravely, like a warrior, and so by all rights shall join our ancestors on the other side without delay."

Ignoring Chiman, Yakal continued to dig a shallow grave in the floor. He placed pieces of maize in Tu'janel's mouth for her journey through the spirit world before carefully wrapping her in a red cotton blanket. He laid her body into the grave. Then he filled several earthen bowls with corn kernels and put them in the hole, as well as a gourd full of water, Tu'janel's backstrap loom, and several balls of yarn. She would need the food and the tools she had used in the village in her new life among the Mayan ancestors. Then Yakal headed outside. The others followed.

Before anyone could stop him, Yakal grabbed a dry branch from the pile of sticks, jabbed it into the nearest cooking fire, and spun around to the hut. He touched the burning branch to the thatched roof. The dry palm fronds caught fire quickly. The men and women moved away from the blaze.

"Yakal, what are you doing?" Chiman shouted as he ordered several youths to the nearby river for buckets of water.

"I'm making sure the portal to the Wayeb is fully closed," he replied. His whole body shook with anger. "The evil ones have taken my Tu'janel; they have cursed me and this hut." He waved his hand at the flames. "They won't take anything else."

Within minutes, flaming timbers fell in with a crash, sending a spiral of black smoke into the air. Tu'janel's body disappeared in the fiery rubble. The stucco walls began to crack from the heat, and pieces bubbled and popped, exposing the bamboo timbers underneath.

Chiman shook his head. "This is not the way of our people. You didn't cover the body or allow me to say prayers for Tu'janel. You may have angered the gods by this act." He turned his back to Yakal and motioned for more water to be thrown onto the fire.

Ajkun held the infant tight in her arms and watched her son-in-law. "Yakal, this has gone far enough," said. "Come to my house, and we'll take care of your daughter together."

"Old woman, my life here is over; I'll return to the lands of my father far to the north and repledge my allegiance to the Cocom of Mayapán."

"But what of your child?" Ajkun said.

"From this day forth, I have no child," Yakal replied as he headed toward his canoe on the river.

Chiman quickly followed Yakal and grabbed him by the forearm. "Yakal, stop! You're like my younger brother. Don't leave in haste." He let go of Yakal's arm. "Come; break the fast with me and my family. In the daylight of this new year, we'll discuss what to do about the girl."

"There's nothing here for me," Yakal said. "I'll return to Mayapán and beg my father's forgiveness." He quickly embraced Chiman. "You've been a good friend, but I can't stay."

CHIMAN

Chiman walked through the jungle from the village center toward the spit of land that jutted into the river. He was glad the Wayeb ceremony was over, but he was worried about the infant girl and about Yakal. *I hope Ajkun can find a wet nurse for the little one,* Chiman thought. *After I eat and rest a bit, I'll need to go see her.* He continued walking on the dirt path toward his house. *Perhaps I should have sent someone after Yakal. I wonder if he'll come back once his grief has passed.* As he entered the clearing, he could hear his wife yelling from inside their three-room thatched house. Her shouts filled the air, silencing the birdcalls and the continuous swoosh of the river as it tumbled over rocks near the hut. He scanned the yard; the turkeys were pecking for grubs inside their barricade of sticks, his clean loincloth and black monkey cape were on the narrow wooden bench by the door with his favorite gray towel and a coconut husk full of soft soap. Chiman paused in his search as he heard a piece of pottery smash against the wall. He looked to the flowering avocado tree planted by his father's father. There he caught sight of his four-year-old son, Tz'ajonel, who sat at the base of the tree, scratching in the dirt with a small branch.

Chiman quickly walked over to Tz'ajonel and squatted down in front of the boy. He laid his quetzal feather headdress on the ground next to him. The child reached out and stroked the three-foot-long, iridescent peacock-green feathers before looking up into his father's lined face.

"What's wrong with *Chuch*?" he asked.

"I'm not sure; perhaps your mother is angry because your Uncle Yakal left the village," Chiman replied. He looked into his son's brown eyes and wondered just how much he could tell the boy.

"Why did he leave, Tat axel?" Tz'ajonel asked his father.

"It's a long story, Tz'," Chiman said, using the boy's nickname as he slowly stood up. "Someday, when you're older, I'll tell it to you, but for now, I must go help your chuch."

"Will Chuch make us breakfast soon? I'm hungry," Tz' said.

Chiman's stomach rumbled, and he nodded his head. "After five days, I'm hungry, too. Stay here while I go find out what's wrong." He patted Tz' on the head.

"May I go see the new baby, Tat axel?" Tz' said as he jumped to his feet.

"You'd like that?" Chiman said, surprised that his son knew of the birth. The child nodded his head and smiled. "Go then, but be back later, so we may eat at the feast together."

Chiman watched as Tz'ajonel slipped his bare feet into his leather sandals, adjusted his loincloth, and took off running down the path that led back to the village. Chiman bent to pick up his headdress and felt a twinge of pain in his lower back. At that moment, he felt much older than twenty-eight and longed for the day when Tz' would begin to take over some of the ceremonial duties of the community.

As soon as he entered the hut, his wife got up from her stool by the window opening and marched toward him.

"How could you?" Chachal cried as she began punching Chiman in the chest. "How could you let that baby live?"

Chiman grabbed Chachal's fists and held them tight. "What are you talking about, Chachal?" Chiman asked as he continued to hold onto her wrists.

She struggled in his arms and finally broke free of his grasp. "Potz' was here just a few minutes ago. She told me what happened. The midwife could be lying about when the infant was born; you should have smothered it when you had the chance," she said. She kicked at the shards of brown and blue pottery on the floor. "And why did you let Yakal leave the village?"

Chiman stared at his wife. He had never understood her strange, erratic outbursts. This time, she shook with the force of it. Then all of a sudden, she slumped on the narrow wooden bed and began to cry.

Slowly, as if approaching a wild animal, Chiman moved toward Chachal. He sat down next to her and carefully wrapped one arm around her plump body. He stroked her long, black hair with his other hand and let Chachal sob against his bare chest. He felt the tears mingle with the dirt and soot on his skin. He needed a bath after the past five days, not this. "Shh, my love, it'll be all right." He continued to stroke her hair and swallowed hard to stop his empty stomach from cramping. "I couldn't force Yakal to stay. He's tired and weak from the fasting, as we all are, and I believe once his anger and grief fade, he'll be back."

Chachal lifted her tear-streaked face and looked beyond her husband to the open doorway. "I know my half-brother better than any of you. He's like our father, stubborn as an agouti, and if he says he's going back home, then that's where he's headed." She began to cry again.

Chiman straightened his back, stood, and walked to the window. The sound of the river soothed him. "If that's the case, then he's deserted all of us, Chachal, not just you," he chided his wife. "He's forsaken his own child and angered the gods by burning down the house before I had time to say a proper prayer for Tu'janel."

"Where is this child of the Wayeb now?" Chachal asked as she wiped her face with the sleeve of her cotton huipil. The white fabric was streaked with grime.

"Ajkun has her; she's trying to find someone to provide milk for the baby. And we don't know she was born in the Wayeb.

Ajkun says the drumming had stopped, and I believe her."

"Humph, you would. I still say the girl should have been buried with Tu'janel," Chachal said again.

Chiman turned and studied his wife's face. He noted the gray hairs beginning to appear around her forehead and the way her mouth always drooped in a slight frown. "Why would you even think that?" he asked. "Even if it's true and the portal was still partially open, we have no idea what that could mean; it could bring great good to the village," Chiman said.

"Or terrible evil; like you say, you don't know. I've seen things, Chiman . . ." Chachal let her voice drift into a whisper, "Terrible things."

"Speak up, you know I can't hear you when you mumble like that," Chiman said. He could feel his hunger and tiredness making him irritable. He took a deep breath and let it out slowly, willing himself to calm down.

Chachal looked around the room and wandered through the rest of the house. "Where is Tz'?" she asked.

"He's gone to see the baby."

"What? You allow our son to mingle with this tainted newborn? Have you no sense at all?" Chachal said as she whirled around and glared at Chiman. "I forbid him to have anything to do with the child, ever."

Chiman straightened his tattooed shoulders. In the dim light of the hut, the deep-blue jaguar spots that covered his arms and back like a cape blended with his mocha-colored skin and he looked half-man, half-jaguar. "Enough of your nonsense, woman. The gods will decide who our son shall see or not see, not you." he said. "Now, bring me hot water, so I may bathe. Then you'll provide me with food, and after I've slept, I'll return to the temple and meditate on this girl. When Itzamná has spoken to me in a vision, then I'll gather the village and announce what shall be done with the child." Chiman looked at the broken pottery on the dirt floor. "And clean up this mess that you've made." He walked outside and motioned for Chachal to hurry and meet his demands.

After he was rested, Chiman walked back to the village center where several of the men were raking out the coals of the previous night's bonfire. They planned to add wood to the embers to roast a peccary and a small deer for the evening feast. Setesik and Banal Bo'j were lowering clay-covered baskets full of turtle meat into a heated pit so the meat could slowly roast for several hours. He nodded to the women seated in a semi-circle preparing tamales and paused to watch as they spread long ovals of warm corn dough on the inner, light green leaves of fresh corn and then added layers of chopped deer meat and fresh figs. They covered the meat mixture with more corn dough and wrapped the corn leaves around the tamale, making a packet that would later be steamed in a spicy blend of tomatoes and chili peppers. Chiman's mouth watered just at the thought of the food he'd feast on later that day. He waved to Acan, the wine maker, and was glad to see he had plenty of gourds full of beverages already lined up for the feast. As Chiman continued walking, he sidestepped two small boys chasing each other in the plaza and turned to admire the village, a place he had lived all his life, just like his father and grandfather before him. He took pride in the clean line of huts tucked among the many banana, mango, and avocado trees. Although only about sixty inhabitants lived in Pa nimá, some much older than Chiman, he felt responsible for everyone, the young and the old, now that he was the official shaman. He shook his head though, as he thought of his young and impetuous friend, Yakal. He had not managed to keep the youth from leaving.

No one in the settlement had been happy when Chiman had returned from a trading trip to the north almost five years earlier with fourteen-year-old Yakal and his half-sister and new bride, Chachal. They didn't see the need for new blood or a bond between the Cocom families, the rulers of Mayapán, and their own, independent tribe of the south. However, as time passed, the elders forgave Chiman as Yakal had proven to be an able hunter and a good stonemason. Many in the village had gained food and housing because of the youth. And Chachal was a loyal, albeit unhappy, wife. Despite the birth of their son, Tz', several months after their arrival in Pa nimá and the fact that she held a position of great power in the small town, Chachal was never satisfied.

The smell of wet soot and wood from Yakal's burned hut rose in the air, blending with that of the fuchsia-colored bougainvillea blossoms that grew in profusion along the roofline of the adobe temple. Chiman removed his leather sandals and entered the sacred space. He sat cross-legged in front of the statue of Itzamná, which had been brought inside at dawn. Drops of dried blood still speckled the stern-faced god staring silently back at him. Chiman placed a small ball of copal in the pottery brazier near the idol and lit it. The incense permeated the air, and Chiman tried to formulate the proper question to ask of his god. But he still had too many thoughts swirling in his mind. *Why is Chachal so upset?* he wondered. *Although, she hasn't been happy for several years, perhaps I shouldn't have brought her to the village, so far from the city. Maybe the elders were right when they said I should have married someone from here.*

Chiman drew a deep breath and let it out slowly. Then another. He felt his heartbeat and placed both hands on his brown chest, willing his body to slow down. Another deep breath and his thoughts revolved back to Yakal. The boy had helped build this very temple, but he had abandoned his child—an act no man should commit.

Chiman shifted his weight and added more incense to the fire. It sputtered and sent spirals of sweet, pine-scented gray smoke into the air. He directed his gaze to the statue in front of him. He concentrated, forcing all thoughts except one from his mind. "This child, is she of the Wayeb, and if so, what is to become of her?" he asked Itzamná. Chiman closed his eyes and waited to sense a response. Several minutes passed in silence, and he resisted the urge to open his eyes. Years of practice had taught him patience eventually brought an answer.

He felt a cool breeze on his face, and multiple images flickered in his mind's eye. He saw the girl as a toddler, crying out in her sleep, then older and gathering herbs with her grandmother, Ajkun, then as a young woman canoeing across the river. Tawny-colored jaguars drifted in and out of each image, crisscrossing with those of the baby and girl. At one point, he saw Tz', now a youth, standing beside the girl, a large pyramid rising up behind them. Visions of the girl and jaguars, yellow and black, blended and blurred until Chiman couldn't tell the difference between cats and child. Eventually the visions faded into blackness, and he opened his eyes. He looked around the temple; the incense still burned in the brazier, honeybees buzzed in the flowers outside; only a few minutes had passed. Slowly, he stood and made his way outside.

Chiman headed down the narrow path to Ajkun's hut to speak to the herbal healer about her new granddaughter. When he arrived, he found Tz' inside with the midwife and infant.

"Chiman!" Ajkun said as she hurriedly stood up from the bed. She was holding the infant in her arms.

"Tat axel," Tz' said when he saw his father, "the baby's to be called Na'om; you must make that her name at her naming ceremony."

"Tz', wait outside," Chiman said. "I must speak to Ajkun."

"But Tat . . ."

"Shh, Tz', it's all right," Ajkun said as she reached into a pot and pulled out a small piece of honeycomb filled with honey. "Run along now, and soon you can see the baby again," she said as she placed the sticky treat in the boy's chubby hand. Tz' grinned at her and skipped out into the bright sunlight.

"So, what of the child, what have you seen?"

"Midwife, how do you know I've seen anything?" Chiman

demanded.

"You send your only son outside, and you smell deeply of incense," Ajkun replied. "Being the shaman, it's logical to guess that you've been to the temple and had a vision."

"Oh, Ajkun, I swear by Itzamná there are days when I think you should be the ruler of Pa nimá," Chiman said as he paced the small hut. "You have more sense than any other woman and most of the men."

"Kind words from the man who once held my heart in his hands," Ajkun said as she looked fondly at her former sweetheart. "But enough flattery, my friend; I want to hear news of my granddaughter."

Chiman sat on the one stool in the room and bowed his head. He paused, trying to find the right words to explain what he'd seen in his vision. "This child is no ordinary girl. The spirit world of the jaguars is very much entwined with hers; we must watch her carefully for signs of anything out of the ordinary." He lifted his head and looked at the first woman he had ever lain with and searched her lined face as he spoke. "You're positive the portal was closed when Tu'janel delivered the child?"

Ajkun dropped her gaze to the dirt floor of the hut. "No," she said. She lifted her face and took a deep breath. "Yakal made me promise to protect the child; he said someone would know of her birth and come looking for her and that I was to lie about her true birth time." She looked at her old friend and lover. "I asked him to explain, but he said there was no time. Do you know what he meant?"

"Not exactly, no. For now, I think it's best that we keep this a secret between us and let the villagers continue to believe the child was born after dawn."

"So, should I teach her the healing herbs and train her to be the next midwife?" Ajkun asked. "Or is her destiny to be something different than that?"

Chiman looked at Ajkun. He noticed the way her white huipil

and emerald skirt clung to her shapely body. Even at thirty-one, she still had the looks and the curves of someone much younger. Her black hair was tied neatly in a braid that reached her mid-back, and her brown eyes were filled with intelligence and wit. She had a few wrinkles in the corner of her eyes, but Chiman knew these to be laugh lines from the many times they had shared a good joke. "Frankly, I'm not sure what will happen. For now, I say you train her to carry on the traditions of this house."

"Might I suggest she receive some extra training from you as well?"

"What do you propose?"

"That she be taught to read and write, to know the movement of the stars in the night sky, and to learn to ask for guidance from the gods."

"Train her like I will Tz'? I can't promise you that. You know the village elders won't necessarily approve of a girl learning such things." Chiman looked at the woman standing in front of him. "Of course, if she should just happen to learn to read and write from someone else who has those abilities, who am I to talk? The gods could have favored her with the knowledge for all I'll admit," Chiman said as he stood up. "Don't think I've forgotten that you weaseled that information out of me years ago," Chiman added as he gave Ajkun a gentle hug. He turned before he reached the doorway. "Have you found a wet nurse?"

"Yes, Kemonel has volunteered. She's still nursing her youngest daughter, Mok'onel. She's promised to bring me the head-binding boards, too, as she's the last one in the village to have used them. I'll wait until after the feast to apply them, though."

"Good, well then, I'll see you at the feast later today," Chiman said as he stepped outside into the bright afternoon light.

The western sky was turning a golden pink when the villagers of Pa nimá gathered in the square for the feast. Chiman motioned for everyone to follow him and Chachal to the temple. He had dressed in a new ceremonial loincloth Chachal had embroidered with sunflowers symbolizing the beginning of the new yearly cycle. His black hair was sleeked back with peccary fat, and he'd stuck a single green honeycreeper feather behind his left ear. His jaguar skin cape was thrown over his shoulders, and he wore new leather sandals on his feet. Dark green jade plugs hung in his earlobes. Chachal wore a new white huipil; the shoulders and square neckline were embroidered with sunflowers to match Chiman's outfit. She had pulled her black hair into a bun and outlined her eyes with black. A long necklace of translucent blue-green, forest-green, and black jadeite beads dangled on her chest and matched the bracelet she wore on her right arm. Chiman noted Ajkun in the back of the crowd, the baby slung from a dark blue shawl on her back.

"My friends and neighbors, it's time to celebrate the beginning of a new cycle," Chiman said as he addressed the crowd. "The Wayeb is over, and the new year promises to be a good one. But before we start to feast, I ask that we have a moment of silence for Tu'janel before we welcome the new addition to our tribe." He motioned for Ajkun to advance to the temple.

Ajkun began to pick her way through the group, but stopped when a voice rang out.

"I'll honor Tu'janel," Potz' yelled. "But as Itzamná is my witness, I'll not welcome the child."

"She was born in the Wayeb," Acan said. "The child must be sent away."

"She'll bring harm to us all," Banal Bo'j said. His wife, Pempen, nodded her head in agreement. The butterfly-shaped birthmark on her left cheek appeared to be flying as she moved her head.

From his place at the shrine, Chiman could see the crowd begin to surge around Ajkun. He stepped into the throng and pushed his way to her side. He touched Ajkun by the elbow, and by pressing his neighbors back with his free hand, he was able to lead her safely to the temple. He ignored the frown on Chachal's face as he stood and confronted his neighbors.

"My lord," Potz' said, "if the child is of the Wayeb, what will happen to us all if she stays?" Several of the men and women agreed with the older woman.

"Who among you knows for sure what time she was born?" Chiman commanded. "Ajkun's the one person in the village who knows, and I believe her when she tells me dawn had arrived before the child." He held up one hand to silence the villagers who had begun to shout again. "I've prayed to Itzamná, and he's sent me visions of the girl and her future. Ajkun will train her granddaughter to become our new midwife and healer."

The crowd pressed forward toward the temple. "And if Ajkun is wrong?" Potz' shouted out.

Chiman ignored the woman. In his mind, he saw the images of Na'om with jaguars circling all around her and wondered what it all meant. He shook his head and smiled at the crowd. "My friends, enough of this talk of the Wayeb and these fears; the child is only a day old and can harm no one. Come now; let's celebrate a new beginning with the good food that's been prepared." He looped his right arm through Ajkun's and his left through Chachal's, and ignoring the looks on his wife's face, led the two women to the palm frond mats spread out on the ground in front of the feast.

SATAL

Satal lay in her hammock, staring at the stucco ceiling. She listened to the tolling of bells, signaling yet another death in the city, and half smiled. She let the weight of her body sink deeper into the cotton mesh, willing her mind and body to relax, to slip into sleep. But for days, she'd been unable to rest. Although it had been several weeks since the continuous drumming in the city had stopped at the close of the Wayeb, instead of feeling relief that the sound was gone, Satal felt tense and on edge, like she did before the summer thunderstorms brought the wind, lightning, and pounding rains. She twisted in the hammock and faced the shrunken head of her great-grandmother.

"I know you felt something in the predawn of the last day," Satal said to Sachoj. "I can tell by the look on your face. What do you think it was?"

Sachoj stared out into the bedroom with her glassy brown eyes. Her puckered lips slowly moved, and Satal strained to hear her words. "A ripple in the Wayeb; a rent in the fabric of the cosmos," Sachoj hissed. Her viper-like teeth appeared as she grimaced at her own words.

Suddenly, Satal heard a knock on her front door. With difficulty, she pushed her bird-like frame out of the hammock, grabbed the candle off the shelf on the wall, and slowly shuffled toward the front door. *Who would bother me at this hour*, she wondered. She could see the light of a torch flickering in the courtyard and the vague shadow of a man. *Bitol, what does he want with me that can't wait until tomorrow's council meeting?* Satal thought as she lifted the door latch. The Commander of the Gates bowed when Satal opened the wooden door.

"So sorry to disturb you at this hour, *Nim-q'ij*," Bitol said. "One of the watchmen spotted a stranger trying to enter the city through the northeast gate. When he was questioned, he turned out to be Yakal."

"Yakal! So, the bastard son of my late husband returns to Mayapán. What's he doing entering the city at this late hour? Did he have my daughter with him?" Satal asked. It had been almost five years since she had seen Chachal, her only living child.

"No, most honored one, the youth was alone. When I heard the news, I came to you straight away."

"Escort Yakal to his mother's hut and leave two watchmen on guard overnight. Then bring the boy to the council meeting in the morning."

"Yes, Nim-q'ij, I'll do as you request." Bitol bowed again and left.

Satal leaned against the carved wooden door and looked out into the darkness. She could still smell the remnants of a thousand cooked meals in the air, the scent of epazote, chili peppers, boiled corn, and roasted turkey made her stomach growl. *Why has Yakal returned, and how is Chachal?* she mused as she shut the door and returned to her bedroom.

Placing the candle back on the shelf so it cast a light across the painted limestone walls, she stood in front of Sachoj. "That was Bitol," she said. "Yakal's returned, but there's no sign of Chachal. Do you think this has something to do with what we felt that morning?"

Sachoj blinked, but didn't reply.

"Some help you are," Satal said. She paced around the room trying to interpret the meaning of Yakal's return. "Perhaps the gods will help me if I ask for guidance," she said as she reached into the wooden cupboard in the corner of the room. She grabbed an old black monkey skin and shook it. A few moths fluttered toward the candlelight, and Satal caught sight of a carrion beetle scuttling into the corner of the cupboard. Three new holes had appeared in the fur, and she made a note to replace the skin with a new one. She laid it on top of a small wooden table, smoothing out the soft pelt with her hands until it lay flat. She placed a small ceramic incense burner in the center of the skin. It was shaped like a kneeling skeleton covered in black spots, the arms and hands stretched outward into the room, palms up, forming a spot to lay balls of copal incense. The skeletal head was oversized, with eyeballs that protruded from its face. It was Yum Cimil, the death god.

Reaching back into the cupboard, Satal pulled out a cloth bag with nine dark blue maize seeds inside, a handful of straw tied in a bundle with a piece of sisal twine, a bag of dried mushrooms and herbs, her clay pipe, and a piece of bark from a ceiba tree. She placed her four-inch-long green obsidian knife on the table along with the other items. The knife was part of a matched set that had belonged to her late husband, Q'alel. The shorter knife fit more comfortably in her hand while the larger, longer knife remained in its sheath in the cupboard.

She pulled one of the narrow yellow straws from the bunch, lit the tip of it in the candle, and set the incense to burn. As the pungent smoke drifted outward into the room, Satal opened the bag of ground mushrooms and herbs, packed her pipe, and lit the end of it. She drew a deep breath of the burning mixture into her lungs and immediately began coughing as the harsh smoke scoured her throat. She coughed uncontrollably; tears edged from her eyes, and she wiped at them with the hem of her sleeve. She took a lungful of clean air, then picked up the pipe and drew on it again, and a third time. She coughed again as she placed the pipe on the tabletop and felt the psychedelic mushrooms begin to take effect.

Looking at the incense burner, she called on the death god.

"Yum Cimil, help me read the signs in the corn; help me learn why Yakal has returned." Using one hand, she pinched her bottom lip so that it stood out from her chin, then reached to pick up her knife. The carved green handle of leaves and vines writhed on the tabletop, and suddenly, a small emerald snake slithered from inside the depths of the obsidian, flicked its forked tongue, slipped over the edge of the table, and disappeared into the shadows of the room.

Satal blinked several times, squeezed her lip again, picked up the now solid knife, and poked the tip of it into the full flesh of her lip. A giant bead of blood instantly appeared, and Satal let it drip onto the piece of tree bark. She let go of her lip and sucked on it a moment, then placed the blood-smeared paper on top of the smoky incense. The bark curled into a tight roll and added its own smoke to that already in the room. Satal picked up the tiny cotton bag, shook the nine sacred blue seeds inside, and tossed them out onto the altar.

Her vision blurred as the magic in the mushrooms continued to pulse through her body. She stared at the corn kernels in front of her. Seven of the nine pieces had fallen in a pile, the eighth piece lay close by the others, and the ninth piece was left by itself, far to the edge of the table. As Satal watched, the lone piece of blue corn began to writhe on the monkey skin. It shimmered and slid toward the other kernels, wriggling its way through the thick black hairs. It paused when it fell into one of the many holes in the skin, then with a quick jump, moved ever closer to the other kernels of corn. Satal strained forward, her eyes watering and blurring; the corn wriggled on the pelt and morphed into a little person dressed in blue. The corn maiden bowed to Satal and began to dance, twisting and twirling with her arms outstretched, her tiny skirt flaring up around her slender shape. Then the corn piece began to shift again, morphing into a black, animal-like creature with a long, full tail, which slunk through the coarse hairs of the monkey skin on all four limbs before changing back into a young girl. Satal closed her eyes and pressed her fingertips into her eyes. She massaged her eyelids and then blinked several times before addressing Yum Cimil again. "Who is this girl in blue?" she asked the skeletal figurine. "What does she have to do with Yakal? What about my daughter?"

Beads of sweat trickled down Satal's brow and dripped to the floor. Her head swayed, and she began to twitch. Her hands and arms jerked and then her left leg kicked out and she hit it hard against the altar. The incense burner wobbled, but Satal managed to steady the ceramic statue before it fell over. She watched as all the corn pieces changed into little people, all dressed in blue. The nine pieces stood up and bowed to Satal, then eight began to sway in pairs, dancing around and around in a circle, with the one maiden standing off to one side. They whirled around, slowly at first, then got faster and faster, until they muddled into a continuously revolving ring of blue. Satal gripped the small table edge and fell over in a faint on the floor.

It was daylight when Satal regained consciousness. Soft light filtered into the room from the hallway, and as she pushed herself up off the dusty floor, she could see the corn pieces lay still on the table in front of her. The incense had turned to a lump of gray ash that fell apart when she picked up the statuette of Yum Cimil and placed him back in the cupboard along with her other divination tools.

"So," Satal heard a voice say, and she turned around to look at her great-grandmother. "You're finally awake."

"You saw what happened; who's the corn maiden?" Satal asked as she turned to the head in the niche in the wall.

"Not Chachal, that's for sure," Sachoj said. "She never inherited your powers." The old dead woman blinked her dusty eyes. "From the looks of it, this corn maiden may have special skills. If that's the case, she's someone you need to find before your own abilities begin to fade."

"Humph, that won't happen for years," Satal said, and she

wiped her hands on her skirt. She yawned and crawled into her hammock. "I'll have found this corn maiden long before then. And the first person I'll question is Yakal later on today."

AJKUN

Thirty-eight moons had passed since Na'om's birth, and Ajkun sighed with relief when she felt the toddler nod off in her arms. Very gently, the midwife reached over and put the three-year-old on the bed they shared. Looking at her, Ajkun noticed the close resemblance to her daughter, Tu'janel. Na'om had the same mocha-colored skin, thick eyelashes, and broad forehead. Ajkun felt a brief stab of grief as she thought of her daughter and then pushed her sadness aside. She watched Na'om's chest rise and fall in a regular pattern before she quietly slipped outside to the fire. She hoped the strong herbal tea she had given her granddaughter would keep the nightmares away for one night.

Just the night before, Na'om had woken in fright. Curled up in Ajkun's arms, Na'om had shivered as she tried to describe what she had seen. "Bright eyes that glowed yellow, like the corn you grind for our breakfast, Ati't," Na'om said as she snuggled closer to her grandmother. "Then, I felt this pain," the little girl paused and pointed, "from here to here," she said as she moved her hand from her eye to her chin. "Then I saw these strange men; they were covered in red paint, and they waved sharp, pointed sticks and shouted at you." She covered her eyes with her tiny hands. "There was a woman with a bad leg, and some old men who begged me to help them . . ." Na'om turned her young face to her grandmother. "Ati't, make them all go away."

"Sweet child, I wish I could," Ajkun replied as she hugged Na'om. "All I can do is continue to write down what you see and then tell the stories to Chiman. He's studied the ways of our people since he was a boy and knows much about the mysteries of this world and the Otherworld." Ajkun had rocked the girl back and forth and gradually felt her relax in her arms. She had looked over the girl's head at the wall, noting the numerous notch marks cut into the post supporting the doorway to her storage room. One mark for each full moon since Na'om's birth, and still there was no sign of Yakal.

Ajkun poked at her fire and threw some more wood on it. The flames sparked and crackled, and Ajkun shifted her stool backwards to avoid the sudden blast of heat. She heard Na'om whimper and started to stand up, but then she relaxed when the deep breathing began again. Ajkun suspected Na'om's nightmares had begun when she was an infant and too young to tell Ajkun what caused her to cry for hours. Warm baths, herbal teas, and rocking and singing always put Na'om back to sleep, but Ajkun was glad when the girl was old enough to describe her visions.

Silently she entered the hut and slipped the monkey skin blanket over Na'om's bare legs. She picked up a small journal made of pounded fig bark, took a turkey feather out of a gourd on the shelf, and went back outside. She poured a small amount of hot water into a coconut bowl and added a piece of charcoal from the fire pit. She smashed the carbon into the water until it formed a deep, black liquid, then took the hollow end of the feather, and dipped it into the ink. Slowly and carefully, she scratched out the details of Na'om's latest dreams into the small journal. She laid the open book near the fire to dry. She would take her notes to Chiman in the morning and see what the shaman could make of them.

"So, what do these dreams mean?" Ajkun asked Chiman the next day. "Na'om has almost the same visions over and over again; surely they must mean something?"

"Ajkun, you're an old and wise healer; in many ways you know as much or more about the world as I do," Chiman said as he paced in the courtyard outside his house. "I wish I could send a messenger down the river to the shamans of the other villages and ask for their advice. They'd help me determine whether Na'om was blessed or cursed by the Wayeb. Perhaps we should have spoken the truth about her birth so many moons ago." He stopped to look at the little girl dressed in a sapphire-blue shift. Her brown eyes peered up at him, and he could see tiny flecks of yellow in them. "I'll kill another rooster at dawn tomorrow and read the entrails; maybe it will give me some more answers," he said as he bent down and picked up Na'om.

Na'om squirmed in his arms, and Chiman gently set her back on the ground. "She's feisty, that one," he said. "Whatever these visions mean, she's strong enough to handle them."

Ajkun noticed movement out of the corner of her eye and laughed in spite of herself. She could see Chiman's son, Tz', sneaking up on them from beyond the turkey pen. Then she saw that the boy of seven was not stalking them, but playing with his pet tayra. Named Chac in honor of the rain god, the large weasel was tracking a tuft of cotton fabric that Tz' had tied to a piece of string. The boy threw the string and fabric and waited until the tayra pounced on it before jerking it away. Toss and pounce, toss and pounce, the boy laughed every time the tayra missed the toy.

Ajkun nudged Na'om. "See what Tz' is doing? Perhaps he'll let you play as well." Ajkun looked at her granddaughter's face and caught the glimpse of a smile. "Go on, it's all right," she said as she saw Na'om look at Chiman and then back at her grandmother. Ajkun gave Na'om a little push, and watched as the girl hurried off on her solid little legs.

"She's too shy," Ajkun said to Chiman. "None of the mothers will allow their children to play with her; they worry that something bad will happen if their children get too close. If she's to be the next midwife and healer, the villagers must begin to accept her presence."

Chiman shook his head, and the black jade plugs in his

earlobes wobbled back and forth. "Despite what we've told them about her birth, the people fear her, especially now that rumors of her dreams are circulating Pa nimá. But I gave you my word that she can be schooled, so you must begin that training at once. I believe if the people see her using her healing arts, they'll grow less afraid."

The two old friends stood side by side and watched the children playing. Tz' swung the string, and Na'om and the tayra ran around and around in circles chasing it. Then Tz' began to spin in place, his arms stretched out to either side. Na'om joined him, and finally the two children fell over in a heap of legs and arms, laughing each time one or the other tried to stand and fell back down.

"I see my son is no stranger to your granddaughter," Chiman said. He looked at Ajkun who bowed her head. "It's all right; I know he's been visiting you and helping you gather your herbs and roots."

"The girl does need one friend," Ajkun said. She lifted her head. "I wonder. . ."

Just then, Chachal appeared in the doorway to the hut. "What in the name of Itzamná is going on here?" she said as she stomped toward the children. "Tz', what're you doing playing with this child? Go inside at once." She grabbed her son and pushed him toward the building. Chachal swatted at Na'om with the towel in her hands, shooing her away like one of the turkeys that had come running to the fence looking for corn.

"If Na'om is to be a true member of this tribe someday," Ajkun said as she scooped up her granddaughter and settled her on her hip, "you'd best begin by convincing your wife that she means no harm."

"Hmm, yes, I suppose you're right," Chiman said, as he watched Chachal storm back into their hut, her hand firmly on Tz's shoulder. But Ajkun didn't hear his answer as she had already disappeared down the jungle path.

YAKAL

Yakal stood near one of the supports holding up the thatched roof over his head. The sun was low on the horizon, and he watched as the other stonemasons placed their chisels and hammers in wooden boxes and stored them for the night against the base of the pyramid. They were headed back to wives, children, and pots of stew bubbling on open hearths. Yakal had been in Mayapán for almost five years and had yet to find a woman to take Tu'janel's place in his life. He was twenty-three, and many said he needed a woman before he grew too old to please one. Then he grinned. *There is Uskab*, he thought. He pictured her waist-length black hair, her wide hips, round breasts, and her giggle . . . oh, her giggle sent tingles down his back. He knew she was seventeen, far older than most men would want for a wife. Perhaps that would be to his advantage. Best of all, she was friends with his younger sister, Imul. The two girls were inseparable and could be at his mother's house at that moment.

Yakal's thoughts were interrupted when he saw his uncle, Bitol, approaching from the Warrior's Palace. Yakal noticed he carried a leather tube of documents in his hand. "Yakal, come share a mug of *balché* with me. It's been a long week; let's have a drink together," Bitol said as he came to stand beside his nephew. He looked at the statue of a jaguar in front of them. "You're doing fine work these days; your father would be proud," he said.

"Huh, I doubt that," Yakal replied. "You know what happened when I said I wanted to become a mason."

"Yes, well, that's all in the past, how about that drink?" Bitol said as he patted Yakal on his bare shoulder. "It's been a vexing day for me, and a bit of refreshment would do us both good."

"Another night perhaps," Yakal replied.

Bitol looked into his nephew's eyes. "I know that look . . .," Bitol said. "Uskab is visiting your sister, yes?"

Yakal felt his cheeks redden. "Is it that obvious?"

"Well, if you want to know the truth, yes," Bitol said as he laughed. "It's good to see you show interest in a girl; I was beginning to fear for you, my young friend. It's time to throw off the sadness of losing Tu'janel and the baby and start a new life, with a new woman."

Yakal swallowed awkwardly as Bitol spoke of the child. He had lied to everyone when he first returned to the city, telling anyone who asked that both mother and daughter had perished during the difficult childbirth at the end of the Wayeb.

"Your father would approve of this match," Bitol said as he watched Yakal. "Uskab is the granddaughter of Q'alel's first sergeant, who was a good warrior and good friend to your father," Bitol said as he shifted the tube from one hand to the other.

Yakal pointed to the container to change the subject away from Q'alel. "More building plans or new orders from the council?" he asked.

"Both, I'm afraid," Bitol replied. He shook his head. "Being a simple stonemason was so much easier than this position of Commander of the Gates. I never wanted anything to do with being a warrior, as that was Q'alel's love." Bitol looked out at the plaza in front of them where several kids were kicking a leather ball. "There are rumors the Xiu are planning another attack, so we need to up the number of sentries on the wall again." Suddenly the ball rolled in front of Bitol, and he kicked it to the boy who grinned and ran back to his friends. "Come by tomorrow, and I'll show you the designs for the new basket workshops."

Yakal nodded in reply. He barely noticed when his uncle left.

At the mention of his father, Q'alel, Yakal had been transported back in time to when he was fourteen.

As head of the military and sworn protector of the city, Q'alel held a high seat on the ruling council. He was well regarded in Mayapán for his leadership, and Yakal knew he fully expected him, as his firstborn son, to follow in his footsteps. But Yakal also knew there were many who disagreed with Q'alel, and the loudest opponent to anything regarding Yakal was Satal, Q'alel's legal wife. He thought of the last time he'd seen his father alive.

"The boy should enter the ranks of the military," Q'alel said as he paced back and forth in front of Satal. Yakal stood in the doorway to the palace that he lived in with Q'alel, Satal, and his older half-sister, Chachal. He watched his father talk about him as if he didn't exist.

Satal was kneeling in front of the fire pit, stirring a bubbling pot of iguana stew. She twisted on her knees to stare at Yakal, hidden in the shadows. "Since you've insisted on this match between our daughter and this shaman, Chiman, the boy needs to go with Chachal and keep watch over her. Who knows what these southerners will do with my baby!" She mixed the soup with a wooden spoon, and a rich, meaty scent filled the air.

"You know that intermarriage with these southern tribes is important to all of us. We need to build relationships with those outside of the Cocom tribe," Q'alel said. "If war breaks out again with the Xiu, we must be prepared and have allies in all regions of the realm."

"But Chachal is in love and wants to marry Alaxel; he's from one of the first Xiu families in Chichén Itzá. What better way to establish good relations between the Cocom and the Xiu than to marry our daughter to this highborn boy?" Satal demanded as she stood up and dusted the dirt from her skirt.

"I would sooner cast Chachal into the cenote than to have her marry a Xiu!" Q'alel kicked his stool, and it fell over on its side. The large knife sheath he carried on his hip thwacked into his thigh, and Yakal could see a red spot appear on his father's leg.

"I am of the Xiu," Satal said as she placed herself in front of her husband, "or have you forgotten that? If you hadn't stolen me in that raid, I would have married Alaxel's uncle, Ajelbal. Instead, I was forced to become your wife!"

Q'alel glared at Satal. "I should never have taken you into my bed that night. I should have sent you to the slave quarters, but I was young and stupid back then. I thought our alliance would help end the conflicts between the two tribes; all it did was to bring more warfare to both cities." Q'alel circled away from Satal at that point and noticed Yakal standing in the doorway. "Chachal will marry the southerner, and the boy will begin his training in the morning," he said.

"That boy is not worthy of the military, being the offspring of that slave girl you slept with," Satal said as she spat on the ground.

Yakal saw his father yank Satal's upper arm.

"Mind your words, woman," Q'alel said. "At least Alom has given me a son; you produced one girl and one sickly boy who died at birth." He pushed Satal away. "And now you are unable to make another child; Yakal is my son and will follow in my footsteps. He'll need a lot of training if he is to become a great warrior."

Yakal stepped out from the doorway and approached his father. "*Qajaw*," he said, using the formal mode of address in the hopes it would influence how his father reacted, "may I be permitted to speak?" He avoided looking at Satal; he knew he would get another beating as soon as Q'alel left the house.

"Go ahead, but my mind is made up."

"Qajaw, I don't want to become a soldier . . ." Yakal shrank back as his father advanced on him.

"And what is it you do want to do?" he demanded.

Yakal shuffled his bare feet in the dusty courtyard and didn't look up as he spoke again. "I've been helping Uncle Bitol and the other stonemasons with the work on the wall. I want to become one of them and help build the temples and pyramids I hear you and the others on the council talk about late at night."

"A mason, you want to become a mason! This is what you want out of your life? When you could become a warrior, fight in many battles, and have your name inscribed on those very stones?" Q'alel stared at Yakal, and the boy looked up.

"Yes, Qajaw, I do. Bitol has taught me some of his methods, and he says I'll be a great sculptor one day. He says I can see inside the stone and release its soul through my hands."

"Bitol, what does he know? He balked at the first fight we were in," Q'alel said. "We should have been standing side by side in the attack, but when I glanced beside me, he was gone. My cowardly brother is the man you want to follow?"

Yakal dropped his head and stared at his feet again. "Yes," he whispered.

Q'alel turned his back on his son, and after a moment's silence, he spoke to Satal. "You'll get your wish. The boy will go with Chachal to the south; better he travels with his half-sister and learns something of these southern ways than he stays here and humiliates me."

"But Qajaw . . ." Yakal said.

"Silence, boy. You'll do as you're told. Now, get out of my sight."

Yakal had watched his father march away without another word. He'd heard Satal snickering to herself, but hadn't stayed in the palace long enough to find out why she was suddenly so happy. That had been the last time Yakal had seen his father. Upon his return to Mayapán, four years after that day, Bitol had been the one to tell him of Q'alel's death at the hands of the Xiu in an unexpected attack by the warriors of Chichén Itzá.

Yakal wiped his eyes. He would have liked to see his father one more time. So many years had passed; there'd been so much anger at the end, and for what? Yakal felt the gods had robbed him of his father's love, just as they had cursed him with the death of Tu'janel and the birth of a girl instead of a son. But he would regain Itzamná's favor by carving tales of his father's courage and his first wife's beauty into the stones of the buildings he had yet to build.

He stepped out from under the awning, which provided shade for the workers during the heat of the day, and stared at the pyramid in front of him. This side was deep in shadow, and only the very top of the pyramid held the last rays of the sun. Built over an existing pyramid, this new four-sided one rose sixty feet into the air and had a small wooden temple at the very top. Only the highest shamans of the city were ever allowed up there now, but Yakal was proud to think that he had been the one to lug the final stones that formed the flat platform where the shamans prayed to the gods. No one else in the city could claim such a feat, as the limestone rocks weighed over a hundred pounds apiece. Yakal grinned again, remembering how the sweat had poured off his body as he had struggled up the sixty steep steps with each stone tied to his back. And how later that night, several eligible young maidens had offered to rub his scratched back and sore thighs with cinnamon-scented salve to ease his pain. But Yakal had refused them all. The pain had felt good to him; it had made him feel alive for the first time since leaving the jungle village of Pa nimá, since he had banished all feelings from his body and mind on that fateful early morning. And then he had met Uskab, and everything had changed.

Yakal checked once again to make sure he had put his tools away; there was time enough tomorrow to finish chiseling in the head and fangs of the jaguar. He glanced to his right, at the round observatory building, and noticed a procession of elders entering the domed building. Special slots built into the ceiling allowed them to study the night sky and plot the movements of the stars. Yakal was glad his day of work was over, not just beginning. He adjusted his loincloth and brushed his hands through his shoulder-length black hair. There was no time to bathe before dinner;

Uskab would see him covered in stone dust. *But* he thought, *if she's to become my wife, she'll have to get used to that.*

A steady drumbeat filled the air as the military guard changed sentinels at each of the gateways. Yakal could hear a whistle blow as other guards continued their training nearby, in front of the Temple of the Warriors. He pressed his hands to his ears to block out all the sounds. Even after all these years of living among the thousands of inhabitants of the city, he was still not used to the endless noise of humanity. There were days when he longed to return to the quiet jungle near Pa nimá where he had been able to hear himself think.

Yakal dropped his hands as he looked again at the darkening sky. Thousands of stars pierced the blue-black darkness, and he knew he was late. He hurried past the marketplace, still busy with traders even at this hour. Torchlight cast bright spots onto the many piles of blankets, baskets, and hollow gourds for sale. Smoke from small cooking braziers drifted in the evening breeze, bringing the scent of roasted deer and boiled turtle to Yakal. His stomach grumbled, and he continued toward his mother's house, located on the outer edge of the city, one hut among hundreds in the section reserved for the day laborers. Yakal didn't mind that they lived in this crowded section of the walled city. He preferred the company of the masons, tanners, and salt harvesters to that of the rulers. He had had enough of living in a palace when he was a child. He waved as he quickly walked past several of his coworkers who were already enjoying their evening meals.

Just then, his little sister, Masat, ran up to him. Yakal scooped the seven-year-old up in his arms and tossed her in the air before settling her on his shoulders. Of all his sisters, Masat was his favorite. She giggled and kicked her heels against his chest, and Yakal broke into a trot. As he jogged, he realized with a start that his own child would only be a couple of years younger than Masat, and the notion made him stop in mid-stride.

"Run, Yakal," Masat begged as she kicked her heels again.

"No, little one, that's enough for one day," Yakal said as he let the girl slide to the ground. "I'm weary after a long day of work, and you're getting too big to carry on my shoulders!" The two continued to walk hand in hand until Alom's house came into view.

"Chuch, here he is," Masat said as she ran to Alom, who stood wiping her hands on a soft white towel.

Yakal walked to his mother and stooped to kiss the older woman on the cheek. She held out the towel to him. "Wash up quickly, I've made your favorite dish for supper," she said as she pushed Yakal toward a turtle shell basin full of warm water.

Yakal heard giggling from inside the small hut and poked his head inside. By the light of several candles, he could just see his sister, Imul, and Uskab sitting on palm mats in the corner. Imul was braiding small yellow marigolds into Uskab's long black hair, and Yakal felt a twinge in his groin at seeing the girl. He stepped back outside before the girls noticed him.

"How did your work go today?" Alom asked as she handed Yakal a glazed pottery plate piled high with roasted iguana meat and cooked chaya.

"Grroud," Yakal said as he shoveled another spoonful of the succulent dark meat into his mouth.

"Shush now, I didn't raise you to talk with your mouth full of food," Alom said as she sat down next to Yakal on the pounded dirt of their tiny courtyard.

Masat came and sat in her mother's lap. Yakal's other sister, Binel ja' quickly joined them. Yakal looked at Binel ja' as she gathered her dark blue skirt around her legs. She had been a little girl of only seven when Yakal had left for the south with Chachal. Now she was a grown woman and set to be married at the next full moon.

Movement out of the corner of his eye made Yakal turn his head, and he watched as Uskab and Imul joined the group near the cooking fire. Imul grinned at her brother as he continued to eat, but he noticed Uskab refused to look in his direction. *Perhaps she'll look at me,* he thought, *if I tell them all a story about the sacred ceiba tree when I'm done eating.*

"Where is Tikoy?" he asked as he wiped his mouth and set the empty plate on the ground. His little brother reminded Yakal of himself at age ten.

"He was watching the soldiers training in the central square," Alom replied. "But he should be home by now," she added as she glanced around the dark courtyard. Torchlight from the nearby huts flickered in the darkness, but did not reveal the shadow of the young boy.

"I hope he steers clear of Satal's house," Yakal said. "That witch will scoop him up and drop him into her black potion pot if she sees him." He heard Uskab and Imul giggle.

"Shush, Yakal, you're scaring the girls with that kind of talk," Alom said.

"Chuch, it's no secret that she's a witch," Imul said. "All you have to do to is look at her scarred lips and tongue and her ragged ears from all the bloodletting she's done to know that she's evil." She giggled again.

"Imul, be nice. You never know who's listening to idle talk. With Satal on the council, she wields a lot of power in the city."

"Yakal should have been given Tat axel's seat on the council when he returned to the city," Imul said. "Uncle Bitol thinks so as do some of the others."

"Ah, sweet sister," Yakal said, "I have no desire to spend my days in boring meetings discussing the number of baskets of maize harvested or the amount of salt collected in any given day," Yakal said. "I much prefer to work the stone and help build the city. Now that Uncle Bitol has been made Commander of the Gates as well as head mason, he'll keep us informed of the ins and outs of the city and make sure we're all safe. Besides, Satal would never relinquish her position after all these years, and if anyone tried to make her leave, she'd cast a spell on them."

"Careful Yakal, you don't know who's listening," Alom said. She looked around the darkness and readjusted Masat on her lap. "Come; tell us another one of your stories."

At that moment, a dark shape raced into the group and plopped on the ground next to Yakal.

"Tikoy! Where have you been?" she asked as she turned to look at her son.

"Sorry I'm late, Chuch, but when Nimal saw me watching the training, he asked me to stay."

"Nimal, what did the head of the regiment want with such a little guy as you?" Yakal said as he playfully punched Tikoy in the arm.

"He's asked me to become his personal assistant," Tikoy said with pride, as he dodged another swing of Yakal's hand. "He says I've inherited Tat axel's strength and agility and expects I'll make a fine warrior someday. He wants me to begin my training tomorrow . . ." Tikoy looked around the group, "but told me I must ask your permission, Chuch, and that of Yakal, since he is the oldest and man of the house now that Tat axel is gone." The boy looked at his mother and then at his brother. He fidgeted on the ground and kicked up little puffs of dust with his heels.

Yakal and Alom looked at each other, and Yakal spoke first. "Chuch and I will talk after you've gone to bed, Tikoy, and let you know of our decision in the morning." He turned his head to face Uskab. "Did I tell you the story of how the ceiba tree got its thorns?" he said.

"Yakal," Alom said as she interrupted her son. "You know your father would have wanted this," she said. "Tikoy, if you promise me you'll stay out of the mock battles and only act as Nimal's scribe, then you have my permission. And I'll talk to Nimal in the morning so he knows you're not to participate in the drills until you're much older."

Tikoy jumped up, ran over to his mother, and hugged her around the neck before kissing her on the top of the head.

"*Maltiox*, Chuch, I knew you'd say yes." Binel ja' and Imul grabbed Tikoy by the arms and pulled him down to hug him.

Why does Tikoy get what he wants right away? Yakal thought. *I never had it so easy.* He felt his face grow red with anger, and he stood up abruptly. He stalked off into the darkness and didn't notice Uskab watching him as he hurried off.

Long after the others had gone to bed, Yakal returned to the two-room hut he shared with his siblings and mother. They were all asleep on mats spread across the floor, and Yakal tiptoed past them to his spot against the wall. But he tossed and turned, his thoughts tumbling from Uskab to Tu'janel to his baby girl and the fear that someday Satal would find her. He thought about the night he'd returned to the city, of being sent in front of Satal and the council the next day, and how he'd lied to them all about what had happened to his wife and his infant child. He'd even convinced Satal that Chachal was happy in Pa nimá.

Weary of rolling about in his blankets, Yakal finally got up before any roosters began to crow. He slipped into his loincloth and sandals in the semi-dark hut and stepped outside. The morning air was cool and smelled of the ocean, even though the city was several miles from the sea. He hesitated in the doorway, wondering if he should go back inside for his blanket. But he didn't want to risk waking the others. And he didn't want to talk to his mother about Tikoy.

As he poked at the embers in the fire pit and tried to get a blaze going, Yakal thought of what Bitol had told him when he first returned to Mayapán. As soon as he had left with Chiman and Chachal for the south, his father had regretted sending him away. But Yakal wondered if that was true. *Perhaps Tat forgot about me,* Yakal thought as he blew on the dry wood. *After all, several years passed, and there were no visits and no letters, even though the traders from the villages along the river near Pa nimá came to Mayapán on several occasions. I wrote Tat several times and never heard a word. Only Chachal received news from Satal, begging her to return home where she belonged.* He blew on the wood again, a flame shot up, and Yakal quickly added more wood before placing a clay pot full of water near the flames. He turned at the sound of shuffling feet on the dry ground.

"Chuch, what are you doing up so early?" Yakal said as he saw his mother step from the doorway into the first rays of light. Her graying hair was pulled back into a single plait, and she had a dark green blanket wrapped around her shoulders.

"I heard you get up," Alom said as she readjusted the blanket and gently pushed her son from the fire. She poked at the base of the fire, broke several sticks in half, and fed them into the flames before moving the bubbling pot of water off to one side of the coals. "Hand me your mug, child," she said as she took an old towel and picked up the hot water. She poured the liquid into Yakal's earthenware cup. Then she stirred in some ground cacao beans and frothed the mixture with a wooden spoon before handing the beverage to Yakal. "So, are you going to tell me why you couldn't sleep?" She waited while Yakal sipped his cocoa.

"Too many things on my mind . . ." Yakal paused. He wondered if he should confide in his mother and tell her the truth about the baby he left behind. Then he shook his head. *No one will ever find out, so why even bring it up,* he thought. "Did Tat axel ever speak of me after I left?" he blurted out.

"Your father never stopped talking about you, Yakal," Alom said as she placed her dark brown hand on top of Yakal's. "He so wanted you to be a soldier . . ." Her voice drifted off. She shivered and wrapped the blanket tight around her shoulders. She looked at Yakal. "You have his brown eyes, and your eyebrows slant just like his did." She poked at the fire. "Your father was shocked when you told him you wanted to follow your uncle's path. He saw that as a sign of weakness in himself. He felt that he'd done something wrong in raising you so you'd prefer a chisel in your hand instead of a spear." Alom smiled. "But he loved you very much and realized as soon as you were gone that he'd been too harsh with you."

"Why did he never send me a letter or come get me, if all was forgiven?" Yakal said.

Alom looked directly into her son's eyes. "But he did send you letters, many in the first months and then less and less as he realized you'd never answer him."

"I never received any letters!" Yakal said. He choked on the bitter chocolate drink. He spat out one word, "Satal!"

"Satal? What does she have to do with this?" Alom asked.

"Don't you see? She never wanted Tat to be with you, never accepted me as Tat axel's child. She must have done something to his letters to perpetuate the rift between us."

"Oh, she is an evil one, that woman," Alom said.

Yakal stood up and tossed the last drops of his cocoa in the fire where they sputtered and burbled. "I'll have a word with that *itzinel*. That witch will regret ever crossing this family," Yakal said as he started to walk away.

"Yakal, wait, you mustn't act in haste," Alom said as she hurried to step in front of her firstborn. "She's too powerful these days; no one dares cross her. We must just wait and pray she heads to the land of the ancestors soon." She guided Yakal back to the fire, and they sat in silence for a few minutes, watching as the clouds overhead changed from salmon pink to light blue. "Come now, we have other, more important matters to discuss."

"Tell Tikoy I'm sorry about last night. He'll make a fine soldier one day."

"And what shall I tell Uskab?" Alom asked as she watched Yakal's face. It reddened to match the color of the sky. "Ah Yakal," Alom laughed, "It's no secret to any of us that you have feelings for the girl."

Yakal smiled, showing his white teeth. "What about Uskab? Has she said anything to Imul about me?" Yakal asked. "Would her parents agree to the match?"

"Agree? They've already spoken to the shamans and been told it's a favorable joining for everyone involved." Alom stood up and patted Yakal on the shoulder. "They're just waiting for you to ask Uskab." She handed Yakal a small basket of tamales for his lunch. "Your sister, Binel, weds at the next full moon, which is only three weeks away. We could make it a double wedding, but you must hurry and ask Uskab!"

Yakal grinned and bent down to kiss his mother on the cheek. "I'll ask her tonight as soon as I get done with work," he said. He picked up his lunch and hurried off to work. An image of Tu'janel on the birthing bed, the baby tucked in by her side flitted across his mind as he walked. He kicked at a rock and sent it spiraling across the dusty ground as he pushed the image far back in the recesses of his mind. There was no time to dwell on things in the past.

NA'OM

It was a few days after her name day, and seven-year-old Na'om sat down in the shade of the lime tree in her grandmother's courtyard. She adjusted the strap that wrapped around her waist, through the backstrap loom in front of her, and to the base of the tree. She leaned backwards, and the rope grew taut. Picking up a wooden shuttle, she passed the white cotton thread through the gap between the two sets of warp threads and packed the thread tight with a straight piece of bamboo. She pulled up on the stick attached to the heddles, making a new gap in the warp threads, and slowly passed the shuttle back the other way. She didn't really enjoy weaving, but Ajkun wanted her to know how to make clothes as well as gather the herbs they used to heal the villagers. She worked for a few minutes and watched as the fabric slowly grew under her hands. Then her shuttle got wedged among several threads; she yanked on it and broke a warp thread in the process.

"Ati't," the girl called, "I need your help." She waited a moment and called again. It was only in the ensuing silence that she heard someone snicker and looked around quickly to see who it was.

"Tz'," she cried out when she saw the twelve-year-old boy standing in the shadows near the gate to the courtyard. "What are you doing here? How long have you been watching me?" she asked. Her eyes searched his lean face for an answer.

"Long enough to know you'll never be a great weaver if you don't learn some patience," the boy replied and laughed. He bumped the square leather pouch he wore around his waist as he held up a mahogany paddle slightly taller than his five-foot frame. "Come to the river and watch me learn to paddle one of the canoes."

"You know I can't," Na'om said as she tried to knot the two broken threads back together. "Your mother still won't let us be together, despite what your dad says. And you'd be in trouble with the elders if they thought you were trying to teach me stuff only the boys are supposed to know. Besides, I promised Ati't I'd try to get another three inches woven today, but at this rate, I don't think I will." Na'om put the shuttle on the ground and started to untie the loom strap from around her waist. "I'd rather come with you, but Ati't says I need to know how to make my own clothes as well as learn about herbs." She struggled to stand up and got tangled in the rope.

Placing his paddle against the side of the lime tree, Tz' stepped behind Na'om and placed his hands under her elbows. In one motion, he lifted the girl to her feet. Her black, waist-long hair brushed against his bare arm, and he leaned in to smell the vanilla oil she used to make her hair shiny. He stepped backwards as Na'om spun around.

She looked at him with curiosity as she pushed a strand of hair behind her ear. "Maltiox," she said as she brushed the dirt from her turquoise skirt.

The boy picked up his paddle and started to leave. "I don't care what Mother or the elders think; Father is shaman of the village and tells me all good leaders must befriend everyone. But if you're afraid," Tz' shrugged, "well, suit yourself," he said. "I wish you were a boy; it'd make it so much easier to spend time together."

As he hurried off, paddle in hand, Na'om saw the bone whistle Tz' always carried with him slip from his pouch and land on the ground. "Tz', wait," Na'om cried as she hurried to get the small flute. But the boy only waved and ran on down the path. The girl picked up her loom and carried it to the hut. She stepped into the semi-darkness and saw her grandmother was still lying on the bed.

"Ati't," she said, "Tz' dropped his whistle; may I go to the river to give it to him?"

Her grandmother didn't answer. Na'om hurried to her grandmother as she struggled to rise from her side of the bed they shared. "Are you all right?" Na'om asked.

"Hand me the basket of dried nettles, child," Ajkun said.

Na'om reached for the basket on the top shelf in the corner of the hut. It was a long stretch for the little girl, but she was just able to snag the basket with the tip of her finger. She caught it before it fell to the floor. "It's empty," Na'om said as she looked inside the tightly woven reeds. "But I know where there are more. When I was playing, I found them just yesterday . . ." the girl paused; she wasn't supposed to wander off the paths around the village if Ajkun wasn't with her.

"It's all right, Na'om," Ajkun said, "You're growing into a big girl; more and more, you'll need to roam this area alone, I'm afraid. Your ati't is getting old and weary." She slipped her calloused feet into her leather sandals and headed toward the doorway. "Run and fetch the nettles for me, my poor old bones need some tea. And while you're gone, I'll fix that broken thread."

Na'om bent down and kissed her grandmother's wrinkled skin. *She tastes like dark honey,* Na'om thought, as she handed the bundle of threads to her grandmother. "I'll be back quickly," she said as she skipped down the path toward the river. She held the empty basket in one hand and still clutched Tz's whistle in the other. She glanced at the crystal-clear blue water as it burbled alongside the path and could hear the shouts and laughs of the young men as she grew closer to the clearing where the canoes were stored.

She thought of bringing Tz' his whistle, but then realized that would only get him in trouble. *The elders mustn't know Tz' stopped by the hut on his way to practice,* she thought. Her mind made up, Naòm tucked the flute into the pocket of her skirt and backtracked up the path to where she had found a shortcut to the manioc fields. It led diagonally away from the river, cutting through thick jungle, and came out a short distance from where she had found the nettles.

Glancing all around her to get her bearings once again, Naòm stepped into the tangle of liana vines that hung from the nearest ceiba tree. She focused on a large mango tree in the distance and started walking in that direction. The jungle closed in on all sides, and Naòm could no longer hear the river gurgling or the men as they called out instructions to the new paddlers. She concentrated on keeping the mango tree in her sights. The air grew warmer as the closeness of the trees and grasses pressed in on Naòm. She stopped and looked behind her. Only the twitching of a bush as it sprang back into place marked the way she had come. She felt a bead of sweat trickle down her back and wished she had brought a gourd of water with her. Continuing forward, she stepped over a trail of leafcutter ants. One line of ants, with nothing on their backs, marched head to toe into the grass to the left, while a parallel line of ants, each carrying a wedge of green leaf that was two sizes bigger than the ant itself, disappeared into the grass to the right.

A quick flash of bright orange and black caught her eye, and Naòm peered into the foliage to catch sight of the bird. She knelt down, scanned the trees ahead, and finally saw the male hooded oriole perched on a limb; it sang *chut, chut, chut, whew, whew* before flying off. Naòm searched for a nest, but the glare of the sun was too bright. All she could see was darkness against the bright blue sky. She squinted, blinked, and rubbed her watering eyes. She started to return the way she had come, unsure she'd be able to make her way to the other side of the thicket. But looking around, she realized she didn't know exactly which direction led back to the river as the bushes all started to look the same to her.

The heat of the sun pressed down on her head like a heavy hand, slowing her steps. She stopped and turned in a full circle, sighted in on the tall mango tree, and continued to press forward.

She caught another flash of yellow and black, this time low to the ground. She crouched, hoping to see the female oriole in the brush. Suddenly, Na'om stiffened as she heard a low growling near her. She twisted around slowly and placed the basket for the herbs on the ground. The growls continued, growing louder. Na'om stood still, not sure whether to move or not. She glanced to her left and right, but couldn't see through the dense scrub on all sides. Again, she thought of returning the way she had come, even though that would delay getting the nettles for Ati't. Then, out of the corner of her eye, Na'om caught another glimpse of something tawny and black before a searing pain ripped into her. She clutched at her face as blood began to flow from the wound.

A jaguar limped out into the dirt directly in front of her. Na'om could see the broken piece of an old arrow shaft hanging from the jaguar's left flank. Pus oozed from the red wound, leaving a dark trail of dirt and grime on the beautiful yellow and black-spotted coat. Na'om swayed on her feet, but stood her ground. The jaguar's head lowered, her ears went back flat against her head, and Na'om looked directly into her eyes. They glowed like the yellow stones in the riverbed. She touched her cheek, and her fingers came away covered in blood. The jaguar growled again and bared her white teeth.

Na'om continued to stare into the jaguar's eyes. They hypnotized her, golden orbs full of light that sparked and danced. The heat of the jungle pulsed in her head, and she rocked on her feet, first to the left, then to the right. The cat shifted its weight in rhythm with Na'om, and Na'om felt a strange tingling warmth spread throughout her body. Then, a wave of tiredness and pain washed over her, and Na'om just wanted to lie down, to curl up somewhere cool and dark to lick her wounds . . .

Just then, a small black jaguar ran out from under the bushes and bumped into his mother. The she-cat turned her head, breaking her gaze with Naʼom, who watched as the kitten, his black spots barely visible on his cocoa-colored coat, tried to suckle from his mother's elongated teats. Naʼom felt a peculiar ache in her chest as the kitten sucked a moment before being cuffed by the mother. With a squeak, the kitten ran back into the brush, his right ear ripped and bleeding.

The mother jaguar faced Naʼom and growled. She crouched lower to the ground, her hindquarters ready to spring. Her tail swished rapidly from side to side, and she bared her fangs again. Bracing her feet shoulder-width apart, Naʼom stood as tall as she could. She felt drops of blood dripping on the front of her shirt, but ignored them. She swallowed several times. And then, Naʼom growled back. It came out as a squeak, so she swallowed again and growled. The cat snarled. Their eyes locked. Another wave of pain and fatigue swept through Naʼom's body. The cat sank lower, her belly almost flat against the ground. Naʼom stood on her tiptoes and brought her arms forward in front of her. She held her hands out, palms down, toward the wounded cat. The jaguar dropped her head so her chin touched the dirt. She lay like that for a moment before backing up a step, where she turned and slunk away into the underbrush.

Naʼom plunked down in the reddish dirt. She removed her deep blue sash from around her waist and bunched the cotton up against her face to stop the bleeding. She felt woozy and lay down, curled up in a ball among the sticks and rocks, her hand pressing the cloth tightly to her face. The sun was directly in her face, and she kept her eyes tightly closed against the brightness.

She must have slept, for the sun was no longer in her eyes when she finally opened them. With difficulty, she sat up, her right arm asleep from being lain on for so long. Her right cheek throbbed with pain, and the sash had stuck to the wound. She got to her feet and swayed there, as the blood rushed from her head. She took several deep breaths and headed back in the general direction of the river, all thoughts of finding the nettles driven from her mind with the pulsating pain in her face. Her right eye watered, making her sight blurry, and she stumbled through the bushes.

All of a sudden, Tz' came crashing through the brush, calling her name. "Naom, what happened?" he said as he rushed to Naom's side.

"A jaguar," Naom said and fainted into Tz's arms.

Tz' lifted Naom in his sturdy arms and carried her back to Ajkun's hut. Naom woke up as he laid her on the bed. She couldn't see out of her right eye, but heard Tz' speak to Ajkun.

"I must tell Father of the jaguar," he said. "We'll hunt for her, and when she dies, I'll have the skin," he said proudly as he headed off to the river.

Ajkun approached Naom with a basin of warm water, which she used to soften the sash dried into Naom's wounds. She gently removed the cloth and looked at her right cheek. Four deep gashes ran from just below Naom's eye to the corner of her mouth. Naom winced, and tears leaked from the corners of her eyes as Ajkun washed the wounds. When the gouges were clean, she applied a warm poultice of creeping chaffweed leaves; they would help stem the flow of blood that had restarted. Ajkun wrapped Naom's face in a clean white cloth, which she tied under her chin.

"You should rest now, child," Ajkun said as Naom struggled to sit up higher on the narrow bed. "In a few days, you'll begin to feel better. Shh, don't try to sit up," she said as she laid a hand on Naom's shoulder and pushed her gently back onto the mattress. "You've lost a lot of blood from that cat scratch."

There was a knock on the doorway, and Chiman appeared in the entranceway, Tz' at his side. "I must speak with the girl," Chiman said as he entered the room. He didn't wait for a reply, but approached the bed. He looked down at Naom who glanced up into his kind face with scared eyes. "Don't be afraid, Naom, I mean you no harm," he said as he sat down on the edge of the bed. "Tell me what happened this morning; Tz' says you were attacked by a jaguar."

Na'om looked quickly at Ajkun who nodded her head. She looked back at Chiman. "Yes, there was a jaguar; she was hurt, an arrow hung from her side, and I could feel her pain . . ." Na'om's voice drifted off as she thought about the strange sensation that had swept through her body. She didn't want anyone else to know about it. She cleared her throat. "She was hurt, and there was a kitten, too, which she swatted at," Na'om paused again, seeing in her mind's eye the ripped ear that dripped blood and mingled with her own blood in the dirt. She struggled to sit up again.

"The girl needs rest now, Chiman," Ajkun said as she moved to the doorway and held the covering aside.

Chiman stood looking at Na'om and motioned for Tz' to wait outside. "One more question, in private, then I'll go," he said. Ajkun followed Tz' outside. Chiman turned back to Na'om. "You said you felt the jaguar's pain, what did you mean by that?"

"Only that I could see the arrow wound and so I guessed she must have been in pain," Na'om said quickly. She didn't know exactly what she had felt, but she didn't want to try to explain it to the shaman.

Apparently satisfied with her answer, Chiman left the room, and Na'om drifted off to sleep.

It was almost dusk when Tz' returned to the hut and burst into the room where Ajkun was changing the poultice on Na'om's face. He carried the jaguar skin draped over his shoulders. The tail dragged on the ground behind him, and the front paws extended midway down his chest. "Grrr," he said as he prowled across the room. He stopped his joking and looked directly at Na'om when she didn't respond. "Tat axel's given me the skin, since I'm the one who found the dead cat. It's a great honor to wear a jaguar skin, you know," he said as he twirled in front of the bed. He grinned at Na'om, but she looked away when she recognized the wound in the side of the fur.

"How did you find me this morning?" she asked as she faced the wall, unwilling to look at the skin or to let Tz' see the wounds in her face.

"I came back for my whistle, and Ati't told me you had gone for nettles." He shifted the slippery skin on his back. "I thought you might try to use the shortcut you came across last week. Aren't you proud that I found this cat that hurt you?"

"No," Na'om said. "She was sick, probably dying when I saw her, so what you did was no act of bravery." Na'om remembered the glazed, yellow eyes of the cat, how they had stared into her own brown eyes and held her gaze until she felt herself melting into the cat, becoming one with the jungle creature.

Tz' pulled the skin from his body and bundled it into a large ball that he carried in his arms as he turned to leave.

"Tz', wait, I'm sorry," Na'om said as she turned to face her friend. "You are brave; you knew the cat was wounded when you went out there, so thank you for saving me." She held out her hand to Tz' who approached the bed. She pulled Tz' toward her and innocently planted a quick kiss on his cheek.

Tz' quickly turned his head, tugged his hand out of hers, and left the hut without saying a word. Na'om lay on the bed, wondering what she had done to make him leave so rapidly.

That night, Na'om dreamt of the jaguar. She was back in the brush, the sun beating down, the jaguar facing her. A tingling sensation rippled through her body as she felt the ground under her bare feet, the motion of wind across her face, the burning as claws ripped into her cheek. She felt an aching hunger in her belly and a deep pain in her left side and tightness in her teats swollen with milk . . . She woke from the fearful dream to find Ajkun holding her tightly. She touched her face and felt the bandage on it.

"You were moaning, Na'om, but you're safe now; I have you," Ajkun said as she held the girl and rocked her in her arms. She helped Na'om lie back down on the bed.

Na'om pretended to go back to sleep and eventually heard the gentle snores of her grandmother. Too restless to sleep, she thought of the jaguar's glowing yellow eyes, so like those in some of her dreams. Of how the pain in her face matched that of her earliest dreams. *How many other things have I dreamt of will come true,* she worried as she waited for the light to grow stronger outside. *Ati't calls it a gift, but I don't want it. I want to be like the other girls in the village.* She fretted the rest of the day and only picked at the stew Ati't brought to her. That night, Na'om was afraid to go to sleep, afraid of the dreams that might come to her.

After two days of bed rest, Na'om could not lie in the hut any longer. "Ati't," she cried, "I must get up and move around outside."

Ajkun came into the room and removed the poultice of fresh herbs and flowers. There was no sign of infection on Na'om's face, just deep gashes that had scabbed over. "Some sunshine on those cuts will help with the healing," Ajkun said as she helped Na'om to her feet. "We'll rub calendula salve on your face day and night to help prevent some scarring," she paused as she pulled an earthenware pot from a shelf, "although I'm afraid you'll be marked forever."

Later that afternoon, while Ajkun dozed in the hammock outside, Na'om took a chance and ran down the path and into the bushes where she had first spotted the jaguar. She crept through the liana vines, searching for signs of the black jaguar cub. She tried making chirping noises, whistling a short tune, standing still and listening, but nothing came out of the jungle to greet her. Then Na'om thought of something else. She swallowed, then growled as she had when facing the mother jaguar. She waited a few minutes and growled again. This time she was rewarded with a tiny meow.

Na'om got on her hands and knees and pushed the bushes aside. There, in the deep grass, was the black kitten. It mewed at Na'om. She removed her blouse and quickly snatched up the cub, wrapping him firmly in the shirt so he couldn't claw or scratch her. He lay still in Na'om's arms, too frightened and hungry to move.

Na'om hurried back to the house she shared with her grandmother. She cautiously opened the gate and crept into the yard, careful not to make any sound so as not to wake her grandmother who was still dozing in the hammock. Na'om scurried to the hut with the cub still wrapped in her shirt and looked around the room for a place to hide it. Spying the small basket where she stored her extra set of clothes, she dumped the clothes out, placed the kitten inside, and tossed the clothes back on top. Na'om had just put the lid back on when she heard Ajkun beginning to wake outside. She looked around for something to feed the tiny cat.

Two tamales, filled with ground peccary meat, were leftover from the morning's meal. Na'om pulled apart the cornmeal paste in one, exposing the lump of cold and greasy meat inside. She brought it back to the basket, removed the lid, and held the meat out to the kitten whose head peeked out from the bundle of clothes. The cat grabbed at the food, almost biting Na'om's finger in the process. She laughed, though, as his raspy tongue licked her fingers, searching for more of the food. She quickly grabbed the remaining tamale and fed it to the kitten. Then she filled a coconut husk with clean water from the gourd hanging on the wall and let the cub drink. She gently rubbed him behind the ears and felt a low rumbling below her fingers as the kitten began to purr before falling asleep in the basket. Na'om hurried to cover the baby jaguar when Ajkun appeared in the doorway.

All evening, Na'om watched the basket out of the corner of her eye; she worried the cat would push the lid up or make a noise, alerting Ajkun to his whereabouts. But the kitten didn't make a sound, and finally Na'om and Ati't climbed into bed.

Before the mourning doves began to coo the next day, Na'om was up and out of bed, eager to find a new hiding spot for the kitten before Ajkun woke up. But when she searched the basket, the cat was gone. Na'om glanced around the small hut and began to laugh. The jaguar was half in, half out of the cooking pot by the door, his hind legs scrabbling in the air. He was licking up the remnants of the evening's turkey stew.

"What's so funny, Na'om?" Ajkun said as she sat up in bed. She brushed her long gray hair out of her face and let out a cry when she saw the kitten in her cooking pot. "Na'om, where did that come from?" she demanded.

Na'om hung her head and mumbled into her shirt.

"Speak up, girl."

"I found him where the jaguar struck me. I knew he wouldn't leave the area," Na'om said as she scooped the jaguar from the pot. She rubbed him behind the ears and a low purring filled the room. "I've named him Ek' Balam." She put the kitten on the ground, and he wound around her legs, leaving tiny black hairs on Na'om's white skirt.

"You can't keep it, Na'om, let alone name it," Ajkun said. "It's a wild animal and will grow into a big cat someday. You have to get rid of it; take it back into the jungle, before it gets any older."

"He'll die out there on his own," Na'om cried. "He's my friend, and I'm going to keep him." Na'om grabbed the cat by the scruff of the neck and hurried outside. She grabbed the old cloth Ajkun used to handle hot pots by the fire and wrapped the kitten in it. Cradling him in her arms, she hurried down the path, away from Ati't who stood calling for her from the courtyard.

The cat squirmed and wriggled in Na'om's arms, and suddenly a tiny paw shot out and clawed her stomach. She dropped the bundle on the ground, and the kitten shook the cloth off his body. She raised her shirt and saw tiny beads of blood appearing in a thin line across her stomach. Bending down, she spanked the kitten on his tiny black nose, picked him up again by the scruff, and looked into his golden-green eyes. "You're not going to hurt me ever again," she scolded the kitten. "I'm your mother now, and we'll live together forever." Then Na'om blew into the cat's nose. He hung by his neck, all four big paws dangling in the air like a limp rag doll, and Na'om instantly felt sorry for swatting the kitten. She hugged the cat to her, and he began to purr. Na'om turned as she heard feet approaching on the path. It was Tz'.

"What have you got there?" Tz' asked. He leaned on his canoe paddle and eyed the bundle in Na'om's arms.

"Nothing, go away," Na'om said as she tried to shield the kitten from view. The jaguar wiggled in Naom arms, claws extended, and she had to place him on the ground.

Tz' laughed when he saw the cat. "So, you're going to play mother jaguar, are you?"

"Someone has to take care of him, now that his real mother is dead," she said. "Besides I felt . . ." Na'om hesitated, "oh, never mind." *It's better not to tell Tz' about the surge of power and energy I felt the other day,* she decided.

"You felt what?" Tz' asked. "Come on, Naom, you can trust me; I promise not to laugh." He reached out to pet the jaguar, and the kitten laid back his ears and growled at him. "Ha, ha, ha, you're a fierce little thing, aren't you," Tz' said as he jerked his hand back.

"Silly, you have to be gentle, look, like this," Naom said as she caressed the soft fur behind Ek' Balam's ears, making him purr again. "I've named him Ek' Balam."

"And what does Ati't say about you having a jaguar for a pet?" Tz' asked as he looked at the girl and the cat.

"She wants me to return him to the jungle and let him fend for himself. But I'm going to keep him. She'll see; this jaguar will be our protector one day." Naom gazed at Tz'. "Promise not to tell anyone?" she asked.

"You know this is one secret that won't be kept for long, not in this village," Tz' replied. He shook his head. "You're a strange girl, Naom, no doubt about that. Just make sure that cat knows we're friends, all right? I don't want to be eaten someday!"

"Let him sniff you," Naom said as she held the kitten in her arms. "That way he'll recognize your scent." She watched as Tz' bent his face down to the cat and laughed when Ek' Balam licked Tz's cheek. "Now you're safe," she said as she hugged the kitten again.

"Let's hope the rest of the villagers are, too," Tz' replied before hurrying on to the river for his next canoe lesson.

CHIMAN

By the next morning, news of Na'om's pet had travelled throughout the village, and a long line of men and women were waiting to speak to Chiman when he stepped outside his house to wash in the river. He sighed, placed his towel and pottery bowl full of soft soap on the bench by the door, and went to greet his neighbors.

"Well, well, what brings all of you here so early and on such a fine morning," Chiman asked, trying to make light of the situation.

"The girl," several people shouted. "She's got a jaguar in her grandmother's house; you must force her to get rid of it."

"What will happen when the cat gets bigger," Potz' said, "and it tries to eat one of my children? The girl and the jaguar must go!"

"You promised us years ago that this child had not been born in the Wayeb," Acan stated, "but this surely is a sign that she was. Why did you deceive us?" he demanded. He looked around at his neighbors. "The girl should be sent from the village, immediately." Several people in the group nodded their heads in agreement.

"My friends, neighbors, come now, don't be so harsh. Na'om is still a little girl; she's been through a lot in the past few days." Chiman brushed a stray strand of hair out of his eyes. "I admit, I did hide Na'om's true birth from you, but only because there were no real signs that it made any difference." He paused as he saw Tz' step out from the open doorway to the house. The lithe and muscular boy came and stood beside his father. Chiman noted with pride that Tz' did not shrink back from the anger in the air. *He will make a fine leader one day,* Chiman thought. He turned back to the villagers. "I know you're all worried, but I take this as a great sign from Itzamná himself," Chiman said. "The jaguar is our most sacred animal; only the highest priests can speak to them and shape-shift into them. Naom was singled out and marked by the great cat for a reason, of this I'm sure. I believe she possesses a power that we have yet to identify—how else would she be able to tame a jaguar cub?"

"But what of us?" the crowd said. "How are we to feel safe with this Wayeb child and her cat in our midst?"

Chiman looked out at the group. They had trusted him and yet, he and Ajkun had deceived them. They demanded a resolution, but he couldn't force himself to send Naom away. "The girl will remain in the village until the time of her first moon blood." He held out his arms to silence the cries that erupted. "Then she'll be sent to live across the river where she can do you no harm."

"She's being trained as the next healer," Potz' shouted. "I demand someone else learn the art. I don't want my medicines coming from that witch." Her neighbors nodded in agreement.

Kemonel stepped forward, her young daughter, Mok'onel, by her side. "Mok'onel is only a few months older than Naom. I suggest she be trained as the next midwife alongside Naom. That way, if anything should change in the future, the village will have a healer."

Chiman took a deep breath and held up his hands to silence the murmurs. "Thank you, Kemonel. That's a good idea. I'll talk to Ajkun and Naom, and I'll pray to Itzamná for guidance. Now, please," Chiman said, as he began to herd the people from his yard, "you must go back to the village and your work." He turned his back on the group, put his arm around Tz's shoulders, and led the boy back to the house.

Chachal stood in the doorway and watched as her husband

and son approached. "I overheard what they said," she said to Chiman. "They're right, you know, it's absurd to let this girl keep the animal. Drive the cat away, kill it if you must, and then force the girl out of the village."

"Surely you can't expect me to banish her while she's still so young . . ." Chiman said.

"Chuch—" Tz' began, but Chiman put his hand on his arm and shook his head. Tz' fell silent.

"Go to the river and bathe; I'll be along shortly," Chiman said as he handed Tz' the soap and towel. He watched as his only son scuffed through the dirt toward the water, his bare feet leaving small marks in the dry path. He turned to face his wife.

"You'd do well to keep that tongue of yours silent," Chiman said as he pushed past Chachal into the house. "From the moment Na'om was born, you've been against her, but she comes from a good family. And I've seen glimpses of her future. Her destiny is entwined with ours and more importantly, with Tz's. I'll not let you destroy what the gods have ordained."

"All these years you've been lying to the villagers and more importantly to me, your wife," Chachal said as she swatted at a sweat fly on her arm. "I told you to smother the girl at birth, but no, you saved her, and for what? So she can now bring destruction down on our heads?" She smacked another fly with her hand and wiped the stain on her skirt. "What are you writing down in that notebook of yours every time Ajkun comes to visit?"

"Na'om's dreams," Chiman replied. "We decided we needed to keep track of them, to see if any of them ever came true."

"And?" Chachal said. "Was this jaguar in one of her dreams?"

"Hmm, yes, I believe so," Chiman replied. He grinned at his wife. "Exciting, isn't it?"

"Exciting? Have you lost your senses? Don't you see how dangerous this girl will be?" Chachal said. She rubbed the beads of her necklace with one hand. "And what of Tz'? He'll be leader of this village someday; he can't be friends with someone tainted by the Wayeb."

"I still don't understand why you're so afraid, Chachal. No harm has come to any of us, ever. No. My mind is made up. The girl remains on this side of the river until her first moon blood has passed, and the cat may stay as well." Chiman picked up his cotton towel and headed out the door toward the river.

"You're a fool, Chiman," Chachal called to his retreating back. "You've let your feelings for Ajkun get in the way of making good decisions for the people of Pa nimá. The girl and the cat will bring nothing but trouble to us all."

NA'OM

Na'om and her new pet were inseparable, the kitten like a small black shadow of the girl. The villagers shook their heads and muttered among themselves of how foolish it was to allow the two to remain. Many walked a wide circle around Na'om whenever she appeared on one of the many winding paths around the small town or at the river, with the rapidly growing cat running alongside her. When they came to Ajkun's hut for salves or a healing tea, they waited outside the gate until Na'om had placed Ek' Balam inside the hut and stood guard in front of the door. But the people of Pa nimá knew better than to approach Chiman again. He had made his decision, and Na'om was still considered a member of the town.

Initially, at night, the small cat curled up next to Na'om on her side of the bed, purring gently as she stroked his soft head and rubbed his ears until they both drifted off to sleep. However, as the cat continued to grow, he took up more and more space until finally even Na'om had to admit it was difficult to sleep wedged between the cat and her grandmother. Over the course of several days, she trained Ek' Balam to spend the nights on a small woven palm frond mat on the floor, still within reach of her hand so she could continue to pet him before sleep.

As the weeks passed, the red scratch marks on Na'om's face slowly faded to white scars, which stood out against her dark face. She did her best to hide them by letting her long hair hang loose. She avoided looking directly at anyone, especially Tz', and tilted her head to one side so her hair fully covered that side of her face whenever he was around. Aware that most people in the village were afraid of her cat, Na'om and Ek' Balam spent more and more time alone, among the hibiscus, philodendrons, and ferns that grew around the village. Hidden by the plants, they were able to observe without being seen. Hours passed as they sat and watched the people go about their daily work, or as Na'om studied the habits of the leaf-cutter ants, praying mantises, and giant millipedes and centipedes that shared the tropical rain forest with them. Other times, the two crept through the brush on the trail of a small agouti or a squirrel, and Na'om watched as Ek' Balam pounced, crushing the tiny animal in his powerful jaws.

One afternoon, when he was done with his studies, Tz' found Na'om and Ek' Balam sitting in the shade of the large lime tree outside Ati't's hut.

"What are you doing here?" Na'om asked as Tz' plunked down on the ground beside them. "Won't your mother be mad if she finds out you've been visiting?"

"Father says the gods look favorably upon us and has given me permission to come see you whenever I want," Tz' replied. "Unless you'd prefer I didn't come," he added as he watched his young friend's face.

"Silly," Na'om said as she playfully punched Tz' in his right arm. "Of course I want to see you; besides Ek' Balam, you're the only friend I have." Na'om picked up a tiny stick on the ground and started to break it into little pieces which she let drop to the ground. "Everyone else is too scared of me and of Ek' Balam. As if either of us would hurt them." She leaned back against Ek' Balam and felt his side move in and out with his breathing. "Mok'onel is so nervous that she can't concentrate on anything Ati't tries to teach her."

"Well, she does have a lot to learn to catch up to you," Tz' said.

Na'om grinned. "She still can't tell the difference between nettles and plantain, and they don't look anything alike. I don't see how she'll ever become a midwife."

In silence, the three of them watched as two humming-birds fought for control of the nearby pink and white hibiscus blossoms. The tiny iridescent green and red birds whizzed and whirred at each other, dive bombing and attacking as they battled for the sweet nectar in the flowers. Ek' Balam's eyes darted from bird to bird, his tail swishing rapidly from side to side on the ground.

Tz' pulled his bone whistle out of his leather pouch. Placing it to his lips, he imitated the chirps and squeaks of the little birds until they believed he was a rival bird and attacked. They flew directly at his head, and Tz' ducked to avoid being hit.

Na'om laughed as Tz' swatted at the birds with his hand. "Ha, ha, that'll teach you to trick them," she laughed as she stood and brushed some dry leaves from her skirt. She motioned for Tz' to play his whistle and began to dance and twirl in time to the music.

Suddenly, she grabbed Ek' Balam and hoisted the half-grown cat into her arms. She cradled him and tried to twirl him around. But the cat was too heavy, and his back feet slipped from her grasp until they touched the ground. Na'om towed him around in a semi-circle, his long tail dragging on the hard-packed dirt. The cat growled and squirmed.

"He doesn't look too happy," Tz' said as he stopped playing.

"Well, you can't dance with me, since you're the musician," Na'om said as she let the cat down. "So, Ek' Balam has to learn to be my dance partner." With that comment, Na'om motioned for Tz' to resume playing. She picked up the cat's large, front paws, placed them on her shoulders, and covered them with her own hands, holding the feet in place.

Ek' Balam's tail swished from side to side. But he remained standing on his hind feet.

Na'om stared into the jaguar's chartreuse-colored eyes, and their gaze locked. Slowly she took a step backwards and felt the cat stiffen. "Come on, boy, it'll be fun," she said as she took another step. First one foot, then the other, she led the cat around in a wide circle while Tz' played.

"What in the name of Itzamná is going on here, what are you doing with that cat?" Ati't demanded as she appeared in the courtyard with two full gourds of fresh water.

"Just dancing with him," Na'om said as she dropped the cat's paws. Ek' Balam paced to the shade of the lime tree and flopped down into the dirt. He began to lick himself.

Na'om took the water from Ati't and hung the gourds by the door. Then she popped inside, grabbed a dried fish from their small storeroom, and tossed the treat to the cat. "Your reward for dancing with me," she said as she knelt down and rubbed behind the cat's ear. She leaned against his side, and her black hair fell away from her face, blending into Ek' Balam's pelt.

"I should go," Tz' said as he stood up. "Come to the river with me, and we can play in the shallows like we used to," he said. He held out his hand and pulled Na'om to her feet.

"Can I go, Ati't? Please?" Na'om said.

"Mok'onel is coming later, Na'om," Ajkun said. "You need to be here to study with her."

Na'om ran over to her grandmother and hugged her. "Please?" she said again.

"We'll be back by mid-afternoon, I promise," Tz' added.

Ajkun looked at her granddaughter and then at Tz'. "You'll soon pass your thirteenth name day, Tz'," she said, "and then, there'll be no more time to play. Go on, both of you, but be back in an hour, or your mother will have my head." She laughed as Na'om and Tz' both hugged her and ran off.

***

The months passed, and Ek' Balam continued to grow. Sometimes Na'om heard the cat rise from his mat by the bed and move outside the hut at night; she could hear his feet padding back and forth across the small dirt courtyard, and she knew her friend was guarding them from anything harmful in the dark.

As the weather grew hotter with the approach of the rainy season, the two went almost daily to the river to swim and play in the cool water. Na'om learned to hang onto Ek' Balam's soft fur and ride with him as he swam from one side of the river to the other. The men of Pa nimá had been to the opposite shore, crossing the water in one of the small, dugout mahogany canoes to hunt in the jungle, but none of the women had ever been there. Na'om liked exploring a territory they hadn't seen. Although she remained in sight of the river, she discovered many new patches of nettles and ceiba trees laden with seed pods, their fluffy insides used to stuff the mattresses in the village. Sometimes she spent the whole day collecting them. She'd place the leaves or pods in a basket and balance it on top of her head while Ek' Balam pulled her through the currents to the village side of the river.

Often she returned just as Ati't and Mok'onel were finishing a lesson. One afternoon, Na'om watched as Mok'onel looked up from the herbal ledger, tears of frustration on her face.

"How do you keep these plants all straight in your head?" Mok'onel said. "I can't do this!" she cried and threw the book on the ground. "Chuch should never have insisted I learn."

"Shh, child, it's all right," Ajkun said as she wrapped her arm around Mok'onel's shoulder. "I'll speak to your mother and to Chiman; not everyone is gifted with the art of healing. Your talents lie elsewhere; no one can force you to become what you're not."

From then on, Na'om returned to being Ajkun's sole student. She was glad she didn't have to share Ati't anymore and spend time with Mok'onel. It was so much easier to move through the brush looking for herbs with Ek' Balam at her side than with the heavy-footed girl.

One morning, Na'om woke and stepped outside, fully expecting to see Ek' Balam sprawled in the dirt in the shade. But he wasn't there. Several hours passed with no sign of the cat, and

Na'om found it impossible to concentrate on the herbs Ati't was trying to show her.

"Na'om," Ajkun said, "Sit down and study these drawings. You need to learn to recognize these plants and the ailments they treat." She held out the pounded fig bark journal full of black and white ink sketches of various plants.

Na'om took the book and set it on her lap, but every time she thought she heard something, she glanced up from the page to scan the surrounding area for Ek' Balam. She suddenly knew how Mok'onel had felt that last day of her training. "I can't concentrate, Ati't," Na'om said. "Please let me go to the river and look for him," she pleaded.

Ajkun took a deep breath and let it out slowly. "All right, you may go, but be back before dinner, ready to learn at least one new plant for today. You'll never be able to take over for me someday if you don't."

Na'om jumped up and ran down to the river. Kemonel and Mok'onel were washing their clothes in the water, along with Potz', Chachal, and several of the other women and their daughters. *Ek' Balam won't be here*, Na'om thought as she listened to the chatter and gossip and the *thwack, thwack, thwack* of the clothes as the women pounded the fabric on the smooth rocks before laying them over any available bush to dry. She turned to leave, but Mok'onel caught sight of her. She nudged her close friend, Sijuan, who touched another, and slowly all the women stopped their work to stare at Na'om.

"What do you want, girl?" Potz' called out. "We're busy working here. Come back later."

Na'om said nothing.

"What's the matter with you, girl?" Chachal called out. "Didn't you hear us say 'go away'?" She and Potz' turned their backs on her. Na'om watched as Mok'onel and Sijuan splashed each other playfully with water.

Kemonel shook her head and chided Mok'onel for being rude

before giving Naóm a brief smile. The others continued thumping the washing on the rocks.

Naóm waited until she was around a bend in the path before she let the tears gush forth. She scurried into the underbrush and only stopped crying when she felt a jumping spider land on her leg and crawl up under the hem of her skirt. She swatted at the insect, wiped a dirty hand across her face, and hurried back to Ajkun.

Without a word, she plunked down in the dirt near the fire, picked up the herbal book, and tried to learn the multiple uses for the brilliant orange-red flowers and root of the local blood flower. "Root has pain-eliminating properties and can be used to treat ringworm and bleeding," Naóm muttered to herself. "The white, milky sap is poisonous, but used in tiny amounts, may help with a severe toothache." She paused as images of Chachal floated into her mind, the other women, and even the girls laughing at her. She could see Chachal's open mouth, her white teeth glistening . . .

"Any sign of your cat?" Ajkun asked when she noticed Naóm had returned.

Jerked out of her memory, Naóm simply stated, "No."

"What's wrong?" Ajkun said as she knelt down in front of Naóm. She tilted her granddaughter's face up to the sky. "You've been crying! What happened?"

"Nothing, it doesn't matter," Naóm said. Ajkun shook her head and went back inside the hut. Chachal's face floated in front of Naóm's eyes. "Stupid old woman," Naóm muttered under her breath.

By nightfall, Naóm was worn out and refused the bowl of stew Ajkun handed to her. "He's never been gone this long," she cried as she stared into the flames in front of her.

Ajkun awkwardly got down on her knees near Naóm and hugged the girl around the shoulders. "I knew this day would come sooner or later," she said as she rocked back onto her heels.

"Ek' Balam's a wild animal and has probably gone off to live the life of a jungle cat. I never thought he'd stay with you as long as he has."

That night, for the first time in months, Na'om didn't fall asleep stroking the head of her friend. When she did finally drift off, she had a series of terrible dreams. In one, she saw Ek' Balam locked in a wooden cage, his usually thick and glossy pelt full of tiny sticks and seed burrs. His eyes were glazed over, his strong body gaunt from lack of food. In another nightmare, she watched as Tz' endlessly retreated from her, fading into a deep blackness, forever slipping away just as she was to grab hold of him. In a third dream, she cradled a baby boy in her arms, but the child was dead. Black wasps buzzed about her ears and eyes, and no matter how far or fast she ran in the dream, the black wasps followed her.

At breakfast, Na'om picked at her bowl of corn mush until Ajkun spoke.

"Come child, you've got to eat; you skipped dinner last night. You can't let your worries over Ek' Balam affect you this way."

Na'om put her bowl on the ground. "It's not just that," she said as she crawled up into her grandmother's lap. "I had more bad dreams last night." She told Ajkun what she had seen. "What do they mean? And will they come true?"

Ajkun placed her granddaughter on the stool, went into the hut, and returned with the ledger. She began to write down what Na'om had told her. "It's been many moons since you've had any dreams," Ajkun said as she looked at the small child in front of her. "I think they're caused by your worries over this cat of yours." She handed Na'om her bowl of porridge. "You have to eat. It'll do you good."

Na'om picked at the mush and managed only to eat a few spoonfuls. "I'm going to check the river again; perhaps, if I call, he'll come from the other side." She placed her bowl on the ground, gave Ati't a peck on the check, and ran down the path, her black hair flying loose behind her head.

As she approached the river, Na'om slowed down and crept toward the water, leery of running into any of the villagers. But the riverbank was empty of people and her cat. Na'om looked across the shallow water to the opposite shore only thirty feet away. *I can swim that,* she thought, and she quickly stepped into the water. Her huipil and skirt sucked up the water and clung to her legs and arms, but Na'om persisted. She kicked her feet and paddled with her arms toward the nearest rock. She reached the rough surface and held onto it for a moment, feeling the current of the river pulling at her. She took a deep breath and let go, kicking harder this time as the flow of water continued to tug on her clothes, dragging her farther downstream. She bounced into another rock and clutched at it. She tried to put her feet down on the sandy bottom, but the undercurrent here was too swift, and she felt her young body being steadily drawn out from under her. Na'om glanced back at the village side of the river; she was more than halfway to the opposite side. *I can do this,* she thought. She edged her way around the rock and pushed off it with her feet, launching out into the river in a rush of water. Within minutes, she was in the shallows and able to climb up on the riverbank. Dripping wet, she took a few minutes to catch her breath. "Ek' Balam," she called. "Where are you?" Silence answered her. "Ek' Balam," Na'om shouted again, her voice high and thin. She shivered in her wet clothes and began to walk along the river, but her way was quickly blocked by a series of large rocks covered over with shrubs and vines.

She was farther downstream than she had ever been, and after one last glance at the village side of the river, Na'om proceeded to push her way through the thick undergrowth. "Ek' Balam," she cried. Nothing, just the sound of the water as it gurgled over the rocks. Even this was quickly swallowed as Na'om pushed her way deeper into the jungle. She meandered, pushed aside small branches, stepped over twisted tree roots, and was surprised to find a small clearing a few hundred feet from the stream. Surrounded by tall mahogany trees, the circular area was free of the dense vegetation nearby, the area only crisscrossed by a number of thick vines. Na'om stepped in between the trees, into the ring, and headed to the exact center where a shaft of sunlight penetrated the canopy overhead. Stepping into the warmth, she removed her wet clothes and laid them on the ground. She shivered and hugged her thin, still girlish body. Closing her eyes, she lifted her face to the light and felt the sun slowly warming her chilled skin. The heat soaked into her, filling her with energy. She felt tingly all over and slowly revolved in the spot, a sense of excitement building inside her. She held her arms out to her sides and turned faster, then faster, spinning in one spot, her body whirling in the heat. Her ears filled with a buzzing that blocked all noises. Suddenly images began to flood her mind; she was in a dense thicket, a small agouti hidden in the brush just a few yards in front of her. She could smell its fear and sensed its heat and her mouth watered as she thought of the taste of fresh meat. She felt the weight of her body brushing the rough ground, the swish of her tail as it flicked ever so gently . . . Na'om opened her eyes. Dizzy from spinning, she fell down on the rough, thick vines, scraping the back of her left leg. She lowered her head and took a deep breath, and as she did so, she caught a glimpse of her arm out of the corner of her eye. Her skin was outlined in deep purple that pulsated and shimmered in the light. She jerked her head up and looked directly at her arm. It was just her normal brown arm. Na'om tilted her head to one side, and again, she just caught a peek at the iridescent purple outline hovering around her skin. It quickly began to fade as her breathing returned to normal.

Her ears still ringing with a high-pitch sound, Na'om pushed herself up off the ground and reached for her shirt. It was still wet in spots, but she pulled it on anyway, tugging the blouse down over her bent knees. She crouched in the opening, with her arms wrapped around her knees, and tried to make sense of what had just happened. The air around her vibrated in the heat, and slowly her hearing returned to normal. Exhausted, she lay down in the warm dirt, curled into a ball, and fell asleep. She dreamt of Ek' Balam and her grandmother.

The sun had moved far away from the center of the circle when Na'om finally woke up. She brushed the dirt from her shirt, leaving several spots in the fabric. She tugged on her skirt and hurried back to the river where the sun blazed on the rocks. Holding her hand up to her eyes, Na'om searched the opposite shore for movement. She was surprised to see Tz' working his way along the riverbank in a small canoe.

"Tz'," Na'om called. She waited, but he didn't turn his head. "Tz'," she called again, "it's me, Na'om," she cried loudly.

Tz' twisted his body in the canoe, looking along the shoreline in front of him. "Where are you?" he cried.

"Over here, on the other side of the river," Na'om said. She watched as Tz' jerked around in the canoe, sending the small boat rocking back and forth in the water. "Give me a ride."

Tz' dipped his paddle into the water and quickly brought the canoe to rest in the shallows near Na'om. "What in the name of Itzamná are you doing over here?" he said as Na'om awkwardly stepped into the tippy canoe.

"Looking for Ek' Balam," Na'om said. "I told Ati't I'd be gone only a short time, but I wound up falling asleep."

"Wait, he's not with you? Then how'd you get over here?" Tz' asked as he back paddled the canoe out into the river again.

"I swam," Na'om replied. "Promise me you won't say anything to Ati't," she said as she turned in the boat to look at Tz'. "She'd be worried stiff if she knew I'd swum across the river by myself."

Tz' shook his head. "You're one crazy girl," he said as he straightened the bow and pointed the canoe toward the other side. "Grab that other paddle and dig into the water with it; if you're going to keep crossing the river, maybe you'd better learn how to use a canoe."

"You know that's not possible," Na'om replied.

The minute the canoe touched land, Na'om leaped from the boat, gave Tz' a quick peck on the cheek, and raced up the path toward her grandmother's hut. She fumbled with the latch on the gate and quickly hurried toward the house.

"By all the gods, where have you been, child?" Ati't said as soon as she saw Na'om. "I've been looking all over for you. Chachal has a terrible toothache, and she needs some bloodroot sap. The vial we had is all dried up, so I'll need you to go look for more," Ajkun paused. "Na'om, are you even listening to me?" She stared at Na'om, taking in her dirty shirt and damp skirt. "Where have you been all day? Out looking for that cat of yours? Well, never mind, you're safe, that's all that matters," she said as she scooped the young girl up in her arms and hugged her. "And look who's here," she added as she held back the deerskin covering the doorway.

Na'om peered into the dark interior and saw a shape lying on the floor by the bed. "Ek' Balam!" she cried as she hurried to his side. She buried her head in his soft fur and instantly felt him begin to purr. "Where've you been?" she asked as she nuzzled his neck. She turned and looked up at Ati't. "When did he come back?" she asked.

"Shortly after you left," Ajkun replied. "He must have been out hunting, as his muzzle was all covered with blood."

Toward dusk, Tz' came by to say hello. He grinned when he saw Ek' Balam. "So, your mighty cat has returned," Tz' said. "I suspect he was off finding himself a lady friend for a few hours." He reached over to Na'om and gave her a hug. "Don't be surprised if he disappears again from time to time." Then Tz' walked over to the jaguar, squatted in front of the big cat, and looked the animal in the eyes. "My friend," he said as he rubbed Ek' Balam's ear, "we need to make a pact, so our Na'om doesn't worry so. When you take off for a few hours or days, I'll watch over her, and if I should be gone off hunting, then you're to remain in the village and guard her."

Ek' Balam shifted his weight and suddenly licked the side of Tz's face.

"I take it that means we have a deal," Tz' said as he wiped the drool off his cheek with the back of his hand.

SATAL

Satal poked at her cooking fire and threw more wood on it to bring the embers to a full blaze. The flames pushed back the dark night. There was a smell of rain in the air, and Satal glanced at the sky; no stars were visible. She nodded to herself. *No one will see me when I go out later,* she thought as she placed a small blackened glazed pot on the flames and filled it with water. She added a bundle of dried oregano and chili peppers, a six-inch gray lizard, and a few pinches of coarse pink salt. When the concoction reached a simmer, she moved it off to one side of the fire. Lighting a small twig, she touched it to the wick of a candle. The wax sputtered and caught, and Satal stood up slowly, balancing the candle in its dish on the palm of her arthritic hand.

Barefoot, the old woman shambled into the front room of the house she had shared with her warrior husband, Q'alel. The thick stone walls and roof had kept the hot, mid-day sun from penetrating inside, and Satal enjoyed the coolness of the tiles under her tough, leathery feet. She crossed the almost empty space and entered the hallway. In the semi-darkness, she paused in the doorway to the room where her daughter, Chachal, had lived, vacant now for so many years. Satal had left everything the way it was before Q'alel sent Chachal off to live in the south, far from her mother. By the light of the flickering candle, she could see the hammock still stretched across the room, the pile of woolen blankets folded neatly on top of a wooden trunk. One of Chachal's old dresses, the white cotton now yellow with age, hung from a peg on the wall.

Satal shuffled forward down the hall, entered her bedroom, and went to her wooden cupboard where she kept all her special supplies. She opened the heavy door on its copper hinges and found the bag of black cornmeal she wanted as well as her copper bowl. She picked up the gourd of jequirity beans, but put them back; she wouldn't need them for this particular spell.

"What's the plan for tonight?" Sachoj's mummified head inquired from her niche in the wall. "Are you ever going to find that child?"

"Shush, old woman," Satal said. "You know I've had spies searching the nearby villages for years. No one recalls any child being born that year during the Wayeb."

"Perhaps you're not looking in the right place. Maybe you're not as strong as I thought you were, having to rely on others to do your job," Sachoj hissed. "Your grandmother and mother had my talents; the magic must have skipped a generation or two."

"How dare you," Satal said as she whipped around to stare into the wrinkled face. "If this corn maiden really exists, I'll find the girl, mark my words. In the meantime, I'll continue to make life difficult for Yakal and his family. I warned Q'alel when he stole me from the altar in Chichén Itzá that his family would be cursed, and so far, I've carried out that promise." Satal gathered her supplies in her hands.

"Play all you want at tormenting Yakal; the real work is to find the child before it's too late," Sachoj said.

"You just sit there and keep quiet," Satal commanded her great-grandmother, "or I'll pack you in a box and leave you in the cave next time I'm down there." Satal scuffled back outside to her fire, her feet like slithering snakes on the dry stones in the yard.

Reaching into the bubbling pot with a wooden spoon, she carefully removed the cooked lizard from the broth, setting it aside for a snack once her task was complete. By the light of the flames, she poured a handful of the dried corn flour into the copper bowl and added just a few drops of the hot liquid from the cooking pot. She quickly worked the mix into a paste with her fingers. Then she removed her obsidian knife from a deerskin pouch around her waist. She held the green blade up to the fire, heating the tip of it. Tugging on her earlobe, Satal stabbed herself with the sterilized knife and let the few droplets of blood that appeared drip on the mound of cornmeal. Then she reached into her pouch again and removed a small piece of folded cloth. Tucked inside was a single, long, black hair. She kneaded it with the blood into the maize, and her fingers quickly molded the dough into the rough shape of a young, pregnant woman. She held the tiny sculpture up to the light, squinting at the contours and made a few adjustments before dropping the formed dough into the bubbling stew.

Satal looked skyward when she heard distant thunder and quickly removed the pot from the fire. She wrapped her black shawl more tightly around her shoulders as she felt the first few drops of rain spatter on the stones around her. She covered the warm pot handle with a piece of cloth, slipped into her leather sandals, and walked through the dark night toward the Temple of Cremations.

Only a few torches were visible near one of the gates in the wall as Satal carried her potion past the dark houses and palaces of her neighbors. The rain fell faster, and Satal hurried on toward the quiet marketplace, the stalls silent and empty of people, cloth tarps thrown over the mounds of wares for sale in the morning. She stopped and ducked into a corner booth full of baskets when she saw a lone watchman look in her direction as he patrolled the perimeter of the city. But he didn't see the short, old woman; she was just another black shadow among many. She wound her way through the small alley of stalls and appeared near the front of the temple.

Satal glanced all around before scurrying across the open space between the market and the base of the shrine. Lightning flashed overhead, illuminating the twenty-five steep steps ahead of her, and Satal paused to take a deep breath. *This is far easier than going to the cave,* she reminded herself as she began her ascent. The warm pot banged into her leg at every step, and she struggled to climb the slippery, narrow stones. Her legs were tired, and her left knee was throbbing by the time she reached the tiny temple room at the top. She entered and could hardly see in the dense blackness. This was the first time she had been up on the pyramid in the dark and only knew from past trips that the wooden planks covering the entrance to the shaft tomb were directly in front of her on the floor. She inched forward, feeling with her feet, and bumped into the boards. She put her pot on the stone floor and yanked one of the slats aside. A wet, earthy smell wafted up out of the deep pit that extended far below the pyramid and connected with the series of caves and caverns underneath the city that eventually led to the Underworld.

Picking up her copper container, Satal upended the broth into the dark pit and imagined seeing the slowly dissolving maize figure and bundle of herbs cartwheeling into the blackness. She listened closely and heard a tiny splash far below her feet. She spit into the well for good measure, put the pot on the stones under her feet, and then hurriedly replaced the plank. Lightning flashed, thunder crashed, and the small wooden temple creaked as the rain poured down. Satal wrapped her shawl more tightly over her head. Back outside, the wind whipped the ends of her scarf out of her hands and her stringy, graying hair tossed around her head. The rain came down in slanted sheets, making the steps of the temple even more slippery. Fearing she would fall, Satal sat down and inched her way on her bottom like a small child, from step to step.

Lightning flashed again, and Satal felt the rumble of thunder resonate deep in her chest. She clutched the stones she sat on, and then she groaned. Her blackened pot was missing. Frantically, she felt all around on the step she sat on and on the one above her, but couldn't find the kettle. "I must have left it inside the temple," she mumbled to herself. She tried to think how many steps she had come down and knew she couldn't make it back up the twenty stairs to retrieve the pot. Raindrops pelted her wrinkled face, and she shook her fist at the gods before slipping the last five stairs to the ground. Soaked through and through, she hurried away in the dark.

Once back in her bedroom, Satal stripped off her wet clothes. She stood naked for a moment in the doorway, watching the lightning illuminate the sky in ribbons and streaks of yellowish green, and she muttered to herself about the pot she'd left behind. "It's an old pot, just like any other; no one will suspect me of doing anything," she mumbled as she pulled on a dry huipil. "The rulers will be concerned though," she argued out loud. "No one is allowed into the temple except the priests and elders. But perhaps there's a way to divert any suspicion from me and place it on someone else," she said as she climbed wearily into her bed. She was cold and curled into a ball on her side, trying to get warm. *I'll think about this in the morning,* she thought. *Right now, I need to thaw out.*

Closing her eyes, she tried to imagine her old lover's body wrapped around hers, warming her back with his strong, muscular torso. Ajelbal had been her first and only true love, her betrothed. His flute music had filled her heart with joy each time she had heard it. Then had come the attack on Chichén Itzá, Q'alel leading the raid. She'd never seen her dear Ajelbal again. At first, Satal had despised the serious, war-oriented Q'alel, but with the birth of Chachal, she had warmed to his embrace. It was only after the death of their infant son, when the midwives had told Satal she'd never bear another child, when Q'alel had found the arms of another woman to hold him at night that Satal's fury had returned in force. Satal sighed and curled up even tighter. Too many years had passed; she could not conjure up an image of Ajelbal. She wiped a tear from the corner of her eye and slowly fell asleep as the rain drummed on the roof overhead. Her lizard snack lay cold and uneaten near the quenched fire.

YAKAL

Two days after the storm, Yakal watched as his wife, Uskab, swept the small yard in front of their thatched hut. He helped her load the pile of leaves and dirt into a basket. "I'll dump this outside the city gates later today," he said. He placed his large hand on the small bulge in her belly and grinned at his wife. *This baby will be strong*, he thought. *It will be my first of many sons.* Then he frowned as he thought of the first pregnancy that had ended quickly, so soon after their marriage three years before.

The couple had consulted with the midwives who had assured them that many young girls lost their first child to the gods. "Uskab is strong," the women had told them, "she will bear you many fine sons."

When Uskab had discovered she was pregnant again, Yakal had taken her to the wise women, and they had cast a circle of bones for the couple, which foretold of a sturdy boy. Yakal smiled again. He hoped his son would have Uskab's green eyes and the same little dimple in her chin.

"What are your plans today?" Yakal asked as he watched Uskab pull her long hair away from her face and tie it into a single braid.

"I need to go to the market. We're out of cornmeal and cacao beans for your morning drink. Plus, I thought we might have a small piece of deer meat for supper tonight." She bent to pick up her cotton shopping bag, then walked over to a small palm frond basket and lifted the lid. "I also need more nettles and raspberry leaves for my tea; I want our son to have strong teeth and bones."

"I'll go with you and help carry everything," Yakal said as he put on his leather sandals.

"Don't you need to go to work?"

"I can take a few hours off to help my young, pregnant wife," Yakal said. "The ground is still being leveled for the new palace; I can't set any stones until the area is flat."

The marketplace was already bustling with people when Yakal and Uskab arrived. Vendors were removing the cotton cloths covering copper bowls and plates for sale, and the piles of hollow gourds that had been turned into birdhouses. Uskab paused in front of blankets filled with wooden carved spoons and ladles and baskets of every shape and size before heading on. Some women were busy blowing on cooking fires that sent spirals of smoke up into the air, while behind them, others sat on palm frond mats, patting maize dough into tamales, or chopping vegetables for large pottery urns full of fresh turkey soup. Ducking into a small alley, Uskab waved to an older woman standing behind a pyramid of ripe tomatoes. She picked out several and placed them in the bag Yakal carried.

They entered the meat section, and Yakal watched as Uskab went from one booth to the next, sniffing the various deer carcasses that hung from hemp ropes in the area. Finally, she found one that smelled extremely fresh. She pointed to it and told the vendor, "I'll take this much." She showed the butcher just where she wanted the cut taken from. The man wrapped the meat in a green banana leaf, and Uskab placed the package next to the tomatoes.

"What else do you need?" Yakal asked.

"My tea and cacao beans," Uskab replied as she moved deeper into the market.

The air grew cooler, and the rich smells of cooking food were replaced by the spicy scent of cinnamon and chili peppers. Strings of hot peppers of all different shapes and colors hung from the bamboo poles that held up the roof; below were baskets piled high with small white onions. Uskab selected a rope of red, green, and yellow peppers and added a few white onions to her bag.

"Are you all right?" Yakal asked as he saw Uskab wobble a bit.

"Yes, I'm fine; your son is squirming around a bit, though."

"Let's find your herbs and get you back home," Yakal said. Uskab nodded in reply.

It was while they were waiting to pay that Yakal saw Satal out of the corner of his eye. The old woman stood near the fringe of the market, staring out into the brightening day. "I wonder what she's doing," Yakal said.

"Let's go see," Uskab said as she moved closer to the woman.

"Careful, Uskab, you're not safe around her," Yakal said as he placed a hand on Uskab's arm, slowing her pace. "She's like a black wasp, eager to sting and poison all that brings life and love into this world."

"Her mouth is moving, but there's no one near her to hear what she's saying," Uskab said and then groaned. She placed her hand on her stomach.

"Leave the witch alone, we need to get you back to the house," Yakal replied as he turned Uskab in the opposite direction. He took one last look at the older woman before guiding Uskab away, but he failed to see Satal pivot and look directly at their retreating backs.

"Rest now," Yakal said as he placed all the food in the cool interior of their hut. "I'll be back in a few hours to check on you," he added as he gently kissed Uskab on the cheek.

When Yakal returned to the house at lunchtime, Uskab was sound asleep in the hammock. He found some leftover tamales and ate them quickly, washing them down with a small amount of lukewarm water. The gourds were almost empty, so he took them with him back to the job site. *I'll fill these at the cenote before I return for dinner,* he thought as he took one last look at Uskab.

Yakal ignored the giggles of the women gathered around the

city's well as he stood in line to fill his water gourds. Other than the four young male slaves who threw wooden buckets into the fifty-foot round opening to the blue-black water fifteen feet below, he was the only man at the cenote. He peered over the edge as he waited. The sheer vertical walls were rubbed smooth by the passage of thousands of buckets, and Yakal couldn't see the bottom. No one knew how deep the cenote actually was, and he stepped back from the slippery edge. *No wonder the shamans say these wells are entranceways to the Underworld,* Yakal thought as he hefted the cords on the now heavy gourds to his shoulder. It was dusk when Yakal returned to his house.

Uskab held out her hands for the gourds. "You'll bring shame on my name, if the women catch you filling these again," she said as she hung them from a wooden peg near the door to the hut. "Come, your stew is ready," she added, and she ladled a big scoop of the deer soup into a coconut bowl and handed it to Yakal.

She sat down and watched as Yakal blew on the bits of chopped tomato and hot pepper on his spoon.

"Aren't you eating tonight?" Yakal asked when he noticed Uskab's hands were empty.

"I'm not hungry," Uskab replied. "I'm just so tired; all I want to do is lie down again."

Yakal placed his half-eaten bowl on the ground and stood up in front of his young wife. "Come, let me help you to bed," he said as he held out his hand. Uskab grasped it, and Yakal pulled her to her feet. "You must rest, and maybe later, you'll feel like eating," he said as he guided Uskab inside the hut. She climbed into the swinging hammock they shared, and Yakal covered her with a soft deerskin blanket.

"Maltiox, my love," Uskab said as she twisted onto her side. "Now go and finish your stew before it gets cold."

In silence, Yakal quickly ate his soup. From where he sat, Yakal could see many of his friends as they entered their own yards and sat down to meals with their wives and children. After washing his bowl, he checked on Uskab. She was sound asleep. He let the thin blanket that covered the doorway at night drop into place and went back outside. *Perhaps Chuch will know what might be ailing Uskab,* Yakal thought as he headed toward his mother's house.

As he approached the market area, he noticed a large crowd had gathered at the base of the Temple of Cremations. The people were all staring at the top of the pyramid where one of the city shamans was holding up a blackened pot. "What's going on, my friend?" Yakal asked as he tapped a young boy on the shoulder.

"The elders have found a kettle inside the temple," the boy answered. "They say someone has been performing black magic up there . . ." The boy shuddered at his own words.

"And they have no idea who this person might be?" Yakal asked. He began to push to the front of the crowd to get a better look.

At that moment, he noticed a break in the throng. Satal was standing in the middle of it, a wide space between her and the others who had gathered at the temple base. She was staring intently at the vessel in the shaman's hand. Satal turned and saw Yakal staring at her.

"What, fool?" she asked.

Yakal noticed her swollen, red earlobe and felt Satal's intense gaze burning into his chest. He blinked. "Nothing," he muttered to the woman. "I was just out for a walk and saw the crowd. He looked away from Satal and back up at the pot held so high above their heads. Then he spun around and strode back the way he had come, eager to get as far away from the witch as possible.

Back at the hut, he immediately went inside to Uskab who only groaned when he kissed her lightly on the nose. He lit a candle on the shelf on the wall and then stepped back toward Uskab. Yakal gasped. The ground underneath the hammock was covered in blood. He pulled back the blanket. A large puddle of bloody bits and pieces lay between Uskab's legs. "Uskab," Yakal said as he shook her by the shoulder, "Wake up!"

Uskab's eyes flickered open and shut, and Yakal ran for his mother.

Within minutes, the two were back at the house. "Make a big pot of hot water, Yakal," Alom said as she pushed her son toward the fire pit. She whirled around and moved to the hammock. She held a vial of pig urine under the girl's nose, and Uskab gasped for breath. She blinked and opened her eyes. And immediately began to cry as she felt the wetness all around her.

"Come, child, we must see what's happened," Alom said as she gently pulled back the blanket. Blood covered Uskab's skirt and legs. She slowly helped the girl to her feet and threw the blanket back over the small fetus in the hammock. "Bring the hot water, Yakal," she called through the doorway as she tugged Uskab's wet dress off over her head.

Yakal appeared with a large turtle shell full of warm water and soft cloths, which he handed to his mother. He took one look at Uskab's bloody thighs, at the tears streaming down her face, and spun around without a word.

"Yakal," Alom cried, "where are you going?"

"To deal with the witch who did this," Yakal said as he hurried out into the night.

Satal was sitting hunched in a corner of her front room munching on an ear of roasted corn when Yakal shoved open the door and strode across the room. He towered over the woman as she struggled to rise to her feet.

"How dare you enter this house without my permission," Satal shrieked as she looked up at Yakal's stern face. She raised her arm as if to strike the youth with the corncob.

Yakal grabbed Satal's wrist and twisted her arm painfully behind her back. "Listen to me, old woman," Yakal said and saw the corn drop to the floor. "A long time ago you had the strength to hit me when my father was not around, but those days are long gone." He felt Satal squirm in his grip. "I know you cast another one of your spells on Uskab; that's why she's just lost our child. But this time your magic will come back to hurt you. The shamans and elders want to know whose pot was discovered in the temple today, and I intend to tell them it's yours."

Satal yanked her arm free and faced Yakal. "You have no proof of any of that, you stupid boy. Why, that pot could belong to a thousand different people . . . what makes you so sure it's mine?"

"I saw the way you were looking at it tonight, at the temple. And I can see your ear is puffy from some evil bloodletting that you did."

"Ha, all just guesses and conjectures." Satal shifted her weight. "Why, I could have been stung by a bee; that's why my ear is swollen. And yes, I was in the crowd, staring at the pot, so what? Many others were there tonight as well, also gawking at it. That doesn't mean I was up at the top of the temple." She pointed to her swollen knees. "Do you think any of the elders will believe your story when they take a look at this old body? How could I have climbed all the way up to the top of the pyramid?"

Yakal looked at the floor. He knew she was right. *No one will accuse her or try her for witchcraft,* he thought. *All the men on the council fear her evildoing, but no one is going to risk being hexed by her in order to charge her with this.* "You may never be found guilty," Yakal said as he drew in a deep breath, "but I swear by Itzamná that if any harm comes to another person in my family, I'll kill you myself, with my bare hands."

Satal spit on the floor. "Get out of my house before I call the guards and have you locked up."

Frustrated with his inability to do anything, Yakal picked up the corncob from the floor and threw it against the stucco wall where it splattered, sending bits of corn kernels across the room. "Stay away from me and my family," Yakal yelled as he strode from the room.

SATAL

The blackened cooking pot was sitting on the ground in front of Satal's door when she opened it the next morning to let in some fresh air. She hurried out into the common ground between her house and the next, hoping to catch a glimpse of who had left the object behind. *It must be someone on the council,* Satal thought as she slowly bent down, retrieved the pot, and took it inside. *They're the only ones who would be able to get it from the shamans.* She turned the pot over in her hands and noticed a large *X* had been scratched into the soot-covered bottom. *Why would anyone do that?* she wondered as she paused in the large empty front room to catch her breath. When Q'alel had died, Satal had had most of the furniture removed; only two round leather chairs made from the tanned hides of peccaries sat in one corner, with a table made of the same leather and split bamboo wood. Satal liked the room empty; it made it easier to clean.

She placed the pot on the table and sat down, the leather crackling underneath her. *I must remember to oil these chairs,* she thought as she stared at the pot in front of her. *Do I take this thing to the council meeting this morning and demand to know why someone left it on my doorstep, or do I stay silent and keep an eye open as to who might have returned it?*

Satal slowly got up and padded into her bedroom when she heard the drum roll announcing the changing of the guards at the various gates. She pulled off her white cotton nightgown and stood naked while she decided what to wear to the meeting.

Something that commands attention and expresses authority, she thought as she looked at one dress and then another in her wooden wardrobe. Finally, she slipped into a dark blue cotton dress with turquoise and rose-colored blossoms embroidered on the shoulders and around the neckline. *I mustn't let anyone forget who I am,* Satal thought as she smoothed the fabric over her sagging breasts and small paunch.

She heard a snicker in the room and turned to face Sachoj. "What?" she demanded of the mummified head.

"You should get rid of that pot," Sachoj said.

"Why?"

"The scratch in it, you fool."

"It's just been banged about a bit that's all. It doesn't affect the inside, so there's no need to waste good cacao beans on a new one."

"Playing the fool once again, Satal," Sachoj hissed. She changed the subject. "I know you slept poorly last night; I heard you whimpering."

"I ate a bit of undercooked peccary, that's all," Satal said. She refused to admit her great-grandmother was right. In her dreams, she'd shape-shifted into a black wasp. She'd had visions of the Wayeb child and of jaguars that ripped and tore at her when she was in her wasp state. One wing had been badly damaged, and Satal had fallen to the ground, only to wake up on the floor underneath her hammock. Her right elbow still hurt from where she'd banged it on the tiles.

"If you want to remain on the council, you must make those men fear you," Sachoj said. "Use your powers today and command them to obey you."

Satal bowed to Sachoj. "Yes, you're right, I'll demand respect from them all." She hurriedly brushed her grey-streaked hair and pulled it back into a large bun at the back of her head.

She ate half an avocado sprinkled with salt and lime juice and a few bites of ripe mango before heading to the Warriors' Palace.

Perfect, Satal thought as she looked at the angle of the sun in the sky. *I'll be just a few minutes late.*

As she expected, the other council members were all seated when she arrived, chatting among themselves. Several of the men were checking their notes, shuffling leaves of pounded fig bark covered in tiny markings, while others sipped from coconut husks filled with cool limeade. Several servants leaned against the stucco walls behind them, whispering of local gossip. All fell silent as Satal approached, and the ten men stood up and bowed respectfully as she took her place at the large wooden table. With difficulty, she wiggled into the high wooden chair. With her short, four-foot frame, she looked like a young child in the seat since her feet didn't quite touch the ground.

"So, what's the first order of business?" Satal asked as she looked at the men. She waited for someone to speak, and finally Bitol broke the silence.

"The priests are calling for a special ceremony and sacrifice to cleanse the Temple of Cremations," he said. The others in the group nodded their heads in agreement.

"Ah, yes, I heard the rumors," Satal said as she carefully watched each member. *One of you knows far more than you're revealing,* she thought. "Nasty business, black magic, and so on. Of course, let's do a special ritual, make it a public holiday so the crowds can come and watch."

"Excellent idea, Nim-q'ij," Bitol said. "The priests recommend holding the rite during the next full moon. Is everyone in agreement on this?"

The men and Satal nodded their heads.

Satal decided to see if she could catch her silent visitor of the early morning. "I heard there was some kind of pot left behind; this is how the priests knew anyone had been up to the temple." She looked around the room and watched each man in turn. "What became of the vessel?"

No one said anything. The men shifted their papers and

looked anywhere except at Satal.

"Well, I guess that doesn't really matter," Satal said. *All of you must know,* she thought as she adjusted her weight in the hard chair. "What else is on the agenda for today?"

Matz', in charge of keeping track of the number of baskets of corn used each week by the thousands who lived inside the city walls, directed his one good eye at Satal. "We've used three hundred baskets of corn this week, Nim-q'ij," he said.

"So, where does that leave our supply level in the granary?" Satal asked.

"It's getting quite low, I'm afraid. The rains are coming just in time."

"Cut back the amount given to the slaves; that should ease the need. Give them time to forage for greens outside the city walls to replace the lack of meal; the chaya plants should be large enough to harvest now that we've had some showers."

"As you wish, my lady," Matz' replied.

"Who's next?" Satal demanded.

Kubal Joron cleared his throat as he stood up. His large belly pushed against the edge of the table, and he stepped back to accommodate his girth. "The cenote is slowly refilling, but the water is murky from all the runoff. Several people have gotten sick, and I fear there will be more."

"Give the usual command, tell everyone to boil the water used for cooking and drinking," Satal said as she shook her head. "Each year it's the same, why don't they ever learn?"

"Many of the sick are newcomers to the city, my lady," Kubal Joron said as he wiped his face with a pale lilac-colored cloth he had tucked inside the deep purple sleeve of his shirt.

"That was not really a question," Satal said as she glared at the face of the man near her. *He even looks like a water jug,* she thought, *with that thick neck and bloated belly.*

"Yes, Nim-q'ij," Kubal Joron muttered as he sat back down.

The hours slowly passed as the rest of the men gave their

reports on the number of baskets of salt harvested, how many new peccary piglets had been born, and the names of the elders who had passed and gone to join the land of the ancestors. The servants refilled their glasses, but no one wanted to break for lunch.

Nimal, in charge of the warriors, showed the council the new arrows he had commissioned for the troops. "We'll use three black feathers for the regular warriors and three white feathers for the boys in training."

"And what will the officers use?" Bitol asked.

"I've given them compensation so they can purchase their own arrows from among the many fletchers in the city. Many are trading with Xik', as he's the best arrow maker in the city. Each man receives his own design of colors and feathers, with no two alike. That way, when a Xiu is killed, we'll be able to identify who shot the man and reward him accordingly."

Satal felt her stomach gurgle, and she hoped the meeting was over. "Is there any other business to attend to?" Satal asked as she prepared to stand up. Her empty stomach growled, and the noise echoed in the spacious hallway.

"Yes, actually, three more things," Bitol said, as he tried to ignore Satal's stomach noises.

Satal sighed and eased back down in her seat. *I must remember to tell one of the servants to provide me with a ceiba pillow for this hard chair before the next meeting,* Satal thought. "Well, let's get on with it."

Matz' stood up and braced his hands on the table as he leaned in toward Satal. "The Xiu have been sending raiding parties deeper into the lowlands. They're capturing the young men and women for slaves and sacrifices, killing the elders, and destroying the crops. We need to increase the number of warriors we have and then send them in to protect these people," he said.

"How far south are these raiders traveling?" Satal asked as thoughts of her daughter's safety swept through her mind.

"Actually they're headed more to the east, closer to Tulum, my lady," Bitol said from his seat.

"Then why should we protect them?" Satal asked. "Most have refused to swear allegiance to the city, preferring to remain independent from us. If the Xiu attack them, what concern is it of ours?"

"My lady," Kubal Joron said as he heaved his body upwards again. "The people of the southern lowlands fear the Xiu will eventually head in their direction. If we offer these southerners protection, then they'll swear loyalty to us. In return, they've agreed to pay us in goods that we would normally have to buy or barter. For instance, we'd no longer have to purchase copal or quetzal feathers for the shamans, and one tribe has promised us some of their rare blue jade in exchange for their continued safety." He wiped a bead of sweat from his brow and sat back down.

"So, we send our young men to fight their battles and perhaps lose a few people, but fill our coffers with their natural resources. That does seem like a fair trade," Satal said. "How many youths are we talking about here?"

"Two hundred, maybe three," Bitol said. "I suggest we start with patrols along the known travel routes of the Xiu, and when they appear to be heading too far south, our men will engage them and send them back the way they came."

"Good, work out all the details, and I'll expect a report next month. But when the first shipments of goods arrive, I want to be notified at once. The jade, in particular, will need to be kept in a safe place. What else is there, as you did say three more things, didn't you?" Satal said.

Bitol motioned to a servant who quickly left the room. "With the number of inhabitants of Mayapán growing almost on a daily basis, I find it too difficult to be Commander of the Gates and Head Mason, so I propose that I turn the title of Head Mason over to Yakal."

"Yakal, why him?" Satal demanded. "Surely there's someone more worthy of that rank among the hundreds of masons."

Bitol looked at the men around him who nodded encouragement. "Yakal is the best of all the masons; we actually decided on this before you arrived. Since you were late to the meeting, we started without you, voted, and the result was unanimous. Basically, we're just telling you of the decision."

"I see," Satal said. "And what else did you discuss while I was out?"

At that moment, the servant returned, with Yakal just behind him. Bitol motioned for his nephew to approach the table.

Yakal nodded respectfully to all the men, but deliberately avoided looking at his stepmother.

"Yakal has information on the new pottery workshops being built. We felt that since he's now Head Mason, he should join the council, and submit his own reports," Bitol said as he leaned back in his chair. He nodded to Yakal.

The youth stepped forward and uncurled a large sheet of paper with drawings of the layout of the buildings on it. "My lords, my lady," Yakal said, "the foundations are laid and my workers are beginning to build the walls. But we'll need far more stone and far more thatch than originally planned as we've added another section to the buildings so that each potter may live with his family behind the main workshop. That way, they won't need to navigate the crowded common ways morning and night to get to and from work, which will increase productivity."

"Whose idea was this?" Satal said.

"Mine," Yakal replied as he looked at Satal's scarred face.

"It will raise the cost of the whole project, you do understand that?"

Bitol interrupted. "Yes, Nim-q'ij, we've factored that in and figure the savings will be had when each potter can throw an additional two pots a day."

"Well, I guess it's all settled, and you didn't really need me here for this last bit," Satal said as she stood up. The men stood as well. "This meeting is over," she said as she hobbled out into the late afternoon sun.

As she slowly walked back to her palace, she thought of how easily Bitol and Yakal had challenged her. And then it struck her. "Of course," she muttered, "it was Yakal who left the pot at the house; Bitol had access to it, he could have easily given it to Yakal. I'll have to watch those two more closely now that Yakal is part of the council."

She entered her courtyard and wandered over to the thatched outdoor kitchen. There was no food inside the wooden and mesh-covered cupboard. The half an avocado and mango eaten that morning had been the only things left. Satal sighed. She would need to go to the market for food at some point, but all that sitting had made her tired. She needed to lie down.

Too tired to walk as far as her own room, and unwilling to discuss the meeting with Sachoj, Satal stepped into Chachal's room and slipped into the hammock. She gently swayed, letting her thoughts drift. *Perhaps I should get a slave, someone to do the shopping, cooking, and cleaning for me,* she thought. *No, then I'd need to feed, clothe, and house them on a daily basis. That would cost too much and destroy my privacy. No, not a good idea.* She didn't need anyone around on a regular basis, someone who might see her when she was performing her magic.

Like Chachal? she heard a voice in her head say.

Satal struggled to sit up in the swaying hammock and looked around the room. It was empty.

Just because I'm in the other room doesn't mean I can't connect with you, Sachoj said. *We both know Chachal saw you shape-shift when she was younger; she was terrified when you turned into a giant wasp. No wonder she didn't fuss too much when Q'alel sent her away.*

Shush, you hear me, Satal thought. *Chachal wanted to stay with me; she was in love with Alaxel. It's Q'alel's fault that she left. m*

Ah, Q'alel, I wonder what he would have done if he'd known the true story behind Chachal and Alaxel, Sachoj pondered. *Would he have sent her with that southerner? Or allowed Chachal to marry the father of her unborn child? Sachoj stifled a cackle. Perhaps her child is the one you seek!*

Satal scrambled out of the hammock and hurried into her bedroom. She confronted her great-grandmother. "What did you just say?" she demanded.

"You heard me the first time," Sachoj said and grinned, showing her viper-like teeth. "It's time you sent more men to search for the Wayeb child. Find a way to send them farther afield."

"The council plans on sending patrols out to protect the people from the Xiu; perhaps I can find a spy or two to help me," Satal said. She grinned at Sachoj. "You're right; we must find this jaguar-child."

Na'om

Once she knew Ajkun was sound asleep, Na'om crept from the hut and hurried down to the river, Ek' Balam padding softly by her side. The pounding of a single drum from the village echoed off the water, sounding hollow to Na'om. The dark sky was filled with stars, and a sliver of a moon shone on the river, barely illuminating the numerous rocks. Na'om walked beyond the village bathing area and pulled a fat log out from the riverbank. Straddling it with her legs, she used her hands to push across the expanse of black water to the far side, the jaguar swimming silently alongside her. After that first nerve-wracking swim two years earlier, Na'om had figured out this clumsy and slow method to cross the river that didn't require swimming and being stuck in wet clothes all the time. She pulled the log up into the grasses on the opposite bank while Ek' Balam shook the water from his pelt. The two hurried down the path to her sacred circle.

Na'om stood on the edge of the ring and surveyed her handiwork in the dim light. Over the space of many months, she'd snatched tiny bits of time to work on the area. She'd cleared all the vines covering the ground, built a small fire pit, and constructed a simple lean-to out of branches and palm fronds, which shielded the fire from view and provided much needed shelter. She could sit in the shade of the simple shed during the hot, dry months, had protection from the heavy summer rains, and best of all, she was hidden from the prying eyes of the villagers.

Na'om hummed as she dragged some dry sticks and branches to her fire ring. She piled them up on top of some shredded coconut fibers, and after striking two rocks together several times, she managed to get a fire going. The flames felt good against her bare legs and feet, which were still cold from the river. Ek' Balam plopped down in front of the fire and began to wash his face. Na'om smiled at him and reached into the lean-to for a leather bag full of dried fish. She tossed one to the big cat who caught it and ate it in one bite. "You're supposed to chew, silly," she said as she rubbed him behind his ear. She reached for the water gourd and shook it. It was empty.

Dusting off her hands, she quickly walked back to the river to fill it. She approached the bank with caution, afraid even at this late hour that someone from the village might be on the other side of the river. But the area was empty. Then Na'om grinned. *It's my tenth name day,* she thought. *The last day of yet another Wayeb, so the women are ensconced in their huts, and the men are at the temple, dancing around a bonfire to the sound of that single drum. Even Tz' has joined the dance this year, now that he's come of age.* After Na'om filled her jug, she checked to make sure her special log was still hidden in the brush.

Back at her shelter, Na'om poured some of the river water into a hollow coconut bowl and drank deeply before setting the bowl on the ground for Ek' Balam. The big jaguar drained the rest of the water and lay back down in front of the fire. "You're on guard duty, my friend," Na'om said to Ek' Balam as she settled herself in the shelter.

She sat cross-legged and placed her hands on her knees, palms up. Taking several deep breaths, Na'om willed her body to relax. She envisioned a white light entering the top of her head, creeping ever so slowly down her face, neck, arms, through her torso to her thighs, calves, and feet. Once she was fully coated with this invisible white light, Na'om opened her mind to the Otherworld.

Instantly impressions began to fly across her mind's eye; she saw her seated figure in front of the fire, Ek' Balam beside her, the river and the village of Pa nimá, then the men at the bonfire. She smiled as she saw Tz' in the group, his chest dripping beads of sweat as he danced and danced, and noticed that he glanced around him, as if he sensed her presence. She pushed outward with her mind into the dark jungle, and visions of giant bats and skeleton figures with bulging eyes, puddles of blood and vomit, and a giant wasp floating over a pool of water in a dark cave rushed at her, only to be repulsed by the shroud of white light protecting her spirit. Na'om ignored them all and pressed onward into the pulsating, gyrating darkness, searching for answers.

Ever since those first heady moments when she'd spun round and round in this very spot and seen the jungle through the eyes of Ek' Balam, she'd been practicing her meditations. Over time, she'd learned that she received clearer pictures if she was seated and patient. She drew another deep breath and pushed forward into the blackness.

Visions of a vast city with thousands of inhabitants filled her mind. She could see the tops of hundreds of one and two-room stucco huts, a steep, four-sided pyramid, a dome-shaped building. She zoomed in closer and began to see individual people, women and children asleep in swaying, multicolored hammocks and men in full leather armor marching in unison along the perimeter of a wall. She concentrated and focused her attention on one sector of the city. But every time she drew near, the images went black, and a painful buzzing filled her ears. Frustrated, Na'om opened her eyes.

She looked out from the lean-to and saw Ek' Balam sprawled on the ground, fast asleep. "Some guard cat you are," Na'om said as she stood up and stretched. "I guess I have to do this the hard way," she said as she added some sticks to the fire and set a pot of water to boil. She picked up a basket and threw a few pinches of herbs into the hot water. She let them steep a few minutes, and when it was cool enough, drank the tea, herbs and all.

She settled down near the fire, preferring its warmth to the darkness of the lean-to. She realigned herself with the white, protective light and felt the herbs begin to tingle throughout her body. She pushed her spirit back into the void, flying past the myriad of strange and evil entities that floated in the ether, and arrived back at the foreign city. Instead of going directly to the area blocked from view, she continued to circle, zooming in now and then for a close view of some family, then back out. She flew high over the giant bonfire built at the base of the pyramid and noted the tens upon tens of men moving counterclockwise around the fire. One man in particular kept appearing in Na'om's mind, but he danced by so rapidly she never could quite see his face.

Na'om roamed through the city once more and approached the one large palace that caused her ears to buzz and sent black sparks into the night sky every time she moved close to it. She pressed forward, despite the increasing pain in her head, and caught a glimpse of a puckered brown face grinning at her from inside a wall.

I see you, the head said.

Na'om jerked her spirit back into her own body and opened her eyes. She was back in front of her fire, and Ek' Balam was lying by her side. He picked up his head and looked at Na'om.

"I'm all right, boy," she said as she reached over to pet him. "I'm not sure what that thing was, but I pray to Itzamná that I never see it again," she said as she poked at the fire. Sparks popped in the air, and the burning wood settled down into a heap of bright red coals. Na'om stared into the fire, pondering the visions she'd just had.

I've been experimenting for a couple of years now and keep coming back to that one palace, but I've never seen that face before, Na'om thought. *Perhaps it's time I shared these images with Ati't; maybe she knows if this city really exists, and if it does, what these images mean.*

Her mind made up, Na'om quickly stood up and poured the remaining water from the gourd on the fire, which hissed and sizzled and sent a cloud of ashy smoke into the air. "Come on, boy," Na'om said to Ek' Balam. "Time to head back before anyone notices we've been gone."

Just a touch of daylight hugged the horizon as Na'om paddled her log back across the river. But the single drum continued to pound, so Na'om knew the men were still hard at work, keeping the foulness of the Wayeb at bay. The shadows lay deep along the path, and Na'om kept seeing that strange brown head out of the corner of her eye. Every time she did, she jumped and jerked around, expecting to see a whole person standing in the brush alongside the path. But no one was ever there.

She approached Ajkun's hut with care and carefully slipped under the covers. But the damp hem of Na'om's skirt brushed Ajkun's leg, and she woke with a start.

"Na'om, you're freezing cold," Ajkun said as she sat up in the narrow bed. "Are you ill, child?"

"No, Ati't, everything's fine; I just went outside to pee and must have gotten dew on my skirt," Na'om lied.

"Why do you have your clothes on?" Ajkun said now fully awake. In the faint light, she could just see Na'om. "What mischief have you been up to?" she demanded.

"Shh, Ati't, calm down," Na'om said as she placed a hand on her grandmother's arm. "Come and lie back down, the day has yet to arrive. I'll explain everything in the morning, I promise," Na'om said. She yawned. "I just need a few hours of sleep."

Na'om closed her eyes and only vaguely heard her grand-mother get up and move about the two-room hut. She drifted off into a deep sleep and woke several hours later when the smell of hot cocoa wafted into the room. She sat up in bed and yawned, stretched, and stepped onto the cool dirt floor. She brushed her clothes down; they were wrinkled, but she had to wear them for the day, as her other set of clothes needed to be washed.

Barefoot, she padded outside into the bright of day. Ajkun was sitting on her wooden stool by the fire and didn't notice Naʻom until she walked right up to Ajkun and hugged her around the shoulders.

"Morning, Ati't," Naʻom said as she sat cross-legged on the ground near her grandmother's feet. "What shall we do today?" she asked.

"We'll start by you telling me what happened last night," Ajkun said sternly. "It was the last day of the Wayeb; what were you doing outside?"

Naʻom looked around at the ground, found a small stick, and began breaking it into tiny pieces, which she threw into the fire. "Please don't be mad at me," she began. "I'll tell you everything, but promise me you'll let me finish before you say anything." She looked up into the dark brown eyes of the one woman who had ever cared for her. Naʻom's biggest fear was hurting her grandmother in even the smallest way. She took a deep breath. "I found a special spot, on the other side of the river, a place where I've been able to have more dreams—well, I think they're dreams, although I'm not really asleep." Naʻom paused and found another stick to break. "I guess you'd call them visions. Anyway, I go there, meditate, and see all kinds of things. Last night, after you were asleep, I did a meditation, and I saw something." She paused again, and a shiver ran through her body as she recalled the wrinkled old face. "I saw a city, a place I've been able to visit on other occasions, but this time, I saw this old, old face grinning at me, and then I jerked back into my body." She looked up at Ajkun who was staring directly at Naʻom.

Naʻom waited for her grandmother to speak. But she just continued to stare at her. "Ati't, are you all right?" she asked.

Ajkun shook her head, but forced herself to smile. She patted her lap, and the young girl climbed up into it and snuggled against her warm chest. "By the all-powerful Itzamná, I've never heard of somebody being able to do what you just described," Ajkun said as she hugged Naóm. "I don't know what any of it means. I think we have to tell Chiman; perhaps he'll understand these visions you've had."

"So, you're not angry with me?" Naóm said as she tilted her head toward her grandmother.

"Angry? No, confused, yes, scared even, but I could never be angry with you. You're the only family I have these days . . ." Ajkun's voice drifted off, and she shifted the girl's weight on her lap. "I do want to know how you've been able to cross the river, though. That worries me."

"I use a log, or sometimes I swim alongside Ek' Balam. He lets me hold onto his back and helps me across."

"Well, that can't continue," Ajkun said, and she pushed Naóm to her feet.

Naóm put her hands on her hips and stared at her grandmother. "I'm not going to stop going over there," she said. "You can't make me quit."

Ajkun laughed. "You sounded just like your mother just then; she had the same wild spirit in her. No, we'll talk to Chiman and explain what's been happening, and I'll insist he give you one of the smaller canoes to use. That would be much better than you swimming each time."

Later that afternoon, when the villagers were preparing for the new year feast, Naóm and Ajkun walked to Chiman's house. As they approached the hut, Chachal met them on the path.

"May Itzamná bring you great happiness this year, Chachal," Ajkun said as they faced the woman.

Chachal put down her basket of tamales, blocking the pathway. She stared at Naóm who stood just behind her grandmother. "What are you doing here?" she demanded. "And why is she with you?" she added as she pointed at Naóm. She leaned toward Naóm. "Stay away from my son, you little witch, you."

"We've come to speak to Chiman, is he home?" Ajkun said.

She shook her head ever so slightly at Na'om, who remained silent.

"He's home, but tired from the past five days. I have to get these tamales to the women so they can be cooked for the feast. But I'll be back shortly. I expect to find you both gone by the time I return." Chachal picked up her basket, and with one last glance at Na'om, she hurried on toward the village center.

"We'll have to be quick about this," Ajkun said. "The last thing we need is Chachal to hear about your special powers."

"Powers, what powers?"

Ajkun and Na'om both jumped as Tz' stepped out of the brush just ahead of them.

"Tz'ajonel!" Ajkun exclaimed. "You gave me such a fright; what on earth are you doing spying on us?" she demanded.

Na'om laughed. "He wasn't spying, Ati't, look, he was checking his trap line," she said and pointed to the three mice dangling by their tails that he held in his right hand. "A treat for Chac?" she asked, referring to Tz's pet tayra.

"Exactly," the youth said. "He's going blind in one eye, so I try to help him out with some extra food. Have you come to see Father? I think he's in the hut."

Na'om nodded.

"See you at the feast later?" Tz' asked as he started to walk toward the riverbank where Chac was lying in the sun.

Na'om nodded again. *At least one person will want me there,* she thought as she went with Ajkun to the doorway of the hut.

"Ajkun, Na'om," Chiman said when he saw them. "Come in, come in, have a seat," he said as he waved his hand at the four wooden stools arranged around a leather-topped table. He settled his lean frame on one stool, adjusted his loincloth, and motioned for them to sit. "Something's happened, surely not more trouble with the villagers," he said as he looked from Ajkun to Na'om.

"No, my friend, nothing like that," Ajkun said. "Na'om needs to tell you, as I fail to understand what's transpired." She placed her strong brown hands flat on the table and looked at Naʾom. "Child, you're safe here," she said, encouraging Naʾom to speak.

Naʾom nodded, swallowed, and looked up at Chiman's face. *Tzʾ doesn't look anything like him,* she thought before she quickly pushed the idea away. *Concentrate and tell the man what you've seen,* a voice from deep within urged. "My lord, I've been to the other side of the river many times, and I've seen things, strange and wonderful things. Last night, I saw this city and this face . . ." Naʾom paused and shuddered as the sight of those puckered lips floated in front of her eyes. She couldn't talk about it. She swallowed again and continued. "There's a city full of houses, and one section is almost always black to me and buzzes when I approach it, but last night, maybe because of the Wayeb, I saw more details, even though it hurt my body to go near the place." She looked at Ajkun and back at Chiman.

The older man furrowed his brow and both women remained silent, waiting for him to speak. Chiman stood up and began to pace the room. "How did you learn to spirit travel?" he asked as he stopped in front of Naʾom.

"I don't know; I just get really quiet and then feel my spirit slip out of my body," Naʾom said. "Is that part of the evil of the Wayeb?" she asked.

"No, not at all, but if what you say is true, then your gift is stronger than I ever believed possible. It takes a shaman years of training to learn that skill," Chiman said. He knelt in front of Naʾom. "This city you keep seeing, does it have a wall around it?" he asked.

"Yes, a high wall, with men in armor patrolling in front of big doors or gates," Naʾom said. "Why?"

"From what you describe, that's the city of Mayapán, where I met Chachal," Chiman stopped and looked at Ajkun who shook her head a tiny bit. "Tell me more about how you've seen these images."

"Well, once I get still, I cover myself in white light, and then

I just push my spirit out into the blackness. Sometimes, like last night, I drink some poppy seeds in my tea, and I can go farther or deeper, I guess you'd call it. With the tea, I can see faces of people, rooms in houses, and other stuff . . ." Na'om said.

Just then, Chachal appeared in the doorway. Her heavy frame blocked the light, and the three turned to see her standing there. She pushed a wisp of her gray-black hair off her face and clutched at the jadeite necklace she always wore. "Still here, I see," she said as she entered the room. Her deep blue skirt rustled as she walked toward Chiman.

"We were just leaving," Ajkun said. "Come Na'om, we have things to do before the feast."

"Good, I need time with my husband," Chachal said as she patted him on his bare arm.

Chiman shrugged off Chachal's hand. Ignoring her, he stood up, and his head almost grazed the ceiling of the low room. "We'll talk more tomorrow, Ajkun," he said as he stepped outside in front of the women.

Na'om trailed behind Ajkun, followed by Chachal. She could feel the woman's eyes boring into her back.

Tz' came running up to the group when he saw them leaving the hut. "See you later," he said to Na'om.

She nodded, smiled, and followed Ajkun toward the village center.

As they left the clearing, Na'om could hear Chachal's strident voice above the sound of the nearby river admonishing Tz' for being friendly to her.

"But Chuch," she heard him say, "she's my friend."

"It's high time you made new friends, Tz'," Chachal's voice drifted to them. "In fact, I've spoken to Kemonel, and I want you to pay attention to her daughter, Mok'onel, at the feast tonight. You're almost fifteen, old enough to marry. The girl is eleven, and by next summer, she'll have reached her moon time."

Na'om and Ajkun paused on the path, just out of sight of

the hut, and continued to listen to the conversation. They heard Chiman speak, but his voice was too low for them to understand the words. Then Chachal's shrillness came to them on the light breeze.

"That girl is unsuitable for Tz'. He'll begin to take note of Mok'onel and that's that."

Na'om kicked a rock in the path and sent it flying into the bushes.

Ajkun looked at Na'om. "Don't fret; Chachal won't get her way," she said.

"But how do you know, Ati't?" Na'om replied as the two began to walk slowly along the dirt path. She scuffed her bare feet, and little clouds of dust rose at each step.

"I may not be able to see like you do, but I know more about Chiman than any person in this village," Ajkun said as she stopped and placed her hands on Na'om's shoulders. "If he wants you to be with Tz', then you will be, no matter what Chachal says. Just remember that anytime doubts begin to creep into your mind." She looked along the path, at the shadows that stretched from one side to the other. "Come, there's much to be done before the feast." She picked up her pace, and Na'om had to run to catch up with her.

Later that afternoon, as the sun dipped below the edge of the jungle, Na'om followed her grandmother to the evening's festivities. She had changed into a new set of clothes that Ajkun had made her, a dark blue cotton skirt and matching shirt, both embroidered with deep purple morning glories that trailed across the shoulders and hem on vines of forest green. The stitching was subtle against the deep blue fabric, and Na'om liked that it was so different from the clothes of the other girls.

Lit torches lined the central plaza, and the whole village had gathered in the opening. The smells of peppers, tomatoes, and fresh cilantro mingled with that of roasted deer meat and the sweet scent of steamed corn tamales. Na'om stayed to the edge of the central plaza, letting Ajkun be drawn into a group of older women who hustled her off in a wave of chatter. Keeping to the dark purple shadows, Naʼom avoided the clusters of people gossiping and chatting as they ate the stews prepared by the women of Pa nimá. She quietly made her way around the outskirts of the gathering toward the temple. She stopped by one of the many huts when she noticed Mokʼonel and a group of other girls had stationed themselves near the shrine, close to where Chiman, Chachal, and Tzʼ were seated. Mokʼonel had pulled her black hair back from her face and braided it. The long plait was coiled on the back of her head, and sheʼd intertwined fresh marigolds in among the loops. The yellowish-orange blossoms matched those embroidered on her white shirt, and Naʼom noticed sheʼd rubbed her cheeks with annatto paste; the reddish tint highlighted her high cheekbones and accentuated her small white teeth.

The girls laughed, and Naʼom watched as Tzʼ turned his head in their direction. She saw Chachal lean in to Tzʼ and whisper something to him. He nodded his head and slowly rose to his feet. He adjusted his new loincloth and threw his spider monkey cape across his shoulders before approaching the group of young girls.

Naʼom sighed as Tzʼ hugged each of the girls in turn and then remained standing beside Mokʼonel. The two were of the same height; Tzʼs body was strong and muscular, Mokʼonelʼs just showing the first hints of womanhood in the slight curve to her hips and the petite breasts that pushed against the fabric of her shirt.

Sheʼs so pretty, Naʼom thought, *and they look so nice together. No wonder Chachal wants Tzʼ to be with her . . .*

"Naʼom, what are you doing here, hiding in the shadows?" Ajkun said as she touched Naʼom on the arm. "Come eat with everyone; itʼs a new year, a new beginning."

"You know I wonʼt be welcome, Atiʼt," Naʼom said. "No one wants me here."

"I want you here and so does Chiman," Ajkun said as she looked closely at Naʼom. She followed her granddaughterʼs gaze to the cluster of girls and Tz'. "Is that what's bothering you?" she asked as she nodded her head in that general direction.

Na'om looked at the ground and mumbled, "Yes."

Ajkun put one finger under Na'om's chin and lifted her head until their eyes met. "What did I tell you earlier?" she demanded. "Go over there and show them who's in control here. You have power, Na'om, use it."

Emboldened by her grandmother's words, Na'om straightened her back and stepped into the torchlight. She took three steps and then stopped as she saw Tz' turn in her direction. He flashed her a big smile and beckoned with his hand.

Na'om grinned and hurriedly crossed the span between them. She laughed inwardly when she saw Mok'onel step away from her, leaving just enough room for Na'om to wedge her body between Tz' and Mok'onel.

Tz' wrapped an arm around Na'om's shoulder and gave her a quick sideways hug. "'I'm so glad you're here," he whispered in her hair as he bent and placed a quick kiss on her cheek. "These girls were beginning to bore me."

Na'om grinned and moved her feet just slightly, forcing the older, bigger Mok'onel to back away some more. *Ati't was right,* Na'om thought, *I do have power. And from now on, I plan to use it.*

The next morning, Na'om and Ajkun were just finishing their chores around the house when Chiman arrived. He motioned for Ajkun to remain seated on the one stool and squatted by the fire. "I won't stay long," he said and held his hands out to the flames. "I just wanted to hear a bit more about where Na'om has been having these visions."

Na'om placed the broom she'd been using to sweep up leaves against the hut and came and sat next to Chiman. "I found a circle of trees on the other side of the river. Over the past couple of years, I've cleaned the ground inside the ring and built a simple lean-to out of sticks to shelter me from the rain and sun. It's in that space that I meditate and see things."

"Across the river, you say? How in the name of Itzamná are you getting over there?"

"She's been using a log or swimming with that cat of hers," Ajkun said. "I believe it's time for Na'om to be taught how to paddle a canoe."

"Yes, I agree. Tz' has gotten quite good at it. He can teach you when he has a chance. And I'd like to see this ring of trees; perhaps this is where your permanent home should be built," Chiman said. He looked as Ajkun and Na'om. "I'm sorry, but the day will come when you'll have to leave the village, Na'om." Chiman stood up and flexed his legs to get the blood flowing again. "Chachal and the others will insist that you move; it sounds like you've found the ideal spot, though," he said as he patted Na'om on the shoulder.

"You won't make her move right away, will you?" Ajkun said as she placed a hand on Chiman's bare arm.

"No, not until her moon blood appears, as I promised," Chiman said. "In the meantime, Na'om, I want you to continue telling me of these visions." He leaned in closer to Ajkun. "You should continue to write them down and teach Na'om how to write, so she can do the same. We have to have a record of this for the sake of everyone's future."

SATAL

Dressed in an ash-colored skirt, plain white shirt, and wearing her third best pair of sandals, Satal prepared to enter the crowded living quarters of the less fortunate citizens of Mayapán. Despite her resolve to immediately hire new spies to help find the jaguar-child, it had taken Satal a full week to find the time to actually make the trip into this part of the city. Even though the common people lived there, she was familiar with this section of Mayapán, as she often visited one or two shops in the sector that sold the herbs she needed for her potions. Since she was a member of the council and was well recognized by many in the city, she couldn't spend her days outside the walls gathering plants and roots to dry as she had in her youth. *It's just as well,* Satal thought. *These old bones of mine are so sore; any amount of time spent afield would only make them ache worse.* Although rumors circulated among her elite neighbors that the citizens of this section were trustworthy and hardworking by day, but thieves and worse by night, Satal felt reasonably safe. *They could steal the very clothes off a person's back especially one as old as me,* Satal thought, *but they also have heard rumors about me and my powers.*

Even though the day was bright and sunny, Satal had slipped her small, green obsidian knife in its sheath into her pocket. She also carried its mate, the knife with the eight-inch blade, and a fist-sized cotton bag full of cacao beans in a leather satchel. Satal glanced behind her, at the wide expanse of open space near the

Temple of Cremations and the market before picking the first alleyway that led into the heart of the residential section. A pack of dun-colored dogs raced past her, chasing a small rat, which disappeared into one of the many one-room huts lining the street. Satal checked her pocket and held the shaft of her knife in her hand. She liked the weight of it, the feeling of safety it provided.

Women dressed in shabby clothes stood in the doorways to the houses and stared at Satal; none spoke to her as she slowly walked by, and she heard them shush their young naked children who peeked out at Satal from behind their mother's skirts. She knew there was a public house in the district, a place where the potters and salt workers went after a long day to drain a glass of fermented berries. She wasn't sure exactly where it was, though, and hoped the street widened into a courtyard or market area where there might be a sign of some sort. She felt all the pairs of eyes pressing into her back, but refused to stop and ask for directions.

Seeing an opening off to her right, Satal turned the corner with relief. This passage was wider, and the houses were set farther apart, each with its own tiny courtyard, but it led deeper into the maze of paths and huts rather than back to the main marketplace. She hurried along and avoided eye contact with the people she met. Women had babies slung in shawls on their backs or clutched them in their arms, suckling the infants openly, while men with pack baskets full of wares edged around her, bumping her with their wide loads. Satal slipped the knife from its sheath. A bead of sweat ran down her back, and she fought the urge to scratch at it. As she advanced deeper into the throng, the dust and noise in the air grew thicker, and she stifled a grimace as she noticed a number of men clustered in a group, filling the lane from one side to the other. They were hunched over, staring and shouting at some event near the ground.

Satal looked left and right and knew she had to pass through the crowd. She watched as one man with a bundle of sticks on his back just pressed into the bodies; they parted reluctantly and let the man through, sucking him into their midst where he disappeared from view. Satal paused and waited for another vendor. I'll follow right on his heels, she thought, and let him part the throng for me. Two men carrying a deer carcass upside down on a pole approached the group, and Satal fell in step behind them. The first man prodded with the tip of the pole, and men fell aside, letting them pass. Satal hurried after them and felt the swarm of warm bodies close behind her. The men towered over her four-foot frame, blocking out light and fresh air. Satal silently urged the deer hunters to hurry, to reach the other side of the mob. But they stopped. They shifted the deer to the other shoulder to get a better view of the two cocks fighting in the dust.

Move, Satal prayed as she felt more sweat trickle down her back. Through the tangle of arms and backs, she could see the two birds flapping and flying at one another, their deep bronze and golden feathers glistening with fresh blood. Eager to see the final killing swipe of spurs, each time one cock advanced, the men leaned forward, pulling Satal with them. Warm, dirty bodies pressed against her back, on her arms, against her chest, and she smelled the rank scent of blood and men's sweat. She withdrew the knife from her pocket and poked the deer hunter just in front of her with the very tip of the blade.

He jumped at the sharp prick and quickly glanced over his shoulder. Satal looked at him with wide eyes and motioned with her one free hand. He frowned at her, said something to his companion, and they moved on, with Satal just behind them.

She took a deep breath once she reached open space and silently put the knife back in her pocket. She turned another corner and finally saw the wooden sign for the bar hanging on the wall, Silowik Tukan. The Drunken Blackberry, how appropriate, Satal thought.

With a quick glance up and down the crowded lane, Satal stepped into the dark interior. Leather-topped tables were arranged around the room, each with wooden stools placed beside them. A wooden counter ran along one wall. The three shelves on the wall behind it were lined with various gourds, each with a different colored string tied about its neck. The other three walls were painted in lurid reds, greens, and browns depicting half-naked women dancing with men in loincloths. The painted figures of the men held jugs up above their heads, and lines of red droplets flowed from the vessels to their open mouths. Many of the paintings were scratched or altogether gone where the stucco walls had been chipped or cracked. The place appeared empty, as no one stood behind the counter, but Satal noticed a young man seated across the room, his back against the wall where he could see anyone and everyone who entered and exited the bar. As she walked toward the youth, she adjusted the bag on her shoulder and double-checked that her small knife was still handy. It wouldn't do any good to have had that stolen in the cockfight crowd, Satal thought as she felt the satisfying weight of the handle in her hand.

The young man, about eighteen years of age, was dressed in a simple white shirt and loincloth. His hair was greased with peccary fat and spiked on top, part of the new style favored by the younger men of Mayapán. He stood up as Satal approached and pulled out a stool for her to sit on. "Nim-q'ij, to what do I owe this honor? Please, sit down; let me buy you a drink." The youth rapped on the tabletop and shouted, "Another glass of balché and one for my friend, here." He motioned to the stool beside Satal and sat down again.

Ignoring the glances of the bartender who had appeared from a back room at the sound of the boy's cry, Satal sat down and leaned toward the youth. "I need your help, Ilonel," Satal said. "I hear you're the man to come to, as you're the best in the business."

"That depends on the business, my lady," Ilonel said. "Surely someone in your position can command anyone in the city to do your bidding . . ." He paused as the bartender put two mugs of balché on the table. "Put it on my bill," Ilonel said and waved the man away. "To your health, my lady," he said and took a deep pull on his mug of fermented tree bark and honey. "Ahh, as I was saying," Ilonel continued as he wiped his mouth with the back of his hand, "you sit on the city council and can order anyone to do almost anything, so whatever this business of yours is, it must be suspect, in which case, you've come to the right man." He thumped his empty mug on the table and eyed the second one.

"Go ahead, I have no desire to drink that swill," Satal said. "I need you to find someone, someone very special."

"And where am I to look for this special someone?" Ilonel asked.

"To the south. I want you to sweep the countryside; go from village to village, as far as our distant cousins in Tikal, if you must, but you are not to return until you find this child."

"Ah, the mystery thickens, for it's not just a person, but a child. And how will I recognize this special child?" Ilonel asked as he drained the second mug of balché. "And, more importantly, what's in it for me? What you ask sounds like a lot of walking; I might even need to buy a canoe to travel the distances you mention." He folded his arms across his chest. "It's pretty cozy, sitting right here, enjoying a simple drink from time to time."

Satal reached into her bag and pulled out the sack of cacao beans. "This should get you started; there's more when you need it. Hire men to help in the search; have them report directly to you, and you will report directly to me." Glancing around, Satal checked to see that they were alone. The bartender had gone back into the other room of the bar. She pulled out the larger green obsidian knife from the satchel and laid it on the table in front of Ilonel. "When you bring me the child, this will be yours. I don't need to tell you how much someone with your connections would pay for this on the black market."

Ilonel whistled softly between his teeth as he drew the knife partway out from its leather sheath. He eyed the etchings on the blade and the twisted vines and leaves carved into the handle. "This child must be very special indeed, my lady." He pushed the blade back in to the hilt, but did not return the knife to Satal. "I know some men who will help me, but we need more information. Do I search for a boy or a girl?"

Satal looked into the young man's unlined face. "I believe a girl," she said.

"Tell me more about this child; otherwise, it'll be like searching for a stingray spine in a pile of straw." Ilonel took another sip of balché, his hand still firmly on the knife.

"She has some kind of connection to jaguars."

"Oh, ho, now I search for a jaguar-girl. The mystery deepens. I suspect anyone with those kinds of powers must be very valuable indeed."

Satal reached across the table for the knife.

Ilonel grinned and gripped the handle more tightly. "Oh, no, my lady, this stays with me," he said as he removed the knife from the tabletop and placed it in his lap.

Satal took a deep breath and let it out slowly. "You're pushing your luck, Ilonel," she said as she stood up and brushed off the back of her skirt. It was sticky with stale balché that had spilled on the stool, and she looked at her hand with minor disgust. "I expect reports every month or two until the child is found."

"As you wish, Nim-q'ij," said Ilonel. "We shall find your mystery child, have no fear."

Satal walked across the dimly lit bar and stepped back out into the daylight. The sun made her squint, and she hesitated before turning to her left, to find her way out of the maze of shops and huts. Her head down against the sun, Satal was unaware of those around her until a voice spoke directly to her.

"Nim-q'ij, what are you doing here?" a nearby woman asked.

Satal turned to find Uskab approaching her. Uskab looked around and hurried to Satal's side. "This is no place for you, my lady," Uskab said. "Come; let me lead you back to the marketplace."

"Yes, that would be most helpful," Satal said. She looked at Uskab. "Perhaps you can help me. I need a trustworthy girl to come do chores for me, two or three times a week. I thought I might find someone if I wandered into this area," Satal lied. "But," she paused, "I got stuck watching that cockfight back there and felt a bit weak, so entered the shop for a drink of water."

"I doubt they even know what water is in there," Uskab said as she meandered in and out of the lanes, leading Satal farther and farther from the crowd.

Satal hurried after the young girl, grateful Uskab had believed her little lie.

Uskab slowed and waited for Satal to step beside her. She pointed down a narrow street. "There's the market and just beyond, the Temple," she said. "You should be safe now, my lady."

Satal looked around her. She knew this street; the alley was lined with shops and huts owned by the market vendors, many of whom supplied the herbs she used. "Thank you, Uskab, you've been most helpful." She reached into her pocket and withdrew a small bag of cacao beans. "Here, let me pay you for your trouble," she said as she pulled out two beans. "I always pay my debts."

"Nim-q'ij, save your money," Uskab said as she pushed the woman's outstretched hand away. "I was headed in this direction anyway." She turned to enter one of the shops, which sold a variety of medicinal potions and amulets. "If I hear of anyone looking for work, I'll send her your way."

Satal nodded and headed back to her palace. *Now that he's been handsomely paid, Ilonel had best find the child,* she thought as she reached the market. The smell of turtle soup caused her stomach to rumble, and she stopped at one of the many stands for a quick bowlful.

Later that afternoon, as she halfheartedly swept the front room of her palace, she heard a knock on the door. She laid the straw broom against the wall and sighed as a small piece of plaster fell off the wall and onto the freshly swept tiles. *By all the gods,* she thought, *this place is going to fall down around my ears if I don't get someone in here to fix it.* Another knock interrupted her. "Coming, coming," she called, "I'm not as young as I used to be, you know," she said as she pulled open the heavy door.

A young girl of about thirteen or fourteen stood in front of her. "Yes?" Satal asked, as she looked the girl over from head to toe. *She appears clean, her dress is a bit worn, but her nails are trimmed,* she thought as she stood there.

"Nim-q'ij, my sweet sister-in-law sent me. She said you look for a servant girl . . ."

"What's your name?"

"Masat, my lady, I'm the youngest sister of Yakal; you ran into my brother's wife today in the alleyway. Uskab said you need a girl to clean and perhaps to cook?"

"Yes, yes, I do; come in, child," Satal said as she stood to one side.

Masat hesitated and then stepped through the doorway. She paused just inside the front room and looked around at the wide hall.

Now why would Uskab send me one of her relatives, when she knows I can't stand the family? Satal wondered as she walked past the teen and sat down in her worn-out leather chair. "Your mother and brother don't mind you working for wages?" Satal asked.

"I near my fifteenth name day, my lady," Masat said. She looked down at her bare feet. "I'm small for my age, but I can clean and cook many dishes, I can run fast to the market, and I know many of the vendors, who always give me a fair price, without the need to haggle."

"You didn't answer my question."

Masat blushed and paused before answering. "I'm to wed soon and need money to purchase items for my new home, my lady. Chuch understands this."

"And what of your brother, Yakal? Is he in favor of this situation?"

"My brother doesn't know I'm here," Masat said.

"And what happens when this wedding takes place? I fear I'll be left to fend for myself again," Satal said.

"No, no, honored one, no. I would come here still, that is . . . once I had tended to my own home," Masat replied.

"Um, yes, well I doubt that," Satal said as she pushed herself up from the chair. "I suppose I can find another girl to replace you once that time arrives." She walked over to the broom and picked it up. "Well, don't just stand there, girl, there's work to be done. Clean in here while I figure out a market list," Satal said.

"Yes, Nim-q'ij," Masat said as she began to sweep.

Satal headed outside, away from the dust floating in the air. *This girl may be useful in more ways than one,* Satal thought as she looked inside her baskets and bags near the fire pit. *Perhaps if I promise her some extra trinkets for her wedding, I can encourage her to tell me what goes on in Yakal's house and that of the mother. The more eyes I have working for me, the better. Yes, this may work out quite well,* Satal thought, and she smiled.

AJKUN

Ajkun lay in bed, still tired after a full night's sleep. *I'm getting old,* she thought as she shifted her weight and felt her bones creak. *Today's my forty-fourth name day, and so many years have passed since I last held my sweet girl-child, Tu'janel.* She rolled over and bumped into Na'om. The girl was on her back, deeply asleep, her arms flung wide. *She's grown into a woman in thirteen heartbeats,* Ajkun thought as she looked at her granddaughter. Her waist-length black hair had fallen away from her face, and Ajkun could see the white scars etched into her face. *So many moons have passed since that first encounter.* Ajkun sighed and heaved herself out of bed.

Ek' Balam lay right outside the doorway. *This cat's been part of the family for over five years, and I still don't feel comfortable with him nearby,* Ajkun thought. "Shoo, go on now," Ajkun said, and she waved a hand towel at the jaguar. Ek' Balam yawned, stretched, and paced over to the lime tree where he lay back down in the sun. Ajkun stepped outside and went to void her bladder in the bushes. Then she went down to the river to wash. She loved the sight of the stream in the early morning on days like this day when the river water was warmer than the air, and mist swirled along the water's edge and across its width, obscuring the other side. Ajkun felt wrapped in a cocoon, the sound all muted by the fog, the rush of the day still ahead of her. She took her time washing up and reluctantly turned back to her house.

When she returned, Na'om was already up and had the fire

going. Ajkun watched as her thirteen-year-old granddaughter placed the pot on the cooking stones to make hot water for their morning tea. "Morning, Naʼom," Ajkun said as she sat down on her wooden stool. She wrapped her gray shawl around her shoulders. "There's a little chill in the air this morning. The heat of the fire feels good on these old bones," she commented as she held her hands out to the flames.

"Some hot tea will warm you," Naʼom replied. "And I'm making us a pot of corn porridge as well. We still have some of that dark honey Tz' brought the other day; I'll add a spoonful of it to your bowl."

Ajkun watched as Naʼom moved about the fire, preparing the meal. "You remind me so much of your mother at this age," Ajkun said. "She liked to help me like you are, making the meals, carrying the water, gathering firewood. You look like her as well, the same long legs, the curve of your hips . . ." Ajkun paused. "Naʼom, has there been any sign of your moon blood?"

Naʼom dropped her head and refused to look at her grandmother.

"Come child, you mustn't be afraid; it's the most natural thing in the world," Ajkun said as she reached out to hug Naʼom.

"I'm not afraid of that, Atiʼt," Naʼom said. "But the villagers will force me to leave you once they know I've become a woman."

Ajkun set her hot coconut husk full of tea on the ground to cool. "Ah, yes, I'd forgotten that," she said. "Well, it's time we talked to Chiman again. Perhaps as part of their training, the village boys can build you a permanent house where your lean-to stands now."

"Will they all need to help?" Naʼom asked. "I don't want them to disturb the energy of that space." She stirred the pot of cornmeal on the fire and ladled some into another coconut shell, which she handed to Ajkun.

Ajkun smiled at her granddaughter and blew on the hot mush. "I do wish you didn't have to live alone," she said. "Perhaps

I should move over there, too."

Na'om swallowed a spoonful of porridge before answering. "Ati't, I won't be alone; Ek' Balam will be with me all the time. Besides, your place is here, in the village. I'm the only one allowed to be an outcast." She laughed nervously.

"Well, I still don't like it," Ajkun replied. "The village needs you even if they don't see that yet. And you need to put more faith in your ability to foresee things."

"I don't see how these stupid dreams I have will ever be of use to anyone," Na'om said. "They've never helped me, that's for sure. All they do is force everyone away from me so that I've never really had any friends except you and Ek' Balam and Tz'." She picked at her food. "Maybe Chachal was right, and I should have been smothered at birth."

Ajkun dropped her spoon on the ground. "When did she say that? Why I'll wring . . ."

Na'om handed her grandmother her spoon. "She didn't say it, not out loud anyway," she muttered. "Don't worry, Ati't, I just won't be so visible anymore, which might be a good thing."

"You've hardly been visible lately, child, the way you and that cat can disappear into the undergrowth without a sound; it's spooky," Ajkun said. "I never know when you'll pop out at me." She blew on her tea and took a sip. "We'll go see Chiman as soon as we're done eating."

They met no one on the path to the shaman's house, and Ajkun was glad to see that Chachal was not at home. *The less that woman knows about Na'om and her whereabouts, the better,* Ajkun thought.

"Chachal's in the village center, doing needlework with some of the other women," Chiman said as he motioned for the midwife and her granddaughter to take a seat. "What brings you here today, my friend? Surely not more dreams," Chiman asked as he looked at the young girl in front of him.

"No, nothing like that," Ajkun replied. "Na'om informed me

this morning that . . . hmm, how shall I say it? That her moon time has come," Ajkun blushed.

"Ah, I thought as much, the minute I laid eyes on you," Chiman said as he looked directly at Naʼom. "You've grown into quite the pretty young lady; I can see why Tzʼ talks about you nonstop."

Ajkun watched as Naʼom's face turned red. Her granddaughter looked down at the floor and shuffled her bare feet on the cool stones.

"Come child, no harm in telling the truth, now is there?" Chiman said as he gently laid a finger on Naʼom's chin and raised her head. He looked directly into her eyes. "I know you're shy, afraid to show your face because of your scars, but I'm here to tell you that your marks are the signs of a warrior, and you should be proud of them. Hold your head high, and let the world know you're a force to be reckoned with." He turned away from the girl and let the deerskin cape across his shoulders drop to the floor. "See these spots of mine? They took many painful months to tattoo, but they hold no real power. Your scars command attention. I envy you." He picked up the fur and placed it on the edge of the bed. "Come, sit, we have much to discuss at this point." He made room for Naʼom, who sat on the edge of the bed with him.

Ajkun sat down on a three-legged wooden stool. The smooth and leathery peccary hide creaked as she adjusted her weight. "I should let Naʼom speak, as it's her idea." Ajkun nodded at Naʼom as she pulled the shawl from her shoulders and folded it into a neat bundle on her lap.

"I wondered if Tzʼ might be the one to help me build my permanent home on the other side of the river," Naʼom said as she plucked at the blanket on the bed. "I don't want just anyone in my sacred circle, but I trust Tzʼ. The other village boys might disturb the energy there." She looked into the brown eyes of the shaman and waited for his response.

"Hmm, yes, a good idea. Tzʼ needs the experience as his last attempt at building a structure didn't last more than a week!" Chiman laughed. "Many of the village boys are old enough to marry and are already building houses of their own; Tz' is the only one not engaged at the moment. He can certainly help you."

None of them noticed when Chachal stepped into the doorway. Her plump body filled the space. She frowned when she saw Na'om sitting on the edge of her favorite monkey skin blanket. "How dare you speak of Tz' in front of her," she hissed to Chiman. "I plan to announce our son's engagement soon. I don't understand why you've let her into our house!" She placed her basket of embroidery on the floor and stared at the three of them.

"No one was speaking of marriage, Chachal," Chiman said. "Na'om needs some help with a project, and Tz' is the perfect person to do it."

"Never fear, Chachal," Ajkun said as she stood up and tucked her shawl under her arm. She nodded to Na'om who hurried to her side. "We were just leaving." She winked at Chiman. "Until later, Chiman," she said as she quickly paced to the door with Na'om just behind her.

"Ati't," Na'om whispered as they rounded the bend in the path. "Did you see the look on Chachal's face when she saw me sitting on the bed?"

"Yes, but it wasn't as funny as the look she gave me when I called her husband 'Chiman' instead of 'my lord,'" Ajkun said. "I don't know of anything Chachal hates more than to be reminded that Chiman and I were friends long before she came into the village." Ajkun laughed. "I know it's wrong of me, but I do love to torment that woman."

Later that afternoon, Chiman, Ajkun, and Na'om met at the river. Chiman motioned to one of the canoes, and Ajkun held the dugout steady while Chiman knelt in the bow. Then she motioned for Na'om to sit in the middle.

"But who shall guide the canoe across the river?" Na'om asked as she settled herself.

"Why Ajkun, of course," Chiman said as he nodded at the older woman.

Naʼom watched as her grandmother deftly pushed the canoe off from shore, and then with a bit of difficulty, she hopped into the boat as it glided across the clear shallow water and into the river.

"That was a lot easier to do twenty years ago, I'm afraid." Ajkun laughed as she picked up her paddle and carefully guided the canoe into the current.

"Atiʼt, when did you learn to paddle a canoe?" Naʼom asked as she continued to watch her grandmother steer the boat across the river.

"That's just one of many things your grandmother learned from me," Chiman said with a laugh. "She knew just the right words to get me to teach her things that no woman is supposed to know."

"Enough of our past, my friend," Ajkun said. "Naʼom, dip your paddle in the water; we'll never get to the other side of the river if you don't begin to help."

Naʼom shifted her attention back to the front of the canoe and plunged her blade into the water. She pulled back and felt the resistance of the water against the wood in her hands and then the slip of the canoe as it eased a bit farther forward in the river. Within minutes, the dugout was on the far side of the river, and Naʼom hopped out onto the sandy shore. She held the canoe steady while Chiman and Ajkun stepped into the ferns growing along the water's edge. The three of them pulled the boat onto higher ground, and Chiman tied the canoe's bow rope to a nearby ceiba tree.

"All right, Naʼom, lead the way," Chiman said.

Naʼom nodded, got her bearings, and pushed into the undergrowth that grew along the shoreline. Within minutes, the three arrived in the small natural clearing.

Ajkun looked at the cleared space inside the large mahogany

trees. "And all this time I thought you were over here gathering ceiba pods and blood flower and other herbs. Look at what you've done to this place." She wandered around the thirty-foot circle, peeked into the small shelter, and smiled as she noted the precision with which Na'om had built her fire ring.

"There's definitely good energy in this spot," Chiman said as he approached Na'om. "It's almost like a vibration under my feet."

"I feel it, too," Na'om said as she looked up at the shaman. "And that's why I don't want just anyone to wander through here."

"Well, I guess it's settled, then," Ajkun said. "Although I'm sad, I know it's for the best, and I have to admit this spot is magical."

"I'll have Tz' come over tomorrow," Chiman said as he headed back toward the canoe. "If Chachal has had her way, word will have traveled through the village by now, so the sooner your home is built, the better."

Na'om

Na'om put down the last basket from the canoe in the middle of the new house. It had taken three months to build, but she finally had her own place to live. She liked the clean, white stucco walls, the hard-packed dirt under her feet. She could do whatever she wanted in the space, and she twirled around on the spot. But she stopped when Ajkun blocked the light coming in through the doorway. She quickly removed the pile of blankets from her grandmother's arms.

"The only thing left to bring from the canoe is the mattress," Ajkun said as she took a deep breath. She looked around the small space, at the jumble of baskets and wooden crates that filled the room. "I guess you'll have to lay it on the floor for now," she said.

"I don't mind," Na'om replied. "I'll be closer to Ek' Balam that way." She draped the bundle in her arms over everything and went to give Ajkun a hug. "Don't worry so much, Ati't, I'll be fine."

"I know, I know, it's just that you're still so young," Ajkun said, "and there's still so much you need to know." She held Na'om tightly to her chest.

Na'om took a deep breath; her grandmother smelled of hot peppers and herbs, of sun-bleached cotton and coconut juice. "Let's get the mattress and go back across the river for something to eat, then I can come back and try to make some sense of this mess."

They stepped from the small room into the outdoors. With Tz' in charge, the two childhood friends had built a thatched roof over the fire ring and a small wooden table beside it to the right of the hut door. Several glazed pots were piled haphazardly on the ground, and three water gourds hung from strings around their necks from one of the support posts. The two women walked to the river, and with some effort, they picked up the bulky cotton bag filled with ceiba fluff. Na'om had spent weeks collecting enough kapok to fill the sack before sewing the end shut. They put it inside the hut and returned to the river.

Ajkun stepped into the bow of the canoe, and Na'om took the stern. With ease, she pushed off and jumped into the already moving boat. Deftly, she dipped her paddle and held it against the side of the vessel, guiding them through the current to the opposite shore. It had only taken Tz' a few days to teach her the tricks of steering a canoe with a paddle, and Na'om was glad her log-riding days were over.

Back at Ajkun's hut, Na'om entered and looked around to see if she had forgotten anything. The only thing was Ek' Balam, and she knew he would follow her if she offered him his favorite treat, the dried fish he loved to eat.

"Come and sit, child," Ajkun said as she ladled some fish stew into a hollowed gourd. "I have things I need to tell you, things I should have told you long ago, but never found the chance."

Intrigued, Na'om hurried to sit on her palm frond mat. *I'll need to weave some of these for my house,* and she smiled at the thought. She took the bowl of stew, blew on it to cool it, and waited for her grandmother to sit down on her stool.

Ajkun leaned forward, her arms cradled on her knees. "You know your mother died, giving birth to you, but what I've never told you was that your father was here as well."

"You said he was out hunting and was captured by the Xiu," Na'om said.

"No, he was here that night, participating in the rituals for the Wayeb. He was so upset at the loss of your mother, Tu'janel, that he turned his back on everyone here, including you. He acted as though you were cursed for being born during the Wayeb . . ."

"Like everyone else here," Na'om muttered.

"Yes, like everyone else, except Chiman and Tz," Ajkun said. "But your father said something strange to me that night; he made me promise to protect you because someone might try to harm you."

"Who was he referring to?"

"I don't know, and that's why I've never told you this before." Na'om started to speak, but Ajkun held up her hand to stop her. "There's more, I'm afraid. Chachal is your father's half-sister. Chiman went to Mayapán to barter various items, and he fell in love with Chachal. He brought her back here, even though rumors say she was in love with someone else at the time. Yakal came with them, although I'm not sure why," Ajkun said.

"So, where is my father now?" Na'om asked.

"Back in Mayapán, living among the Cocom, I think."

"And because he left and didn't take Chachal with him, is that why she's always so mad at me?" Na'om stirred her stew and took a small bite.

"Chachal's been a bitter woman ever since the day I met her," Ajkun said. "Chiman should have left her in Mayapán and found someone here to marry."

"Like you, Ati't?" Na'om asked with a grin.

"Hush, child, whatever gave you that idea?" Ajkun said.

"I see the way you two are together, you like each other a lot. You always smile more when he comes around, and Chachal must dislike you for some reason other than just me," Na'om said.

"Yes, well, those days are gone, what might or might not have happened in the past is behind us now," Ajkun said as she pointed to Na'om's bowl. "Eat now, while I go get you something." The older woman stood up slowly and walked stiffly into the hut. When she returned, she had a finely woven covered basket in her hands. She pulled off the tight lid and lifted out a turquoise and black jade necklace. "This necklace belonged to your mother,"

Ajkun said. "I took it from her the night she died and have saved it for you to wear." She stepped behind Na'om and clasped the jewelry around her neck. "Your father carved the jade jaguar head as a wedding present for your mother. She wore it on her wedding day and every day until she died."

"It's beautiful," Na'om whispered as she felt tears forming in her eyes. She wiped them away before reaching up to finger the smooth stones. She bent her head enough to catch sight of the jaguar; its teeth were bared in a slight snarl. "It looks like Ek' Balam."

"Yes, it does," Ajkun replied. "Your mother also had a way with animals, although she never tried to tame a jaguar!"

Na'om rubbed her fingers along the side of her face, tracing her scars, before touching the necklace again. She held it up to the light, and the black jade glistened. Na'om could see tiny specks of green jade had been inset into the face for the eyes. "It really does look like him, even down to the slightly tattered right ear." She let the necklace drop back to her chest and felt a slight buzzing as it touched her skin, like the energy she felt in the air right before a thunderstorm. Na'om looked at her grandmother's wrinkled face and knew this day was difficult for her. Although excited about the move, she realized it would be very lonely for Ati't once she was gone. "I'll visit every day, I promise," Na'om said as she stood up and wrapped her grandmother in a big hug. "I should be going, though, as I have lots to do before it gets dark." She whistled to Ek' Balam who padded over to her. She gave him a dried fish and watched as he swallowed it whole.

Ajkun nodded, and the two women and the cat walked slowly down to the river. Na'om stepped into her small canoe and waved to Ajkun as she steered into the current. Ek' Balam slipped into the water and gracefully swam to the opposite shore. Na'om needed to pay close attention to the water, but she was pleased to see her grandmother still standing near the water's edge when she arrived on the opposite bank. Na'om waved and blew Ati't a big kiss and watched as the older woman slowly made her way back toward the village. Na'om stared at the empty riverbank for several more minutes before turning away.

With the steady passage of feet in the past few months, a trail had been made from the riverbank to Na'om's hut, and she skipped down it to her house. Everything was as she had left it. Ek' Balam claimed a sunny spot underneath a nearby mahogany tree. In the light, his dark fur looked like melted chocolate. Upon entering the clearing, Na'om spun around in a circle, her arms stretched out wide at her sides. Her bare feet kicked up puffs of dust as she turned and turned and turned. Finally, Na'om collapsed on the ground, too dizzy to stand. She sat quietly to catch her breath and felt a strange tingle of energy throughout her body. She took several deep breaths and closed her eyes. Free-flowing swirls of colors passed behind her closed eyes, and Na'om tried to concentrate on the patterns, hoping for an image to appear. But nothing manifested. She heard a buzzing in her inner ear and focused on the sound. It grew louder and louder as she thought about her father and his fears. *Why would he need to leave in order to protect me?* she wondered. It made no sense. The buzzing intensified, and she opened her eyes again, half expecting to see a swarm of bees flying nearby.

She looked around at the work ahead of her, and thought, *No more childish behavior now, I must act like the grown-up woman that I am.* She stood and brushed the dirt from her skirt and set about getting her kitchen area in order. She rearranged the three cooking stones so they held her smallest pot and the largest one with ease, and once the few gourds and baskets were placed just so, Na'om went into the hut and began moving things around.

She dragged the mattress to one corner and smoothed the blankets on top. The spot looked so inviting that she flopped down on the bed. She stared up at the thatched roof overhead and at the white walls around her. *I'll need to make some shelves and a bed frame,* she thought as her eyes slowly drifted shut.

Within minutes, she dreamt she was propelling a canoe down a wide river. Tall mahogany trees overhung the water, and she paddled past a large rock covered with about fifty foot-long baby crocodiles. They squirmed and wiggled over and under each other, vying for space in the direct sun. A strange boy crouched in the bow of the boat, his back covered with scratches. Her arms ached, and her hands were sore from the wooden paddle; her dress was dirty and torn in places. The sapphire-blue water stretched ahead of them, and she had no idea where she was going, just that she had to keep paddling and paddling and paddling . . .

Na'om woke with a start and sat up on the bed, confused as to her surroundings. The hut was dark, only the small amount of light coming from the doorway delineated the inside from the outside. She looked around for Ajkun and then remembered. She was alone. Suddenly, the gravity of the situation hit Na'om, and tears slipped from her eyes. She hugged herself tightly and pretended she was wrapped in Ajkun's arms, that her grandmother was holding her and telling her everything would be all right, that she'd just had a bad dream. Na'om thought of the vastness of the water in her dream and knew it must be the big river that Chiman and the other traders traveled to reach the large cities in the north. She shivered and forced herself up from the bed.

She hurried outside to the kitchen area. She found her fire rocks, struck them together several times, and caught a spark in a dry pile of coconut husk. She blew on the embers and laid the smoking bundle in the fire pit. Quickly, she added tiny sticks and twigs and soon had a blaze going. The light and heat chased away the jungle darkness, and Na'om put a container of water on to boil for chamomile tea. Ek' Balam padded over from his spot under the mahogany tree and stretched out against the side of the hut, his belly exposed to the heat from the fire. Na'om leaned against him, and he began to purr. She thought about the dream some more, but already tiny details were beginning to slip away. *I'll need to ask Chiman for my own ledger and record them myself,* she thought. *If I wait to tell them to Ati't, I might not remember everything. And since I still can't write very well, I'll just draw pictures to remind me of what happened.* With that problem resolved, Na'om relaxed a bit. She lifted the jaguar necklace her grandmother had given her off her chest and felt a prickle in her fingertips as she caressed the smooth stone carving. *I wish I'd gotten a chance to know you, Chuch,* she thought as she rubbed the stone jaguar's tiny nose.

And I you, replied a voice in her head.

"Who's there?" Na'om cried out as she looked around for the woman who had spoken.

Your mother, Tu'janel. You wear my necklace, and through it, I can speak to you from the Underworld. Don't be afraid; I mean you no harm. I'll help you when I can.

The voice went silent, and Na'om touched the necklace. The feel of the cool jade in her hand was soothing, and she didn't feel quite so alone.

Na'om listened to the forest around her. She could hear the river slipping over the rocks, the flutter of a bat's wings as it flew by chasing bugs, the grunting of some animal farther downstream, which caused Ek' Balam to perk up his ears before laying his head back down. "It's still just you and me, old friend," Na'om whispered to the cat. "But then, it's always just been you and me here in this world." She sipped her tea and began making a list of projects to work on the next day. First on the list was to ask the shaman for a pounded bark leaf ledger and some ink. She put more wood on the fire and watched as the sticks sizzled and sparked.

Just then, she felt Ek' Balam stiffen underneath her, and he quickly got up. "What is it, boy?" Na'om said as she struggled to her feet. She couldn't see anything in the darkness; the flames still danced behind her eyes. Ek' Balam began to growl, and she felt the hair bristle on the back of his neck. Na'om bent down to her pile of wood and grabbed the largest piece. She moved up against the hut; the solid wall felt good behind her back. "Who's out there?" she cried.

The hoarse whistle of a pauraque bird filled the air as the brown- and chestnut-colored nightjar flew past. "It's just a bird, silly," Na'om said, as much to herself as to her cat. She chucked more wood on the fire, and the flames leaped higher, driving the darkness backwards into the ring of mahogany and ceiba trees. Picking up a sharp-pointed stick, Na'om dragged it in a wide semicircle from one edge of the hut, out and around the kitchen area, to the path to the river, and back to the other side of the hut, marking a solid line in the dry dirt. "Whoever crosses this line, without my permission," Na'om said to the black night, "shall suffer greatly." She tossed the branch back in the woodpile, and the nightjar flew by again, startling Na'om. Her senses were heightened, and she knew it would be many hours before she'd be able to relax. *I should have skipped that nap,* she thought. "I wish I knew an actual protection charm," she said to Ek' Balam. "Then we'd really be safe out here."

The jaguar just yawned and closed his eyes. "Hey, no going to sleep on me," Na'om cried. She tugged on the cat's front paws, forcing him to stand. "Come on, now, we haven't had time to practice our dancing lately," she said as she carefully lifted the big cat's front feet and placed them on her shoulders. The weight of his body pressed down on her, but Na'om began to hum and shuffled several steps backwards while Ek' Balam awkwardly followed her on his hind feet. "I know, it's no fun without Tz's music," she said as she let the cat go. Ek' Balam took up his spot by the fire again.

Na'om twirled around by herself several times and felt the same prick of energy she'd sensed earlier course through her body from her bare feet to the ends of her hair. She closed her eyes and spun slowly, her arms held out from her sides. With each revolution, pins and needles moved up and down her spine.

The buzzing returned in her ears, and she shivered. Opening her eyes just a crack, she caught a glimpse of her outstretched hand. Vibrant purple light shimmered off her fingers. She stopped in her tracks and turned her head to look directly at her hand. It appeared normal. Then she moved her head and looked at her limb with her peripheral vision. It still glowed with color. She grinned, as this hadn't happened to her in a long time. Fascinated, Na'om tried peering at other parts of her body, and they also shone the color of jacaranda blossoms. Still absorbed in looking at the weird purple light surrounding her body, Na'om took little notice of Ek' Balam as he walked toward the path to the river, his tail swishing from side to side.

The pauraque bird whistled again, and the jaguar growled and crouched low to the ground, ready to pounce. The noise brought Na'om back to herself, and the strange light vanished. "If someone's out there, you'd better say something before Ek' Balam makes you his supper," Na'om shouted as she grabbed a piece of firewood again. The bird screeched and flew off through the trees.

Unexpectedly, she heard scuffling in the dry underbrush, sticks breaking, and then the quick patter of many feet running toward the river. "Go boy," Na'om said as she patted the cat on the back. The jaguar darted down the path. She ran just behind him and caught a glimpse of three boys as they jumped into a canoe and pushed off from shore. One youth, Kon, dipped his hand into the water and pulled up a fistful of rocks, which he began to throw at Ek' Balam.

Na'om waved her stick in the air. "Stay away from here," she cried. "Or next time, I won't warn you about my cat."

Laughter drifted back to her on the night air. "You watch out, Na'om," Kon cried. "We know that cat isn't always by your side; we'll be back."

CHIMAN

The shaman was surprised to see Na'om sitting outside his gate the next morning when he started toward the village center. "What brings you here so early, child?" he asked as he helped the girl to her feet.

"A thousand pardons for disturbing you, my lord, but I thought you should know two things that occurred yesterday," Na'om said as she looked at the ground. "I moved into my new hut and . . ."

"Ah yes, moving day," Chiman said, "That explains why Ajkun was so sad last night. So, what's the other thing?"

"No, my lord, the move wasn't what I wanted to tell you about," Na'om replied as she shuffled her feet. "I had a dream yesterday that I need to write down and also . . ." Na'om paused and looked up into the older man's face. "Kon and two of the other boys from the village were spying on me last night. I chased them away, but they threatened to come back."

"Hmm, I see," Chiman said. "Walk with me to your grand-mother's and tell me of this dream."

"What of the boys?"

"I'll speak to the elders; from now on, that side of the river shall be off-limits except to the hunters. No one is allowed near your house without my permission. The people of Pa nimá insisted on kicking you out of the village, and I've listened to their demands. Now they must obey a few rules as well." Chiman walked in silence while Na'om respectfully stayed a pace behind and told her story.

"Have you been practicing your glyphs?" Chiman asked the girl.

"Not really, Ati't has always written everything down. But I thought if I drew the images . . ."

"Hmm, yes, that might work. As long as you put in plenty of details so I can see what these dreams might mean. I'd send Tz' to practice with you, but he's getting ready for his first trading voyage and is too busy studying the maps and star charts."

"When does he leave?"

"Within the month, before the heavy rains swell the rivers and make the passage difficult."

"Will he be gone long?"

"Oh, I expect him back in time for the new plantings. I plan to let him lead the ceremony in the new corn fields, so they must be back by then." Chiman stopped walking and looked at the girl. "This dream of yours, you're sure you were in the canoe with some strange boy, not Tz' and some of the others?"

"No, my lord, this one wasn't about Tz'."

"So, other dreams have been?" The shaman watched as Na'om blushed. "It's all right, child, I've known for a long time that you have feelings for my son. Unfortunately his mother knows it, too, and is already planning his wedding when he returns from this trip." He looked at Na'om, but she didn't speak. "Come, I must talk to Ajkun," Chiman said. His stomach growled, and he laughed. "Besides, she makes the best hot chocolate in the village, and I could obviously use some."

As soon as they neared Ajkun's hut, Na'om skipped ahead and entered the courtyard. "Ati't, I'm here," she called.

Ajkun pushed aside the deer hide over the doorway and stepped out into the early morning light. "Na'om," she said as she wrapped her granddaughter in a hug. "Are you all right, did you sleep well?"

Na'om tugged on her grandmother's sleeve. "I'm fine, Ati't,

but we . . . you have a visitor," she said as she pointed to the gate where Chiman still stood.

"Chiman, come in, come in," Ajkun said as she beckoned with her hand.

"He wants hot cacao," Na'om whispered to Ajkun as she hurried to start the fire.

"Hot chocolate, eh?" Ajkun said as she eyed Chiman. "Something tells me your visit this morning is not about breakfast."

"No, dear woman, it's not, although I wouldn't mind a cup, if you have some," Chiman said as he looked around the yard. "We've promised the Cocom a variety of goods in return for their protection from the Xiu. The elders thought a supply of medicines might be a good item to barter, so I've come to you to see what you might be able to provide."

"When do the traders leave?"

"Before the rains."

"So, we have less than a month to prepare," Ajkun said as she handed Chiman a coconut husk full of frothed hot cacao. "With Na'om working with me, we can pull together some salves and tinctures. Are you going?"

"No, I'm getting too old to travel that far; Tz' is going, though. He needs to see other parts of the world and get to know other people." Chiman sipped from his cup.

Ajkun took a drink of her tea. "And find a bride other than Mok'onel, perhaps?"

"Ah, so you've heard of that plan," Chiman said. "Why doesn't that surprise me?"

"That's all the women talk about when they come here for medicines, how Chachal has picked Tz's bride, how he'll marry Mok'onel before the end of the year; frankly, I think it's a bunch of nonsense. Tz' needs to pick his own mate, like any other man."

"Or woman," Chiman said. He looked at Ajkun's lined face and could still see the young woman he had loved for so long.

"Don't poke at old scars, not in front of the girl," Ajkun said.

She leaned closer to Chiman and whispered, "You know why I chose Tajinel for my husband."

Chiman nodded and kept silent. He drank the last drops of cocoa and set the cup on the ground. "Thanks for the cocoa; send Na'om to the house when you have sufficient supplies, and I'll have Tz' and the others come pick them up." Chiman stood up and walked to the gate. "Oh, Na'om," he said as he turned around. "Come by the house later, and I'll give you that blank journal and ink."

"Yes, my lord," Na'om replied.

Chiman walked into the village center, nodding to several of the villagers as he passed their huts. There was so much to do to prepare Tz' and the other youths for this trip as well as for the upcoming planting season. He wasn't sure where to start. Thinking about how his own life had evolved, he knew he would wait until after the trip to tell Tz' of the sacrifices he'd need to make for the planting ceremony. Too much information this soon would only make the boy nervous and might jeopardize the entire trip. They needed to establish good connections with the Cocom if the village was to avoid a raid by the Xiu.

NA'OM

As the days turned into weeks, Na'om slipped into a routine. At first light, she hurriedly ate breakfast, gathered firewood, and filled her water gourds before canoeing across the river to the village where she went directly to Ajkun's hut. There the two women worked side by side for several hours pounding roots and grinding leaves to make a variety of salves, herbal teas, and tinctures for the traders. The shelves in Ajkun's storeroom slowly filled with pottery vials, bowls, and coconut shells sealed with beeswax.

After lunch, while Ajkun napped in the hammock in the courtyard, Na'om did her grandmother's chores before venturing out into the jungle to look for more berries, roots, and bark. Ek' Balam stayed by her side and kept her company while she filled her basket with palo de arco bark or bundles of orchid tree root. She was kept so busy that it was always evening by the time she paddled back to her side of the river. But regardless of how late it was, she still managed to find a few minutes to pull out her ledger and draw in a few more pictures of her dreams. Slowly the pages were filling with black and white images, and she promised herself that as soon as the men left on the trip, she'd spend more time on each picture and fill the lines with color.

Many nights her dreams were filled with images of Tz', of him playing his flute while she tried to dance with Ek' Balam or of Tz' canoeing on the river with a group of other men. One night she dreamt he tried to kiss her, and she woke when she felt the softness of his lips against hers.

That dream left a strange ache in her heart, and she spent the time doing her chores wondering what she would do if he did try to kiss her; the thought made her smile and nervous at the same time. She did miss seeing her one true friend, but knew he was busy with his own preparations for the trip. She tried not to think of him getting married on his return. *Perhaps he'll find someone else to love,* Na'om thought, *and he won't be stuck with Mok'onel. Not that she isn't a pretty girl, because she is,* Na'om considered as she bent to fill her water gourds. She paused and peered at her own reflection in the still pool of water. She reached up with one hand and brushed her long, black hair away from her face. Her scars stood out on her dark skin like lines of chalk on pottery. She stared into her brown eyes and noticed tiny spots of gold in her right one. *Tz' will marry anyone who is prettier than I am, someone he and the other villagers can respect, not an outcast.* Na'om dropped the gourd in her hand into the water, shattering the images and let the river carry her thoughts away like the many, many air bubbles that rose to the surface as the jug filled. *This day will go by as fast as all the others,* she thought as she hung the water gourds by her fire pit. *Tomorrow, the men leave on their big trip. I hope I can at least say good-bye to Tz' before he goes.*

Na'om was at Ajkun's hut later that morning when Tz', Kon, and another youth arrived with large open baskets for all their supplies. Na'om avoided looking at Kon when he passed her as she held open the flap covering the doorway. But she felt his arm brush her small breasts as he sidled by. Ajkun pointed the way to the many shelves filled with the jars and bowls that were to be taken, each labeled with a tiny tag to identify its contents and medicinal uses.

"Itzamná, you've been busy," Tz' exclaimed upon seeing the supplies. "I'm not sure we can take all of this and still have room for all the other things Tat axel wishes to trade."

"Well, take as much as you can," Ajkun replied. "What's left can be used by the villagers over time."

Na'om watched while their work was carefully stacked into each basket between layers of cotton cloth to protect and pad the fragile pots. She grinned when Tz' strained to pick up the load. "Here, let me help," she said as she lifted one handle of the basket off the ground.

Tz' hefted the other side, and the two friends carried the full basket down to the river, where they placed it in the middle of one of the three twenty-foot-long trading canoes. The elders of the village and Chiman were also at the water, supervising the packing of stacks of tanned furs, bundles of bird feathers, and yards of cotton cloth being sent to trade for salt, pieces of obsidian needed for spearheads and knives, and protection from the warring Xiu. Kon and the other boy arrived from Ajkun's carrying a hamper between them and set it on the ground.

"Load that one in a different canoe," Tz' ordered. "We'll go get the last container." He nodded at Na'om who followed him back toward Ajkun's hut. As soon as Tz' was around the first bend in the path, away from the eyes of all those loading the canoes, he stopped. "I'm sorry there hasn't been much time to visit these past couple of weeks," he said.

"You've been busy, so have I," Na'om shrugged.

"How do you like your new house?"

"It's all right, different," Na'om said. "I miss Ajkun's company, someone to talk to, as Ek' Balam doesn't really carry his side of a conversation." She gave a half-hearted laugh.

"Look, there's not much time," Tz' said, ignoring Na'om's attempt at a joke. "I just wanted to talk to you about Mok'onel," Tz' said. He looked back toward the river as he heard voices approaching.

"Marry her or not, what difference does it make to me?" Na'om said as she started to walk again.

"Well, that's just it," Tz' said, but he was interrupted when his friends appeared.

"Tz', come on," Kon said. "Your dad is waiting for the last hamper, so they can fill the canoe and cover it all with a canvas tarp." He looked at Naom and grinned.

Tz' looked at Naom. "I have to go; will you come to the launch tomorrow?"

"I'll be there," Naom said as she watched Tz' run to catch up with his friends. She walked the rest of the way to Ajkun's by herself and stood aside at the gate while Tz' and Kon hurried through with the last basket.

She plopped down on her mat by the fire and poked at the embers with a stick. Ajkun hobbled over to join her. "What's wrong with your knee, Ati't?" Naom said as Ajkun sat down on her stool.

"My arthritis again; we've been so busy getting things ready, I've forgotten to drink my nettle tea every day." She rubbed her leg with the palm of her hand. "I'll be fine in a day or two, now that we can rest a bit."

"I'll be glad to have a break, too," Naom said. "I still haven't finished unpacking things in the house. It's been nice to work with you, though."

"You deserve some time to yourself," Ajkun said. "And I think some of our neighbors are even beginning to see that you're not such a threat after all."

"I wouldn't go that far." Naom laughed. "They still jump aside when Ek' Balam and I appear on the path from the river." She dropped the stick and stood up. "I should go, Ati't, it's getting late, and I need to make my supper." She bent down and kissed the older woman on the cheek. "I'll be back in the morning to see the men off, will you come say good-bye?"

"Yes, I suppose I should," Ajkun said. She rubbed her knee again.

At the river, the three canoes laden with goods sat on the shore, the piles covered tightly with tarps held down by thick hemp ropes. Naom walked the shoreline to where she had hidden her own canoe in the bushes. She untied the bow rope and gently started to ease the boat into the water when she heard voices. She peeked between the leaves of a small trumpet tree and saw Mok'onel and Chachal approaching. She crouched low in the stream and listened.

"He'll be gone for a month, six weeks at the most," Chachal said as she sat on the riverbank and dangled her feet in the water. "While he's gone, you'll work for me at the house. If Chiman sees you on a daily basis, he'll begin to appreciate what a fine, young, capable woman you are and see what a good match you'll make for Tz'."

"What about Na'om?" Mok'onel said. "Begging your pardon, my lady, but doesn't your husband see Na'om and her grand-mother on a regular basis?"

"Leave the outcast to me; I'll invent some ailment that will require a special tea, one that will send the girl far away in search of roots and bark. With any luck, she'll get lost in the jungle on the other side of the river and never come back. Then, when Tz' returns, all you'll have to do is be there, and he'll forget all about his old playmate and her stupid cat. But enough of her. Get undressed and scrub your skin with this soft sand as I've taught you. You want to be as smooth as glazed pottery tonight when you visit my son in his bedchamber."

Na'om's legs began to ache from crouching for so long, but she didn't dare move. The two women would see her the moment she stepped from the bushes and into the canoe. They'd know she had heard every word. So, she waited and waited. She watched as Mok'onel removed her huipil and skirt and slipped into the water. Chachal handed her a small bag filled with sand, and Mok'onel rubbed it up and down her legs, arms, and around her breasts. *She really is quite beautiful,* Na'om thought as she studied the girl. *She's a little heavy in the middle, but has wide hips, which will make childbirth so much easier; I'm sure Tz' will want many children, considering he's an only child.*

Finally, as the light began to fade, and the air grew cooler in the shadows, Chachal told Mok'onel to stop. "Come with me to the house," she said as she handed the girl a towel. "I have a new outfit for you to wear and will braid that long hair of yours after I smooth it with vanilla oil." She scooped up the girl's clothes into a bundle and tucked them under her arm. "We must hurry, before my husband and Tz' return from the temple; we can't have them see you like this, at least, not yet."

Na'om waited an extra few minutes before standing up. The blood rushed from her head, and she bent over to let the dizziness pass. Quickly she stepped into the canoe and pushed off. She looked at her wet feet in the dim light; they were wrinkled and cold, like those of an old woman.

Na'om built a fire and heated up some leftover turkey stew. As she ate, she felt a buzzing in her ears. She tried shaking her head on one side while hopping up and down, in case there was water in her ear, but the sound remained. She picked at her soup and quickly gave Ek' Balam her bowl to lick. He looked up with the last drops of soup clinging to his whiskers. "That's it, boy, there's no more food," Na'om said as she leaned against the hut. She tried to block out the weird ringing by placing her hands over her ears, but that just seemed to intensify the noise. She closed her eyes, and instantly black shapes swooped toward her in her mind's eye. She looked up when she felt Ek' Balam stretch out beside her. She rubbed his favorite spot behind his ear. "So, you know Tz' is going away tomorrow, which means you'll need to be here with me, right?" she said to the cat. Ek' Balam lifted his head and looked at her, then shook himself, and stood up. His tail swished from side to side as he paced toward the dark bushes beyond the clearing. "Where are you going?" Na'om cried. The cat gave her one more glance and disappeared into the underbrush. "Great; now what?" Na'om said. The constant drone in her ears was tiring, and although it was still very early in the evening, Na'om decided to go to bed.

She stacked the dirty pot and bowl together to wash in the morning. Then she rubbed her gums and teeth with a tiny piece of rough cloth, rinsed her mouth with water, and went into the hut. She lay on the bed and watched the light of the fire as it threw shadows on the walls. She thought about what she'd seen and heard at the river that day, of the conversation that Tz' hadn't been able to finish. *I wonder what he wanted to say about Mok'onel,* she thought as she gazed at the flickering black shapes dancing on the stucco beside her head. *It looks like a couple, moving to some unseen music,* she reflected as the forms shifted and changed. Just then, the light changed as a darker shape appeared on the wall. "Ek' Balam?" Na'om called out. There was no answer. She watched the shadow grow larger. "Who is it?" she said as she jumped up from the bed. She looked around the small room for a weapon. *If it's that stupid boy Kon again, I swear by Itzamná, I'll hit him with something if he comes near me.* She picked up a bowl full of peccary fat and hid by the doorway. The shadow on the wall grew larger and larger, and Na'om was just about to jump out when she heard a voice.

"Na'om, are you home?" Tz' said as he poked his head through the doorway. He saw Na'om swinging the pot in her hand as she stepped through the open space to the outside.

"Easy there, girl, you could have hit me with that!" Tz' said as he grabbed Na'om's arm and pushed it to one side.

"Tz'! What are you doing here?" Na'om asked as she looked at her friend.

"I came to see you, of course. Now, are you going to tell me why you tried to hit me with that pot?"

"I thought you might be Kon," Na'om said as she moved toward the fire. "He was here a few weeks ago with a couple of his friends." She poked at the sticks and blew on the flames before adding more wood. The flames leaped up, throwing back the darkness.

"Oh, so you were expecting him?"

"No, silly, that's why I had the pot in my hand; never mind, it doesn't matter now." Na'om gestured to the pounded dirt floor by the wall. "Care for a seat?"

Tz' looked around the area. "Don't you have anything comfortable to sit on? My back is sore from carrying all those heavy baskets you helped fill."

"Ha, ha, no, the only thing I have is my mattress. We could move that out here, but you have to promise to help me move it back before you leave. It's like dragging a dead deer around if I try to move it myself." The two entered the hut and each grabbed an edge of the cushion. They lugged it outside and placed it against the wall. Tz' sat down on it and leaned back.

"Ah, that feels so much better," he said as he tilted his head back and looked up at the stars overhead. "So, how do you like living over here by yourself?" He looked around the clearing. "Where's Ek' Balam? I thought I'd get a chance to say good-bye."

"He took off earlier. The minute I said you were leaving tomorrow, he up and left," Na'om said.

"Smart cat, he's probably off to get some food, maybe a bit of loving before he takes over guard duty. Don't worry; he and I made that pact years ago, and neither of us has let you down; you'll always be protected by one of us." Tz' patted the mattress. "Come, sit with me."

Na'om plunked down on the pad next to her friend. She looked at him sideways, at his bare, muscular chest, his strong arms. She could smell vanilla oil on him and wondered if that was from Mok'onel. "How come you're not at home? I heard Mok'onel was supposed to pay you a visit tonight," Na'om said as she picked at the hem of her skirt.

"Where did you hear that?" Tz' demanded. He twisted to stare at Na'om. "Chuch told me no one would know about Mok'onel." He reached out his hand and turned Na'om's face to his. "You overheard them talking at the river tonight, didn't you?"

Na'om looked at the mattress and nodded her head.

"So, you must know she's ready to have a child as well. Chuch expected me . . . us . . . to, well . . ." Tz' stopped and shook his head. "I couldn't do it, not with her. I think Chuch figured Mok'onel might get pregnant, and then I'd have to marry her when I return from this trip." He picked up a stick and began breaking it into tiny pieces. "She's always meddling in my business as if I'm some little boy," Tz' said as he threw the handful of twigs away. "But I'm not, I'm almost eighteen and a man, and I'm able to pick my own wife."

"Maybe you'll find someone on this trip, like your father did with Chachal," Na'om said as she plucked a string from her blanket.

"Maybe," Tz' said as he touched Na'om face again. "Or maybe I've already found someone." He tried to push Na'om down on the mattress. "Don't be afraid," he said as he tried to push her again, ever so gently, down on the bed.

"What are you doing?" Na'om demanded. She shoved against Tz's bare chest and felt the oil on it slip under her fingertips. She scrabbled to the far side of the mattress and wiped her hand on the blanket. Her white scars stood out in stark relief against her reddened face.

Tz' reached out and tried to run his fingertip down the length of them.

Na'om grabbed his hand, pushed it away, and then jumped to her feet. "I think you should leave," she said.

"Why? What'd I do?" Tz' said as he also stood up. "I thought we were friends, no, more than friends." He kicked a small stone and sent it flying into the darkness of the jungle. "You hide your scars and your pain from everyone, including me, and yet it was the day when you got those scars that I knew I wanted to marry you."

Na'om looked at Tz' and searched his brown eyes to verify the truth. "How could you know that? You were only twelve. Besides, you knew I'd be cast from the village, ineligible to marry anyone, especially you." She threw a piece of wood on the fire and watched the flames. "Is that why you came tonight, you figured no one else would want me, so you'd take me for yourself before you leave, only to come back and marry Mok'onel when you return?"

"No, of course not," Tz' said. "I love you, I always have, and when I return, I intend to ask Tat axel for the right to marry you."

"So, what were you trying to do just now? Mark your territory before you go?" Na'om stood back from the heat, crossed her arms, and said again, "I think you should leave."

"Na'om, stop, why are you mad? I came here because I wanted to be with you, don't you understand that? I could have taken Mok'onel tonight and made her and my mother very happy," Tz' said as he paced in front of the fire. "I wanted to be with you, to spend my last night with you. Ahh, this is so stupid, I'm so stupid. You probably wanted Kon to show up, just like he was bragging about to the others tonight."

"Wait, what did he say?" Na'om demanded.

"That he took you the other night and that others have been here as well."

"Leave me, now!"

"So, it's true?" Tz' asked. "I thought I would be the first . . ."

"Go! Now!" Na'om screamed. "I never want to see you or your stupid friends again."

Without another word, Tz' slipped on his sandals and hurried off into the darkness.

Na'om kicked the mattress with her bare foot and winced as her toes met the compacted padding. She plunked down on the bed and rubbed her foot, still mad at Tz' for making assumptions that weren't true, and more importantly, mad at herself for not giving in to what her heart and body had really wanted from him. *That Kon, he's the real troublemaker,* Na'om thought. *I hope he dies!*

As Na'om sat and stared into the embers of the fire, Ek' Balam appeared out of the darkness and sprawled on the ground near her. She reached over, rubbed him behind his ear, and felt the rumble of his purring under her fingertips. "At least you'll always be here for me," she said to her cat. "I can't say the same about Tz."

AJKUN

At daybreak, Ajkun made her way down to the river along with the rest of the villagers. She nodded to Banal Bo'j, Setesik, and Potz' and glanced up and down the line of people for Na'om, but there was no sign of her granddaughter. Once at the water's edge, she scanned the far side of the river for Na'om, but there was no still no sign of her. Ajkun watched as Chachal gave Tz' a hug before he stepped into his loaded canoe. The other youths pushed their boats into the current, and everyone waved to the group as they rounded the bend in the river. Despite the cries of good luck, safe passage, Na'om still didn't appear. *I'm surprised she didn't come say good-bye to Tz',* Ajkun thought as she slowly walked back to her hut. *If she doesn't come across the river later, I'll have to go see what's happened to her.*

Several hours went by as Ajkun puttered at her daily chores of gathering firewood, sweeping the courtyard and her hut, and grinding corn for her morning gruel. Every now and then when she heard footsteps approaching, Ajkun lifted her head, hoping to see Na'om, but it was always one of her neighbors in need of a salve or an herbal tea for a stomachache.

Just as she was going to walk back down to the river and use a canoe to cross, Na'om swung open the little gate and stepped into the courtyard. Ajkun looked up from grinding roots in her heavy pottery bowl. *She looks like she's been crying,* Ajkun reflected. *Did she oversleep? Is that why she missed the farewells?* "Come sit, child, you look tired," Ajkun said as she patted the ground beside her. "Is everything all right?"

"I guess so," Na'om said as she plopped onto the mat beside her grandmother. "I had this strange sound in my ears that didn't go away all night. I feel better now, though."

"I missed you at the river this morning," Ajkun said. "Were you standing among the reeds on the other side where I couldn't see you?"

"No, I didn't see them off . . . Did everything go well?"

"Well, yes, there's not much to tell, really, Chachal made a big show of hugging Tz', which only embarrassed the poor boy, the men got into their canoes, they started paddling down river, we all waved, and then they were gone. But never fear; they'll be back before we know it, and the seasons will start again. The new cornfields will be ready by the time Tz' returns, and he'll conduct the planting ceremony this year, or at least that's what Chiman says." Ajkun picked up her pestle and began to grind the roots again. "We'll see what Chachal has to say about that."

The two women sat in silence for a bit. Na'om picked at the hem of her skirt and watched her grandmother pour the powdered roots into a soft deerskin bag.

"So, are you going to tell me what's bothering you, or do I have to start guessing?" Ajkun said. "Speak child, was it another bad dream?"

"I wish it had been a dream, truly I do," Na'om said as she shifted her weight on the mat. She tucked her legs under her skirt and leaned against Ajkun's side. "I'm not sure where to start." Na'om plucked a piece of straw from the ground and began bending it back and forth, breaking it into small pieces, which she let drop to the ground. "I was at the river last night and heard Chachal and Mok'onel speaking, then Tz' showed up at my house, smelling like vanilla oil and then . . . oh Ati't, what have I done?" Na'om buried her face in her hands.

Ajkun patted the girl's shoulder and felt her silent sobs through the press of Na'om's body against her thigh. "Shh, whatever has happened, we can fix it, but you must tell me the whole story . . . Did Tz' hurt you?" she demanded.

"No, nothing like that. You see, Mok'onel was supposed to go to Tz' last night and . . ."

"Chachal, that crafty woman," Ajkun said as she interrupted Na'om. "Sorry, go on."

"And when she appeared, Tz' pushed her away. But then he came to me, and he tried to kiss me . . ." Na'om paused.

"Did you make love?" Ajkun said as she sat up straight on her stool.

"No, we didn't, because I pushed him away. Oh Ati't, I was so confused, he was acting so different, and I didn't know what he wanted and then we argued . . ."

"Argued? Now you truly do sound like a couple." Ajkun laughed softly. "I'm sure whatever happened between you will be long forgotten and forgiven by the time Tz' returns."

Na'om threw the pieces of straw on the ground. "I told him I never wanted to see him again," she said and wiped at her eyes. "I doubt he'll forget that." She rubbed her sleeve across her face. "I should have made love with him; then maybe I'd be carrying his child right now, and he wouldn't have to marry Mok'onel when he returns."

Ajkun readjusted her position on her stool and rubbed Na'om's shoulder with her hand. "He won't marry Mok'onel, trust me on that." Ajkun paused and took a deep breath. "You did the right thing by not letting him take you last night. Let me tell you a little story, one that's never been told before. Once you've heard it, you must promise not to repeat it. Perhaps then, you'll see why a pregnancy now would just complicate matters." She sat back down on her stool and prodded at the fire with a long stick. "Many, many years ago, when I was a young girl like yourself, I, too, was in love, in love with someone who by all rights could not marry me . . ." Ajkun's voice drifted off.

"It was Chiman, wasn't it?" Na'om asked.

"Yes, Chiman. We had eyes only for each other, but Chiman's mother wanted him to marry anyone but the village midwife; the lines of bad blood between our families go back many generations, I'm afraid. Chiman was such an impetuous boy, he always wanted what he couldn't have, and even though he had just become a man, we met in the jungle night after night to make love with one another. However, I was to marry Tajinel, one of the farmers; his first wife had died, and he needed someone to take care of his house, cook him meals, bear his children. But I didn't want him. I thought he was too old, and he had horrible warts on his hands. The thought of those hands touching me made me shiver. I only wanted Chiman. Then my moon cycles stopped, and I knew Chiman and I were in trouble. I desperately wanted the child, though, so I married Tajinel as quickly as I could and bore him a daughter, your mother, Tu'janel. But I knew the girl was Chiman's child, not Tajinel's.

"But then that means . . ." Naom paused and looked at her grandmother's lined face. "Chiman is my grandfather?" Naom asked. "Is that why he's always been so protective of me?"

"Maybe. I never told him Tu'janel was our child, but I suspect he knows. He always wondered why I turned away from him so abruptly, but he was too young to marry me, and we drifted apart. A few years later, when Tajinel died from a hunting accident, Chiman wanted to marry me then, but I said no. I guess I thought my feelings for him were over. The years passed. Chiman kept asking me to reconsider his proposal, and I stupidly kept saying no. Finally, he went away on a trading voyage and came back four months later with Chachal."

"Would you have wed him if he'd been older?"

"Probably, although we would have had to fight his mother over the idea. Anyway, my point is," Ajkun said as she poured hot water into a coconut bowl and handed the tea to Naom, "if we had been patient and trusted the timing of things, we might be together now, but we were young and hasty, we didn't ask the gods for guidance, and moved of our own accord. Things happen for a reason, but everything has its proper time and place," Ajkun said as she motioned for Naom to drink the herbal mixture.

"So, where does that leave me with Tz'? If Chiman is my grandfather, the blood lines are too close for us to ever be together," she said as she swallowed some of the tea. She grimaced at the bitterness.

"Ah, but what if they're not," Ajkun said as she looked around the courtyard. "Being the only midwife, I attended to Chachal during her birthing of Tz'." Ajkun looked around again and leaned closer to Naom. "She went into labor several weeks earlier than what Chiman and I had calculated based on their time together and . . ."

Suddenly, Mok'onel appeared at the courtyard gate. "Ajkun," she said, "hurry, my mother's waters have broken, the baby is on its way." She looked at Naom and nodded. "Please, both of you, you must hurry," she said before running back down the path, her bare feet scudding on the packed dirt.

"Oh Ixchel," Ajkun said, "this is Kemonel's fifth child; if her waters have broken, there's no time to lose. Run child, and count the contractions as I've taught you while I gather my herbs. I'll be there as quickly as I can."

"Why can't Mok'onel deliver the child?" Naom said as she sipped at her tea. "We did that training together. Besides, I doubt Kemonel wants me there."

"You know as well as I do that Mok'onel dropped the bag of flour we used that day on the ground." She laughed. "What a mess that made!" She tugged on Naom's arm and pushed her toward the gate. "Go help Kemonel, and remember, count slowly and make sure there is hot water on hand when I arrive." Ajkun hurried into the hut, pulled her leather medicine pouch off its shelf, and began stuffing it with various salves and teas. She plucked her small statue of Ixchel, the goddess of childbirth, off its pedestal and placed it into the satchel as well. Then she walked as quickly as she could to the village center.

A small gathering of women hovered at the doorway to Kemonel's hut. They kept peeking through the opening, but moved aside when Ajkun arrived.

"Why is the girl in there?" Potz' said as she turned her one good eye toward Ajkun.

"That girl is my apprentice, as you well know, Potz," Ajkun said as she stared at the older woman's cataract-filled eyes. The left was completely white, earning her the nickname of One-eyed. "She must learn to birth a child just as your son must learn to throw pots; it is their destiny." Ajkun glanced at the fire ring and was glad to see a large kettle of water on the boil. Kemonel let out a groan, and Ajkun stepped into the dark hut.

Kemonel lay on a small mat on the floor, and her daughter, Mok'onel, held her hand. "Breathe, Chuch," she said as she stared into her mother's eyes.

Na'om turned from where she was squatting next to Kemonel when she heard Ajkun set her bag on the dirt floor. "The pains are only four breaths apart, Ati't," Na'om said as she moved out of the way.

Awkwardly, Ajkun squatted in front of Kemonel. "I'm going to check you," she said to the woman. "And when I say push, you push." Kemonel nodded and scrunched up her face as another labor pain hit her. Ajkun turned to Na'om. "Come child, you must learn what it looks like from this angle," she said as she pulled up Kemonel's skirt, exposing her thighs. "The baby is already starting to appear; see there, that black spot," she said as she pointed to a small patch between Kemonel's legs. "That's a bit of hair, the head is down, and he or she is ready to come out." Ajkun looked up and said to Mok'onel, "Help your mother into a squat, she needs to push soon. You hold her on one side, and I'll support her on the other."

"But Ati't, who will catch the child?" Na'om said as she watched the women shift positions.

"You will. Hold the head under the neck to support it, and let Kemonel push the baby into your hands. The child will be slippery, though, so make sure you don't drop it." She gave Na'om a quick grin before looking down at Kemonel. "All right, we've been here many times before; you know what to do."

Kemonel nodded and strained with all her might.

Na'om watched as the round head topped with black hair popped out, and she hurried to place her hands under the slippery, wet neck. Another push and one shoulder slid through, then the next, and with one final push, the rest of the baby flopped into Na'om's arms. She looked up at Ajkun and Kemonel. "It's a boy," she said as she lifted the child up so Kemonel could see him.

"Another son, your husband will be pleased," Ajkun said as she took her knife and cut the umbilical cord. She folded it into a piece of cloth and handed it to Na'om. "Throw this into the fire outside and bring in the hot water." She took the infant from Na'om and placed him in Kemonel's arms. She nodded to Mok'onel. "Help me get your mother into a more comfortable position and then bring me a large bowl so I may wash the baby."

Na'om returned with the water and washed her arms and hands after Ajkun. She threw the dirty water outside and refilled the basin so Ajkun could bathe the infant in the warm water. Ajkun wrapped him in a thick cotton blanket and handed him back to Kemonel. "We'll bring the binding boards by later today," Ajkun said. "For now, try to get some rest; once the boards are attached, you won't get much sleep due to his screaming."

She nodded at Na'om who stepped outside. Slowly the two walked back to Ajkun's hut.

"You did a fine job back there," Ajkun said as she wearily climbed into the hammock in the courtyard.

"Well, at least I didn't drop him," Na'om said, and they both laughed. She tucked the blanket around her grandmother's small body. "He has such big brown eyes; I never knew a baby could have such big eyes."

"Someday you'll have a child of your own, and then every-thing will change," Ajkun said.

"I doubt that will happen, not in this lifetime, anyway," Na'om said as she laid a kiss on her grandmother's cheek. "Rest now, I'll get the binding boards from Chiman for Kemonel."

SATAL

Satal paced back and forth in her bedroom, waiting for the sound of the drums that signaled the changing of the guards at the gates. She needed to meet Ilonel again, but it had to be late at night, so no one would see her at The Drunken Blackberry. They'd agreed to meet after midnight. She stopped in front of Sachoj.

"I know what you're thinking, old woman," Satal said to the shrunken head in its nook in the wall. "It's been three years since I hired the boy, and all he's done is take my money. We're no closer to finding this jaguar-child I keep dreaming about than we were the day she was born." She stared at her great-grandmother, expecting an immediate response, but the open eyes remained fixed on some distant spot that only Sachoj could see.

"Humph, some help you are tonight," Satal said as she resumed her pacing. In the distance, she heard the striking of drums and knew it was time to leave. She threw a black shawl over her gray-black hair and wrapped it tightly around her body. It blended with the black skirt and shirt she wore. For safety, she placed her small knife in her pocket. She didn't know who or what she might encounter on the way.

With one last glance at Sachoj, who still appeared lost in another dimension, Satal blew out the candle in the room and walked through the dark house to the doorway. She paused as she pulled the heavy wooden door shut as its rusty hinges screeched in the night, and she heard the neighbor's dog begin to bark. She listened to muffled voices, then a *kathunk* as something heavy hit the wall, and the barking quickly changed to a whimper.

Satal tucked her shawl more tightly around her body and hurried through the silent streets of Mayapán, past the dark houses of her neighbors, past the silent marketplace, and into the narrow alleys of the seedy part of town. She had no trouble navigating the dark streets as she had taken this route many, many times over the past few years, always meeting Ilonel in the same bar, always walking away empty-handed as he explained yet again why he hadn't found the child.

A young couple was entangled in each other's clothes ten paces from the swinging wooden sign marking the entrance to the Silowik Tukan. A few other people loitered on the street directly in front of The Drunken Blackberry, but Satal saw they were too busy with their own shady bits of business to pay much attention to her, and she popped inside. The tables and stools in the front room were filled with men of all ages playing games of dice. They shouted as they rattled the carved bone playing pieces in coconut bowls before spilling the contents onto the tabletops while a group of drummers played in the corner near the serving counter. She glanced around and caught the eye of Q'abarel, the barman, who gestured toward the back room. She nodded and pressed her way through the crowd, pushed aside the heavy leather flap covering the doorway, and stepped through into a much smaller room. It was dimly lit by candles in sconces attached to the stucco walls, and Satal noticed the ceiling was blackened with soot above each spot. The room was partitioned into wooden sections with a walkway down the center. For privacy, each enclosure had a thin dark curtain near it, which hung from a hemp line that ran from one end of the room to the other. A slave girl dressed in a simple white dress stood near the doorway, waiting to serve those inside.

Satal noticed most of the compartments were occupied, their curtains drawn, the inhabitants' soft whispers masked by the pounding of the drums just on the other side of the wall.

She knew where Ilonel would be seated, though, as he always picked the same spot, farthest from the door on the right side of the room.

She pulled back the curtain and slipped inside the gloomy space. Several empty mugs sat on the scuffed leather table. "I see you've been here awhile," she said as she nodded at Ilonel. She noticed that his normally spiked hair lay flat against his head, tied in back in a small queue with a thin piece of leather. His white shirt was stained, the long sleeves ripped at the cuffs. "For what I pay you, you could afford some better clothes."

His back pressed against the wall, Ilonel grinned at Satal. "The shrewd man knows when not to appear too well off. You're not my only customer tonight and," he paused and gestured to the mugs, "one must extend a certain amount of hospitality to those you do business with. Can I order you something, a frothy mug of hot cacao, perhaps?"

Satal nodded, and Ilonel leaned out of the booth and snapped his fingers. The slave girl hurried to him. "Cacao for my friend and another balché for me," he said. "Add it to my bill; I'll settle up tomorrow morning." The girl nodded and silently drew the curtain back in place as she left.

Satal and Ilonel sat in silence until the girl returned and placed their two mugs on the table. "May Itzamná guide you," Ilonel said as he picked up his mug and drank.

Satal sipped at her cup. The beverage was hot, but lacked flavor. *The beans they used must be stale,* she thought as she pushed the mug to one side. "So, what news do you have?" she demanded.

"My informants have been as far south as Chicanná and Chetumal and as far east as Tulum. No one has heard of this Wayeb child you speak of. Are you sure he or she even exists?"

"She exists and appears to be gaining power," Satal said. "I need you to find her! An expedition is headed out the day after tomorrow toward the southeast. They'll be collecting tribute from the villages along the southern Usumacinta River and the smaller rivers that feed into it. I want you to follow this group with a party of your own, one that you will lead. I'm not paying you good cacao beans to sit in this booth all day and conduct business; I expect you to get this girl and bring her back to me." Satal reached into her pocket and removed a pouch full of cacao beans, which she placed in Ilonel's hand. "This should be sufficient payment considering all that I've already given you over the years."

Ilonel hefted the bag and whistled softly between his white teeth. "This girl must be extremely special, my lady. But at what point do you concede defeat? Three years we've been searching, and no one knows of the girl. If she exists, she's well hidden. I can't just walk into a village and take her."

"You can, and you will! If that means killing the villagers who hide her, then do so. But I suspect someone as clever as you already knows that the slavers in Chichén Itzá will take anyone off your hands that you bring them. Do what you must; just bring me the girl." She leaned in closer to Ilonel. "This is the last time we'll meet; if you return empty-handed, don't bother to hide. My magic will find you." Satal slid from her seat and walked quickly through the front room to the outdoors.

Once in the street, she took a deep breath of fresh night air. The stale smell of fermented berries hung on her clothes, and she hurried home to bathe and change. Only cold water remained in the turtle shell basin in the outdoor kitchen, but Satal stripped off her clothes anyway and scrubbed her wrinkled skin until it hurt. She left the pile of clothes on the ground for Masat to wash in the morning. Naked, she entered her bedroom, pulled on a clean shift, and lay down in her hammock. She rocked to and fro and was just about asleep when Sachoj's scratchy voice filled the room.

"I've seen her again," Sachoj said.

Satal placed her bare foot on the floor and stopped the hammock. "Do you see where she is?" she asked.

"Nothing is familiar looking. She's reached her womanhood,

though. And is only just beginning to understand the power she has. This spy of yours needs to find her quickly so we may tap into her strength and turn her to our side before it's too late."

"I've sent him in a new direction and told him to do whatever it takes to find her," Satal said. "She'll be in our hands within a few months." Both women smiled at the thought. They needed fresh blood to keep their magic alive.

YAKAL

Yakal yawned as he slipped into his clean loincloth and draped his squirrel-skin cape across his shoulders. The sun was barely over the city walls, the courtyard in front of his hut still in shadow when he stepped outside. *Why did Satal summon me at such an early hour?* he wondered. He looked back at Uskab still asleep in the hammock. They'd been married over five years, and he still loved to look at her and hear her soft breath as she slept. He hurried through the quiet city, nodded to a few early risers, and knocked on Satal's door.

"It's open," Satal said.

Yakal stepped inside the dark, almost empty front room and saw Satal in a worn-out chair in the corner. His footsteps echoed in the large room as he approached the old woman.

"Nimal is leaving tomorrow on an expedition into the south," Satal said. "The villages near where you used to live are offering their contributions to the city in exchange for protection from the Xiu of Chichén Itzá. I want you to go with these men, as you might know some of the villagers from your youth."

"But Nim-q'ij, I'm no soldier," Yakal protested as he stood in front of Satal. "And I'm a married man, what will happen to Uskab if I go?"

"She can move in with your mother. You're the only one in the city who has travelled that far south. We need someone who knows the waterways to meet with these villagers, someone who understands their methods and customs." Satal glared at her husband's illegitimate child. "Much as I don't trust you, you're the only one I do trust to bring back the green jade these southerners are said to possess. Anyone else would gladly trade it to the Xiu for any number of things. And one of the villagers may carry news from Chachal, which you'll need to deliver to me as soon as possible."

"My younger brother, Tikoy, is in the regiment now; surely he can deliver this news?" Yakal looked at Satal's scarred and wrinkled face. *Why do you insist that I go? What's in it for you?* he thought.

Satal tilted her head back to look up into Yakal's brown eyes. "I swear by Itzamná that you do this for me, and I'll make sure Uskab is safe throughout her next pregnancy."

Yakal peered into the older woman's disfigured face. He didn't know whether to believe her or not.

"You'd like a son, I'm sure," Satal said. "Every man does, and you've been trying for years with no success."

Instead of answering, Yakal looked around the empty room, at the walls painted in elaborate battle scenes, the warriors dressed in full regalia. They waved spears and knives as they clashed with the enemy, their leather shields and body armor were spattered with blood, their blue and green feather headdresses brilliant against the white stucco. *Any one of these men could be my father, Q'alel,* Yakal thought, *leading his men into a contest against the Xiu. Will my son one day paint pictures of me on a set of walls?* He turned back to Satal and slowly nodded his head. "I'll bring back your jade and any letters."

"Good, Nimal leaves first thing in the morning. That leaves you tonight to be with Uskab," Satal said with a leer.

Yakal didn't bother to reply; he simply left the room and headed to work. He was lost in thought much of the day, wondering if anyone from his past would be among those carrying supplies to the city. The baby girl he'd left behind popped into his head, his stone chisel slipped, and he chopped off the beak-shaped nose on the statue of Chac, the rain god, that he'd been carving for over a week. He smashed the remaining sculpture with his stone mallet and quickly pushed all thoughts of the child away. He feared Satal might discover his thoughts. He hated to feel Satal's fingers meddling in his life, but knew she had the power to assure a safe pregnancy for Uskab. Of all the events he regretted in his life, abandoning his daughter at birth still unsettled him the most, and he vowed to be a better father, if the gods allowed him the opportunity to be one again.

"Why the long face, my love?" Uskab asked as Yakal entered their tiny courtyard after work.

Yakal didn't look at his wife and entered the hut without a word. He pulled his extra shirt and loincloth from the pegs on the wall and rolled them up in a blanket.

"What are you doing? Yakal, answer me," Uskab demanded when she saw him.

"I'm going with the regiment, to the south," Yakal replied as he flopped into their hammock.

"But why . . ."

"Shh, my little honey bee," Yakal said as he held out his hand to his wife. "Don't speak; it's best you don't know; come, sit with me." He tugged on her hand and watched as Uskab walked shyly toward him.

"How long will you be gone?"

"Hmm, a month, maybe six weeks; it depends on the rains." Yakal stroked his wife's head and longed to run his fingers through it, but she had it all plaited into a braid. He slowly reached down, untied the blue string at the bottom of her hair, and began to ease the strands apart.

"Yakal, I still need to prepare dinner," Uskab said as she felt his hands in her hair.

"That appetite can wait," Yakal said as he continued to unravel her long locks. He leaned into the tresses and breathed deeply. He could smell frangipani blossoms with a hint of spicy pepper.

He touched his wife's small breast through the rough cotton shirt and heard her sigh.

"Yakal," she murmured, "it's too soon."

"Shh, trust me, this time it'll be all right," Yakal said as he pulled Uskab to his lips.

It was dark outside when the couple awoke after their lovemaking. Yakal watched as Uskab cooked pieces of iguana on a spit. He noticed she held her belly with her right hand as she turned the meat with her left. "Are you all right? I didn't hurt you, did I?"

Uskab twisted on her feet and peered into Yakal's face. "No, my love, I'm cradling our son so he stays with me this time," she said as she slipped the meat onto a wooden platter.

"You'll stay with Chuch while I'm gone; she'll make sure you're healthy," Yakal said as he bit into a piece of the hot, greasy meat. "It's tough," Yakal said as he chewed.

"I should have cooked it longer," Uskab said as she watched Yakal swallow the lump of lizard. "That's what happens when you don't let me prepare the meal properly!"

Yakal reached out and grabbed Uskab by the hand. "I'll eat raw meat if it means I can pleasure you every night." He pulled her onto his lap and fed her a tiny bit of the iguana. "Promise me you'll stay away from Satal while I'm gone." He looked into her brown eyes. She nodded. "Promise?"

"I promise, I promise," Uskab said as she stepped away. "Is Tikoy going with you?" she said to change the subject.

"Yes, although Chuch won't be happy. It's bad enough I have to leave, but she won't be pleased if Tikoy goes, too," Yakal said as he licked the meat juices from his plate.

The next morning, twenty military men dressed in hide armor leggings, armbands, and breastplates led the procession through the center of Mayapán. Behind them came fifty slaves, wearing loincloths and leather sandals. Large pack baskets strapped to their backs were held in place by tumplines across

their foreheads. Behind the slaves, a group of young boys in training marched along, carrying baskets partially full of clothes and
food, followed by another fifteen men in leather battle gear. Yakal
hurried from his hut to join the group, and he stepped in line
with Tikoy and Nimal, the leader of the regiment. The group
passed through the city gates while many of the city's inhabitants looked on. The older men carried spears, bows, and leather
quivers full of brightly fletched arrows slung over their shoulders.
The apprentices had sharpened sticks and small knives grasped
in their hands or slid into pouches tied to their loincloths. Stripes
of red war paint were streaked across their bare chests. Yakal
briefly waved his hand to his mother, Alom, and Uskab who stood
among the crowd of women near the perimeter of the wall.

"Don't look back," Yakal warned Tikoy as he caught a glimpse
of the boy's movement out of the corner of his eye. "Father always
said a true warrior only looks forward, never back."

Tikoy nodded his head and did as his older brother told him.
He readjusted his knife sheath as the bone handle bumped him
in the side.

Outside the gates, long lines of slaves who were headed to
the salt flats near the coast, empty baskets on their backs, stood
to one side and let the regiment march ahead of them up an
eight-foot-wide ramp and onto the white limestone *sacbé*. The
thirty-foot-wide causeway stretched in a straight line for miles,
interconnecting Mayapán with many of the other cities and villages to the north and south. Even at this early hour, the flat road
was packed with people. Women had babies tucked into shawls
that hung from their backs. They carried grubbing sticks and
rakes and were on their way to the milpa and amaranth fields
just outside the city. Youths headed to market carried gutted deer
carcasses slung on poles, which they balanced on their shoulders.
Young boys herded flocks of ocellated turkeys together to let the
group pass. Yakal watched as the blue-headed birds pecked at the
white stone underfoot and bobbed their heads about, looking for

insects. Their iridescent bronze and green feathers glistened in the sunlight. One turkey tried to peck Yakal's sandaled foot, and he kicked at the bird and glared at the boy before marching on.

The group marched in quickstep until they were out of sight of the city gates, and then their leader, Nimal, shouted, "Stop! Ten minutes rest for everyone." He grinned at Tikoy and leaned in toward the youth. "No sense killing ourselves on the first day. We made the impression we wanted, now we can continue at a more leisurely pace." He drank from his water gourd. "It's a long ways to where we're going; I don't intend to hurt myself getting there." He swiped his hand across his mouth and waved to Yakal who hurried over. "So, my friend, why have you joined this group? I expected you to remain safe behind the walls you've so carefully built. What's enticed you to return to the wilds?"

"Not what, but who," Yakal said. "Our dear lady of the council, Satal, issued a command; I'm to bring back any jade and give it, and any letters from my half-sister, Chachal, directly to her."

"Ah, Satal, she does have a way of getting what she wants," Nimal said as he replaced the stopper on his water gourd. "The question is, did she really want you to get these things for her, or did she just want you out of the city?"

Yakal looked at his friend; the same thought had entered his mind that very morning as he hurriedly ate the bowl of corn gruel Uskab had prepared. *Why does Satal insist on me being gone?* he mused. *She's basically promised to protect Uskab while I'm away, so beyond the jade and possible letters, what's in this trip for her?* Before Yakal had more time to think, he heard Nimal speak again.

"Come now, everybody up," Nimal said as he turned to the troops who were sitting along the edge of the sacbé, their feet dangling over the four-foot edge of the causeway. "Come on, now, look lively, we've a long walk ahead of us before we sleep tonight." The men and boys struggled to their feet and resumed the march.

Days passed, each day the same. The men rolled out of the blankets they'd spread on the ground, ate a few bites of food, then hopped up on the causeway and continued walking south. At each village they passed, the residents lined the edges of the sacbé, provided them with bits of food, and refilled their water gourds from the local cenote. At the larger towns, the military men were offered gourds of coconut juice and roasted agouti on sticks, which they ate while they walked. Nimal bartered with bags of salt and received warm tamales for the slaves.

The air grew warmer, more humid, the farther south they traveled. Smaller causeways interconnected with theirs, stretching off to the east and the west, highways to other places and cities like Mani, Labna, and Edzna. The various sedges and grasses pressed in on both sides of the sacbé as it slowly narrowed from thirty feet wide to less than ten. The men needed to walk in pairs, and when the road ended, they continued single file, following dirt paths and animal trails through the dense brush that grew higher than their heads. Only when they began to climb small hills leading into the mountains did the men catch their first glimpse of how flat their homeland really was.

Yakal paused at one open area where the land spread out below them like a tabletop. In the far distance, along the horizon, he thought he could see a strip of blue, perhaps the ocean, but it might have just been the distance playing games with his eyes. The trees below them looked tiny while the ones ahead of them, on the hillside, stretched their branches to the heavens. The air was cooler now that they had gained some altitude, and Yakal knew they were nearing the meeting site.

Yakal wondered if anyone from Pa nimá would be in the group they were to meet, or if any letters and supplies from the village of his youth would just be mixed in with all the other trade goods. Tikoy walked over to his older brother.

"Quite the sight, eh?" Yakal said as he laid his hand on Tikoy's bare shoulder.

"I never imagined the land could look so flat," Tikoy responded. "There's a huge world out here, beyond the confining walls of Mayapán." He looked at his brother. "I envy you; you've seen and done things in your life, been places I'll probably never go." Tikoy scuffed his worn-out sandals in the duff. "I hate being cooped up inside the city; I don't know why you ever came back," he said.

"There are many things you still need to learn, little brother," Yakal said. "The world may look inviting from this distance, but up close, it can be another story altogether. Someday you may appreciate those walls that seem to hem you in." Yakal paused and studied the vastness around them. "There are days I miss the village where I became a man, the quiet where I could hear myself think, but I wouldn't trade the life I have now to go back to the past."

The two brothers stood lost in their own thoughts while the men around them ate, slept, and pissed in the dense bushes. Yakal reflected on what he'd just said. *Itzamná, I can't believe I've been gone so long. If she survived, my baby girl must be fully grown by now, a woman in her own right.*

Four days later, the group of men under Nimal's command set up camp along the sandy banks of one of the feeder streams to the Usumacinta River. They made makeshift thatched roofs out of branches and leaves, enough to keep the direct sun off their tired bodies. Hot, sweaty, and covered in dirt from days of marching, the slaves, apprentice boys, and even many of the older men swam in the muddy water, despite Nimal's warnings that crocodiles lined the river in all directions.

"Crazy fools," Nimal muttered to Yakal as the two men watched as one by one, a line of boys climbed into a tree, grabbed a vine, and swung out over the river, before dropping to the water below. "With all this commotion, someone is bound to get eaten."

"None of them have seen this much fresh water at one time, my friend," Yakal said. "Swimming in the cenotes is forbidden, the ocean is too far away, and when the rains come, the arroyos fill so rapidly, even the best swimmer could drown. Post a guard, someone to watch for any crocs, then if one is seen, we can hunt it and eat it, instead of being eaten," Yakal suggested. "After weeks of tamales and agouti, a large chunk of roasted meat would be tasty right now."

"Right, good idea," Nimal said and immediately set four men to watch the water for any signs of suspicious movement. Within the hour, a twelve-foot crocodile was spotted, causing everyone to flee the river in one mass stampede. "Whoever kills that beast gets the choicest piece," Nimal cried out.

Arrows and spears flew from every direction as the older men tried to skewer the animal, while the boys took turns pushing each other into the shallows, each one holding his knife in his hand. Eventually, a flurry of arrows pierced the animal's hide, and several boys leaped into the water and repeatedly stabbed the beast until it stopped thrashing about in the muck and floated belly up in the blood-filled water.

A bonfire was quickly made, and the men carefully slit the skin from the carcass before hefting the beast to a set of poles built over the fire. Within hours, the crocodile was cooked, its flesh charred and dripping with grease. The regiment feasted on the reptile until no one could eat more.

"So, now what?" Yakal asked as he leaned back against a small stump. He patted his full stomach. "I'm not sure any of us could move, even if we wanted to."

"We sit and wait," Nimal replied as he picked at a sliver of meat stuck between his teeth with the tip of his obsidian knife. "We have no real way of knowing when these southerners will show up, or even if they'll show up. My orders are to meet at this spot and wait until they arrive. Then pack up the goods and bring them all home." He slipped his knife into his sheath. "Seems pretty easy to me."

"Hmm, yes, if all goes as planned," Yakal replied.

That night, as the sun dropped over the horizon and the shadows lengthened along the shoreline, great swarms of mosquitoes appeared, attacking the men from all directions. Many thought of jumping back into the water, but the darkness hid the crocodiles and water snakes from view. "My lord," Tikoy said to Nimal as he rubbed mud on his bare arms and chest to protect his skin, "the men are being eaten alive. What shall we do?"

"Have the slaves gather dry wood and grasses from above the waterline and build a number of smudges up and down the shore. Perhaps the smoke will keep these biting monsters away," Nimal said as he tucked one arm inside his chest plate of armor. "By all the gods, I've never seen pests like these devils."

Several days passed, and the men grew restless with nothing to do but hunt crocodiles and fish. The slaves were kept busy collecting wood for the evening fires, and many of them took turns swimming and jumping off the tree along with the boys. Yakal wandered down from his resting area on the bluff overlooking the river to watch. One of the younger slaves, Memetik, climbed higher than the rest, grabbed a different vine, and swung far out across the river before plunging into the waters below. He popped up, sputtering and shaking his head. Water drops flew on all sides, and he laughed and waved to his friends who beckoned to him. Memetik swam to shore and climbed the tree again. He leaped off, making a big arc in the air before dropping to the water. Yakal watched the river and saw the youth begin to swim to shore. He glanced at the vine-covered tree where several other boys jostled to climb as high as the slave boy. Looking back to the water, Yakal suddenly saw Memetik disappear. Yakal searched the water to see where the lad might pop up, but there was nothing, just bubbles of water.

"Everybody, out of the water, now," Yakal yelled as he scurried down from the embankment toward the river. Slaves and boys pushed toward the bank, slipping in the soft mud and sand underfoot.

Finally, Memetik bobbed up several yards downstream. "Help me," he cried. "A crocodile . . ."

Yakal pushed through the throng and waded out into the water. He paddled toward the slave boy, grabbed Memetik under the arms, and half-pushed him to the riverbank. Memetik's left leg from below the knee was missing. Blood pulsed into the murky water, turning their footprints red. "Get me a rope," Yakal cried as he laid the boy on the ground. Someone thrust a piece of hemp into his outstretched hand. Yakal wound the rope around and around the stump as tightly as he could while Memetik screamed with pain.

Memetik looked at Yakal with wide eyes. "Am I going to die?" he asked.

"Not if I can help it," Yakal said. He looked around at the crowd hovering nearby. "You there, and you," he said as he pointed at two youths, "carry him up on top of the riverbank so he can lie down more comfortably. Everyone else, stay away from the water." Yakal stood up and hurried back toward his camping spot. He plucked handfuls of yarrow as he walked, ignoring how the tough stems cut into his hands as he pulled up the flowers, roots and all.

"Eh, what's this, gathering flowers now, are we?" Nimal joked. Then he took a closer look at Yakal's wet loincloth, the blood splattered on his arms and legs. "What happened? What was all that noise?"

"A crocodile bit off the leg of one of the slaves," Yakal said as he reached for his pack basket. He pulled out his spare shirt and laid it on the ground. He filled the fabric with the yarrow. Screams suddenly filled the air again. "They must have jarred him when they laid him down," he said. The screams rose higher and higher, masking the sounds of the river, of the birds flitting from one side of the river to the other as they swooped down on bugs.

"Well, he'll never make it home," Nimal said. "Someone should slit his throat and put us all out of our misery."

"He's just a boy," Yakal said as he bundled up the shirt full of stems and blossoms.

"A slave boy, you mean," Nimal said. He looked at Yakal. "What concern is he of yours?" he asked as Yakal stood up to leave.

"An old grievance with the gods, my friend; perhaps a good deed here will balance the equation," Yakal replied. He grabbed another piece of hemp from his pack. "I'll make sure he makes it home or will quiet him myself."

Yakal hurried back down the river, slipping in the soft sand. One of his sandals caught on a piece of wood sticking out of the dirt, and he stumbled, but he managed to scramble up to the crowd gathered around the injured slave. "All right everyone, give the lad some room to breathe," Yakal said as he pushed through the group. He knelt down in front of Memetik who groaned when Yakal lifted his wounded leg. Yakal opened his shirt and held up several of the yarrow blossoms to the crowd that hovered nearby. "See these flowers? I want you all to collect as many of them as you can find. Look all along the riverbanks and bring them back to me." He pointed to two of the warrior apprentices. "Both of you, come here," he said. "Watch how I pack these flowers around the wound. They'll need to be changed every few minutes until the bleeding has stopped. Is that understood?" The two boys, who looked like they might vomit at any moment, just nodded their heads. Yakal placed his shirt under the stub and pressed the yarrow blossoms all around the wound. Then he took another piece of rope and tied the shirt tightly around the leg. "As soon as the bleeding stops, send someone to fetch me." He looked at Memetik. "We'll have to burn the wound if you want to live." The youth closed his eyes and laid his head back down in response.

"So, will he survive?" Nimal asked when Yakal finally walked back to the bluff.

"It's in the hands of Itzamná now," Yakal said. "But if I burn the stump, he may make it through the night."

"So, what was that thing with the flowers?" Nimal said.

"My first wife's mother is midwife and healer of Pa nimá,

the village where I lived for several years. I used to listen to the women as they discussed various herbal remedies while they cooked and worked around the hut we shared. I remembered the yarrow because it has such a pungent smell to it. It should help with the bleeding."

"You certainly are a man of many talents, if not a few mysteries," Nimal said. "Well, if that slave does live, he should rightfully become your ward since you saved his life."

"And what would the likes of me do with a houseboy?" Yakal said.

"Having a slave to attend to you is a popular thing to do these days, didn't you know?" Nimal replied. "Not just the elite have their special attendants; just about anyone can visit the market when the slavers arrive and pick and choose from the thieves, the orphans, the captured women. Some take a concubine, others want house servants, and some use their slaves as sacrificial offerings to the gods, in exchange for all manner of things."

"Well, if Memetik does live and does make it back to Mayapán, I'll set him free and let him return to his family where they can take care of him. The last thing I can afford is another mouth to feed."

"Oh, have no fear, my young friend, I suspect Satal will reward you handsomely for bringing back her precious jade."

Too restless to eat again, Yakal huddled near a smudge, his one blanket pulled up over his head so the mosquitoes couldn't bite his face, with only a small hole through which to breathe. This left his feet exposed every time he stretched. He tried curling into a ball under the fabric, but found it so hot he broke out into a sweat. He watched as the sky gradually changed from the soft golden light of dusk to the deep velvet blackness of night. As the first stars appeared overhead, a young boy ran up the embankment to Yakal.

"My lord, the bleeding has slowed, and Memetik is asking for you," he said.

Yakal threw off his cloak and let the fresh air ripple across his sweaty skin. *I'd wash in the river, but I know that croc must still be around,* he thought.

He walked back to Memetik and removed the bloody shirt and yarrow compresses. The bleeding had stopped, for the moment, anyway. Yakal knelt beside the slave and looked at his youthful face. "Why were you enslaved?" he asked.

"I was indebted for a year for stealing a baby goat from the birthing pens; my little brother just wanted a pet, and now I'm going to die," Memetik said. His deep brown eyes filled with tears. "I volunteered for this mission, so my debt would be reduced by six months." He groaned as another spasm of pain hit him.

"You won't die, not yet, anyway," Yakal said. He walked back to the fire and grabbed a burning branch. He tamped out the flames on the damp ground. The stick smoldered and glowed a deep red. He nodded to the two boys who had stood vigil over Memetik for the past few hours. "Hold him down, as tightly as you can." They nodded, but looked away when Yakal placed the hot branch against what remained of Memetik's leg. The boy screamed and then passed out. Yakal shook the bloody flowers from his shirt and retied it loosely around the cauterized stump. The flesh was red and needed washing, but Yakal would tend to that in the morning.

"Keep him covered with blankets tonight," he told the two guards. "Wake me if he shows any sign of fever." The two boys nodded in reply, and one added another stick to the fire.

Wearily Yakal walked back up the river. He paused briefly to wash his legs, arms, and face in the shallow water before heading to his bedroll.

"You couldn't warn us you were going to do that?" Nimal said to Yakal as he returned.

"I just wanted to get it over with," Yakal replied. "Now the boy may have a chance."

The two men shared a few cold tamales, and Yakal dozed off,

a half-eaten piece of cornmeal still in his hand.

The sun was barely above the horizon when Yakal felt Tikoy shaking him by the shoulder. "Brother, wake up, the villagers are coming," Tikoy said. He turned to Nimal who sat up and yawned. "Seven, maybe eight canoes," Tikoy said as he slipped off his sandal and wiped the mud from the bottom of his foot before replacing his shoe.

"At last! I was beginning to wonder if we'd ever return home," Nimal said as he struggled to lift his heavy body off the down-trodden grassy patch. "Grab your ledgers and your squirrel fur brushes, Tikoy, my boy," he said. He took the youth's proffered hand and was yanked to his feet. "Now's when you finally earn your keep."

Tikoy hurried off to grab his pouch of writing tools, while Nimal adjusted his loincloth. Yakal walked with him down to the river. Nimal bent and smoothed down his black hair with some water. "This humidity makes even the straightest hair curl," he said as he patted at his head and retied the hemp string around his small braid. Nimal turned to the men under his command. "All right everyone, on your feet; we've got company coming and want to make a good impression. Get the fires going, and cook whatever food we have left so we can offer them a meal." Nimal turned to Yakal. "See if there's any balché left in that small jug in my basket. We can at least offer one swig to the leader of this group."

Yakal nodded and headed back up to where the two men had been sitting. He rummaged around in the basket and pulled out a stoppered gourd. He shook it, but could hear almost nothing inside. *Just as well,* he thought, *no sense getting everyone drunk right away. Besides, they might bring some of their own, as a gift to us. Perhaps I can slip this tiny bit to Memetik to ease the pain. I should go check on the boy, but that will have to wait.* Yakal placed the basket back in the shade, stood, and looked down at the river where he could see the group of canoes. *Hmm, I wonder if I'll*

recognize anyone from Pa nimá, or if anyone will recognize me.
Probably not, since it's been so long.

He slid back down the embankment and took his place by
Nimal's side. One by one, the canoes beached onto the sand, and
the canoeists hopped out. Everyone helped pull the loaded boats
higher on to the bank.

The group of twenty paddlers gathered together and
approached Nimal. The leader, a young man with a series of
raised, dot-like scars running from one side of his face, across the
bridge of his nose, to the other cheek, stopped in front of Nimal.

"Nim-q'ij, my name is Yukanik, and we have brought many
goods to honor the great Cocom leaders of Mayapán." The youth
took a deep breath and exhaled slowly. "We request protection
from your warriors against the Xiu raiders. Our villages look to
you to save us from the slavers and those who would steal our
women and children for sacrifices." Yukanik motioned to the men
behind him who began to untie the hemp ropes covering the
wares.

Yakal scanned the group, trying to recognize anyone, but
most had their faces turned away from his line of sight. One
young man did look familiar, but Yakal could not be sure.

"Come, my friend," Nimal said as he placed an arm around
Yukanik's shoulder. "You and your men have had a long journey.
Come eat with us; let my men unload the canoes." He waved to
several of the warriors who lined the riverbank, and they stepped
into the shallows to remove the tarps. The warriors formed a
brigade and starting handing off each basket and bundle while
Nimal led the canoeists to the central fire.

Yukanik nodded at Nimal and then glanced back at the
canoes. "You there," Yukanik called out to one man as he saw
one basket edged with red ribbon being placed on the ground.
"Bring that one to me." The warrior brought the basket to the
series of stumps laid out as stools near the large cooking fire
where Yukanik, Yakal, and Nimal all sat. "Maltiox," Yukanik said.

"These are for the city council leaders," he said as he lifted out a deer hide packet. He untied the ribbon wrapped around the package and removed several bundles of fig bark sheets of paper, all tied together with yet another piece of cotton.

Yukanik turned to the men who sat on the sandy bank behind him with banana leaves full of roasted crocodile and fresh fish on their laps. "Tz'," he said, "Where's the special packet from that woman, what's her name again?"

"Chachal," Tz' replied as he stood up and walked over to the group.

Yakal's head jerked up at the sound of the name. *Is that really little Tz'ajonel, all grown up now?* he wondered as he looked at the youth in front of him.

Tz' reached into the basket and removed another deer hide packet. "Her letters are in this bundle, marked with the green string." He handed the package to Nimal. "These are to be sent directly to some woman named Satal."

"Give them to Yakal," Nimal said as he pointed in Yakal's direction. "He's the special carrier of that precious cargo."

Yakal looked at Tz', but couldn't tell if the boy recognized him or not. *I'll wait until later, when I can speak to him alone,* Yakal thought, *and ask him about the village. Perhaps he knows what happened to my child.*

By the time the men were done talking, shadows stretched across the river again. The smudges sent giant clouds of smoke into the air when Yakal headed up the riverbank to check on Memetik. He was surprised when Tz' stepped into line with him.

"Mind if I join you?" Tz' asked. He carried a coconut shell sealed with beeswax in his hand.

"No, not at all, but I hope you have a strong stomach; what you're about to see won't be pretty."

"I'll be all right; Nimal told me about this slave boy. I'd like to meet him," Tz' said. "I brought some flax salve to rub on the wound, and I'd like to talk to you, if that's possible." Tz' handed the bowl of salve to Yakal.

"Of course, of course, let's check on Memetik, and then we can go someplace private to speak," Yakal said as he climbed to the bluff. He was pleased to see Memetik was sitting, propped up by a latticework of branches and sticks. "So, how are you doing?" Yakal asked as he bent down in front of the boy.

"Better, my lord," Memetik replied. "I owe you my life and swear by Itzamná that I'll be your servant from this day until the day I die."

"Stop, there's no need to do that," Yakal said as he slowly unwrapped Memetik's leg and rubbed some of the healing balm on the burnt stub. "I don't expect you to serve me. When we get back to Mayapán, you'll go back to your family so they can tend to your needs properly."

"But my lord," Memetik said, "I still owe a debt to the goat herder whose kid I stole; if you were to accept me into your service, then my debt would be repaid, and I could tend to your needs instead."

"First, we have to get you back to the city, which is a long ways away; if you survive the trip, then we'll see." Yakal patted the boy on the head. "Try to rest now, we leave in two days' time." He straightened and nodded at Tz', who stood a few feet away.

The two meandered down along the riverbank, away from the crowds of men and boys sitting around the smudges.

"You probably don't remember me, as you were just a little boy," Yakal said as he stopped beside a large mahogany tree. "I lived in Pa nimá for several years before returning to Mayapán."

"But I do remember. I can dredge up how hard my mother cried the day you left," Tz' said. He looked at the older man's lined face. "I remember how angry my father was with you, the way the smoke from the fire you started filled the village and made it hard to breathe." He paused and smacked a mosquito on his arm; it left a splotch of blood on his skin, which he wiped away with his hand.

"Itzamná, I was a fool that day," Yakal said. "Young and stupid, hungry and tired from the Wayeb ceremonies, then the baby came . . ." he shook his head and looked at the stars overhead. "What happened to the child?" he asked Tz'.

"Oh, with Chiman's protection, Ajkun raised her, and she's learning the ways of the midwife," Tz' said. "But she's been cast out from the village and now lives alone on the other side of the river. The villagers have always feared her and her pet jaguar."

"A jaguar for a pet?" Yakal said. "No wonder everyone is afraid!"

"Oh, Ek' Balam is a good cat; he wouldn't hurt anyone in the village," Tz' said with a laugh. "I think her dreams cause more trouble than anything. My father and her grandmother try to protect her, but she still has to stay away most of the time." Tz' looked at Yakal. "Don't worry about Naom, though, she's tough and can definitely take care of herself."

"Sounds like you've run into some trouble with her," Yakal said. "Naom; it's the name Tu'janel wanted if we had a girl. Tell me more about her."

Tz' scuffed the dirt with his feet. "She's beautiful and different from the other girls. She likes to be alone, foraging in the jungle for medicinal plants. My father says she can see into the Otherworld in her dreams. He writes them down in a ledger so they aren't forgotten."

"So, the power of the Wayeb is shining through, perhaps?" Yakal said. "When you return, will you carry a message to her from me?"

"With pleasure, but only Itzamná knows whether she'll accept it, especially from me."

Before Yakal could question the youth some more, one of the warriors from Mayapán came toward them. "My lord," he said, addressing Yakal, "Nimal needs you, there's some problem with the trade goods; he says to come at once."

Yakal stood up, and he wiped the dirt and dried grass from

his loincloth. "May the gods be good to you, Tz," he said as he gave the youth a quick hug. He turned and hurried after his fellow citizen.

As he approached the regiment leader, he could see that most of the baskets from the canoes had been emptied, and the wares had been repositioned into the numerous pack baskets of the slaves. Bundles of furs and bunches of feathers still lay on mats on the damp riverbank. *Itzamná, how shall we transport all this?* Yakal thought. He tried to catch his breath from running along the river. "What's the problem, Nimal?"

Nimal waved the boy away, and after checking to make sure no one was nearby, he pulled back a blanket lying on the ground near his feet. "Satal told me the original agreement was to send green jade, a large amount of it," Nimal said. "But look at this; it's not green, but blue-green, with flecks of white. She won't like this," he surmised.

"No, she won't," Yakal agreed and then grinned. "She'll love it, as this is an even rarer form of the stone."

"Are you sure? Of course you are, you're a stonemason! No wonder she insisted on you coming with us; she knew you'd recognize this rock."

"That, my friend," Yakal said as he pointed to the pile spread out on the damp ground, "is far more than rock. That represents power and wealth beyond anything either of us will ever obtain. You must set a guard at once, someone you trust implicitly. If word gets out to the Xiu that we have this, we'll all be dead within the week!"

Nimal whistled and waved his hand. Tikoy stood up from in front of a basket with his ledger in hand. "Tikoy, come here at once," Nimal called.

Tikoy nodded at his older brother. "Yes?" he asked Nimal.

"You know the squad as well as I do; pick two people you trust to guard this pile day and night with their lives, and tell them if it reaches Mayapán, they'll receive a handsome reward and a promotion. And tell them they must not speak of the contents of this blanket to anyone."

Tikoy grinned and hurried off.

"Well, that should get the other men talking and wondering," Yakal said. "Let's hope we all make it back home in one piece."

NA'OM

The first summer rains that had fallen during the night had cleared the mugginess, and Na'om stepped from her hut to breathe in the fresh air. She loved the clean, earthy smell and the way the trees and bushes looked new and green and freshly washed. She finished tying her hair in a long braid and was thinking of Tz' and the others who had left so many weeks ago when she heard a noise on the path from the river. "Ati't, what are you doing here?" she said as she walked forward and gave her grandmother a hug.

"I brought you some food," Ajkun said as she handed Na'om a cloth-covered basket. "Extra tamales, some stuffed peppers, and a bit of leftover soup for that cat of yours," she said as she looked around. "Also, the men are back from their trip; Chiman has asked us both to come to his house so we can hear what Tz' has to say about it all."

"I was just thinking about them. They made good time," Na'om said as she placed the containers of food inside a rectangular wooden box she'd made. She put the lid back on and placed a large rock on top of it. "It keeps Ek' Balam from eating everything when I'm not here," she said when she noticed Ajkun looking at her. "Chiman wants both of us there? That doesn't make much sense."

"Whether it makes sense or not is not the point, how are you going to be, seeing Tz' for the first time since the argument?" Ajkun asked.

"I'll be fine. As you said weeks ago, he probably pushed because of the heat of the moment. I still have feelings for him, but he may have found someone else by now or decided Mok'onel is a better mate. I don't plan to encourage him, if that's what you're implying. I think you're right, we have to leave some of this up to the gods, and so far, I haven't had any signs from them regarding Tz'."

"But you've had other signs?" Ajkun said.

"Hmm, more sensations than anything, the constant droning in my ears when I'm here, but which seems to go away when I cross the river. A few dreams, but nothing really that I haven't dreamt before, you know, the strange men covered in stripes of red paint, the wounded crying for help . . . Although there's been this giant wasp, a black, hairy thing that's five or six feet tall that keeps appearing, and I have to fight it," Na'om said. She picked up a gourd full of mango juice and poured some into two coconut shell cups. She gave one to Ajkun and sat down on the ground near her grandmother.

"Why haven't you told me of this new dream?" Ajkun said. "I'll need to write it down."

"Oh, no, I've been practicing my drawing," Na'om said as she jumped up. She disappeared into the hut and came back with her fig bark ledger. "I still have trouble with all the glyphs, all those lines look like so many squiggles to me, so I'm drawing out all the dreams. Here, take a look," she said as she handed the book to her grandmother.

Ajkun carefully turned the stiff, whitewashed pages of bark. Each side was covered in fine black ink drawings that Na'om had hand painted with a variety of colors, and black paw prints ran up and down the margins of each page, as if a tiny cat had walked along the edges of the book. Ajkun could see half-naked warriors holding spears and bows crouching in the green brush, images of the giant black wasp towering over a drawing of a girl dressed in a blue shirt and skirt outlined in purple, and one two-page spread had a finely detailed close-up of a jaguar's face on it. "You're getting quite good at this, Na'om, I can count all of Ek' Balam's whiskers in this one." She handed the book back. "You should show this to Chiman, he'll be pleased to see how well you're doing."

"All right, but I won't do it today," Na'om said. "When do we need to go see him?"

"When the shadows reach across the central courtyard. He wanted Tz' to have time to rest before this meeting." Ajkun placed her empty cup on the ground. "Come have lunch with me; it's been too many days since you and I had a nice chat. I miss having you in the house."

"We could just eat here; after all, you did just bring a lot of food," Na'om said with a laugh. "I'm sorry I haven't been spending as much time with you. I've been busy drawing, collecting herbs, and arranging things in the hut. Come, let me show you," she said as she pulled her grandmother to her feet. "What do you think?" she said as she stepped inside the doorway after Ajkun.

"It's beautiful, Na'om, truly beautiful," Ajkun said. "I had no idea this was what you were up to. And here I thought you were hiding, moping over the loss of Tz'. I should have known better." She sank down on the ceiba-filled mattress on the floor and looked around at the curved walls. The white limestone had been sectioned off with bits of string tied from the rafters to small rocks laid out on the floor, creating a grid on the wall. Inside each square, Na'om had started painting brilliant teal, deep emerald, and lime-green vines and bright golden-yellow and marigold blossoms that twined and twisted from floor to ceiling. Ajkun could see more charcoaled lines drawn on the white walls of images that Na'om had yet to paint. "You'll be living inside a vast flower garden when this is done."

"It makes me happy, helps me forget what the others think of me, and helps pass the time," Na'om said with a shrug. "Plus, when I'm in here, I feel perfectly safe. Like the plants are hiding and protecting me, just like the ring of trees outside." She shook her head and said, "I guess that sounds kind of silly, now that I'm a grown woman and all." Na'om's stomach growled just then, and she laughed. "Let's eat!"

After they ate, the two women spent several hours fussing around the outside of Na'om's hut. Ajkun helped her rearrange the cooking stones in the fire pit so that a variety of pots could be placed over the coals at one time. With Ajkun's assistance, Na'om was able to put together a small bench she had started making by lashing various straight branches she'd collected with bits of hemp twine. She laughed when she sat down on it, as she had to tuck her feet underneath the seat; otherwise, her knees were bent at an awkward angle. "I guess I forgot to measure the height of the legs," Na'om said as she stood up. She walked into the brush, returned with two flat rocks, and went back for two more. She placed a stone under each leg, and the bench rose by three inches or so.

"That's a little better," Ajkun said as she sat down. "It works for someone as short as me." She looked up at the sky. "It's growing late, we should go meet Chiman."

They walked to the river in silence, and Ajkun stepped into the small canoe she'd used while Na'om steadied it for her. "Ready?" Na'om asked, and she gave the boat a push.

Ajkun knelt in between the thwarts. Then she grinned as she picked up her paddle and suddenly pushed off, cutting right in front of the bow of Na'om dugout canoe. "Catch me if you can, or you're a rotten mango," she yelled as she dipped her paddle into the water.

"Ati't, that's not fair," Na'om cried with a laugh as she pushed off from the rocks. She dug deep into the water, but her grandmother had a head start, and Na'om saw a gap opening between the two canoes. *She's not going to beat me,* she thought as she paddled furiously. The space narrowed, and both canoes touched the opposite shore at the same time. The two women laughed and hugged as they pulled the boats up higher on the bank. "You little monkey," Na'om said as she pinched her grandmother gently on the cheek. Suddenly, Na'om stopped when she saw a group of women approaching from the village. The smile fell from her face, and she looked at the ground as she walked past them.

"Potz', Kemonel," Ajkun said as she nodded at her neighbors. "How is the baby? Did that salve help his rash?" she asked as she touched Kemonel on the sleeve of her yellow huipil.

"Oh, yes, Ajkun, it helped a lot, and now that the binding boards are off, it's so much easier to nurse him. He did fuss so as the boards pressed his head into the proper shape. Mok'onel is taking care of him right now, but you should come see him. After the corn's been planted, Chiman has promised to do the naming ceremony." Kemonel motioned for Potz' to continue to the river without her. "We've chosen Tze'm for his name as he laughs so much. Na'om, you should come, too, you did such a great job at the birthing. I'd like you to see the baby."

"Thanks, we'd enjoy that," Ajkun said.

Na'om looked at the woman in front of her and felt her eyes swell with tears. *I won't let her see me cry,* she thought, *but those are the first kind words I've heard from someone other than Ati't in a long time.* She looked directly at Kemonel and said, "Thanks, I'd like that, I'd like that a lot."

"Well, I need to get these gourds filled," Kemonel said as she lifted the trio she held in her hand.

Ajkun nodded and hurried up the path with Na'om.

"Ati't, how come Kemonel is being so pleasant to me?" Na'om asked.

"She was your wet nurse for six months," Ajkun replied. "She must be remembering those early days of feeding you and Mok'onel now that her new child has arrived."

"How come you've never told me this before?" Na'om said as she stopped in the path and looked at her grandmother.

"Does it matter?" Ajkun said. "How would anything be different if you'd known this sooner?"

"I might have realized not everyone is afraid of me, and maybe I'd have tried harder to become Mok'onel's friend. I don't know; it just seems like something I should have known, that's all."

Ajkun didn't say anything, just turned and continued to walk toward Chiman's house. The two women met other villagers as they passed through the central square, but none spoke to them, and Na'om felt their eyes on her back as she hurried after her grandmother.

"Just ignore them," Ajkun said. "Someday they'll all appreciate you, mark my words."

Chiman, Tz', and another young man whom Na'om didn't recognize were all sitting outside under the large avocado tree when they arrived. They were looking at an open ledger on Tz's lap. Na'om felt her heart beat a tiny bit faster at the sight of her childhood friend. Only a few weeks had passed, but it felt like years since she'd last seen him. The rush of the river behind them masked their voices, but Na'om saw Tz' touch the young man's arm and point in her direction as they approached.

"Ajkun, Na'om, it's so good of you to come," Chiman said as the three men stood up and offered the women the bench to sit on. "This is Tikoy," he said as he pointed to the visitor.

Ajkun gave Tz' a big hug and nodded to the stranger before sitting down. She insisted Chiman sit with them, while Tz' and the other youth sat cross-legged on the ground.

Na'om avoided looking directly at Tz', but glanced every so often at the stranger. *He's a nice-looking young man,* Na'om thought, *with those deep brown eyes and long hair, but I wonder what he's doing here.* Then Na'om choked a little as her mind raced through the possible reasons. *Maybe some arrangement has been made, and Chiman has decided I'm to be his wife, so Tz' can marry Mok'onel. Then this stranger will take me far, far away from here, away from Ati't, back to his home in Mayapán where no one knows me or knows the history of my birthing.* Her heart beat even faster, and she did all she could to shield the scars on her face from his view.

Chiman continued to speak. "Tikoy's come from Mayapán. He wanted to see a bit of the world before going back to the city, so Tz' invited him to stay with us through the rains. Once the dry moons arrive, he'll head back north and take some of the villagers with him, so they may experience a bit of the city."

Naom's heart skipped a beat. *This must be why Chiman insisted I come today; he's bound to announce our engagement soon. But I hope he waits until Tz's not around.* She looked at Tikoy and then at Tz'. *They're of similar ages and builds, both muscular and handsome in their own ways. But will I be able to love him, this Tikoy, when I don't know anything about him?*

Ajkun was the first to speak. "Tz', tell me, how did the exchange go? How many were in the envoy, and did they like all the herbs and salves we sent with you?"

"Ati't, it all went well; the fifty or so slaves the men brought were well laden by the time their baskets had been filled. One young slave boy had a mishap before we arrived, his leg bitten off by a river crocodile, but Yakal was there and placed a poultice of yarrow blossoms on the wound . . ." Tz' said.

"Yakal!" Ajkun exclaimed. "I never expected him to be among the group."

"My brother says it's thanks to you, the fact that he learned of some of the healing plants while living here, that the slave boy will live," Tikoy said.

"Your brother . . . ah, of course, now I see the family resemblance," Ajkun said and laughed. She leaned over to Naom. "Say hello to your uncle, child."

"Uncle?" Naom said. "I, I don't understand, I thought . . ." she shook her head and fell silent.

Chiman laughed. "I guess I forgot to mention that detail. My apologies, Naom, this is your father's younger brother, and he's brought a message for you, from your father."

Tikoy stood up and walked to the side of the house where his pack basket leaned against the wall. He rummaged around for a minute and returned with a couple of sheets of bark tied together with twine. "From your father," he said as he handed the package to Na'om.

Wordlessly, Na'om accepted the parcel. Her mind was reeling. *He's my uncle, not my future husband; my father is alive and well and has even written me.* She looked at Ajkun, but didn't know what to say.

"Na'om, are you all right?" Tz' asked. "You've turned almost white. Father, tell her the rest of the news, of my decision," Tz' urged.

"I think Na'om has had quite enough surprises for one day," Chiman said as he looked closely at the girl. "The rest can wait until after the corn planting ceremony."

"Yes, I quite agree," Ajkun said, "We both need some time to adjust to all of this news," she said as she stood up. She offered her hand to Na'om and helped her granddaughter to her feet. She reached down and kissed Tz' on the top of his head. "It's good to have you back, young man; we missed your smiling face." She looked at Tikoy, "And, it's very nice to meet you, you must come visit us soon." She turned to Chiman, "And as for you, old man, you should know better than to surprise an old woman so." She punched him playfully in the shoulder. "We'll talk later, yes?"

"Yes, yes, of course," Chiman said as he rubbed his sore shoulder. He looked over at his wife, Chachal, who was approaching the group from the house. "You'd best go, Chachal is acting very protective of her son just now, but not to worry, I won't let her make any arrangements without your consent."

Ajkun linked arms with Na'om and led her to the path. Once they were around the corner and out of sight of the others, she asked, "Are you all right? This news has been quite a shock for you."

Na'om began to laugh. "I'm fine, just stupid, that's all. When I saw Tikoy, I had it in my head that Chiman had arranged for me to marry him, so I was sitting there trying to imagine whether I could ever love him or not, and then I find out he's my uncle." She laughed again. She handed the bundle of papers to Ajkun. "I'm not sure I want to read this, though. You take it and read it, and if it's good news, then tell me, if not, I don't want to know."

"Are you positive?"

"Absolutely," she said as she hugged her grandmother. "After all, what could my father say to me now that could bear any importance in my life?"

"Hmm, that's what I wonder," Ajkun replied as they continued toward her hut.

CHIMAN

"I won't discuss any kind of marriage arrangement until after the corn planting ceremony," Chiman said as he stood in front of Chachal. *This woman has a one-track mind,* he thought as he glared at his wife. *If she had her way, she'd marry my son off to that silly girl, Mok'onel, without any regard as to whether it's the best thing for the village or what the gods intend to have happen.*

"But Tz' is well beyond the rightful time to be wed; surely if he waits any longer, someone else will snatch Mok'onel away, and who is a better mate for him than her?" Chachal said as she looked into her husband's scarred face. "If you mean to wait and have him marry that jaguar-girl, then you'd best think again. I won't have Tz' tainted by her. And I want grandchildren before I'm too much older, and we know what happened with you after one of the corn ceremonies. Certainly Tz' can wait another year to perform the sacrifice, giving him time to wed and bed Mok'onel?" Chachal sidled up to Chiman and rubbed her hand down his bare arm. "You remember what it was like, don't you, my love?" she cooed. "When making love was so pleasurable for both of us?"

I remember long afternoons spent in the arms of a woman, but she was not you, Chiman thought as he tossed off his wife's arm and moved to stand in front of the doorway. "The scarring that happened to me won't happen to Tz'," Chiman said. "Ajkun will prepare the proper healing salve for his wounds; Tz's sacrifice won't limit your chances for a grandchild."

He watched as Chachal plopped down with a soft sigh on the

edge of a stool. Her long gray hair was pulled back in a tight braid, and he could see the many wrinkles that marked her face, lines she tried to hide by applying a variety of powders and creams to the rough skin. Her dark blue huipil and skirt were tight around her middle, and her breasts sagged beneath the fabric of her shirt. Breastfeeding and age had taken their toll. "Besides, Tz' has made no indication to me that Mok'onel is the one he wishes to marry," Chiman said. "And I've received no confirmation of this match from the gods, either, so we'll wait."

Chachal sighed again. "As you wish, Chiman, you have the final word."

"Good, then that's settled; now, I must go explain to Tz' what will happen and help him prepare. There's to be no food for the boy for the next twenty-four hours; he must fast and purify himself before offering himself to the gods." Chiman picked up his jaguar cloak and threw it over his shoulders as the air was cool and damp, a sure sign the evening rains were coming. The villagers needed to get the newly prepared field blessed and planted with corn, beans, and squash to ensure ample food for the coming year. Chiman walked to the corner of the room, to the shelf where all his ledgers were stored, and retrieved the one with the corn planting ceremony marked in it. He tucked it under his arm, picked up an empty water gourd, and headed to the village center.

He nodded to several of his fellow neighbors as he searched the central courtyard for Tz', but there was no sign of the boy. He finally found his son down at the river, in the bathing area reserved for the eligible bachelors of the village. Tikoy was with him, and Chiman watched as the two youths tousled in the water, wrestling and sparring playfully, sending handfuls of water arcing through the air toward each other, which created miniature rainbows in the bright sunlight. *He should have had a brother,* Chiman thought as he continued to watch unobserved. *Did something go wrong with me as Chachal always implies, or does the fault lie with her that we had only one child?* Chiman pondered. He clapped his hands together and got the attention of the two young men, who pushed their way through the thigh-deep water to the riverbank. They stood in the sunlight and let the air dry their skin.

"Tat axel, what brings you to the river looking so serious?" Tz' asked.

"You must make ready for tomorrow, when you'll lead the ritual for the corn planting," Chiman said. "I've brought the ledger which explains everything; there's much to be done in the next few hours." He bent down and filled the gourd in his hand with river water.

"Better you than me, my friend," Tikoy said as he slapped his hand on Tz's shoulder. He reached down, picked up his dark brown cotton loincloth, and tied it around his waist. "I think that's my cue to go visit my niece and her grandmother for a bit," he said as he slipped his feet into a pair of worn leather sandals. "See you after tomorrow's ceremony," he said as he nodded to Tz' and Chiman.

Chiman stood in silence as Tz' slipped into his own clothes and shoes. He studied his young son's face, searching for signs of fear or reluctance, but Chiman saw nothing except interest and excitement in Tz's eyes. "Come, we must prepare the sweat lodge for the purification ritual, and then you must fast in the temple until it is time to assemble at the new field."

The two men walked side by side back to the village square and approached the sweat lodge. Built of round river stones, the small building's arched roof was only four feet off the ground. Tz' had to crawl on his hands and knees through the narrow entryway, which permitted access to the dark interior. He took the beeswax candle Chiman offered him and placed it on the stone floor. A large bundle of sticks and branches was piled in one corner of the lodge, located under a small opening in the roof. Using the candle, Tz' lit the pyre of wood and coughed as smoke began to fill the room before finding the outlet in the ceiling. He crawled back outside and helped Chiman place a heavy wooden door over the entrance.

"We'll return in an hour or so, after the fire's died down a bit," Chiman said. "For now, you must begin to learn the phrases you'll speak at the ceremony and drink as much water as possible so you sweat in the lodge and purify your body and soul." He led Tz' to the temple, and they removed their sandals before entering. He handed Tz' the water and motioned for his son to sit.

Chiman lit a ball of copal in one of the many pottery incense burners that lined the walls of the room before sitting down as well. He opened the book to the corn ceremony and handed the ledger to Tz'.

"You understand what is asked of you?" Chiman said after Tz' had studied the glyphs and drawings on the page.

"Yes, and I'm not afraid, if that's what you're asking," Tz' said. He looked into his father's deep brown eyes and held his gaze. "Sacrifice is a part of life; the gods mixed their blood with maize to create the first people; we must honor them by offering our blood in return."

"You'll be given balché to help with the pain, and Ajkun has many salves to help you heal quickly. I'll aid you as much as possible." He picked up the water gourd. "Drink and then it's time to enter the sweat lodge. When you're swallowed by the heat, empty your mind of all thoughts except that of the corn. Envision it growing tall, green, and full of ears of corn. Once your thoughts are clear, I'll bring you back here for the evening and stay with you. Then tomorrow, I'll help you dress for the ritual."

"I'm honored, Tat axel, that you place such confidence in me," Tz' said. "Many in the village will question your decision, though, since I have yet to wed." He shifted his weight on the coarse mat under his legs. "They'll consider me too young for this task."

"Leave the worrying to me, Tz'; frankly, I'm growing too old for this particular ritual." Chiman drew in a deep breath and let it out slowly. "You know your mother wishes you to wed Mok'onel; she spoke of it again just this morning. But I told her no decisions had been made."

"But we'll tell Chuch and the others what I've decided after tomorrow, yes?" Tz' said.

"It'll be my pleasure to finally tell your mother your decision," Chiman said with a wry grin. "Now, no more thoughts on any of that," he said as he stood up, offered his hand to Tz', and pulled him upright. "Off to the sweat lodge with you!"

NA'OM

The afternoon and evening passed quickly for Na'om and Ajkun after Tikoy showed up at Ajkun's hut. He entertained them with tales of life in Mayapán, of his training as a scribe and soldier, and spoke of his sisters, mother, and Na'om's father, Yakal.

Na'om smiled to herself as she stepped into her canoe to cross the river to her hut. *I'm so lucky to live here, despite the conditions the villagers have forced on me,* she thought. *I can't imagine living inside high walls, among so many people, unable to venture out into the jungle to forage and be alone.* The moon was high in the sky, illuminating the river, and Na'om had no trouble avoiding the numerous rocks on her crossing. She stepped onto the opposite bank and pulled her canoe high into the bushes. She'd heard rain in the distant mountains and knew the river might rise overnight. She didn't want to be stranded on the wrong shore.

Ek' Balam was waiting for her when she arrived at her shelter. She could see he'd pushed against the box where she stored her food, but had been unable to budge the heavy rock placed on top. "Hey boy, it's so good to see you," Na'om said as she rubbed the big cat behind his tattered right ear. He began to purr. "I wish you had come with me today; you'd like Tikoy. Plus, he still doesn't believe that you even exist since he's yet to see you. Tomorrow, you must come to the corn planting ceremony," Na'om said. She removed the rock from her food stash and pulled out the cooked peppers stuffed with black beans and onions that Ajkun had left for her. Once the fire was going, she placed the peppers in a small pot and set them to heat. She sat down on her new bench to wait and noticed Ek' Balam pacing along the path to the river. "Hey boy, what's the matter?" she asked the cat. He just continued to walk back and forth, his tail swishing from side to side. At one point, Na'om saw him stop and cock his head to one side, and then he returned to patrolling the perimeter of the clearing. Na'om listened to the normal night sounds all around her and noticed the droning had returned in her ears, a constant backdrop to her thoughts. She hadn't noticed it earlier in the day. *Perhaps the river is rising, and the sound is magnified here.* "Ek' Balam, come here," Na'om called to the cat. He turned to look at her with his big yellow eyes. "I have something for you," Na'om said as she reached into the food box and removed a leather satchel full of dried fish. She took one out of the bag and held it up near the fire so the cat could see it. The cat came and gently took the fish from Na'om and sat down near the hut. He licked the salt from both sides before biting the fish in half and swallowing it. He laid his head down on his paws and closed his eyes. *Well, there, maybe he was just hungry,* Na'om thought as she helped herself to the hot peppers. *All that pacing was making me nervous.*

Na'om ate and quickly got ready for bed. She lay down and tried to sleep, but her thoughts kept revolving around all the strange things Tikoy had told her about Mayapán. When sleep finally did come, her dreams were jumbled together and flowed rapidly from one vision to another. She dreamt she was near the edge of a limestone well; its round walls were pitted and cracked, and ferns and vines grew out of crevices in the sheer sides. A mammoth black wasp hovered over the mouth of the wellspring. And then suddenly, she was surrounded by men who lifted her high over their heads and pitched her into the deep, sapphire-blue water. She felt herself falling, falling, until she splashed into the cool water and sank below the surface, deeper and deeper into the cenote. As her dream-self drifted ever downward, she opened her eyes and saw Ek' Balam next to her. She continued to sink past openings in the rock walls, passageways that led upward into the dark earth, and she watched as Ek' Balam swam toward a tunnel. As her lungs grew tight from the lack of air, Na'om kicked with her feet, pushed skyward, and reached out and grabbed Ek' Balam's tail trailing in the water. She began to swim with the jaguar toward the black recess in the wall. There was darkness all around her, but she felt the roughness of the tunnel floor under her bare feet, the water slipping away, and suddenly, her head broke the surface, and she was able to take a breath . . . and the wet fur in her hand turned dry and warm, and abruptly she was wide awake, with Ek' Balam growling at her as he pulled his tail from her grasp.

"Sorry, boy, I didn't know that I'd really grabbed you," Na'om said as she realized what she'd done. She lay there in the dark, unable to go back to sleep. *Why do I keep dreaming of that ugly wasp?* she wondered. *What does it have to do with me? Who were those people, and why did they sacrifice me?* She kept shifting her position on the mattress and fussing with the blankets, but sleep eluded her. Frustrated, she lit a candle and quickly sketched this latest dream into her ledger. She drew the water and the dark tunnels and herself slowly swimming to reach the mouth of a cave so far above her. *I'll fill the outlines in with color later,* Na'om thought, and she yawned. She put aside her work and blew out the candle. Just as the first mourning doves began to coo, Na'om fell into a deep, dreamless sleep.

The sun was high in the sky when Na'om woke up, and she instantly realized if she didn't hurry, she'd be late for the corn planting ceremony. Skipping breakfast, she quickly changed into a bright blue huipil and skirt embroidered with cornflowers, brushed her hair, and pulled it back into a braid. She looked around for Ek' Balam. "Here boy," she called as she ran to the river. But there was no sign of the jaguar. She dragged her canoe out of the bushes, pushed off, and instantly noticed how much stronger the current was than the night before. It took much more strength to keep the canoe in a straight line, and the rocks that normally protruded above the water were now invisible to the eye. Na'om reached the opposite shore, looped her bow rope over a tree branch, and took off at a run for the new field where she could hear the sound of drumming.

All the villagers were gathered in the center of the oblong field when Na'om arrived, but she held back from mingling with any of them. Tikoy and Ajkun stood near the edge of the field beside the pile of tools and seeds to be used after the ceremony, and Na'om hurried over to join them.

"You almost missed this," Tikoy said.

"I overslept," Na'om replied.

"Busy night?" Tikoy questioned with a laugh.

"No, bad dreams," Na'om replied.

Ajkun looked at Na'om. "Anything serious?" she asked.

"I'll tell you later," Na'om said as she kissed her grandmother on the cheek. "But that buzzing is back in my ears."

"Maybe you have water in it," Ajkun said. "Try tilting your head to one side and shaking it, while jumping up and down on one foot. That might help."

"Have you seen Ek' Balam?" Na'om asked as she hopped about in a small circle.

"We figured he was with you," Ajkun said. She patted Na'om on the hand. "Relax, he'll be fine. Shh now, we must hear what Tz' has to say."

Na'om stopped jumping and looked back to the field. A tier of carefully stacked stones, each with a small pottery brazier at its base, had been built at the four cardinal points of the area. Thick clouds of copal smoke billowed up from the mouths of the incense burners, and the pungent scent wafted across the assembled crowd. She looked to the center of the field again, toward another tier of stones, and another, larger brazier. Chiman was dressed in his jaguar cape and matching loincloth and had painted his face and body with blue spots to represent Chac, the god of rain. On his head was his quetzal feather headdress; the blue and green feathers towered four feet above his black hair before arching delicately toward the ground. Chachal stood next to him, dressed in a deep green huipil and matching skirt, which glistened in the sun from the hundreds of macaw feathers she had sewn to the fabric. She wore her favorite jadeite necklace and matching bracelet. She represented the garden of corn when it would be ready for harvest. And between them stood Tz', but Na'om hardly recognized him.

His naked body had been rubbed from head to toe with a yellow clay paste scented with honeysuckle blossoms, transforming his normal brown skin into that of lemon gold. His black hair, streaked with the same yellow clay, had been greased and pulled into a tight point on the top of his head. Three emerald-green parrot feathers were tucked behind his right ear. A thick, jagged line of black paint extended from his left brow, across his cheek, to the right side of his jaw. He was Cinteotl, god of the maize.

Tz' motioned to the drummers seated near the tower of stones, and the slow drumbeat stopped. In the silence, Tz' raised his hands above his head and greeted his neighbors and friends.

"My friends, my family, once again, it's time to sow the fields with the sacred maize. We are born of the maize, in the image of Hun Hunahpu, father of the Hero Twins. We must pray and sacrifice to ensure a good growing season and harvest. As Hun Hunahpu gave his own blood to bring life into the maize-filled bodies of our forefathers, we must give some of our blood for the growth of the corn."

Tz' turned to the pile of stones and the brazier at its base. He picked up a small gourd filled with ground blue corn and sprinkled it into the fire. Then he knelt down. Chachal stepped forward, removed a long, gray stingray spine from a small basket by the fire, and handed it to Chiman. She pulled a piece of flattened ceiba bark out of the basket as well and placed it on the ground in front of Tz' while Chiman held the sharp spine over the flames, heating the barbed tip of it. Chachal gave Tz' a mug full of balché, which he drank in one long gulp. He handed back the mug to his mother, and Naom saw him sway just slightly.

All that fermented juice on an empty stomach must have gone straight to his head, she thought.

Chiman motioned to the drummers, and they began to beat out a rapid rhythm. He handed the stingray spine to Tz'. He nodded to his father, then swiftly reached down, lifted his penis into the air, and pushed the red-hot spine all the way through the tip of it. He dropped the bloody spine on the ground. He let blood drip onto the piece of ceiba bark before struggling to his feet. He handed the piece of bloody bark to his father who tossed it into the burning brazier. Slowly, Tz' and Chiman walked to the four corners of the field where Tz' let his lifeblood drip into each fire, blessing the field for the coming year. He swayed again at the farthest turn, and Chiman steadied him with his hand before leading him back to the center of the field. Tz' knelt, and Chachal handed him another mug, this one full of thick atole. He drank the sweet, porridge-like corn drink and stood back up.

The villagers cheered. Chiman clapped Tz' on the back, and Chachal handed her son a golden-colored loincloth to put on. Tz' quickly tied the cloth over his now swollen member and limped toward a stool placed in the shade of a nearby mahogany tree. The villagers quickly dispersed to the edge of the field to collect their tools and baskets of seeds.

"I'm going to check on Tz'," Tikoy said. He started to move away from the women, but Ajkun placed a hand on his arm.

"Wait just a minute, let me give you the salve he'll need for that wound," she said as she rummaged in a basket at her feet. She pulled out a small, glazed pot. A piece of blue cloth was tied over the mouth of the vessel with hemp twine. "Tell Tz' to apply this first thing in the morning and last thing at night," she said, "and also after every time he urinates. It should ease the pain and help prevent any scar tissue from forming." She handed the pot to Tikoy.

"Right, well, I'll see you ladies in a bit," Tikoy said. He gave Na'om a quick hug. "Later, I want to hear about those dreams you had," he said as he headed toward Tz' and Chiman.

"So do I," Ajkun said, "but first, we must help with the planting." She picked up a basket of corn seed and handed one of beans to Na'om. She started to walk into the field where each man was ramming the fire-hardened, pointed end of a long, wooden stick deep into the dry soil to make holes. Meanwhile, four women followed along behind, one carrying a basket of dried corn, another with dried beans, and the third with squash seeds. Each woman dropped a seed into the hole and moved on the next. The fourth woman followed behind each group to scuffle dirt over all the seeds with her bare feet. Ajkun stopped when she saw Na'om wasn't following her.

"I don't think they'll want me to help, Ati't," Na'om said as she placed the basket back on the ground. "I'll go to the river and fill some of the water gourds; the men will be thirsty before too long."

Ajkun adjusted the basket on her hip. "All right then, I'll see you in a bit," she said as she turned back to her working neighbors.

The empty gourds banged against Na'om's leg as she walked, and she shifted the leather straps in her hand. As she approached the river, she sensed movement out of the corner of her eye, and Ek' Balam appeared from the bushes. He fell in step with her, paced all the way to the river, and lay down on the bank for a drink while Na'om filled each gourd. She carefully stoppered each one and piled them on the grass. She splashed water on her face and shook her head, trying to alleviate the constant droning in her ears.

Suddenly, Ek' Balam began to growl. His ears went back against his head, he rose to his feet, the hair on his tail bushed out, and he swished it from side to side. Na'om looked around the area, but could see nothing out of the ordinary. The river flowed swiftly by, and a light breeze ruffled the surface and stirred the leaves of the mahogany trees.

"What's bothering you?" Naʼom said as she placed the last gourd on the ground. "You were acting strange last night, but I thought it was just because you were hungry." Just then, two female hummingbirds streaked past them, squeaking and chirping to one another. They zoomed in and out of the nearby morning glory vines, their wings whirring in the air. Naʼom laughed to see the birds dart in and out, up and down. "Just some birds, silly," she said as she petted Ekʼ Balam. A crow cawed in the distance, and two more answered it. Naʼom searched the sky, but couldn't see them. "There's nothing wrong," she said to Ekʼ Balam, but he just swished his tail and disappeared into the brush near the trail.

Picking up the full containers, Naʼom walked slowly toward the field. The full gourds were heavy, and Naʼom stopped on the path to readjust the heavy cords between her hands. She could smell the copal smoke from the braziers and see light clouds of dust rising over the bushes as the men pounded the earth with their sticks. She put the gourds down again and went into the brush to relieve her bladder. The whirring in her head grew louder and louder, and she swayed on her feet as she squatted in the dirt.

She was just about to step back into the bright sunlight of the clearing with the water jugs when two dozen men burst out of the trees on the other side of the field. Their faces and torsos were smeared with red, and many had black stripes painted across their cheeks. Some held whips in their hands, which they cracked in the air, while others carried long bows and quivers of arrows. The women and children screamed, dropped their baskets of seeds, and began to run.

Naʼom dropped the water gourds, and one of the plugs popped out, spilling cold water onto her feet. She started to dash toward Ajkun who was intent on placing a corn seed in a hole.

She doesn't hear the attackers, Na'om thought. She felt a sharp pain near her throat, and she hurriedly grasped the necklace around her neck to keep it from banging into her chest.

Suddenly a voice shouted in her head. *Stop! Hide!* It was Tu'janel, Na'om's mother.

Startled, Na'om stopped and saw Ajkun flicking her hand at her, motioning her to run into the brush.

Without thought, Na'om did as she was told and watched wide-eyed as the village men threw their digging sticks at the invaders who fought back with their whips. The long leather strands hissed and smacked, raising welts on the villagers' bare flesh, and the men of Pa nimá tried grabbing the whips with their bare hands, while some threw stones from the ceremonial tier. Na'om saw one stranger fall to the ground, his head split open and bleeding. Arrows whistled through the air, and two villagers fell to the ground. The village women on the far side of the field beat at the men with their baskets, and Mok'onel, Potz', Ajkun, and some of the others started to run toward the river, but they were quickly grabbed by the hair and dragged back to the group.

A black shape darted out of the brush. Ek' Balam pounced on one intruder, landing on his back. The cat sank his sharp teeth into the man's neck, the man screamed, and his fellow companions ran from the jaguar as Ek' Balam turned and slashed at another man with his wide paw. Although he was bleeding from a gouge on the shoulder, an invader notched an arrow in his bow and let it fly, but Ek' Balam sprinted into the undergrowth, and the arrow whizzed harmlessly into the trunk of an avocado tree. A minute later, the jaguar rushed back into the open, attacked another man from behind, and jerked him off his feet. He leaped on the man's throat and ripped it open with his teeth while more arrows flew all around him. One hit Ek' Balam in the left flank, and the jaguar let loose a roar before dashing off into the trees again.

"No!" Na'om cried out loud and started to sprint into the

clearing.

Stop, Tu'janel said.

Na'om sprawled on the ground as she tripped over a root. Prostrate in the dusty dirt, grit in her teeth, but hidden by the brush, Na'om watched as Tikoy helped Tz' struggle to his feet. Then, her uncle ran into the crowd, brandishing his obsidian knife. He slashed at one man who fell, clutching at his stomach. Tz' picked up a nearby stick and hobbled as quickly as possible into the fight. He swung at one of the strangers and received a blow to the head with the butt of a bow. He dropped to his knees, blood rushing down his face. As Tikoy helped Tz' stand, the stranger hit him broadside with the bow across the back of the knees, and Tz' slumped to the ground. Then the man drew a knife and slashed a deep gash across Tikoy's thigh. He fell to the pounded dirt, clutching his thigh as his blood stained the earth a deep red. Tikoy managed to reach out and trip the man, who fell on top of him, and the two wrestled in the dirt, the flash of knives glinting in the bright sunlight.

Chachal ran toward Tz', but a single arrow in the back stopped her in her tracks. She fell face forward into the dry dirt. The string on her necklace broke as she landed, and Na'om watched the blue-green, forest-green, and black beads roll into the dust. Chiman beat at the man holding him by the arms and hurried to Chachal. He placed his hand on her neck and then rapidly pulled the arrow from her. He charged the nearest invader with the bloody missile and slashed the man's face before being knocked down by a quick swing of a wooden club.

Tz's arms were yanked behind his back as he struggled to sit up. His hands were tied together with a piece of hemp rope, and he was pushed to join the other men who knelt on the ground. Their hands and feet were bound by rope, and they were tied one to another into a long line.

The children screamed and pressed their faces into the legs of their mothers, who sobbed and tried to quiet them. The raiders cracked their whips, and the two groups grew silent. They marched among the women, separating the older ones and the ones with infants from the girls near Na'om's age. Mok'onel and her group of friends were pinched and poked, and one man forced Mok'onel's mouth open and checked her teeth before binding her hands behind her back. The village men struggled against their ropes, spitting and snarling at the intruders, who whipped them about the shoulders and backs as the village grandmothers and mothers with the youngest children were lined up in a row. Na'om covered her eyes, but still heard the twang of bowstrings and the zing of many arrows. Then the screams and pleas for mercy stopped. A silence hung over the field except for the harsh tones of the intruders as they gathered the villagers in a group. Na'om opened her eyes and was relieved to see Ajkun among the living. Her grandmother was gesturing to the wounded men, and then pointing to her basket of herbs and salves still on the edge of the field.

Na'om wanted to rush out into the opening again, but knew there was nothing she could do. She dropped back down into the liana vines as the raiders scanned the whole area for movement. She took a deep breath and started to think out loud. "I must be very careful and crawl as quickly and as quietly as possible away from here; they may use this path to reach the river," Na'om whispered. "After all, what can one half-grown woman with no weapons other than water gourds do against so many men trained in the art of surprise attacks?"

Sick to her stomach, Na'om forced herself to crawl away on her hands and knees from the field, even as her neighbors' screams and cries filled the air. She stiffened when she heard Tz's voice shout out, "Na'om," and almost turned back, but she thought of Ajkun motioning her to hide, shook her head, and continued to crawl. She went deeper and deeper into the jungle, angling away from the river until she came to a thick patch of bamboo. She wound her way deep into the thicket and remained there, hidden among the reeds.

"Chuch," she whispered as she clutched her jaguar necklace, "what do I do now?"

Stay hidden, and you'll be safe. Pray to Itzamná for guidance.

Naʾom stayed in the bamboo patch until the sky overhead turned pale purple, and the shadows deepened. She held onto the necklace on its leather thong around her neck, but didn't hear any more words from her mother. Naʾom prayed to Itzamná that her jaguar friend and the others were safe.

Tired, bug-bitten, and hungry, Naʾom cautiously returned to the cornfield. In the light of the rising moon, she saw that it was empty of life. Baskets of seeds lay strewn on the ground, broken gourds lay in muddy puddles, and several drums were punctured. The bodies of the dead villagers had been piled near the now cold brazier where Tz' had tossed his bloodstained piece of ceiba bark. Chachal's feather-covered dress glinted in the moonlight, and she could see multiple arrows protruded from the bodies of Potz', Kemonel, and her infant boy, Tzeʾm, who were all lying together in a small group. Kemonel's little girl, Poy, still clutched her small cornhusk doll in one hand, her fingers entwined with those of her mother. Banal Boʾj and Kon were among the men who had died. Kon's throat had been slashed open. Naʾom retched in the trampled dirt. Three dead intruders had been left behind by their friends.

Naʾom stepped out into the open and slowly began to walk across the field. She bent down and picked up an unbroken basket, still half-full of corn seeds, held it a moment, and then carefully put it back down on the ground. She stumbled over a water gourd and barely felt the water trickle across her feet. She knelt in the muddy field and turned her face to the sky. Tears streamed down her face as she looked to the heavens. "Why Itzamná, why?" she keened to the sky and the gods.

All of a sudden, Naʾom heard a groan, and she hurried toward the pile of bodies in the thickening darkness. She searched among her fellow neighbors and found Tikoy partially propped up on the far side of the tier of stones.

"Tikoy, are you all right?" she asked as she knelt in front of the youth. He had numerous knife slashes across his chest and legs.

"Na'om! You escaped? It must be by the will of Itzamná," Tikoy said. "Never mind, there's no time for explanations. I feel the spirit of my father, Q'alel, calling me from the Underworld." He scrabbled in the dirt by his side and pressed a long, bloody knife into Na'om's hand. "You must travel to Mayapán and find your father. Give him this knife. He'll know what to do."

"I don't understand," Na'om cried as tears ran down her face. "What has this knife or the attack got to do with my father? I have to get you back to the river and patch you up," she said as she tried to lift the youth by one bloody arm.

"Shh, Na'om, it's all right, leave me," Tikoy said as he sank back into the dirt. "Go to Mayapán, tell my brother the slavers were not . . . Tell him, tell him Sa . . ." Tikoy's head dropped to his chest.

Na'om leaned her ear against her uncle's body and listened for a heartbeat, although she knew he had already passed to the other side. She slowly stood, and clutching the knife in her hand, searched the ground around the area for anything that might help her identify who had done this. But in the darkness, she couldn't see anything. She whistled for Ek' Balam, but there was no response. In a daze, Na'om walked to the stool Tz' had sat on. She could see traces of golden clay on the seat. The small jar of salve lay on its side, its contents spilled into the dirt.

Na'om let out a small groan and sank down on the wooden stool. Still clutching the bloody knife in one hand, she wrapped her arms around herself and began to rock back and forth. "Just like in my nightmares, when I was little . . . I should have paid more attention, I should have warned Chiman and the others," she moaned.

She sat hunched over for a long time, too numb to move. Her hand slowly moved to the jaguar necklace hanging around her throat. Tu'janel's voice appeared again.

Move, she directed Naom. *Check the river, then go to your hut.*

In a daze, Naom did as she was told. She stood up and walked back down to the river. At the water's edge, she could see the footprints of many people in the sand and mud, and scuff marks where canoes had been hauled up on to the soft ground. A few of the flat rocks in the area were covered with spots; on closer inspection, Naom could see that they were drops of dried blood. "I hope that's from their dying comrades and not from some of our people," she said out loud.

She made her way to the central plaza, but it was empty. "Everyone was at the ceremony," Naom said. She sat down again in the dirt, but the rumble of distant thunder put Naom in motion. With caution, she went back to the river. Seeing the way was still clear, she tossed the knife in her six-foot canoe, paddled across the rising water, trotted down the path, and hid in the bushes while she scanned the clearing. It looked empty.

"It's safe, and I need some tea and food," Naom said to herself. Keeping busy, moving her body was the only way she could avoid the waves of anger and sorrow that pressed against her skull. She bent down to light the fire and placed the water pot on to boil, but she pivoted on her feet when she heard a noise from inside the hut. Grabbing a burning branch, she crept forward and then jumped into the hut, brandishing the torch in front of her. She waved it around the small room, and she heard a low growl as the light passed over a dark shape in the far corner. "Ek' Balam," Naom cried as she put down the torch and hurried over to the cat. "Oh, Ek' Balam," she shouted. She noticed the broken arrow sticking out of his side.

Naom knelt by the cat and gingerly touched him. He bared his teeth at her, and she flinched. This was the first time the jaguar had ever shown her his teeth. "Come on, boy," Naom said. "It's me." She rubbed him under his chin. "Don't worry, I'll fix you up," she said as she pulled a basket of dried yarrow off a shelf. She placed it on the ground, went back outside, and returned with a bowl of warm water and placed the herbs in it to steep. Na'om gently pulled the wooden shaft from the jaguar's side and then placed a warm cotton towel filled with yarrow over the wound. She held it there with one hand while she ripped some strips of cloth to use as a bandage. "Now don't you go trying to chew that off, you hear me," she said to the cat as he tried to turn enough to gnaw at the fabric. "You can lick it later, after it has healed some."

Na'om went back outside, washed her hands, and fixed herself a cup of tea. She reentered the hut and sat down in the dark next to the now sleeping jaguar.

"What do we do now?" Na'om said.

The only reply was the steady drumming of heavy rain on the thatched roof.

YAKAL

Tired and hungry, Yakal avoided the stares of the guards at the gates of Mayapán as he passed through into the city with Nimal and what remained of the regiment. It had been two weeks since they were attacked by Xiu tribesmen shortly after the convoy had left them along the banks of the river. Yakal's hair was ragged and dirty, his shirt and loincloth were torn, and his right arm was wrapped with bloody cloths. Memetik hobbled along beside him on a pair of makeshift crutches fastened from branches. Yakal stopped just inside the gates and placed his good hand on Nimal's shoulder. "I need to have my mother look at Memetik's leg."

Nimal clasped Yakal in a quick hug. "Have her check that wound of yours as well. I'll call the council members together. But I'm not looking forward to facing Satal."

"She'll be as mad as a wasp over what happened, and the others will probably push for war." Yakal took a deep breath and let it out slowly. "I'll meet you in two hours at the Temple of the Warriors," he said as he prodded Memetik to start walking again.

They wound their way through the crowds toward Alom's house. Inpatient to see Uskab, Alom, and the rest of his family, Yakal refused to stop to talk to anyone and kept poking Memetik in the back until the boy stumbled and fell down in the dirt. Yakal looked at the slave as he struggled to stand back up. "Here, give me your hand," he said and he pulled the boy upright.

"Sorry, my lord, I . . ." Memetik said.

"Shush, it was my fault, and don't call me 'my lord.' Call me Yakal, or I'll send you back to the slavers," Yakal said as he headed into the throng again.

"Yes, my lor . . .Yakal," Memetik cried as he hurried to catch up.

Yakal spied Masat swinging in the hammock outside his mother's house and waved.

Her voice carried back to him as she shouted, "Chuch, Yakal's back." He scooped her up in his arms and winced as the weight of her body pressed into his sore arm, and he gently put her back on the ground.

"What happened to your arm, Yakal?" Masat said.

Yakal didn't answer. He stared at the hut, where Uskab stood in the doorway, her hand caressing the small mound of her belly. Leaving Masat and Memetik alone, he half ran to the house, dropped his pack basket, and wrapped Uskab in his arms. He pressed his dirty face into her long braid and breathed in the smell of jasmine. "I thought I'd never see you again," he said. He held her tight for another minute and then stepped back. He placed his hand on her stomach. "Boy or girl?" he asked.

"You're hurt," she replied, as she led Yakal to a stool by the fire pit. "Let me look at your arm." She slowly unwound the dirty bandages and winced when she saw the ragged slash that extended from Yakal's hand, up the inside of his arm to the elbow. "What happened?" she asked as she poured some warm water into a bowl to wash the gash.

"The Xiu attacked us on the way back here. They outnumbered us two to one," Yakal said. He winced as Uskab dabbed at his arm. "They took many of the slaves and almost all of our cargo, including the jade Satal demanded." He stood up quickly, spilling the bowl of water when he saw his mother, Alom, approaching with a basket full of fresh vegetables.

"My son, what happened?" Alom cried when she looked at his arm.

"They were attacked, Chuch," Uskab said as she pressed Yakal to sit down again.

"And Tikoy?" Alom said.

"He's fine, Chuch, he wanted an adventure, so he went with the southerners to Pa nimá. The attack came after we left the river." Yakal looked around the courtyard and saw Memetik standing outside the gate. He waved to the boy to enter. "I haven't much time to explain, as I must bathe and meet Nimal at the temple for a council meeting. This is Memetik," he said as he motioned for the slave to sit down.

"Did he lose his leg in the attack as well?" Alom said as she looked first at the boy and then at Yakal.

"No, there was a crocodile in the river; it's a long story," Yakal said. "I have many things to tell you, both of you," he said as he placed his good hand on Uskab's arm and held her against him. "Some things I should have explained long ago, but right now, I need you to watch over Memetik."

"Surely his own family will want to see him after being gone so long," Uskab said as she wrapped a clean cloth around Yakal's arm.

"Look, I must hurry and wash up, Memetik will tell you his story while I'm gone, right Memetik?" Yakal glared at the slave boy, who nodded his head. Yakal picked up a clean bowl of warm water and headed toward the hut. "We haven't eaten in over a day," he shouted to the women outside. "I need something in my belly before I have to face Satal and the others with this news." He hurriedly washed the grime from his face and body. *Time enough for a real bath later,* he thought as he pulled on a clean shift and loincloth. He hurriedly brushed his hair and hoped it didn't appear too dirty. He stepped out into the sunlight again and kissed Uskab on the lips as she handed him two tamales wrapped in a banana leaf.

"We'll have a proper meal waiting for you when you get back," she said as she hugged him. "And the shamans say it's a boy," she called out as Yakal hurried through the courtyard to the street beyond.

He ate as he walked, barely noticing the taste of the spicy meat inside the cooked cornmeal as his thoughts tumbled around. *Nimal and I will just tell them what happened and let the council decide what to do . . . A boy, I'll have a son . . . I must tell Uskab and Chuch about Tz' and Na'om . . . Why didn't I ever tell them I had a child? . . . The council will demand we go to war . . .* Yakal finished the tamales and looked around for someplace to throw the banana leaf. Nearing the market, he found one of the many refuse baskets and added the leaf to the growing pile of half-eaten corncobs, turkey bones, and mango peels. He wiped his hands together and headed toward the temple.

Nimal was waiting for Yakal outside the building. "You look worried, my friend," Nimal said. "I've decided we have nothing to fear from that old witch of a woman. I've spoken to the others, and they all agree that we are in the clear."

Yakal gave his friend a half-smile. "And yet, I'm the one who has to break the news to Satal that her satchel of letters has gone missing, along with the jade . . ."

Just then Kubal Joron and Matz' walked up the temple steps together, dressed in matching outfits. "Sorry we're late," Kubal Joron said. "It's my fault; I couldn't find my notes from the last meeting." He looked at Yakal's bandaged arm. "Wounded in battle or attacked by a crocodile, like that young boy of yours?" he asked.

"Battle," Yakal replied as he stared at the man in front of him. "How did you know about Memetik?"

Matz' laughed. "Surely you know my friend here has spies at every gate in the city. Word arrived at the house within minutes. And about that boy, we might be able to take him off your hands," Matz' said. "Wouldn't we, Kubal, my dear?"

"Well, the guard did say he was quite handsome, but he's missing a limb, my pet. How would he manage to take care of us with only one leg?" Kubal Joron fluttered a small fan in his hand, and the smell of honeysuckle filled the air.

"The boy is not for sale," Yakal said. "If I don't keep him at the house, I'll send him back to his parents. They'll provide for him, being his blood relatives."

"Come now, Yakal," Kubal Joron cooed. He pointed to the gold threads woven into his long-sleeved shirt and loincloth and the black howler monkey skin draped across one shoulder. "We have plenty of money and a large house, far more than the parents of a slave boy. We'd take care of Memetik's every need and then some, and if he offered us a little entertainment now and then or did a little work for us, well, that would only be a fair exchange, don't you think?" He fluttered the fan again.

Yakal took a closer look at the man in front of him. *His eyes really are lined with black, as my sister is wont to do,* he thought. *And he does have gold lacquer on his nails.* He looked to Nimal who only shrugged his shoulders and shook his head ever so slightly. "Yes, well, I'm sure you could dress Memetik in the finest clothes and sandals, but like I said, he's not for sale."

"Pity," Matz' said. "We could have used a little amusement, and we'd so love a houseboy of our own; life has been rather dull around here these days." Matz' clapped his hands together. "Well, we mustn't keep the others waiting; do come tell us all about your adventures into the southern lands and about those horrible Xiu who attacked you." He grabbed Nimal by the elbow and linked arms with him. "Do the Xiu really have piercings all over their bodies?" he asked as he walked with Nimal into the temple.

Yakal shrugged his shoulders at Nimal who half-turned to look at him before crossing the threshold into the large room.

They quickly took their places at the council table. Satal was already seated and tapping her fingernail impatiently on the wooden arm of her chair.

"So, I send you out to collect tribute, and you lose not only all of that, but most of our men, too," Satal said. "What do you have to say for yourselves?" she demanded.

"It's nice to see you, too, my lady," Nimal said as he sat down in his chair. "We were attacked, outnumbered two or even three to one. We're lucky any of us returned to warn the city that the Xiu are systematically plundering every convoy that travels from north to south or vice versa. We must prepare for war against them, or they'll soon be battering down the city gates."

As Nimal sat back down in his leather chair, he nodded at Yakal.

With his good arm, Yakal took a long sip of cool water from the mug in front of him before addressing the members of the council. "They were well-armed and seemed to know what our cargo was as well as the best time and place to attack," he said. "I suspect we have spies in the city telling the Xiu all our plans."

Satal laughed. "The only ones who know any plans are seated right here, around this council table," she said as she waved her hand at all the men in front of her.

"Surely you can't mean one of us," Kubal Joron said as he flicked his fan rapidly in front of his face. "Why the very idea is foolishness!" He pulled a handkerchief from the inside of his long sleeve and wiped his sweaty brow.

"Is it?" Yakal questioned. "How else did our enemies know we carried precious cargo?" He turned and looked at Nimal. "What was it the leader said?"

"'Find the jade.' Obviously he knew we weren't just ordinary traders collecting furs and feathers in exchange for salt."

"But what you're saying is one of us is willing to put the whole city in jeopardy," Matz' said as he placed his hand gently on Kubal Joron's arm. "Why would we do that?"

"Some people like rich foods and expensive clothing," Yakal said. "The jade would have bought a lot of that and perhaps paid for a few other indiscretions as well."

Kubal Joron pushed his chair away from the table and heaved his heavy body to its feet. "I won't sit here and be insulted by this,

this . . . mere stonemason!" he cried. "Come Matz', it's time to go! To even suggest either of us would do such a thing . . ."

"Sit down, Joron," Satal said. "No one leaves the council room until I say the meeting is over. If what Yakal and Nimal imply is true, then we have to find this spy or spies and put a stop to them. I don't suspect any of the men in this room and neither should any of you. No, they must be getting their information by some other means." She tapped her nails on her chair. "The question is how." She looked directly at Yakal. "Since you were in charge of the jade, you must find out who this spy is and then report directly to me. Understand?"

"Yes, my lady," Yakal said as he matched Satal's deep gaze. "It'll be a pleasure to bring the person behind this to justice." He nodded at Nimal, and they both stood up. "The meeting is adjourned," Yakal said, and the two men turned to leave the room.

"Yakal, I demand you come back here!" Satal said.

Yakal's stride lengthened, and he straightened his shoulders as he and Nimal continued to march out.

"Yakal, come back here!" Satal demanded. "I'm warning you, you'll regret this!"

Once they were well away from the building, Nimal said, "Oh ho, that went well! And good luck finding the spy. You don't really suspect one of the men on the council, do you?"

"Not one of the men, no," Yakal replied.

Nimal searched Yakal's face and then placed his hand on Yakal's shoulder. "Be careful with your words, my friend. You never know who is listening. Well, if you need help, just let me know; I'll do whatever I can."

Yakal stepped toward the older man and embraced him with his good arm. "I have a few ideas I'm going to work on. Let's meet again in a week and go from there." Nimal nodded, and Yakal watched him disappear into the crowd.

Yakal turned toward home, eager to see his loving, pregnant wife. As he walked, he rubbed his temple, as a dull throbbing had started behind his eyes. *I must be tired,* he thought. He wondered how he would ever be able to connect Satal with this recent attack. *Perhaps she's right, and she had nothing to do with it. If what Tz' said is true about my young daughter, perhaps she can tell me who is behind all this mess. The sooner I send another message to her, the better.*

NA'OM

At first light, Na'om was awakened by the sound of rhythmic licking and was glad to see Ek' Balam was awake and tending to his wound. But she instantly felt the emptiness of the space around her created by the lack of villagers nearby. Tears slipped down her cheek, and she wiped them away impatiently. *No time for tears,* she thought. *I must figure out what to do next.* She petted Ek' Balam on the head and looked at his injury. Thanks to the poultice, it appeared to be healing rapidly. "Good boy," she said as she rubbed him under the chin. She hurried outside and returned with a couple of dried fish, his favorite treat. "You were a big help yesterday," she said as she laid the small meal in front of him. "I hope you're well enough later to go hunting for more food." She returned with a clean bowl of water and set it down where the jaguar could easily reach it.

She pulled on her blue shirt and skirt, and after a quick breakfast of tea and cold tamales, she remembered the knife she'd tossed into the canoe the night before. She hurried to the river. The normal riffles had swollen overnight, and the rocks Na'om usually sighted along to guide her way had disappeared into the deep blue water. Thankfully, her canoe was still high on the embankment where she'd pulled it the night before. The bottom of the boat had a couple of inches of water in it, and she could see the eight-inch knife lying in the murk. She picked it up and cold, reddish water dripped back into the canoe. Na'om bent down carefully over the rushing stream and let the current wash the knife clean. She held it up to the light, fascinated by its beautiful green color and intricate carvings on the handle. She picked a piece of dry grass out from among the intertwined vines and leaves before hurrying back to the hut where she laid the knife near the fire to dry.

While she sipped at her mug of tea, a vision of Chiman's house came to mind, and then the pile of bodies still lying out in the cornfield. She knew she had to cross the river and deal with the dead. She stuck her head into the hut, and Ek' Balam opened one golden-green eye. "I have to go to the village," she said. "Stay here; I'll be back."

Crossing the rushing water wasn't as difficult as Na'om had imagined, but she was grateful to reach the opposite shore. She ran down the path to the shaman's house. A few hungry turkeys squawked as she moved past their pen to the house, which stood silent and empty. She entered the house, half-expecting Chachal to yell at her to go away. Then she remembered. Chachal would never bother her again. She glanced around the vacant house, unsure of why she had come. It looked as if the family had just stepped out for a stroll and would be back anytime. She noticed a bag of grain near the door and filled a bowl with it, which she gave to the turkeys.

Na'om stood and looked at the clean clothes flapping on a line in the light breeze. *I should bring those in once they're dry,* Na'om thought. *Oh, what am I thinking, what does it matter?* She sank to her knees and wept.

With deep reluctance, she forced herself onto her feet again, and with slow, plodding steps made her way toward the new cornfield. She dreaded what she'd see. But when five vultures circled overhead, Na'om broke into a run. The last thing she wanted was for the buzzards to peck at the dead. The field was muddy from the previous night's rains, and everything was splattered with reddish mud. Na'om put her hand over her mouth as the first smell of rot drifted toward her on the wind. She could see the bodies; they hadn't been bothered, yet. She carefully made her way across the ground, searching for any clues that might help her identify who had attacked the village. She picked up a few broken arrows and held the feathered ends in her hand. Mindlessly, she wiped away the muck on the feathers of one arrow on the edge of her skirt and noticed two were pink, the third black. She brushed another arrow against her leg and saw it was fledged with one pink, one white, and one black feather. The third arrow had two turquoise feathers and one emerald-green one. She collected a few more arrows, and they, too, were fledged in different color combinations. She approached Chachal's body and forced herself to remove the elaborate bracelet from her arm. She searched the nearby ground and found most of the beads that had fallen off the necklace as Chachal fell, and placed the mud-encrusted carved stones, the bracelet, and the handful of broken arrows in a neat pile on the ground.

"I can't just leave you all here," Na'om said as she turned to look at the bodies. "And I don't have the strength to bury you." She looked around the empty space, so full of life just the day before. Now the only sounds were a pair of squawking parrots and the wind in the nearby mahogany trees. She listened to the silence; even the buzzing in her ears had stopped. She looked at the trees, and that gave her an idea. She went into the brush and pulled out several large branches, which she dragged to the center of the field. She moved back and forth until she had a large pile of semi-dry firewood. Then Na'om pulled the bodies into a pile on top of some of the wood. She winced as she pulled Kon's body onto the pyre. *Itzamná, what have I done?* she thought, as she remembered how she had wished him dead that night not so many moons ago.

Gently she laid Kemonel's baby boy in his mother's arms as the tears streamed down her face. *I'll never forget catching you as you came into this world, little Tze'm,* she thought as she carefully closed his big brown eyes. She stacked more wood on top of them all. She looked around the tier of rocks, but couldn't find any sparking rocks.

She ran back to the village and entered the first hut she came to. She found a pair of rocks as well as a large bowl of coconut fat. She hurried from hut to hut, collecting as many bowls of peccary and coconut fat as she could carry. Balancing them precariously in a tower, she made her way back to the field. Na'om went around the pile of wood and placed the bowls of semi-liquid grease upside-down on the branches, letting the fat drip onto the wood and bodies below. Then she bent down and sparked the rocks together until a tiny flame shot upward, caught the nearest drops of fat, and burst into a bigger flame.

Na'om stepped back from the pyre as the fire raced from branch to branch. The wind shifted, sending smoke into her eyes, and she moved even farther away. Her eyes watered from the smoke, and she tried to think of something appropriate to say to send these people, her neighbors, off into the Underworld. *I was never able to speak to them in life, what could I possibly say now?* Na'om thought as her mind remained blank.

When the flames had fully engulfed the pile, Na'om picked up the feathered arrows and the jewelry and wandered back to the village center. She looked at all the empty houses, the cooking rings where no flames burned, the large pile of wood stacked in the plaza center that had been collected for the ceremonial bonfire after the planting was complete. None of it mattered now. She meandered down the path to Ajkun's house and stepped inside where the air was cool. Na'om breathed in the familiar smell of herbs and spices. Her first home, where she'd been safe and protected all these years. She saw her grandmother's worn leather satchel and took it off its hook. She placed the handful of arrows and beads in it and glanced around the room again. Her father's unopened letter lay on the shelf by the bed. She thought of reading it. *Why bother,* she thought, as she sank onto the soft bed. *My father abandoned me.* She gripped her necklace in her fist and prayed for a response from her mother.

Not true, Tu'janel finally said. *Your father has worked hard to protect you all these years. Read the letter.*

Reluctantly, Na'om opened the paper package. A two-inch square piece of bark stamped with a red wax seal fell on the floor. Na'om bent down, picked it up, and looked at the embossed design of a four-sided pyramid, a rising sun near its apex. She began to read the glyphs:

My child,

I don't expect you to forgive me for abandoning you. Just know that everything I've done since the day you were born was to protect you. But I grow older, as do those who have raised you, and we won't always be here to watch out for you. Evil is looking for you and will not stop until it finds you, but she grows older, too. You must do everything in your power to stay safe and far away from the city of Mayapán. If you ever find yourself in need, send someone to me with this seal, and I'll come help you.

Your father, Yakal

Na'om put the letter in her lap. "Father, I need you now, but there's no one to send with this emblem," Na'om cried out loud. "Despite what you say about the evil that hunts for me, I have to bring the seal to you myself. But how am I to find this city of Mayapán when I've never been outside the village?"

Follow the map, Tu'janel said.

And suddenly, Na'om knew why her mother had sent her to Chiman's house earlier that day. She scrambled to her feet and ran back to the shaman's house. She burst through the doorway and eagerly scanned the walls. On the far side of the room was Chiman's shelf of ledgers. Na'om crossed the room and one by one pulled each fig bark book from its place and searched its pages. Finally, in the sixth volume, she found what she was looking for, the map she'd seen Tz' and his father and Tikoy looking at just a few days before. Na'om traced the blue lines on the page with her finger. The stream by Pa nimá met a larger river, which eventually flowed into the ocean. From there, a dotted line marked a route overland to the city of Mayapán. She ripped the two-page drawing from the book, tearing the inner edge of one page in her haste. A small piece of bark remained in the book. *Time enough to fix that later,* she thought. *I'll go to the city, find my father, and with his help, petition the rulers to help me. Pa nimá has paid its tribute for protection from the Xiu. The leaders of Mayapán owe this to me, to all of us. I'll demand the city rulers free Ajkun, Chiman, Tz', and the others from the Xiu slave traders of Chichén Itzá who attacked the village.*

SATAL

Although it was broad daylight, Satal went directly from the council meeting to The Drunken Blackberry bar. She entered the large room, and not seeing anyone behind the counter, made her way to the back room. The curtains were all pulled shut, the place was silent, but she checked behind each curtain anyway, searching for Ilonel. In the last compartment, the owner was slumped across the table, sound asleep.

Satal grabbed Q'abarel by the shoulder and shook him. "Wake up, you old fool," she said. "I need to find Ilonel."

The bar man lifted his head and blinked several times before focusing on Satal. He rubbed his eyes and brushed a hand through his hair. "Lady Satal, what are you doing here at this hour?" he said as he sat up straighter in his chair.

"Ilonel, where is he?" Satal demanded.

"He's been gone for weeks, the devil. He owes me quite the sum of cacao beans, which I doubt I'll ever see." Q'abarel yawned in front of Satal, and she could see he was missing several teeth. "Rumor has it he's gone back to Chichén Itzá and is staying with relatives. I knew I never should have trusted that Xiu."

Satal tossed a small bag of cacao beans on the table. "That should more than cover his bill. If he returns, I want you to send a message to me at once."

Q'abarel hefted the bag. "Of course, of course, I'll come myself, the minute I see him," he said as he clutched the sack. He swayed slightly as he stood up. "May I offer you a drink?" he said as he leaned toward Satal.

She held her hand up to her face to ward off the sour smell of old balché. "No, just tell me when you see Ilonel." She turned and left the room.

Back in the bright sunlight, Satal barely noticed the people who stopped and stared at her as she pushed her way through the crowds, past the marketplace, to her house. Masat had left her lunch in the wire cupboard, and Satal carried the plate of black beans, cooked turtle meat, and rice to her bedroom. She needed to consult with Sachoj.

"Ilonel is nowhere near the city," Satal said to her great-grandmother with her mouth half-full of beans. "Do you think he arranged the attack on Yakal and Nimal?"

Sachoj opened her wrinkled, dusty eyelids and blinked several times before answering, "Yes, I'm sure he has his own network of people who would perform such a thing. But he's not in Chichén Itzá."

"Then where in the name of Itzamná is he?" Satal demanded as she placed her empty plate on the cool tile floor. She wiped her hands on her skirt and began pulling her divination objects out from her wooden cupboard.

"No need for any of that," Sachoj said, and Satal turned to see her great-grandmother's viper-like teeth appear in a stiff grin. "From what I see through the haze, he's gone to the Underworld."

"But how can that be?" Satal said as she dropped the moth-eaten monkey skin on the floor.

"It's not clear; the only thing I see plainly is that our jaguar-girl is on her way here. We have to prepare for her arrival."

"I'll tell all my spies to let me know the minute she appears," Satal said, all thoughts of Ilonel banished from her mind. Satal grinned. Finally, after all these years, she would meet the girl who continued to haunt her dreams.

NA'OM

Once her mind was made up, Na'om wasted no time gathering the supplies she'd need to voyage down the river. She found several bags of last year's ground corn and beans in the village, stuffed a sack full of manioc roots, took what dried meat she could find, and placed all the food in a large basket, which she carried to the river. Then she ran back to the village and down the path to Chiman's house. She flicked open the gate to the turkey pen and let the birds out. "Might as well give you some chance at life," she said before running back to her canoe.

She crossed the swollen water, hefted the food basket, and went to her hut. She filled another basket with her extra set of clothes, some salves and tinctures from her meager supply, and an extra blanket. She wrapped Chiman's map in soft deerskin and placed it in a cloth bag coated with beeswax. *Hopefully it'll stay dry,* she thought as she tucked it inside Ajkun's satchel. She stuffed a handful of clean cloths on top. She held up the obsidian knife Tikoy had given her. She'd been unable to find its leather sheath so she carefully wrapped the sharp blade in another piece of tanned deer hide. She placed it in the satchel with her father's letter, the seal, the arrows, and Chachal's jewelry.

She looked around her small clearing to see if she'd forgotten anything. *Oh, a pot or two and my water gourds,* Na'om thought. *Now the only thing I have to do is convince Ek' Balam to stay here, as I can't put him in the canoe with me.* Na'om went into the hut to check on the jaguar, who had remained inside since she'd pulled the arrow from his side.

"Hey boy," she said as she sat down on the floor next to her long-time friend. "I have to go far, far away for quite a while," she said as she checked his wound. It was healing quickly. She stroked the cat under his chin and behind his ears. "You have to stay here, all right? It's a long journey, and you're not going to come. Promise me you'll stay here and watch over things while I'm gone." Ek' Balam purred, and Na'om leaned her body gently against his side. She felt the rumble of his breath against her and lingered in the spot until the hut was dark. She got up and dragged the mattress across the small room to Ek' Balam's side. Then she lay back down near the cat. "I'll leave at first light," she said.

The sun was higher in the sky than Na'om wanted by the time she had packed her canoe, eaten a large breakfast, and checked on Ek' Balam's injury one more time. She spread a generous glob of calendula salve on the spot. "Don't go licking that off right away, you hear?" she said. She took a last look at her little hut, at the walls that still needed to be painted, and her ledger still open to the page where she'd sketched her last dream of falling into the cenote. She patted Ek' Balam and quickly left the house before she cried. She ran down the path and was untying the bow rope on the canoe when she sensed Ek' Balam near her. She turned. The jaguar was limping toward her. He looked at her with his big yellow eyes, and Na'om felt her throat tighten at the thought of leaving him.

She hugged him tightly around the neck. "I'll be back as soon as I can," she whispered in his ear. "I love you," she added, as she stepped into the canoe and pointed it out into the surging water. The current caught the loaded boat, and Na'om maneuvered with her paddle to avoid the few rocks she could see ahead of her. She just had time for one short glance back upstream where she saw Ek' Balam still standing on the riverbank, his tail swishing from side to side, before she was swept around the first bend in the river.

Na'om gasped as her heart cramped, and tears spilled onto her skirt. She quickly ran the bow of the canoe into the bushes and held onto a branch while she cried. She ached to turn around and go back, to live with Ek' Balam in her little hut. "I can't do this!" she cried. "I'm just a girl. Besides, why should I risk my life for all of those who've shunned me?" Anger replaced Na'om's sadness, and she started to twist the boat around so she could head back upstream.

But what about Ajkun? Tu'janel said. *What about Chiman and your good friend, Tz'? Don't forsake them, my child.*

Na'om punched the water with her fist, and her knuckles grazed the gravel bottom of the river. "Why should I save them?" she cried. "What have they ever done for me?" Images began to flood Na'om's mind: Ajkun and Kemonel sharing mugs of tea while Kemonel nursed the infant Na'om, Chiman bringing extra meat and corn rations to Ajkun to feed her young granddaughter, Tz' playing on his flute while Na'om danced with Ek' Balam . . .

She heard Ajkun's voice in her head when she had spoken to Potz' so many weeks ago: *She must learn to birth a child just as your son must learn to throw pots; it is their destiny.*

"But why me?" Na'om cried, and her voice startled a flock of mourning doves pecking for bugs along the riverbank.

My child, you were born in the Wayeb and must accept your powers. Only you can save your people and bring them safely home again, Tu'janel's voice echoed in Na'om's mind.

"But how?" Na'om cried. "My dreams just bring bad luck. Years ago, I wished Chachal had a bad toothache, and she did. I wanted Kon to die and he did . . . Na'om choked on her words and threw up over the side of the canoe.

The answer is in your dreams, her mother said. *Trust in your powers, Na'om.*

Na'om fingered the jaguar necklace around her neck, looked at the familiar river behind her, and then at the jungle and unknown waters ahead. She dipped her paddle into the stream and pushed off from the bank, pointing the bow northward away from everything she had ever known.

Soon, the task of keeping the canoe off any rocks in the river and the sight of new wilderness at every twist and turn kept Na'om too busy to think about Ek' Balam and the distance she was putting between them.

An hour passed and then another. Na'om shoulders ached, and her hands were sore from the twisting of the paddle against the flesh. She ran the canoe into a patch of sand and stepped out into the shallow water, dragging the bow of the boat up onto shore. She stretched and drank some water before relieving her full bladder in the bushes. It felt good to walk around and move her legs after so much time in the canoe. She found an avocado tree and sat down to eat a few bites of dried meat in its shade. Several bees hummed in the branches overhead, pollinating the flowers, and the sound soon lulled Na'om into a light sleep.

The caw of a crow startled her awake. Na'om silently stood up, scanning the riverbank for signs of anyone. The canoe was still pulled up on shore, its bow gently rocking to the pulse of the current. The bees still hummed overhead. And yet, Na'om sensed someone watching her. She looked behind her and could see nothing but jungle. She wished she had the large obsidian knife out in the open. Wary of every little sound, knowing she would be safer on the water, Na'om pushed off from shore and paddled a short distance downstream. She nudged the boat into a crevice in some rocks and quickly retrieved the knife, which she placed by her feet. *I'll make some kind of sheath when I stop for the night,* she thought. She glanced behind her, backed out of the crack in the rocks, and pushed off into the current once again.

Na'om paddled hard for several minutes, and finally the sensation of being watched faded as the canoe rounded yet another bend in the river. Using the paddle to steer, Na'om let the current carry the boat, saving her sore shoulders some of the hard work. She knew she would need to pace herself if she was going to be able to complete this trip. As the sun dipped toward the west, the trees along the shore cast shadows on the water, making it harder and harder for Na'om to distinguish where there might be rocks in the river. She reached into the satchel and pulled out the map. From the looks of it, she was still some distance from the first campsite marked on the bark, and Na'om realized she would not be able to travel that far in one day. Tz' and the other men had shared the burden of navigating the river, and here she was, trying to do it on her own. The enormity of the task ahead hit Na'om hard, and she quickly pulled the canoe to the shore.

Stepping out into the cool shallows and shadows, Na'om waited while her eyes adjusted from the bright glare of the water. The river bottom was sandy in this area, and tiny fish darted in and out of the few rocks. A grove of mango trees was nearby, and the lower branches looked strong enough to support her. She would sleep in the trees, using her blanket to ward off any mosquitoes or other biting insects. She made a ring of river rocks and set a pot of water to boil for tea. Suddenly, she had the sensation of being watched once again. She looked behind her, but could see nothing except unknown jungle stretching into the distance. Then, glancing far upstream, she just caught sight of a young boy scrambling along the opposite shoreline, hopping from one slippery rock to another, trying to keep the canoe in sight.

"To'ik!" the boy yelled. He cupped his hands and shouted again, "To'ik!"

"Stay where you are, boy," Na'om called out as the child finally reached the rocks across from her. He started to wade into the water. "Stay where you are," Na'om said again. "I'm coming to get you." Na'om jumped into the canoe and quickly paddled across the river. As she drew closer and closer to the child, she could see that he was very thin; his ribs protruded from his chest. Dirt streaked his face, and he looked as if he had been crying recently.

Na'om wedged the canoe into some rocks and stepped out of the boat. She cautiously approached the strange child of five or six. "What's your name?" she asked him as she knelt down in front of him.

The boy looked at her with wide brown eyes and mumbled, "Lintat."

"Lintat, that's a nice name. Are you hungry? Na'om said as she took out a packet of tamales from the canoe. She held one out to the boy. "Would you like to come eat this with me, over there?" she said as she pointed to her camp on the other side of the water. "I can make you some tea . . ." Na'om watched as the boy snatched the tamale and began to eat it in quick bites. She touched him on the shoulder, and he didn't flinch, so she picked him up and set him in the bow of the canoe. "Just sit still," she said as she quickly pushed off from shore and guided them back to the other side. She could see her water boiling away in the pot and ran to remove it.

The boy stepped out of the boat. Using the palm of his hand as a cup, he sipped some of the river water. His brown eyes followed Na'om's every movement.

"Come, Lintat," Na'om said as she sat down on the ground. She handed him another tamale. "You've been following me today, haven't you?" Na'om asked as she poured hot water into a gourd and added a pinch of dried herbs. The boy nodded, but refused to say anything. "Where are your mother and father? Why did you call out for help?" she asked as she settled herself more comfortably on the hard ground.

Lintat looked at the river, and Na'om saw his eyes begin to water.

"It'll be all right, you don't have to tell me," she said. "My name's Na'om. I live up the river in a small village, with my grandmother, Ajkun." She handed Lintat the gourd full of tea. "A few days ago, strange men came to our village and killed many of the people there and stole all the others away, including my ati't." Na'om saw Lintat look up at the mention of the raiders. "Now I'm going to go find them and bring them back."

Lintat set the gourd on the ground and moved closer to Na'om. He laid his head against her arm. "Strange men came to my village, too. They took my mother and father and my older sister. They killed my baby sister and several of the older men who they said were too old to be of any use." Lintat looked up at Na'om. "But I hid with my grandmother. Every day since the raiders came, Noy has sent me to the river to keep watch for someone going by. But no one ever came." The boy looked up at Na'om. "But Noy, she kept telling me to keep watch for the girl with the scarred face who would come to help us. A week ago, Noy hurt her leg, trying to chop the ground to plant the corn. Grandfather tried to heal her, but he doesn't know what to do. So every day, I've been running between the village and the river, praying to Itzamná to send someone. No one has passed until today, when I saw your canoe. But I've never seen a girl in a canoe before, so I was afraid to call out to you because Noy says there are witches who ride the river and snatch little boys to eat. But then you pulled that knife out, and I knew no witch would need a knife, so then I had to try to catch you and you kept going and going and I was afraid I wouldn't be able to reach you, but then you finally stopped and I caught up with you." Lintat let out a big sigh as the last of the words gushed out of him.

"Tomorrow, in the daylight, we'll go to your village, and I'll try and help your grandmother," Na'om said to Lintat. "But right now, I think you need to take a bath." She pulled Lintat to his feet and led him to the river. "Here," she said as she handed him a dark brown clay pot full of cinnamon-scented soap. She passed Lintat a cloth and instructed him to scrub everywhere, including behind his ears.

While the boy washed, Na'om took the extra blanket from the canoe and laid it in a crotch in the tree. They would sleep together for warmth and protection. She picked up the child's loincloth, which was filthy and torn, and scrubbed it in the river before placing it near the fire to dry. She handed Lintat her shawl to wrap around himself when he stepped from the water. In the firelight, Na'om could see his back was covered in scratches. Lintat grinned at Na'om as she led him to the tree. "Get some sleep, and tomorrow you can show me to your village," Na'om said.

The boy quickly fell asleep, but Na'om sat by the fire for several hours, watching the embers die down to a thick bed of coals. She had been gone just one day, and already her plans had changed. Instead of continuing on her trip, she would need to go back upstream to this village to try and help this sick woman who somehow knew of a girl with a scarred face. Na'om touched the streaks on her cheek and wondered if this was to be another one of her dreams coming true. She thought of the few herbs and tinctures in her pack and questioned whether she even had the right medicines with her to heal a deep wound. But she knew she had to try.

As the first rays of light struck the riverbank in front of them, Na'om and Lintat ate a quick breakfast before loading the canoe with the few supplies they had brought ashore. Na'om helped Lintat settle into the canoe, then pushed off and paddled strongly against the current, heading back upstream. Lintat sat in the bow and called to Na'om when he could see rocks appearing in front of them. Na'om handed him the spare paddle, and the boy used it to push the bow away from the boulders when it looked like they might run aground. He used the tip of the paddle to point out a stone covered in baby crocodiles, all jostling for position in the early morning light.

Within a few hours, Lintat began to recognize his surroundings and instructed Na'om to pull into a small bend in the river. She could see a well-worn dirt path leading off into the liana vines and knew she needed to be more observant in the future, so she would not be taken by surprise again. She strapped her pack basket on and handed Lintat the smaller of the two baskets, which contained her medicines. Lintat skipped ahead, leading the way to his village, calling out as he approached a small clearing.

An old man, his back hunched over from years of work, shuffled forward to greet Lintat and Naʼom. "Ah, Lintat, such a good boy," the man crooned as he patted the child on the head. "I was so worried when you didn't return from the river last night," he said as he motioned to Naʼom to sit on a stool by small fire. "I thought maybe a crocodile had eaten you." He handed Naʼom a gourd of hot water with nothing in it. "I'm sorry, we have nothing really to offer you for food," he said as he slowly bent his arthritic knees and sat down on the ground.

Naʼom looked at the man. He was too thin, the first stages of starvation evident in his sunken face and protruding ribs. She reached into her pack and pulled out the packet of tamales. There were only a few left, but she quickly handed them over, and the man split one in half before trying to hand the rest back. Naʼom shook her head no, and the man placed the package on his lap. She had to look away as he nibbled on the corners of the cornmeal like a tiny mouse. She studied the village around her. It was no wonder she had never heard of it from Tz' or Chiman. Only a handful of huts ringed the clearing, and they were all small, one-room dwellings, barely as large as Ajkun's storage room. No turkeys roamed the area, no smells of cooking came from the huts, no laughter, just an old man and a young boy.

"Lintat, where is your grandmother?" Naʼom asked as she stood up. The sooner she knew what the woman needed, the sooner she could be on her way again. Lintat led Naʼom to the closest house, and Naʼom stepped inside. Streaks of light came through the poorly thatched roof and bare pole walls. An older woman lay on a mat on the ground, covered in a dusty blanket, and for a moment Naʼom wondered if she was too late. But then the woman opened her eyes and let out a sigh.

"Lintat, is that you?" the woman asked as she struggled to raise her head. He knelt by her side and held a gourd of water to the woman's mouth, which she sipped at before lying back down.

"Noy, I found the girl to help you," Lintat said. He motioned for Na'om to come closer.

Na'om knelt down and paused as the woman reached out her hand and touched the jaguar scars on her face. "We've heard of you, the girl who talks to jaguars."

"How can that be?" Na'om asked. "I've never been here before and didn't even know this village existed."

"The river spirits speak to those who listen, and the river carries many stories on its broad back. The tale of the girl and her black feline friend is one of the greatest. They say you are *to'nel*, a witch who helps, a great healer, and for that I'm grateful, for no one here knows how to help me." The woman took a deep breath, and Na'om could see her words had tired the woman.

Na'om turned to Lintat. "Fetch me a bowl of hot water so I can wash my hands before I examine your grandmother." She took the basket of medicines from the boy and set down her own pack before washing in the basin Lintat provided. She pulled back the woman's blanket and gasped. Her lower right leg was swollen, an angry red line running from a deep gash on her ankle up the inside of her calf to just below the knee. Na'om quickly pulled out all the herbs she had with her and found the small gourd of yarrow tincture. She tilted the woman's head to her and forced her to swallow several drops of the anti-inflammatory medicine.

Using some fresh hot water, Na'om mixed in dried yarrow blossoms and made a compress of the white petals for the woman's wound. She wrapped the leg in a clean cloth and helped make the woman more comfortable on her hard spot on the floor. Na'om motioned for Lintat to follow her outside.

"There's no one else living here now?" she asked the boy as she looked at the boy's grandfather sitting by himself at the small fire in the courtyard.

"No, we're all that they left," Lintat said. "My grandfather was off in the jungle on a spirit quest the day the raiders arrived. Noy and I hid in the liana vines and watched as they took everyone away, with all our food." The little boy scuffed his foot in the dirt.

"You're not going to leave us here alone, are you?" he asked as he tipped his head up to look at Na'om.

She stared into Lintat's brown eyes. The boy was eager to help, and with some food on his thin frame, he could be strong again. "I must continue on my journey to find the rest of my village." Na'om looked at the old man again and thought of the woman inside the hut. In a few days, her wound would be healed enough so she could move. But time was vital to Na'om; every minute she delayed was another minute away from Ajkun and the others. "Come, Lintat, I have an idea." She and the boy walked to the older man and squatted on the ground near him.

Na'om addressed Lintat's grandfather. "Several hours back upstream is the village where I came from. There's plenty of food in the huts there. Do you think you could find this village and come back downstream in one of the canoes to collect your wife?" The man looked at Na'om with renewed interest. "If the three of you went there together, you'd have food and more comfortable lodgings and could wait for my return."

The man kept nodding his head while Na'om spoke. Then he said, "You must show me how to take of my wife, and when she's better, I'll go across the river."

"And what of me?" Lintat asked as he tugged on Na'om's huipil.

"You need to stay here and help your grandparents." Na'om said. "My journey is long and hazardous, and I need to move quickly." Na'om could see the disappointment on Lintat's face. "No sadness now, you'll be the man in charge of the entire village. It'll be your job to make sure all the wild animals stay out of the houses, and the place is ready for us when we return. Do you think you can do that?"

Lintat pulled himself up straight and tall. "Yes, I'm almost seven, you know."

Na'om patted him on the head and gave him a quick smile. "Good, well, I'd better be on my way again." She pulled out the packet of yarrow blossoms, and with Lintat and his grandfather, she went back inside to see Lintat's grandmother. She gave the couple instructions on tending her wounds. "When you get to my village, look for the one hut that stands alone, off to the right of the temple. It's where the medicines are stored. Find more of these blossoms and continue placing them on the wound until the infection is gone."

As soon as she was settled into the canoe, Na'om pushed off from the bank and swung out into the current. Lintat and his grandfather were there to say good-bye. "Follow the river," Na'om said to the old man. "Always keep it to your left, and within a full day's hike, you should reach the village," Na'om said.

The man nodded in silent reply and made to push Na'om farther out into the water.

"Wait!" Na'om cried and reached into the basket in front of her. She pulled out a cloth and wiped her face and arms with it. "There's one more thing you must know. My friend is living in the village as well. He's a black jaguar, and you must be kind to him. Let him know you're his friend by holding this in front of his nose." Na'om held out the cloth. "He'll recognize the scent and let you pass."

"May Itzamná be with you, my daughter," the man said as he shoved the canoe back into the water.

Na'om waved and thrust her paddle into the water. It felt good to be on the move again, heading in the right direction.

AJKUN

Ajkun sat with her hands tied in front of her in the middle of one of the twenty-five-foot dugout canoes along with her older women friends, who had similar ropes around their wrists. The younger girls were grouped together in another canoe, and the men of Pa nimá were divided into two groups in two other canoes. They were tied at the wrists and ankles and bound to each other as well. *If one of the canoes tips over, all the men inside will fall into the river together,* Ajkun thought. She looked at the short stick she'd just pulled out from her pocket. Each morning since the attack, she'd made a notch in the wood. Four days had passed with them traveling continuously north. They moved day and night, guided by the sun and the stars. The intruders took turns handling the long dugouts in the current, so some could sleep while others paddled the boats through the water. They only stopped every few hours to let the prisoners stretch their limbs and use the bushes. Food was given to them in the canoes, and they all tried to sleep when they could, but with the hot sun beating down on them during the day, the sudden bursts of heavy rain, and the mosquitoes biting them at night, it was difficult to get any rest.

On one of the stops, Ajkun had talked to one of the raiders and explained she was a healer and was allowed to apply some salve to the knife wounds the raiders each had. That had earned her a bit of respect, and since then, she'd been able to treat the men of the village as well. Their backs and shoulders were covered with lash marks from the whips, and several had bruises and knife wounds on their arms and legs. With the little medicines she had with her and a few plants she'd found along the river, Ajkun was able to take care of the worst injuries.

As her canoe was pulled into a sandy bank, she stepped into the knee-deep dark water. The current here was strong, and she felt it push her against the side of the canoe. She glanced downstream and noted a fine mist in the air. A dull roar filled her ears, and she was surprised to see the men begin to unload everything from each canoe and place it on the sandy beach.

"Why have we stopped?" she asked the man who seemed to be in charge of the whole group.

"Waterfall ahead, we have to portage," Kux replied. "You'll stay here under guard while we carry the canoes downstream, then we'll come back and get you."

"How long will that take?" Ajkun asked as she looked at the gear and the four canoes.

"Several hours, so make yourselves at home," Kux said. He grinned, and Ajkun could see two of his front teeth were missing, and the others were stained bluish-black. His short black hair was greased and spiked on the top of his head, and it sparkled in the sunlight. Tattooed blue dots spiraled down his left arm from the shoulder to his elbow.

He turned around to his men. "Let's get going; we need to set up camp at the pool by dark." Ajkun looked at his bare back, which was covered with old, raised scars.

She wandered over to the group of men where Chiman and Tz' were sitting on the damp ground. She glanced back to see if the raider cared, but he was too busy trying to lift the heavy canoe to his shoulder. She nodded at the other women, and they quickly rejoined their husbands and sons.

Ajkun sank to the ground beside Chiman. "How are you doing?" she asked. It was the first time they'd been able to talk freely since the attack. "Do you recognize where we are?"

"I do," Tz' said. "Having just made this trip only a few weeks ago, I can tell we're only a few days from the ocean. A day of travel along the coast, then a day or two across land, and we'll be in Mayapán."

"Mayapán? I thought these were Xiu raiders from Chichén Itzá," Ajkun said.

"No," replied Tz'. "That man you just talked to—I'm sure he was in the group who met us on the river. I recognize the tattoos on his arm."

"What I keep wondering is, why did they attack our village, when we'd just paid our tribute?" Chiman said.

"My guess is someone in Mayapán other than Yakal knows about Na'om and her special abilities," Tz' replied.

"What makes you think that?" Ajkun said.

"I've been watching how these raiders treat Mok'onel and the other girls; they definitely are afraid of them," Tz' said.

Chiman rubbed at the rope on his ankle where it chaffed his skin. "Yakal sent Na'om a letter," he said. "What did it say?"

Ajkun poked at the sand with a stick. "I don't know; I never had a chance to read it."

The three fell silent, and Ajkun thought of Na'om all alone in the village. She hoped her granddaughter was safe, and that she remained in the village with Ek' Balam. "Is there any way to escape?" she asked as she pulled a small jar of salve out of her pocket. She rubbed a tiny bit on the men's wrists and ankles, red from the rough, wet hemp cord tied so tightly around their limbs.

"I don't think we need to," Chiman said. "If they take us to Mayapán, then we'll demand to be released. Lady Satal will set us free the minute she hears the news."

"I pity these men when she finds out her daughter was killed," Ajkun said. "From everything I've heard about this Lady Satal, she is a mean old woman." She touched Chiman on the arm. "I'm sorry about Chachal; you've lost a wife, and the village has lost a fine person."

"More than one person is gone, I'm afraid," Chiman said. "I just wish we'd been allowed to do a proper burial for them all." He brushed a strand of hair out of his face. "By the time we get back, who knows what will have happened to the bodies."

"I suspect Naom will do what she can," Tz' said. "She's more resourceful than anyone gives her credit."

The three stopped talking again when they saw the raiders come back for another set of canoes and gear.

Chiman shook his head. "This whole business still makes no sense to me."

"We must trust that Itzamná and the other gods know what they're doing," Ajkun said. "Our fate, as always, is in their hands." She gave Chiman another pat on the arm.

She held out the little jar of salve to Tz'. "How's your other wound?"

"The piercing, oh, it hurt like wild bees had stung me for the first few days," he said as he motioned for Ajkun to put the jar away. "But I think I'm over the worst of it now," he replied. "I just wish we could do something other than be dragged along like prisoners, but there's too many of them, and they have all the weapons." He picked up a stick and scraped it across his skin. It picked up tiny amounts of the yellow clay he'd been covered in on the day of the attack, and he then broke the stick into tiny pieces, which he piled on the sand. They glittered in the light. Then he did the same with another stick. "I keep leaving little piles of twigs, so that if anyone follows, they might know we were here."

Chiman laughed. "I wondered why you'd been doing that all this time. I thought you were just trying to get clean!"

As the afternoon wore on, the groups settled down and took naps. All too soon, though, they were roused by the invaders and forced to march single-file along a narrow and slippery path that wound downhill through the trees. The roar of the waterfall to their right blocked any chance of conversation, and Ajkun was glad when they reached the bottom of the steep cliff. Her arthritic knee ached from the long hike. She could see the river water as it dropped sixty feet over a series of rocks and boulders to a large clear pool. Several of the raiders were casting three-foot-wide circular nets into the water, and she saw one quickly pull in a large fish.

Blankets had been laid on the ground near a large bonfire, and the villagers were herded together near the flames.

"We'll feast on fresh fish and get a decent night's sleep before we continue our journey," the leader said. "We want you to be in good condition when we arrive at the slave market!" His men laughed and held up gourds of balché. "To wealth and prosperity," Kux toasted. "And to poor Ilonel, who's no longer with us," he added as he took a long swig of the fermented juice.

Ajkun refused the gourd when it was held to her lips, and she received a smack across the top of her head. She shook her head to stop the ringing in her ear. Despite the stinging pain, she wouldn't drink with these men, no matter what the cost.

NA'OM

Na'om settled into a rhythm of paddling the canoe, but every two hours or so, she pulled into the shady riverbank so she could stretch her tired limbs. She wandered up and down the rocks and sandy banks, looking for tracks and searching for any food that might be growing near the water. As the day wore on and the shadows crossed from one side of the river to the other, Na'om thought less and less about anything except the task of keeping the canoe moving forward. The only sound was the dip and splash of her paddle in the water and the swish of the river as it passed under the hull. The waterway was swollen with the summer rains, and the current was much stronger than on the day she had left Pa nimá.

Na'om worried about her grandmother and the others; the raiders had four days head start, and she knew she wasn't able to travel as far each day as those men, so every day that passed placed her farther and farther behind.

When the shadows made it hard to tell rocks from river, Na'om wedged the canoe onto shore for the night. She built a small fire and boiled water for tea before placing the blankets in a tree. It was a tight fit, but Na'om felt better sleeping above ground than falling prey to any wandering animals that might pass the spot in the night. Within minutes, she was fast asleep.

The days blurred together as she wound her way downstream. Sometimes she thought someone might be following her, but never saw anyone on the water. Twice she stopped at villages marked on the map, only to find most of the people missing. They had been stolen over the past several weeks by men dressed like the raiders who had attacked Pa nimá. The remaining residents told Naʼom of the rumors that the Xiu from Chichén Itzá needed more slaves to build parts of their city and humans to sacrifice to the rain god, Chac; they feared for their neighbors and families. Naʼom, worried about her grandmother and Tzʼ, pushed steadily onward.

One night it rained heavily, and Naʼom climbed into the limbs of a jacaranda tree to try and find some protection from the storm. But the feathery leaves were no match for the downpour. She spent a sleepless night curled in her blankets, Ajkunʼs worn leather satchel clutched to her middle to keep the map and other contents dry. By daylight, she was soaked through. Everything in her pack baskets was wet, including much of her remaining food. She spent a couple of hours trying to start a fire to dry things out, but eventually gave up, dipped the water from the bottom of the canoe, and continued on her journey.

The river gurgled, hissed, and pushed up onto the riverbanks on either side. The water flowed rapidly underneath the boatʼs hull; Naʼom hardly needed to paddle and spent several hours just steering the canoe to avoid what rocks she could see. At one point, she passed a huge mahogany tree whose trunk leaned far out over the waterway. It was so low that Naʼom had to duck as she passed underneath it to avoid some of the branches that stuck down into the river.

As the waterway twisted and turned, a dull roar filled Naʼomʼs ears, and she tried to stop, so she could look at the map. But the water was deep and swift, and she couldnʼt lodge the bow of the boat onto land. The canoe bumped off hidden rocks and spun sideways, tipping to one side, and water swamped the boat. Naʼom grabbed the satchel before it went overboard and threw the strap over her shoulder and across her chest. One pack basket tipped over, and some of her remaining food rolled out into the boat.

She clutched the gunwales as the dugout rocked in the turbulence, and she leaned heavily to the opposite side to right the canoe.

The current caught the underside of the vessel and flipped it over, sending Naʼom into the raging water. She instantly went under, where the flow of the river pulled at her legs, and she kicked and flailed with her arms to reach the surface. Her head broke above the torrent, and she gulped air as she was swirled about by the steady pull of the flooding river. She fought against the undercurrent and managed to crawl up onto the riverbank, where she lay chest down for several minutes to catch her breath.

Naʼom sat up and pulled her legs far above the water. One sandal was missing, the other hung by a broken strap, and she had a large scrape down her right shin, which was bleeding. She searched the river for her canoe, but there was no sign of it. Both her baskets were missing, too. She pulled off the broken sandal and threw it into the brush where it was caught by the broken strap. It dangled from a branch, water dripping from the toe to the wet ground below.

Tears mingled with the water dripping off her wet hair, making muddy rivulets down her face. Her skirt was torn at the hem, and Naʼom reached down, pulled at the rip, and managed to tear off a piece of the blue fabric, which she held against her shin. She winced at the stinging pain.

"Itzamná," she cried. "What do I do now?" The roar of the river filled her head with noise. She rubbed the necklace, which still hung from her neck, and heard Tuʼjanel speak in her head.

Follow the map, her mother said.

"How? I have no canoe, no food, nothing," Naʼom wailed. "It's a wonder I'm still alive."

Silence was her only reply.

"Follow the map, follow the map, some help that is," Naʼom muttered as she opened the wet satchel. By the grace of all the gods, the beeswax bag had managed to keep most of the map dry, and by looking closely at the markings, Naʼom was able to find where she was. "There's the big fallen tree I passed a while back and . . ." She looked at the hole in the page where the bark had torn when she'd ripped it from Chiman's ledger. On the next page, the map showed the river continuing north and east, widening as it approached the ocean and flowed into a large bay along the coastline. A dotted line extended from a point along the shore inland to a pyramid marked on the paper. "That must be Mayapán," Na'om said. She traced her finger diagonally from the hole in the bark to the pyramid. "Looks like if I go across the land rather than attempt to follow the river, I might reach the city quicker." She put the map away and gently pulled the fabric away from her shin. The bleeding had stopped, but much of the surface area along the bone was raw.

Slowly, she stood up and put her weight on that foot; there wasn't much pain so she shouldered the satchel and headed along the riverbank. The rumble of the water grew louder and louder, a heavy mist hung in the air, and the rocks were slimy with black mold, making it difficult to continue. Na'om gasped when she saw the river disappear from view. Cutting inland, Na'om pushed through the dense underbrush and caught a glimpse of the river through the trees as it fell sixty feet or so to a large pool below.

Lucky I fell out when I did, she thought as she pressed onward. Holding onto tree branches and small ferns and vines, she scrambled and slid her way down the rocky, muddy cliff until she was at the bottom of the waterfall. She watched as the water fell in a pounding torrent over the edge and dropped into the frothing, white pool of water. Looking downstream, she caught sight of her canoe. Smashed against the rocks on the far side of the river, it was obvious the boat would never float again. There was no sign of either of her baskets.

The trees on the opposite side were farther away from the riverbank, and Na'om was able to see a ring of stones someone had built in the center of the clearing. *I wonder if Tz' and the others camped there one night,* Na'om thought, and the idea made her throat tighten with pain.

Worn out and still in wet clothes, Na'om moved far enough downstream to be away from the waterfall's spray. She built a small fire and stood naked by the flames while she dried her dirty clothes on branches stuck into the soft ground. She looked around for something to eat, but couldn't find any plants she recognized. She drank water to fill her empty belly and knew she'd need to find some food soon if she was to continue on her journey.

As night fell, she piled more branches onto the fire. Without her blankets, the air was cold, and she fell into a restless sleep on the hard ground. Every few hours, she woke up shivering and added more wood before lying down again in the little hollow her body had formed in the dirt. She shifted and wiggled around, trying to get comfortable and finally settled on her back. Through a hole in the tree canopy, Na'om could see the stars and thought of the nights when Tz' was in training and had taught her to read the night sky, how they'd searched for the North Star, then Venus, then the constellations. She fell asleep again dreaming of her friend.

Only an hour or so had passed when Na'om woke with a start. It was pitch black, the stars now obscured by clouds. Something was rummaging around the area, and Na'om cursed that the fire had died down so she couldn't really see. She didn't dare move, afraid that whatever large animal was rooting near the river would turn on her. She lay as still as possible.

Suddenly, she felt a warm tongue slide along her shin. She shrieked and jerked her leg back, the sound of her cry echoing in the blackness. She grabbed a stick, and swung it out into the darkness. The air was empty around her.

Gathering courage, she sucked in her breath and let out a fierce growl, hoping the animal would be frightened of her jaguar-like sounds. The clouds parted just for a second, and in the dim moonlight, Na'om caught a glimpse of a familiar black shape lying on the ground a few feet away.

"Ek' Balam?" she cried. She scrabbled toward the animal, her desire to see her old friend overcoming her fears. A deep purring filled the air. "Ek' Balam!" Na'om exclaimed as she knelt by her animal friend and hugged his head in her arms. "How in the name of Itzamná did you get here?" She looked at him and noticed his normal glossy coat was dirty and full of burrs and tiny twigs. "I told you to stay in the village," she said. "Oh, how I've missed you, you silly old cat."

Na'om quickly rebuilt the fire into a blaze and sat beside the jaguar, her body leaning into his stomach. The tip of his tail twitched on the ground, and she rubbed him behind the ear, in the tiny spot that he liked so much. His purring filled the air. "What am I going to do with you?" Na'om said. "You can't keep following me."

She turned and gripped the cat in the soft skin between his shoulders. The big head went limp in her hands. Na'om peered into Ek' Balam's eyes. "You have to go back, you hear me?" But just the thought of saying good-bye to her best friend yet again made Na'om's eyes fill with tears. "I told you to stay in the village," she said. "You have to go back."

Ek' Balam just flicked his tail in reply.

The next morning, Na'om drifted in and out of sleep. It was pleasant to just look at the blue sky and listen to the occasional squawk of a parrot while leaning against Ek' Balam's warm body. Soon, she'd need to go visit Ajkun and help her prepare some salves . . . Na'om sat up with a start. She wasn't at home; there was no village nearby. Ek' Balam raised his head as she stood up and left his side. Na'om watched the river flow by while tears slipped down her face. *If I ever reach Mayapán, will my father even bother to help me?* she wondered. She stroked her mother's necklace, hoping she'd hear something, but it was quiet. The only noises were the sound of the river slipping by and the continuous drone in her ears, which Na'om was so used to hearing, she almost didn't hear it.

Ek' Balam lay by the small fire, licking his wound area, and Na'om knelt by the cat. The spot had healed quite a bit, but needed more salve. "I need to get going," she said to the jaguar. At the sound of her voice, the cat got to his feet and stood waiting. "Go on home, boy," Na'om said. She pushed him on the rump. "Shoo, go on now."

Ek' Balam just looked at her and swished his tail from side to side.

Na'om sighed. "Well, I can't leave you here, so come on," Na'om said. She started to walk, and he fell in step behind her.

"At least I don't have to talk to myself anymore," Na'om said. Just having a companion made her feel better, and as the sun rose in the sky, things didn't seem as bad as they had the night before.

Without warning, Ek' Balam darted into the bushes and disappeared. Na'om heard a squeak and then silence. The cat came back to where she stood by the water, licking his lips. "Found something to eat, did you?" Na'om said and patted the cat on the head. The thought of food made her stomach grumble, and she scooped up more water to fill the emptiness.

Several hours passed, and Na'om sat down to look at the map. "We'd better head inland now, away from the river," she said to Ek' Balam, who stopped licking his paws to look at her. "I wish I had some water gourds with me, but there's bound to be water someplace," she said.

She swayed on her feet as she stood up; the world turned gray, and she bent down quickly to let the dizziness pass. "Need some food," she mumbled as she spotted a large tree several hundred yards away and headed in its direction. By placing the sun over her left shoulder, Na'om continued to move northeast, away from the river, and deeper into the interior of the jungle around her.

SATAL

When Satal opened the heavy wooden door to her front room, the bar owner had his fist raised, ready to pound on it once again. "You," Satal said. "What do you want?" She looked around the courtyard to see if anyone else stood nearby. It wouldn't do to have her neighbors see Q'abarel standing at her house. Satisfied that they were alone, she motioned for the man to step indoors.

"Sorry to disturb you, my lady," Q'abarel said. "But you wanted to know when Ilonel returned, so I came at once."

"Ilonel? I thought he was dead," Satal said half to herself.

"Dead? I don't know about that, but even as we speak, his men are in the bar boasting of the new slaves they just delivered to the market. I thought you'd want to know."

"And Ilonel? Did you see him?" Satal said as she looked into the barman's face.

"No, but I doubt he'll be away for long. Probably just making arrangements with the market owners as to when these new slaves will go up for sale." Q'abarel shuffled his worn leather sandals on the floor. "The bar is quite busy, my lady, I need to get back. Only the girl is tending to it all, and she's so easily swayed to give out free drinks . . . All my profits are being given away."

Satal sighed and reached into her pocket. "Here," she said as she placed an old, dried up cacao bean in Q'abarel's hand. "That should more than adequately pay for your trouble." She opened the door, checked the area again, and practically pushed the man outside. "Don't bother to come back; I have the information I need," she said as she shut the door in his face.

If she'd been a young woman, Satal might have skipped down the hallway to her bedroom. She grinned at Sachoj. "New slaves at the market; I'm off to see which one of them is our girl." She quickly pulled her shawl from its peg on the wall and wrapped it around her head and shoulders. She tucked a bag of cacao beans into her skirt and hurried outside.

The slave market was outside the city walls, and Satal slipped through the busy southern gates along with several others. The people in front of her turned off to the manioc fields, and Satal walked by herself the short distance to the hallway and open arena where the slaves were auctioned off. A few men with whips patrolled the perimeter of the main building where the slaves were housed, and as she approached, she could hear angry voices coming from inside the large room used as an office.

"These people are under the city's protection," a man said. "They are not slaves, never were and never will be. I demand you let them go at once."

Satal crept up to the side of the building and continued to listen just outside the door.

"I just paid good cacao beans to Ilonel's men as a deposit for these people," another, deeper voice said. Satal recognized it as belonging to Tarnel, the owner of the market. "How am I going to recoup my losses if you just take them all?"

"That's your problem, not mine. Perhaps you should pay more attention to your business partners. Now, unlock the barricades, and let all of them go, or I'll bring the city guards in here. I'm sure we'll find more than a few infractions to cite you on."

Satal hurried away from the building as she heard footsteps approaching the door. She gasped when she saw who had spoken. Yakal. Satal needed to act and quickly.

"Yakal, oh, I'm so glad you're here," Satal said as she hurried up to his side.

"Lady Satal, what are you doing here?" Yakal said. He looked around the area. "How did you hear the news?"

"Why, Masat, of course," Satal lied rapidly. "The dear girl knew I'd want to know." *Stay calm,* Satal heard Sachoj say in her head. *Just play along and see what happens.*

By now, Tarnel had stepped outside and looked from Yakal to Satal and back.

"Look who's arrived, Tarnel, now do you doubt my authority?" Yakal said. "Surely you'll not argue with the city's lead council member." He pointed in the direction of the pen and motioned for Tarnel to open the locked doors.

Satal could hear multiple voices from inside the building. *Who in the name of Itzamná is inside,* she wondered. She gulped when the first man pushed through the doorway into the bright sunlight. Although much older, she instantly recognized Chiman with his dark blue jaguar tattoos underneath the layer of dust on his skin. She searched the group for Chachal, but didn't see her daughter.

"Chiman, what are you doing here?" Satal said as she hurried up to him. "Where's Chachal?" She looked around the gathering of villagers and noticed Yakal was talking to an older woman and a young man. Several young girls stood with the women, many were crying, and the men had their arms around them protectively. She wondered which one of the girls was her jaguar-girl.

"My lady Satal, by all the gods, it's good to see you," Chiman said as he briefly hugged the woman. "I thought this nightmare would never end."

"I don't understand; what are you doing here?" Satal said as she pointed to the slave arena.

"A little over a week ago, the village was attacked," Chiman said. "Some were killed, and the rest of us were taken prisoner. We've been on the move ever since and were just brought here last night under cover of darkness. Itzamná knows what would have happened to us all if Yakal hadn't come to set us free." He looked at the older woman. "What are you doing here?" he asked.

"Why, I . . . I heard about your arrival and came as soon as I could," Satal lied. "I had to make sure these men did you no harm." She looked around the group again. "But where's my daughter, where's Chachal?"

Chiman looked at the ground. "My lady, I'm afraid she was killed in the attack."

"What? That's not possible," Satal said. She looked at Chiman and then back at the group. "I don't understand." Suddenly, the enormity of the situation hit her. Thanks to the stupidity of the men she'd hired to find the jaguar-girl of the Wayeb, Chachal was dead. Satal groaned and felt anger pulse through her body. In her mind, she heard Sachoj hiss and spit in the quiet space of the bedroom.

Chiman placed his hand on her arm. "Lady Satal, are you all right?"

"I'm fine," she replied as she shrugged off his touch. "I want to know all the details of this attack." She turned to Yakal. "You will find the men who did this and report to the council as soon as you have information."

"As you wish my lady," Yakal said before turning back to Ajkun and Tz'.

"Chiman, walk me back to my palace and fill me in on this attack," Satal demanded.

Once back in her own home, Satal wandered down the hallway and looked into Chachal's old room. Emptiness filled the space, and she felt a few tears slip down her lined face, which she hastily brushed away. She sank down into the hammock still hanging from the walls. She'd never see her daughter again. They had never been that close, especially after Chachal had seen her shape-shift into a wasp so many years ago, but Satal sometimes thought she had loved Chachal and that Chachal had loved her in return. She rocked back and forth in the dusty webbing of the hammock and looked at the cracked stucco ceiling high above her. *I should get someone in here to fix that,* she thought. *Oh, why bother? Now that Chachal is gone, there's no one to inherit this house.*

Not true, she heard Sachoj say. *There's your grandson, Tz'.*

Then she heard Sachoj laugh, and the sound echoed in the empty bedroom down the hall and drifted into the chamber where Satal still sat in the hammock, her feet barely touching the tiled floor.

"What's so funny, old woman?" Satal said as she stood up and slowly made her way to her own bedroom. She stopped in front of the shrunken head and peered at her great-grandmother's dusty head.

Your grandson is the spitting image of Alaxel, Chachal's old lover from Chichén Itzá, Sachoj said. *I'm surprised that fool of a shaman, Chiman, thinks the boy is his.*

"That doesn't matter now. The important thing is to find the girl and extract retribution," Satal said as she slipped her sandals on her feet.

Where are you going? Sachoj asked.

"Back to the bar. I need to talk to Ilonel's men and find out what happened, why they brought Chiman and the others here, and tell them they need to find the girl."

Satal hurried through the crowded streets to the Silowik Tukan. Q'abarel was behind the counter and motioned with his hand toward the back. Satal pushed past the men lounging near the doorway and entered the back room. Most of the booths had their curtains drawn, but steady whispers and occasional laughter filtered through the thin sheets of fabric. Satal marched on her short legs to Ilonel's favorite spot and found one of his men inside, lounging against the wall, a mug of balché in his hand.

"Why Lady Satal, what an honor," Kux said as he stood up, spilling some of his drink on his bare chest in the process. He wiped the sticky drops away with his hand.

"Tell me what happened, why did you go to Pa nimá?" Satal demanded as she plopped down on the slightly sticky bench opposite Kux. "And why were you so stupid as to bring the prisoners here! Didn't you realize people would recognize them? You should have taken the whole lot to the slave market in Chichén Itzá where they really need slaves these days."

Kux took a quick look down the short hallway, drew the curtain, and leaned in toward Satal. "Calm down, my lady, let me try and explain. With me being in the regiment, Ilonel, may he rest easily in the Underworld, contacted me and told me to keep an ear open when the group headed by Nimal met the villagers bringing tribute from up and down the river. At the meeting place, I overheard Yakal speaking to a youth about a young girl with special powers from the village of Pa nimá. I told Ilonel what I had overheard, and he said that's where we needed to go."

"My orders to Ilonel were to find the girl, not bring back several canoe loads of people to the slavers. Not only did you fail in the task, but you killed my daughter in the process!" She stared into Kux's deep brown eyes and watched him fidget on his seat.

"My lady, we didn't expect the villagers to fight back, but they did. I had no idea your daughter lived there," Kux said as he picked at a bubble of green glaze on the side of his almost empty mug. "Things just got carried away, and several people were killed, including Ilonel, poor man."

"Oh please, save your breath, we both know there was no love between you. For all I know, you could have killed Ilonel yourself to get his share of the profits after selling the slaves." Satal poked Kux in the chest with her index finger. "Ilonel made a bargain with me. Now that he's dead, I expect you to finish the deal. You and your men will patrol the land to the south of Mayapán, searching for this girl and her pet jaguar. When you find them, you'll bring the both of them directly to me."

"Itzamná, a pet jaguar, Ilonel never mentioned anything about a cat!" Kux said. "By all the gods, how am I supposed to transport something like that and not raise suspicion? And suppose I do find this girl, what's in it for me?" Kux asked as he drained the last drops of fermented juice from his mug. "Now that our slaves have been released without any further payment, why should I bother to search for this girl?"

"Because if you don't, I'll tell the council you and your men were behind the attack on Yakal, Nimal, and the others. I've already told Yakal to find the spy who leaked the information. It would be a simple matter to bring you before the city leaders and have you made a slave for your treason against the city."

"But, Lady Satal, you have no proof. I could just as easily say you hired me to do this work." The man picked up his cup, looked at the emptiness, and put it back down.

Satal stared at the man in front of her. "Don't think I don't know who you are, where you live, or what you do, Kux. It would be a pleasure to mention to your wife where you spend your days," Satal paused and motioned to the walls around them, "and who shares your hammock at night when you claim to be off working. The barmaid here can easily be paid to tell the truth about your activities. Trust me; you don't want to make me cross." Satal looked at the man's lined face and detected a slight twitch near his left eye.

Kux flexed his left hand around his empty mug, and Satal noticed the way the spiral of dark blue spots tattooed into the skin rippled as he moved his bicep.

"By all the gods, you are a hard-hearted woman," Kux said. "I warned Ilonel not to get involved with you. And now I have to clean up his mess." He pulled back the curtain and snapped his fingers at the slave girl standing near the doorway. The girl hurried down the aisle.

"Another balché," he said. "I'll pay at the end of the night." The girl didn't move. "What? You don't trust me?" Kux said. He reached under the table and pulled out a small pouch. He loosened the drawstring, reached in with his fingers, and pulled out a bead. "Tell Q'abarel I can pay for barrels of this swill." The girl hurried away.

Satal reached across the sticky table and snatched the bead from Kux's open palm. "Where did you get this?" she demanded as she held the blue-green jadeite up to the light.

"I found it on the ground in Pa nimá, along with some others," Kux said as he quickly flexed his fingers, motioning for Satal to return the bead. "Why?"

"Let me see the others," Satal said.

Kux opened the pouch and dumped the contents onto the tabletop. The four carved beads rolled to a stop, and Satal picked each one up carefully, eyeing it closely before setting it back down. Suddenly, she scooped the group of them up in her hand, clutching them in her fist.

"Wait, what are you doing?" Kux said. "I need those to pay my bills!"

"These beads belonged to a necklace that I gave my daughter when she left here many years ago. When you bring me the jaguar and the girl, I'll pay you, but these belong to me." Satal stood up and pushed back the curtain. "I'll settle your bill with Q'abarel on the way out, so you can go straight home and pack for your journey." She didn't wait for Kux to move, but headed back to the front of the bar.

Na'om

As Na'om continued to walk northward away from the river, the air grew hotter and drier. Na'om noticed the trees were shorter, and several were types she had never seen before, more like thorn-covered bushes than actual trees. The landscape was flat, the ground a dusty white, not the lush duff of the jungle she had grown up with. None of the plants and grasses that clung to the rocky soil was familiar to her, and Na'om wondered if it had been a mistake to leave the river.

"Perhaps we should go back," she said to the cat behind her. "It's all so strange and dry and hot, so very hot. With nothing to eat, I'm not sure how much farther I can go."

Despondent, Na'om sank down in the dirt underneath one of the scrubby bushes. It offered little protection from the sun directly overhead. Ek' Balam paced around for a minute and then lay down, his tail switching from side to side, his head tilted at a slight angle. He began to lick his wound, but stopped and turned his head to the left. Na'om watched as he sprang to his feet and sprinted into the waist-high grass. She could hear rustling, scrabbling, grunting, then a long squeal, and thought, *Well, at least one of us can eat.*

A few minutes later, Ek' Balam returned. A fifteen-inch-long black iguana was firmly grasped between his jaws. He dropped the animal at Na'om's feet. Na'om grinned and patted the cat on the head. "Good boy, Ek' Balam, good boy, we'll both have a bite now." Na'om wasted no time in gutting the animal with her knife and quickly had a small fire made out of dry brush and tightly twisted grasses. She cut off strips of the meat, skewered them on branches, and placed the branches near the flames. The smell of roasting meat quickly filled the air.

Too hungry to wait, Na'om ate the first piece while the blood still ran red. She licked the stick and forced herself to postpone eating the next piece until the meat was fully cooked. She gave the head, guts, and tail to Ek' Balam who wasted no time in gulping down the raw flesh. He sat and groomed his face while Na'om ate the charred meat until her stomach hurt. She threw the last few pieces to Ek' Balam who swallowed them whole.

When they'd finished eating, she scraped together handfuls of the rough soil with her bare hands and threw it onto the fire, smothering the flames. "The last thing we need is to set these grasses on fire," Na'om said as she leaned against Ek' Balam. "Let's rest awhile, let the food settle and the sun drop a bit in the sky, and then we'll go on."

The sun had almost set when Na'om woke up. She scrabbled to her feet, dusted off her clothes, nodded to Ek' Balam, and the two continued on their way. The meat had given Na'om new strength, and as the stars came out overhead, she realized she could use the heavens as her guide. "We'll walk through the night and sleep during the heat of the day," she said and patted the cat on the head.

The patches of dry grasses and sedges were dense, and their sharp edges scratched Na'om's arms and legs as she pushed through them, but she ignored the pain, too focused on keeping her sights lined up with the stars overhead. After several hours, though, she was too tired to continue and curled up on the ground against Ek' Balam's warm body.

As she slept, she dreamt. She was in a large room. A hammock, wooden cupboard, and small table were the only pieces of furniture. The black wasp was hovering in the doorway, larger and fiercer than ever. It circled around her, zooming in to sting, time and time again. Na'om swung at the giant insect with her arms, which quickly were covered with welts that oozed black pus. Finally, Na'om reached into her satchel and pulled out the large green obsidian knife. She stood with her back against the wall, waited for the wasp to strike again, and when it drew near, she shoved the knife into its breast just as the wasp stabbed her yet again with its stinger.

Na'om woke up with a start. The predawn air was cool, and she curled more tightly against the cat by her side. But sleep evaded her. The thought of the wasp burned behind her eyes every time she closed them, and she shivered. She looked at her arms in the dim light and noticed the crisscrossed scratches were red and inflamed. "No wonder I dreamt I was being stabbed," she said to Ek' Balam.

Wearily she got to her feet and brushed the dirt from her clothes. Tiny rips and tears were visible in the fabric of her blue skirt, and a long thread had snagged and pulled from the shoulder of her shirt. She cut the dangling string and tossed it into the brush. Her scraped shin was sore, and she wished she had just one tiny pot of salve to use on her cuts. She looked around the scrubby brush, determined to find something that might help her. The dried grasses stretched in all directions, punctuated by clumps of chaparral bushes, spiny acacias, and numerous ceiba trees whose trunks and branches were covered with thorns. Not knowing which plant might help, Na'om chose the chaparral bushes over the others as it didn't have any spines. She pulled off some of the leaves and placed them on a flat stone, then used the back of her knife to pound the leaves into a pulp. An acrid smell filled the air as the plant fibers broke down, and she debated about whether to use the leaves at all. But she scooped up the mush and rubbed the oily mixture on her arms and leg. The smelly poultice soothed the pain, but stained her skin a grayish yellow.

As the daylight grew brighter, Na'om decided to push forward, hoping to get several hours walking in before the afternoon heat forced her to stop. She looked at her feline friend. "Ready?" she asked. In response, Ek' Balam stood up, the tip of his tail twitching ever so slightly.

The hours passed slowly, with Na'om moving ever northward. The ground remained flat, the trees and shrubs the same, and Na'om began to wonder if she was moving at all, as each step felt like the last, each clump of sedge or ceiba bushes looked the same. There was nothing to distinguish this patch of savanna from the one she had wandered through at daybreak. She saw no signs of people or animals, and as the heat of the day pressed down on her, her thirst grew and grew, until her mouth was dry and her vision blurred. She sat down in the semi-shade of a small acacia tree, closed her eyes, and dozed, only partially aware that Ek' Balam paced the ground in front of her before he flopped down in the dusty dirt to rest his big head on his paws. Na'om's head pounded, the steady buzzing in her ears intensified, and she drifted in and out of consciousness.

In her dream state, she heard soft voices, which she ignored, but Ek' Balam's low warning growl jerked Na'om awake. She opened her eyes and noticed several young men standing in a semicircle around her. They carried spears, bows, and arrows, all of which were trained on Ek' Balam, who crouched on the ground in front of her. His tail slashed the dirt from side to side, and he emitted a steady rumble from deep in his throat. Na'om scrabbled to her feet, her back still pressed against the acacia tree, and she grimaced as she felt a spine poke her in the buttock.

"Who are you, what do you want?" she cried. She reached toward the satchel still slung around her shoulder.

"Don't move," one of the older men ordered. He flicked his hand at one of his friends who had an arrow cocked and ready to fly. The arrow zipped through the air, hitting Ek' Balam squarely in his front shoulder. The cat instantly dropped to the ground. Then the man reached forward, tugged the satchel from Na'om's chest, and with one hand, slipped the leather strap across his own body.

"What have you done?" Na'om croaked as she rushed to the jaguar's side. She placed her head against Ek' Balam's chest and could hear a steady heartbeat. She looked at the strangers, one of whom still had his bow and arrow aimed at her.

"He's just been drugged, don't worry, we don't mean him any harm." The man in charge motioned to his friends who quickly cut some sturdy branches from the nearby ceiba tree. They whacked off the spines with their knives and laid the branches on the ground. The older man cautiously approached Ek' Balam, poked him with his foot, and when the cat didn't respond, swiftly tied his front paws together and then his back paws. He arranged the two poles on the ground, spread a blanket across them, and lashed the four corners of the heavy cloth to the poles. Then he and his friends gently rolled the drugged jaguar into the blanket.

"Stop!" Na'om tried to shout. Her voice came out cracked. She swallowed hard, forcing the tiny bit of saliva in her mouth down her throat. "What are you doing? Who are you?" she demanded as she grabbed the man closest to her by his tattooed arm.

"Silence!" the man said. "You'll only speak when we tell you to." He took another piece of rope and tossed it to one of his friends, who yanked Na'om's arms behind her back and secured the hemp around her wrists.

He nodded, and four of the men hefted the poles with the heavy cat draped between them. The blanket was too short, and Ek' Balam's big head almost dragged on the ground.

The leader poked Na'om in the back with his bow tip. "Move," he said as the group of six began to wind their way through the thick brush.

Ignoring his command not to talk, Na'om stood her ground. "I need water," she said, eyeing the gourds each man carried across his chest. "And so does my cat," she added.

Impatiently, the man grabbed his gourd, pulled the stopper, and let the warm liquid drip into Na'om's mouth. She swallowed several big gulps and felt the moisture soaking into her dry body, parched from the constant heat. "Now him," she said and nodded toward the jaguar.

"He'll have to wait," the man said and prodded Na'om again. "Now move."

"Where are you taking us?" Na'om said as she stumbled along behind the group of men in the rapidly fading light.

"To someone in Mayapán, now move! No more questions!" the man said.

Na'om stopped talking and studied the men around her. They were all in their late teens or early twenties. Many had tattoos on their bodies; the leader's left arm had a series of blue dots inked on it that reached from his shoulder to his elbow. Each man had his black hair greased into short spikes on top of his head. They wore simple loincloths and leather sandals, and each carried his own water and weapon.

Several hours passed as they meandered along narrow footpaths that looked unused except by the occasional animal. The men followed the night sky with its waxing gibbous moon, pausing only to drink more water from time to time.

As they rounded yet another clump of tall sedges, Na'om stopped in amazement. In the bright moonlight, she could see a five-foot-high causeway in front of them, stretching in two directions as far as Na'om could see in the dark. Built from the surrounding rocks and covered in smooth, white limestone cement, the walkway was fifteen feet across. Two of the men pulled themselves up onto the pavement and then leaned down to extend hands to help the others. The stones were cool and smooth under Na'om's bare feet, and she was glad to get off the rough ground they'd been walking on before.

She shuffled along in the blackness with the others, staying far away from the edge of the causeway, as she didn't want to trip and pitch off the side. After another hour or more, Na'om saw flickering lights in the distance, and she kept watching them as they grew from tiny dots of light into lit torches lining the walls of a great city directly ahead of them. Men carrying bows with quivers of arrows slung across their backs patrolled in front of a pair of vaulted gates. Naʾom slowed her steps and just caught a glimpse of a huge open space inside the gates before the leader turned and saw her.

"Keep moving," he said. He pushed Naʾom in front of him, and they continued a short distance to a series of buildings and a fenced-in arena. There were several wooden cages and pens off to one side of the area. The guard stopped her in front of one cage, and she listened as the men talked among themselves.

"But I thought you said we were to take her directly to Lady Satal," one man said to the leader as he eyed Naʾom.

"Do you want to be the one to wake Satal at this hour of the night?" the leader said. "No, we'll lock the two of them up here and send a slave boy with the news at first light. Lady Satal has waited this long; she can wait another few hours."

The men pushed Naʾom into a cage and bolted it. She watched through the bars of her prison as they rolled her still-drugged jaguar into a separate cage and then reached through the wooden sticks to cut the ropes wrapped around his paws.

"Can you at least give him some water?" she asked, nodding toward Ek' Balam.

The youngest of the group found an old pot, poured the remaining water from his gourd into it, and set the dish inside the cage. He double-checked the log blocking the doorway before hurrying off to catch up with the others. The leader spoke to the group and then stepped inside the largest building. Naʾom saw a man sitting at a wooden desk before the rough wooden door was closed.

Although exhausted, Naʾom couldn't sleep. She walked over to the edge of her cage and knelt down by Ek' Balam, who was beginning to stir in the other pen. "Hey boy," she said as he rolled onto his chest.

Ek' Balam swung his big head in the direction of Naòm's voice. He blinked a couple of times, got unsteadily to his feet, and paced to the small bowl of water, which he drank without stopping until the vessel was dry.

"Hey boy, come here," Naòm said as she stretched her hand between the wooden slats toward the cat.

Ek' Balam swiped his tongue across his mouth, looked again at Naòm, and then crossed to the far side of his cage. He lay down with his back to her and placed his heavy head on his paws.

"I don't blame you," Naòm said as she returned to the far side of her own enclosure. "It's a fine mess I've gotten us into." The air was humid, and within minutes, large drops of rain plunked on the thatching above her head, a few at first, and then the storm gained momentum. The rain fell faster and harder, and the wind kicked up, sending the water sideways into the cages. Naòm moved as far away from the bars as possible, huddling in the middle of her enclosure, her arms wrapped around her bony knees. The rain drowned out all the other night sounds of the vast population not far from her, the city she had seen in her visions. She wondered who had demanded her capture. She needed to contact her father, but had no idea how, now that his seal and the rest of the contents of the leather satchel had disappeared with the leader of her captors.

SATAL

It was the first day of the Wayeb. The light filtering into Satal's bedroom was still dim when she heard the first of the drums begin to sound in the city, marking the beginning of the five days of prayers that would ensure the city's safety for another year.

"Happy birth day," Sachoj said as Satal got up from her hammock and relieved her full bladder in a small pot in the corner of the large room.

"Humph," Satal muttered as she settled back into her nest of blankets. "Another revolution of the calendar, that's all this is. The seasons continue to advance, I'm another year older, and there's still no sign of the girl, with no chance to renew my powers."

"You've lost faith?" Sachoj said. "I'm surprised. From what I see, the girl will be in your hands before you know it."

"What? Old woman, if you've been withholding information from me . . ." Satal said as she got back up and began to pace the room.

"Go ahead, threaten me," Sachoj laughed. "What do I care? I'm just an old, dusty, dried-up head!" She laughed, and it ended in a long hiss. "So, what have you planned for tonight? When will we go to the cave and summon Camazotz into the world?"

Ignoring her great-grandmother, Satal pulled off her white nightshirt and left it on the hammock. She looked at her naked body in the light, noticing the folds of skin around her mid-section. She no longer had the body of a young woman, and she felt older than her fifty-two years. She took her black huipil and matching skirt from the wardrobe and put them on, smoothed her gray hair, and twisted it into a bun. "I may not go to the cave tonight; it's so difficult to get down that little ladder. Besides, now that the rains have started, the way will be muddy and slippery; carrying a chicken through it all won't be easy."

"My, my, you are getting old," Sachoj admonished. "Well, perhaps you can . . ."

Above the sound of the drums, Satal heard a knock on her door. "Who in the name of Itzamná is here now?" she complained. "I swear by all the gods, I'm tired of being disturbed. Everyone should be preparing to fast or cowering in their homes today, not bothering me!"

She shuffled down the hallway, crossed the large front hall, and pulled open the heavy front door. A young slave boy, wearing only a dirty loincloth stood on the stoop. "Well, what do you want?" Satal demanded. The boy held out a scrap of folded fig bark to Satal who took the grimy paper. The boy dashed off before she could even look at the glyphs on the page.

Satal closed the door and went back to her bedroom. She opened the page and noticed the markings were from Kux. She gasped as she read the note. "The girl is at the slave market!" she exclaimed to Sachoj. "Today may be a good day after all!"

Satal threw her black shawl over her head and quickly hurried outside. The pounding of the drums was louder and steadier, and Satal noticed the throngs of men and youths headed toward the pyramid of Kukulcan, eager to join the circle of shamans already dancing around the bonfire built at the base of the pyramid.

Satal ignored the glances of the few guards at the gates to the city as she hurried toward the slave market. Her mind was reeling with ideas. She was eager to meet this girl, who had tormented her so many times in her dreams, and who had inadvertently caused the death of Chachal. She needed to see her in the flesh, to learn what she knew of the Underworld and the spirits of the Wayeb before sacrificing her to Camazotz and his brothers.

Yakal

With difficulty, Yakal rolled out of the hammock that he shared with Uskab with difficulty. His head hurt, his eyes were tired, and even his bones ached. *I drank too much balché with Chiman and Tz' last night*, he thought as he washed his face with cold water. He peeked back inside his small hut and was glad to see Uskab was still asleep. Tz' and Chiman were rising in the early morning light, and they nodded to Yakal as he stepped back outside. Memetik slept on the far side of the room, rolled up tightly in his blanket. His crutches leaned against the wall within easy reach. The two village men joined Yakal outside, and the three drank from one of the many water gourds hanging by the doorway.

"The drums have already started," Yakal said. "I should join the others at the ceremony."

"I think Itzamná will forgive you if you're a few minutes late," Chiman said as he hugged his friend. "The past several days have not been easy, I'm afraid."

Yakal nodded. Telling his mother, Alom, that her youngest son, Tikoy, had been killed in the attack had been the hardest news to share. He was grateful Ajkun, Mok'onel, and the other women from Pa nimá were bedded down in Alom's hut. They were helping her through her grief. He knew Ajkun had found medicinal herbs at the market to ease his mother's pain. *Now that the Wayeb has started, it's good all the women are together,* Yakal thought. *And once Uskab wakes up, she should join the others and stay until the drums have stopped.*

As he had done every year since leaving Pa nimá, Yakal knew he would pray that Na'om was safe as he danced at the bonfire, especially this year, since he knew she was alone. But once the rains subsided in three months, Chiman and the others could return to Pa nimá and take up their lives again, with Na'om safely back among them.

"Should we join you at the bonfire?" Tz' asked Yakal as he drank some more water.

"No, Tz'," Chiman said. "I think we've both been through enough. You've yet to fully recover from the corn ceremony, the wounds from the attack, and this forced trip. Itzamná knows you've sacrificed enough for one year."

Yakal nodded his head in agreement. The pain behind his eyes was worse as the light of day grew stronger. "I should eat something before I leave," Yakal said as he looked around the small kitchen area for any leftovers. "If you could escort Uskab to my mother's house while I'm gone, that would be a big help." Yakal found a plate of cold tamales covered with a cloth and quickly ate one. He handed the rest to Chiman. "I'll see you in five days, my friend. My house is your house while I'm gone."

Yakal ducked back inside the hut and kissed Uskab on the forehead. She opened her eyes and placed her hand on his cheek. "You're burning up, Yakal," she said as she struggled to rise.

"Shh, relax, it's nothing. I'm off to the ceremony, my little honeybee. Chiman will take you to Chuch's." He placed his hand on her swollen belly. "Take care of my son," he said as he kissed Uskab again.

Yakal joined a group of older men walking to the pyramid of Kukulcan. He noticed Satal leaving her palace and wondered where she was hurrying to at such an early hour, on this, the first day of the Wayeb. But the steady beat of the drums pushed Satal from his mind as he joined the large group circling the bonfire. He stepped in line with two potters and began to move counterclockwise with the rest. The pain in his head pulsed with each drumbeat, and he squinted against the glare of the flames and sunlight.

Having his eyes closed just intensified his headache, so Yakal opened them again and noticed Nimal was only a few spaces away. He maneuvered through the group until he was dancing next to his friend.

"Are you all right?" Nimal asked. "You don't look well."

"Too much balché last night," Yakal said. "At least, I think that's what's gotten to me." He almost stopped moving as he thought back through the many headaches he'd experienced in the past several weeks. "Have you experienced any unusual symptoms lately?" he asked Nimal.

"If you mean a widespread rash and a persistent headache, then yes," Nimal replied.

"And they started soon after we returned from our disastrous trip and had to speak to Satal?" Yakal said.

Nimal shuffled sideways in silence for a minute. "Now that you mention it, yes, that is when the rash first appeared, just after we got back." He stopped dancing and stepped backwards, allowing other men to move past him.

Yakal joined Nimal. "I suspect our dear Lady Satal has afflicted us with something because we dared to defy her." The two men watched their neighbors circling round and round the bonfire, and Yakal wondered how he could ever get rid of the woman who had plagued him and his family for so many years. "Once the Wayeb is over, we should ask the other men who were with us if they've had any similar afflictions," Yakal said. He waved to one of the slave boys who hurried over with a gourd full of watermelon juice. He drank the sweet liquid and felt its cooling properties race through his limbs. He shivered despite the heat from the fire as he handed the vessel to Nimal, who also drank before handing the gourd back to the slave.

Just as Yakal was going to rejoin the dancers, he noticed

Chiman, Tz', and a slave boy running toward the group. He raised his hand and waved, and the three hurried to his side. "What's wrong?" Yakal asked as he noticed the worried look on Chiman's face.

"This boy showed up shortly after you left this morning," Chiman said. "And he had this in his hand," he added as he held out a piece of fig bark.

Yakal could see his own insignia of the pyramid embossed into the red wax on the paper. "Where did you get this?" he asked the slave boy.

"My master, Master Tarnel, found it last night in a bag and sent me to find you this morning. He asks that you come to the slave market right away."

"I don't understand; what's the matter?" Nimal said as he looked at the group. "Why would Tarnel have your seal?"

"I sent this to Na'om months ago and told her to send it to me if she was ever in danger," Yakal said. "I must go at once."

"Who's Na'om?" Nimal said. "What about the ceremony?"

"I haven't time to explain," Yakal said. He nodded to Chiman. "Come with me." The older man bobbed his head in reply.

"I'll stay here and explain this all to Nimal," Tz' volunteered. "Let me know if there's anything I can do to help."

Yakal hugged the boy and clutched Chiman's arm. "Come on; I saw Satal leaving the city this morning, and now I think I know where she might have been going."

The two men ran toward the slave market, passing through the quiet city streets with ease. They arrived at Tarnel's office out of breath and had to wait to speak as they burst through the door. Yakal noticed the worn leather satchel on Tarnel's desk and the pile of items placed to one side. He leaned forward and tried to pluck a large green, carved obsidian knife out from among the broken arrows and pile of beads, but Tarnel clamped his hand over the hilt of the knife.

"I received the seal; where did you get it?" Yakal demanded.

Tarnel put his hands up in front of his chest as if to protect himself. "The seal was in the bag, along with these other items. The minute I saw it, I knew I had no ordinary slave girl in my midst, so I sent the boy to find you."

"Where's the girl?" Chiman said as he headed toward the doorway.

"Why, with Lady Satal, of course. The minute she appeared, I gave the girl and her big jaguar to her," Tarnel said. "I thought it might have something to do with the Wayeb."

Yakal and Chiman both groaned.

"Why, what's wrong?" Tarnel said as he looked from man to man. "I assumed the boy found you, and you sent Satal to fetch the girl, since you were involved in the Wayeb ceremony."

"I was at the pyramid, but Lady Satal is the last one the girl should be with," Yakal said. He reached over to gather the items.

"Hold on, you can't just take those, you know," Tarnel said as he tried to grab the beads and arrows and move them out of Yakal's reach. He snatched the knife off the tabletop and held it at arm's length. "I haven't been paid for the girl or these things, so you'll not be taking anything until I see some kind of payment."

"That knife belonged to my father, you idiot," Yakal said as he tried to grab the blade.

Tarnel jumped backwards, slashing the air in front of him with the sharp knife. "Come back with some cacao beans, and the whole lot can be yours," he said. "Otherwise, I keep it all."

Yakal looked at Chiman who only shrugged. "Come on, I have an idea," Yakal said. He turned back to Tarnel. "If I find you've sold this stuff while I'm gone, expect to spend several months in one of those cages you have outside!" He stormed out the door into the bright light, wincing as the sunlight pierced like a spike into his eyes.

"What do we do now?" Chiman said as he jogged back toward the city with Yakal. "I have no currency, and I suspect you don't, either."

"No, but I know someone who does, and I have something he wants," Yakal said. He ran to his hut and found Memetik sitting by the fire. The boy jumped up on his good leg when he saw Yakal.

"Come on, boy, I need you to do something for me," Yakal said. Memetik grabbed his crutches and hurried after Yakal and Chiman.

"Where are we going?" Memetik said. "Do you want me to take your place in the ceremony?"

Yakal stopped jogging and knelt down in front of the boy. He grasped Memetik's hands in his own. "I don't want to do what I'm about to do, and I will find some way to get you back, I promise, but I need you to go live with some other men for a bit." He noticed the puzzlement in Memetik's face. "There isn't really time to explain, just know that I'll make it up to you, somehow, I promise."

The three continued walking through the empty streets. The occasional dog barked at them as they hurried past, and a flock of turkeys flew up into the air as they rounded a corner near the marketplace. Yakal stopped in front of a large house and approached the wooden door.

He knocked several times and finally heard voices on the other side. The door creaked open on its copper hinges.

"Yakal!" Kubal Joron said as he looked out the door. "We're just on our way, aren't we Matz," he said as he looked back toward the interior of the house. "I know, we're late, the ceremony started hours ago, but one can't hurry if one wants to make an impression," he said as he gestured to the deep blue shirt and loincloth he wore.

"I've come to ask a favor," Yakal said, ignoring Kubal Joron's outfit. "I haven't time to explain, but I need money, a lot of money," he said and looked up into the painted face of Kubal Joron.

"My goodness, what kind of trouble are you in?" Kubal Joron said.

"No trouble, but I need to purchase some things from the slave market, which might help me identify the spy Lady Satal asked me to find, and I can't afford what Tarnel is asking."

"My, my, all this intrigue, please, tell me more," Kubal Joron said.

"Itzamná, I don't have time for this," Yakal shouted. "Will you loan me the money or not?"

"And what do I get in return?" Kubal Joron said. "Since we sit on the city council together, I know your salary affords you little in the way of collateral. I must have some kind of insurance that you'll pay me back."

Yakal gestured to Chiman and Memetik to approach the doorway. "You once expressed interest in the boy, Memetik. If you give me the money, I'll hand him over to you," Yakal said.

Matz' had joined Kubal Joron at the door. "Dearest, look who's come to stay with us," Kubal Joron said as he placed his lacquered fingers on Matz's arm. He turned to Yakal. "Wait right there, while I fetch my purse." He waddled away, his large backside swaying in his loincloth.

Matz' knelt down in front of Memetik. "Don't look so worried, my child. We really mean you no harm. Dear Kubal and I need a houseboy, to do a few little things for us; now that doesn't sound so bad, does it?"

Memetik looked from Matz' to Yakal and back to Matz'. "My lords, would it be all right if my younger brother came to stay here, too?"

Matz' laughed. "Why, of course, what a perfect idea." He turned and yelled back into the interior of the house. "Bring the big purse, Kubal dear, we're going to have two beautiful boys to raise."

Chiman and Yakal shook their heads and waited impatiently for Kubal Joron to return. His face was flush, and several beads of sweat dripped from his forehead as he handed over the large leather pouch full of cacao beans.

Yakal placed his hand on Memetik's shoulder. "I'll be back to get you as soon as I can," he said. The boy nodded.

"Now, my dear boy, what kind of food do you like to eat?" Matz' said as he gently pushed Memetik through the open doorway and into the cool and spacious front hall. Memetik glanced back at Yakal and then continued to limp inside.

"Don't hurt him," Yakal warned as he turned to Kubal Joron.

"Never fear, Yakal. Now do tell me how this all turns out," Kubal Joron said. "This is the most excitement we've had in months."

"You're coming with me. If what I suspect is true," Yakal replied, "you may have to pass judgment on Lady Satal before this day is over."

"Well, I'm not sure I'm ready for this," Kubal Joron protested. "What about it being the Wayeb?"

"That's the reason we have to go, now." Yakal shook his head. "I'll explain later, right now, we have to find Lady Satal." Yakal handed the bag of cacao beans to Chiman. "Go back to Tarnel's and pay him whatever he asks for those items. I'm off to find Na'om and Satal." He hugged his old friend and pointed in the direction of Satal's palace. "Meet us at her house. May Itzamná be with you," he added.

"May he be with all of us," Chiman added as the three men went in opposite directions.

NA'OM

When the first drums started beating, Na'om was instantly awake. She rattled the door on her cage, hoping she could loosen the bar that held it tight, but the piece of wood was securely fastened. Ek' Balam still lay with his back to her, but she could see from the rise and fall of his chest that he was sleeping peacefully.

She leaned back against the bars of the enclosure and closed her eyes. She wondered how long she'd be kept locked up. *Perhaps through the Wayeb,* she realized with a start. *No one will be conducting any business for the next five days. I just hope they remember to feed us during this time.* The morning air was cool, and Na'om imagined she was back in her small hut, surrounded by the walls she had begun to paint. She felt some of the tension drain from her body as she envisioned the rich reds, yellows, and greens of the flowers and jungle plants she had depicted on the walls. *Someday I'll get back there to finish them.*

At the sound of quick footsteps, she opened her eyes. A small woman dressed all in black stood before her along with four well-muscled men. One man placed a bowl full of raw meat in front of Ek' Balam who quickly gulped down the food. He paced the cage for a few minutes, and then Na'om saw him sway on his feet and slowly lie down. His tongue lolled outside his mouth.

"What did you just do to him?" she cried as she stood up and confronted the people in front of her.

"Just a little drug to help him sleep," the woman said. She nodded to two of the men, and they threw a thick blanket over the cage before hefting it up by the bottom. Grunting with the weight, they hoisted the cat inside his crate to their shoulders and proceeded to carry Ek' Balam away.

"Where are you taking him?" Na'om shouted as she shook the bars of her coop. "Let me out of here!" She kicked at the wooden slats with her bare feet.

"If you don't calm down, I'll drug you as well," the old woman said as she peered at Na'om. "Tie her up, and bring her to my house," the woman said to the two guards. "Quickly, now, before the whole city hears her cries."

The men stepped into the cage and caught Na'om around the waist. One tied her hands behind her back while the other stuffed a rag inside her mouth. She choked on the rough cloth and tried to spit it out with no luck. Someone threw a feedbag over her head, and tiny bits of ground corn filtered down on her face as she was pushed toward the cage door.

"Come quietly, and this will all be over soon," the woman said.

Na'om didn't bother to try and reply. She scuffled through the dry dirt with her bare feet, her arms held on either side by her guards. She tried concentrating on the twists and turns they made, but soon lost track of the number of rights and lefts. The only thing she noticed was the sound of the pounding drums, which grew louder and louder with each step. Finally, they stopped, and she heard the woman speak softly to the guards.

Then she was pushed up a few steps, heard a door open, and was shoved inside. Na'om stumbled on the smooth stone flooring and almost fell. Prodded in the back, she carefully felt her way with her feet across a large open space; the constant poking directed her down a hallway and into another large space. She felt the rope on her arms yank upwards, and then the bag was removed from her head.

She was in a large room. The walls were painted with images of warriors in full leather outfits; their spear tips dripped blood as one group charged at another. One end of a hammock hung from a hook in the wall; the other end lay on the floor, and the rope around her wrists had been attached to the second hook. The cage with Ek' Balam inside had been placed in the far corner of the room, and Naʾom was glad to see the steady rise and fall of his chest. *At least he's not hurt,* she thought. Then she shuddered as her eyes came to rest on a shrunken head tucked into a crudely carved niche in the wall. *That's the ancient woman who spoke to me that day so many years ago,* Naʾom thought. She closed her eyes and heard the buzzing of a thousand bees in her head. She shook her head to clear it of sound and opened her eyes.

The old woman was standing in front of Naʾom. "I've waited so many years to meet you," she said to Naʾom. "I almost don't know where to begin." She grinned and nodded, mumbled to herself, and went to the tall wooden cupboard.

Naʾom watched as the woman began to take a variety of items from the shelves and place them on the little table, including a candle, which she lit. Naʾom closed her eyes for just a split second and instantly the black wasp appeared in her mind and she knew she had to find a way to defend herself against this woman. She wished she could reach her necklace and ask her mother for help, but with her hands firmly tied to the wall, she couldn't.

"Yes, yes, I agree," Naʾom heard the old woman say as she put a copper bowl on the monkey skin she'd laid on the tabletop. Naʾom watched as she poured some herbs into the bowl, ground them into dust with a pestle, and packed the powder into a small clay pipe. The woman touched a piece of straw to the candle flame and tipped it into the bowl of the pipe. She breathed in deeply, and a bitter smoke drifted up toward the high ceiling in the room.

Swallowing her fear, Naʾom called out, "Who are you? What do you want from me?"

The woman puffed on her pipe a few more times before coming back to stand in front of Naʾom. She noticed the old woman was short and had to tilt her head up slightly to look into

Na'om's face.

"Who I am doesn't concern you, my dear," she said. "But what I want is another matter. You shall tell me all you've learned about the Underworld."

"And if I refuse?" Na'om said. She wriggled her hands, trying to free her arms.

The woman shuffled over to the table again, picked up the bowl, and then went to Ek' Balam's cage. She held a small green knife in her hand. "Perhaps we'll start by taking care of your friend here; his blood will be a great help to me tonight when I summon my friends."

"NO!" Na'om shouted. She twisted her body, writhing on the ropes. "Leave him alone; he's done you no harm." She heard the woman laugh and closed her eyes again. Instantly, she began to cover herself from head to toe with white, protective light. She felt the air around her vibrating and heard the woman laugh again.

"Good, good, let me see your powers," she heard the woman say.

Na'om pushed the white light outwards, into the room, stretching the cocoon of protection until it wrapped around Ek' Balam's cage. She felt a presence next to her in the whiteness, and the spirit of Ek' Balam appeared beside her, his black coat outlined in white.

"Excellent, my child, wonderful, now let's see what else you can do."

Na'om twisted her head and saw the black wasp hovering several feet off the ground. The wasp hung in space, its black eyes glittering in the light. It floated slowly toward Na'om and Ek' Balam, who edged closer to Na'om, until their sides were almost touching.

Suddenly the wasp darted in and jabbed Na'om with its stinger on her shoulder. She swiveled on the ropes, curving her body away from the piercing sharp probe, as a picture of a young woman clutching her bloody thighs filled her mind. The wasp attacked again, hitting Naʾom on the other side. She writhed in pain and saw this old woman at the top of some temple during a thunderstorm. Naʾom heard Ekʾ Balam growl and sensed him swatting at the insect, which flew up toward the ceiling and out of harm's way.

"Very good, very good," the wasp-woman said as she swooped down for another attack.

This time Naʾom anticipated her movements and squirmed out of the way at the last second, avoiding the huge stinger that extended from the wasp's body. But the ropes held her too tightly, and the insect jabbed again, stabbing Naʾom on her right arm. She shrieked with the pain and heard Ekʾ Balam roar. The men who had attacked the village filled her mind, and she jerked violently as the poison flowed into her arm. Her body crashed into the jaguar. She felt a jolt of electric current run through her as the heat and energy of Ekʾ Balam's life force flowed into her, traveling from the point of contact to her extremities. Her head pounded with a rush of jungle images, smells, and tastes. And in that instant, as her spirit melded with that of Ekʾ Balam's, Naʾom understood everything. She saw her own life in a hundred separate pictures and that of her father and the life of this woman who carried evil like a shawl around her shoulders. Naʾom knew what the woman wanted, and she knew what she had to do to defeat her.

With the combined strength of both their spirits inside her, Naʾom yanked on the cord holding her to the wall and felt it break. She slumped to the floor, her right arm already swollen from the elbow to the shoulder with the toxins the wasp had injected into her.

The wasp zoomed in for another hit, but this time Naʾom was ready. With the speed of a cat, she snatched at the creature with her left arm, snagged the insect by the wing, and tossed her across the room. The bug crashed into the solid wall with a dull thud and slid to the tiles below. Naʾom let the white light all around her recede and opened her eyes.

The woman was standing just a few feet away, still puffing on her pipe. Ek' Balam was awake and had his face pressed close to the bars of the cage. His ears were back, and a deep rumble filled the room in counterpoint to the distant sound of the drums outside. Na'om wriggled her arms, but the rope binding her wrists was still tight against her flesh.

"By all the gods, I've never seen such a display," the woman said as she hurried to place the loop of rope back on the hook high in the wall. She turned to the head in the niche in the wall, a grin on her face. "I know, I know, Camazotz will be very pleased," she said as she began to pace back and forth in front of Na'om and Ek' Balam. "I can't wait until sundown!"

Na'om hung her head. It throbbed from the effort of extending the protective white light out so far into the room. She was so tired all of a sudden, and her arms ached from their awkward angle. She caught a glimpse of the string holding her necklace and tried to catch it with her teeth, but couldn't quite bend her head down that far. *Itzamná, I could use some help,* she prayed, but there was no answer.

The woman was muttering again, and Na'om strained to hear what she was saying.

"Yes, yes, you're right, we should go now," she said to the head in the wall.

Na'om saw her gather the items from the table, and then she carefully rolled the head in a piece of soft cotton and placed it all in a basket. She turned to Na'om, a slight smile on her face. "I suspect you must be thirsty, my dear," she said. "Let me fetch you a glass of water."

Na'om drifted in and out of consciousness while she waited, but felt the spirit of Ek' Balam deep inside her and wasn't afraid.

"Here, drink this," the woman said as she held out a mug to Na'om.

Na'om lifted her head and let the woman pour the liquid

into her mouth. It tasted coppery, like blood, but Na'om drank it anyway. She grew more tired and wanted nothing more than to lie down on the cool tiles and sleep.

With her eyes barely open, she saw the woman approach her with the small green knife and felt the ropes being cut from her wrists. "Come now, child, let me help you stand," she heard the woman say and felt a pair of hands grab her under the armpits.

She swayed on her feet, but managed to stay upright. "Let him out," she said, nodding to Ek' Balam in his cage. "I promise you, he won't harm you."

"No, I suspect he won't," the woman said and quickly set the jaguar free.

Holding her by one elbow, the three moved down the hallway and outside into the bright daylight. The drums beat a steady rhythm, which Na'om felt as a pulsing in her veins. They slowly walked down the large street, and Na'om sensed pairs of eyes watching them as they moved past the houses. She squinted, and as they crossed into another avenue, she could just see the tip of the pyramid over the rooftops and a brief glimpse of the ceremonial bonfire at its base, where hundreds of men circled the flames.

"Quickly child, we must hurry to the gates before any more people see us," the woman said and tugged on Na'om's arm. She turned down another street and then another, twisting her way through the city before leading Na'om out into an open area. The ground was hard underfoot and sloped gently toward the center, toward the fifty-foot round sinkhole that provided the city with fresh water. The area was deserted; no one ventured near the cenote during the Wayeb. Na'om could see the smooth edge of the well, its steep walls, and the water far below. A dark line on the sheer white walls showed how low the water level was. But as the summer rains drained into the vast labyrinth of channels and caves deep underground, the water level would slowly rise.

All of a sudden, Na'om heard people running and glanced behind her. A large group of men was headed in their direction.

"Stop!" a man shouted. The group of men quickly engulfed the trio. Na'om looked at them all and noticed Chiman was in the crowd. Several of the men carried bows and arrows, and Na'om recognized they were dressed like the guards she had seen at the vast city gates.

"Lady Satal, by the powers of the city council, I'm placing you under arrest for high treason and witchcraft against the city and people of Mayapán," the leader said.

"Treason and witchcraft, what nonsense is this?" Satal said as she eyed the men. She pointed with her wrinkled hand at an overweight man. "Kubal Joron, surely you don't believe Yakal in any of this?"

Na'om's head jerked up when she heard the name Yakal, and she looked quickly to Chiman. She opened her mouth to speak, but he caught her eye, and ever so slightly, shook his head no.

Kubal Joron wiped his mouth with a cloth. He slowly looked around the area. "My lady, I'm afraid that I do. All the evidence Yakal has points to some mischief, enough to cause me quite some concern. I'm afraid I'm left with no choice, but to agree with him."

"Evidence, what evidence? I demand to know what you're talking about," Satal said.

Yakal took the satchel off, and Na'om recognized it as Ajkun's bag. He pulled out the handful of broken arrows and the large green knife Tikoy had given her right before he died.

"Humph," Satal said. "You call this evidence? It's nothing but a bunch of junk."

One of the guards tugged the basket from Satal's hand, pulled out the items, and set them on the ground. Yakal reached over and unwrapped one bundle. He held up the shrunken head for all to see. "Isn't this proof of some kind of witchery?" he asked. Then he swung the head by its hair and pitched it far out over the cenote.

Satal gasped as they all heard a faint plop in the water. She pushed Naʼom out into the crowd of men. "Here's who you really need to worry about," she said. "Yakal, tell them who the girl is; I'm sure everyone here wants to know."

"The girl is my daughter, Naʼom, born to my first wife who died in childbirth in the village of Pa nimá. I was a young man at the time and overcome with grief. I left the village and let others raise her."

"Tell the truth, Yakal," Satal said. "Go on, tell them the real reason you abandoned your child. She was born in the Wayeb!"

Everyone looked from Satal to Naʼom to Yakal and back to Naʼom. A ripple of soft murmurs moved through the crowd.

"Is this true?" one of the men said.

Yakal nodded. "Yes, Kubal Joron, I'm afraid it is. But at the very end of the Wayeb, isn't that right, Chiman?" he said as he turned to his friend.

"Beginning, end, it makes no difference," Kubal Joron said. "Anyone born during the Wayeb is a danger and should be sacrificed."

"The girl is no danger," Chiman said, "But she does possess certain abilities."

Yakal spoke up. "Satal has been trying to find Naʼom since the day she was born, to obtain access to the powers she holds. And here is the proof." He held up the large knife with the carved handle. "I'm sure you all recognize my father's knife; he wore it every day of his life. It was given to Naʼom by my brother, Tikoy, the day he died, in the cornfield in Pa nimá."

He held up the arrows and turned to another man. "Nimal, can you tell me where these came from?" he asked.

Nimal took the broken shafts in his hand and examined the feathers. "I'd say they all came from Xikʼ, as he's the only one I know who fletches arrows in these different patterns. Let me guess, also found in Pa nimá?"

Yakal nodded. "The only way these items could ever have been in Pa nimá was if someone from here had taken them there."

"Lady Satal, have you anything to say for yourself?" Kubal Joron asked.

"May blood and pus run from all your orifices!" Satal cried as she pushed Na'om into Yakal and started to run.

"Seize her!" Yakal cried, and several men rushed forward to grab Satal by the arms.

Na'om turned, sprinted after Satal, and managed to snatch the back of Satal's skirt. She spun the old woman around, but lost her grip on Satal's garment in the process.

Satal ducked and scurried backwards, stumbling on the smooth ground. Her left foot thrashed over the edge of the cenote. She flailed her arms in the air, and Na'om caught Satal's hand. Na'om pulled and Satal seemed to float for just a second before gravity took over and the two of them tumbled over the edge.

"Noooo!" Na'om heard someone shout as she closed her eyes and drifted downwards. She took a deep breath of air, heard a splash, and felt water spray on her as Satal sank below the surface. Then a second later, she struck the water herself and opened her eyes. Instantly, there was another splash, an explosion of bubbles, and in the deepening gloom, Na'om saw Ek' Balam swimming strongly beside her. She reached out, grabbed his tail, and felt him begin to pull her through the darkness.

AJKUN

The rainy season was over, and the rivers were finally navigable. Ajkun was eager to get away from Mayapán, away from this spot of so much pain, and back to her village in the jungle. Although she had made some new friends, especially Alom and Uskab, she longed to be back among the plants and animals that she knew so well. The city was too vast, too loud, and too empty for her ever to feel truly comfortable in it.

She hugged Alom one last time and gave Uskab a quick kiss on the cheek. She ran her fingertips through the dark patch of hair on Uskab's newborn son and kissed him gently on the forehead.

Yakal waited his turn. "Thank you for healing me and the others. The fevers are almost gone now."

"Whether it was my herbs or Satal's death that cured you, no one can say; I'm glad you're feeling better, though."

Yakal gently hugged Ajkun good-bye. "I don't expect I'll see you again anytime soon," he said as he held the woman in his arms.

"No, I doubt I'll ever come back here," Ajkun said. "But who's to say; I never expected to come to the city in the first place. Only Itzamná knows what the future holds for any of us."

Ajkun walked over to Mok'onel who stood a little way off from the rest of the villagers headed back to Pa nimá. "Are you sure you won't change your mind and come with us?" she asked the girl.

"No, it's kind of you to ask, but the village holds too many bad memories for me," Mok'onel said. "With Chuch and the children all gone, I don't know if I could ever live there again." She looked over at Alom who nodded. "I have a place to stay here in the city, and I think I may have met someone," Mok'onel added, and Ajkun saw her blush.

"Well, I'm happy for you, my dear, I truly am," Ajkun said and hugged the young girl again. She looked at Chiman and Tz' waiting to lead her toward the river that would take them all home. "I'm ready; let's go."

***

Within two weeks, the villagers had safely pushed their way up the rivers until they reached the area of Pa nimá. As the group got closer to their homes, Ajkun noticed how each person sat up straighter in the canoe and paddled longer and harder. *Of course,* she thought, *they all have their normal lives to return to, but I have no one waiting for me when I get there.*

As they rounded the last bend in the river, and Ajkun saw the familiar sand and rocky beach where they always stored the canoes, she avoided looking at the opposite shore. She didn't want to see the path that led to Na'om's hut.

Chiman and Tz' helped Ajkun from the center of their canoe and steadied her as she struggled up the slight slope to the path leading to the village. "I'll be fine," she said as she shrugged them off. "Just have to get some feeling back in my legs again." The father and son nodded and unloaded what little gear they had brought with them from Mayapán. The three followed the others in the village to the central plaza.

Ajkun stopped and looked about in amazement. "Why, I thought the place would be overrun with animals and jungle vines by now," she said. The square was neatly swept, and a stack of wood stood piled next to a cooking ring, where a bright blaze burned under a large cooking pot. The rich smell of turkey and corn stew drifted to them on the light breeze.

"Hello, who's there?" Chiman called.

An older man stepped from one of the huts, followed quickly by a small boy of about eight. The child ran up to Ajkun. "Where's Na'om?" he asked as he tugged on her skirt.

"How do you know about Na'om?" she said as she knelt down and looked the boy in the eyes.

"She came to my village months ago and helped my noy with her wounded leg. She promised to come back and let me play with her pet jaguar. Where is she? Still down at the river?" the boy said as he started to run down the path.

"Wait, child, come back," Ajkun said. She held out her arms and the boy ran to her. "What's your name?"

"Lintat," the boy said.

"Lintat, that's a nice name for a boy," Ajkun replied as she held the child by his shoulders. "Now you must be big and brave and strong, like your name suggests, can you do that for me?"

Lintat nodded.

"Good," Ajkun said. She took a deep breath and let it out slowly. "Na'om isn't here; she never made it out of the city. Because she was born in the Wayeb, she sacrificed herself to save us. Do you understand?" The boy nodded, but Ajkun noticed the quiver in his bottom lip and the sudden wetness in his big brown eyes. She felt her own eyes tear up at the thought of her Na'om at the bottom of the cenote and hugged the boy to her chest before pushing him away. "Go on, now, I mustn't just stand around here talking, there's work to be done."

Ajkun hurried off to her old hut and quickly stepped through the doorway. Only then did she let the sob trapped inside her chest escape. She sank down on the narrow bed she'd shared for years with Na'om and cried. After a time, she sat up, wiped her wet face with the edge of her sleeve, and looked around her. The hut was neat and clean, the floor had been swept, and all her bottles and pots of salves looked like they'd been dusted recently. But the sight of it all just made the ache in her heart worse, so she went back outside. She nodded to her neighbors who were busy starting fires of their own and wandered back down to the river. She needed to get away from everyone, to find some place private where she could really let out her anguish.

She stepped into one of the smaller canoes and pushed off from shore with the tip of the wooden paddle. She quickly made it to the other side of the river and nudged the bow of the boat up into the bushes. Liana vines stretched across the path to Na'om's hut, and several small branches from the surrounding mahogany trees had fallen into the middle of the clearing. But otherwise, the place looked exactly as Ajkun remembered it.

The short bench she had helped Na'om build stood near the cooking ring, and an old blackened pot balanced on the rocks. Only the box where Na'om had stored food had been knocked over, the pottery bowls inside licked clean by some unknown animal. Ajkun sighed and stepped into the ring of trees. She touched each object, but left it in its place. She didn't want to change anything about this space; it was all she had left to remember Na'om by. She entered the small hut and was amazed again by the brilliant colors Na'om had begun to paint on the white limestone walls. The gridlines and marks outlining the flowers and trees Na'om had yet to paint had begun to fade, but if she closed her eyes, she could see the jungle flora and fauna as Na'om had envisioned it. Ajkun stood for several minutes with her eyes closed, imprinting that thought deep into her mind.

All of a sudden, she heard footsteps outside the hut and turned just as someone filled the doorway, blocking the late afternoon light.

"I thought I might find you here," Chiman said as he entered the room. "Itzamná, I had no idea," he added as he looked at the detailed paintings on the wall. "When did she start doing this?"

"While Tz' was away on the trading trip. It helped her pass the time," Ajkun said, and a sob escaped her.

Chiman held out his arms, and Ajkun stepped into his embrace. They hugged and cried together, their tears mingling on Chiman's bare chest.

Finally, Ajkun pulled away from her friend. "I don't know what to do now," she said.

"I do," Chiman said as he leaned down and kissed Ajkun's round lips. She looked up at him in surprise. "We must go on living; it's what Na'om would have wanted," he said. "We'll leave this the way it is," he added as he scanned the room. He noticed the ledger that lay open on the floor, the pages filled with black and white drawings. He knelt down and flipped through the book, amazed at the images. "How come she never showed me this?" he asked as he looked back over his shoulder at Ajkun.

"She was going to, right after the corn ceremony," Ajkun said. "It's a record of all her dreams as she saw them." She knelt beside Chiman, and they looked at each colorful, detailed drawing until they came to the last two pages. In the sketched black lines, they could clearly see the apex of a pyramid, the round opening of a cenote, and the image of a girl and a jaguar falling into the water. Then the girl was swimming upward, into a tunnel, pulled by the jaguar toward the light.

Ajkun looked at Chiman's lined face. "Do you think it's possible?"

"Only Itzamná knows," Chiman replied, but his wrinkled face broke into a smile, "and Na'om."

GLOSSARY

ati't: An affectionate term for grandmother.

atole: A sweet, thick, cinnamon-flavored drink made from powdered corn meal, usually served hot.

balché: A fermented, honey-sweetened drink made from the bark of the *Lonchocarpus violaceus* tree.

ceiba tree: The sacred tree of the Maya. Considered the world tree, its branches reach into heaven and its roots extend down into the Underworld.

cenote: Natural sinkholes that appear in the limestone terrain and are the source of fresh water in northern Yucatán. They are interconnected by a series of underground caves and tunnels, and many of these tunnels eventually lead to the sea. The Mayans considered cenotes entranceways to the Underworld.

Chichén Itzá: A city in northeastern Yucatán which was ruled by the Xiu tribe.

chuch: An affectionate term for mother.

Cocom: The leading tribe of the city of Mayapán and the enemy of the Xiu.

copal: An aromatic tree resin burned as incense during ceremonies and for purification.

huipil: A loose-fitting tunic made from cotton, often heavily embroidered around the square neckline.

itzinel: A witch.

je′: Yes.

jequirity beans: A type of hallucinogenic bean, toxic in high doses.

maltiox: Thanks.

Mayapán: A city in northern Yucatán which was ruled by the Cocom tribe.

nim-q'ij: Respected or honored one.

noy: An affectionate term for grandmother.

Pa nimá: A phrase meaning by the river; the village where Naʼom is born.

qajaw: Formal word for father, used to show respect.

sacbé: Raised pavements or causeways made from white limestone that connected cities, temples, and plazas.

Silowik Tukan: To be drunk; blackberry; the name of the bar in Mayapán.

tat axel: An affectionate term for father.

to'ik: To help.

to'nel: A witch who helps.

Wayeb: The five unnamed days at the end of the calendar year when the portal to the Underworld stands open.

 The sign for the five-day Wayeb period.

Xibalba: The Mayan Underworld.

Xiu: The leading tribe of the city of Chichén Itzá and the enemy of the Cocom.

ACKNOWLEDGMENTS

I owe a great deal of thanks to the many people who have contributed to the creation of this novel.

A huge thank you goes to my husband, Jeffrey Thomas, who has been with me on this journey every step of the way. He was the first set of eyes to see this manuscript and was willing to read endless drafts, as the narrative morphed from a simple twenty-page short story to this novel. He spent hours working on plot details and gave me ideas on how to tweak aspects in each character to bring out his or her best and worst traits. He also suggested having Sachoj's shrunken head be able to talk, which added just that right touch to Satal's complex character.

A big thank you to my editor, Jennifer Caven, who encouraged me to keep rewriting, even when I felt the manuscript should only be used to start the morning's fire. Her first reactions on reading this book gave me the courage to continue.

A warm thank you to my cover designer, Brandi Doanne McCann, who was able to take the image I had in my head and actually create it. In another life, I want to come back as a graphic artist.

Thanks to my creative writing professors at the University of Maine, Farmington, Gretchen Legler, Pat O'Donnell, and Jeff Thomson, and my Spanish professors, Linda Britt and Marisela Funes, who encouraged me to continue writing about Mexico and its people, a subject that they knew fascinated me.

Thanks to all my beta readers who read the first version and later drafts of this book: Jane Harmon, Judith Fowles, Dodie Lake,

Cher Michels, Angela DeRosa, Scott Thomas, and Lucy Cayard. (My apologies if I've forgotten anyone.)

A big thanks to my parents, Joan and Rod Cart, who first took me to Mexico when I was six, a trip that opened a doorway into a world that I might not otherwise have known existed. Their love of Mexico and the Mexican culture is equaled by my own. I am so glad they introduced me to the ruins at Mayapán a few years ago, as I had been searching for quite some time for a second locale for this book. When I walked through the ancient wall, I knew I had found my setting.

A warm thank you goes to the authors of numerous books on Mexico and the Mayan culture, which I used to create an authentic atmosphere in the book. These include Michael Coe, Linda Shele, David Freidel, Lynn V. Foster, Mary Miller and Karl Taube to name just a few.

Last, I want to thank the Mayan people of the Yucatán, those who lived long ago and those who live there today. Thank you for sharing your culture and for your hospitality.

About the Author

Lee E. Cart is a freelance writer, editor, book reviewer, and publisher for Ek' Balam Press. She lives in central Maine with her husband, Jeffrey, and their two cats. She enjoys reading, writing, cooking, gardening, and traveling to Mexico, Hawaii, and Ireland. She lived in Guadalajara, Mexico for over seven years as a child and loves to return to the city to visit family and friends. She also enjoys traveling in the Yucatán. When she is not writing, she can be found curled up some place snug with a good novel, a cup of tea, and a piece of very dark chocolate.

Printed in the USA
CPSIA information can be obtained
at www.ICGtesting.com
LVHW010239210824
788809LV00008B/225